M000312187

RATS OF
LAS VEGAS

RATS OF
LAS VEGAS

Lisa Pasold

Enfield & Wizenty
(an imprint of Great Plains Publications)
345-955 Portage Avenue
Winnipeg, MB R3G 0P9
www.enfieldandwizenty.ca

Great Plains Publications gratefully acknowledges the financial support provided for its publishing program by the Government of Canada through the Book Publishing Industry Development Program (BPIDP); the Canada Council for the Arts; as well as the Manitoba Department of Culture, Heritage and Tourism; and the Manitoba Arts Council.

Design & Typography by Relish Design Studio Ltd.

Printed in Canada by Friesens

FIRST EDITION

Library and Archives Canada Cataloguing in Publication

Pasold, Lisa
    Rats of Las Vegas / Lisa Pasold.

ISBN 978-1-894283-92-2

    I. Title.
PS8631.A825R38 2009   C813'.6   C2009-902484-5

Lisa Pasold gratefully acknowledges the support and encouragement of the Banff Writing Studio, and also thanks Lauren B. Davis for her mentorship and advice.

ENVIRONMENTAL BENEFITS STATEMENT

Great Plains Publications saved the following resources by printing the pages of this book on chlorine free paper made with 100% post-consumer waste.

TREES	WATER	SOLID WASTE	GREENHOUSE GASES
14	6,528	396	1,355
FULLY GROWN	GALLONS	POUNDS	POUNDS

Calculations based on research by Environmental Defense and the Paper Task Force. Manufactured at Friesens Corporation

Mixed Sources

Cert no. SW-COC-001271
© 1996 FSC

FSC

for Bremner

1

I came to luck naturally. It's an ability, like playing piano or shooting pool. I have an affinity for cards. It's innate, instinctive: you can work it up, but if you're not born with it, there's only so far to go. The cards arrange themselves botanically, as leaves on a particular tree. As each one appears, I place it in my mind along its branch and look at what remains—the gaps, the holes in the foliage, the sky—what is begging to be found. This is the way the world comes to me, something more automatic than chosen. I have no choice.

I looked down at the brown oilcloth of the table, thinking about what cards had been discarded. Dermot coughed; he owned the beer hall and the backroom where we were playing, and he had a cold. He leaned on the door that led to the bar, watching the end of the game. There were three of us left at the table, there were the cards, and there was a collection of empty whiskey glasses alongside my cup of tea, ladylike in pale yellow china. At seventeen, I had no interest in liquor, though I was often frustrated by how quickly my tea went cold. There was almost always a poker game in the backroom of Dermot McMann's Gastown bar. Nothing high stake, just a simple game in a plain room with three painted white walls and one stained wall of once-red wallpaper, the whole décor suffering from more than a decade of tobacco and neglectful housekeeping. Dermot kept the bare light bulb shaded with green paper, his one concession to atmosphere.

I held a nine of Clubs, barely useful in relation to the other cards in this poker game. If I were a gypsy fortune-teller, I could have held this nine and pronounced it a fortunate card, coupled with its dark suit of Clubs—a number representing strong will, great reserves of fortitude. But I held fortune differently. I discarded the nine. Dermot coughed again, trying to smother the sound in his black beard. His beard threatened to take over his head, it grew so far out on either side of his face, but above the beard what you noticed were his kindly suspicious eyes. He wasn't suspicious of me. The long arms which allowed him to deal cards across a wide round table or thwack miscreants on the far side of the smooth wooden bar, those same long arms had picked me up and set me on a bar stool when I was too small to see past the edge of the oilcloth. He said he was just doing himself a favour, taking advantage of local talent, but he was always kinder than he claimed.

I'd played for Dermot for seven years—he introduced me to the game when I was ten. I picked up the rudiments of cards from my mother's upstairs neighbour, but Dermot was the one who gave me a chance at poker, little stick of a thing that I was, and I felt a certain loyalty to him. He was the one who encouraged me to listen to what the cards had to say, and during most games, the cards offered me quite the serenade. The player opposite me, Kevin, almost as short as me, and round like Humpty-Dumpty, had been playing at Dermot's pretty much since I started there. He looked at his cards, bending the slightest corners back from his not-quite-new striped vest, so he could see what he held. Then he folded, because he was tired of bluffing and more important, he had to get home in time for dinner or his wife would tan the skin off his knuckles. In the seven years that I'd played at Dermot's, I'd grown to appreciate players like Kevin. The man didn't know much about poker, but he knew a great deal about life, and every now and then he enlightened me on some subject I hadn't any experience with: traditional marital relations for example. My mother's household was no shining example and I needed whatever education I could find.

When Dermot first sat me on a barstool and handed me a pack of cards, he taught me the different hands of poker, showed me how to figure the simplest odds for a flush based on what had already gone by in the game, and he taught me the need for secrecy, to keep that so-called poker face no matter what my hand revealed. I can't explain why the cards were my perfect key, a password to the world around me. All I know is that I recognized them as my saving grace, from the first moment I held them in my hands. And I might not have known this was unusual, except that Dermot seemed so delighted by my prowess. I soon discovered that the men who played poker in the backroom of Dermot's bar had no feel for cards. They had no idea. I mean, they hadn't the foggiest notion of how to listen to the game. Winning money from them was almost too easy, except that I was a child. Can't imagine that grown men would easily agree to play with a mere girl? You have to imagine Vancouver back then, through the dirty black Thirties.

It was 1938, that spring which was so unseasonably hot, before the War, before so many things. Cars still had running boards. Their hooded shapes cruised along the grand streets of Hastings and Burrard, paperboys running alongside selling headlines for a nickel.

And my nickels, from Dermot's games? Oh, I saved a few coins; the rest, I spent at the movies. On Granville Street I went to see *Top Hat* at the Orpheum Cinema and dreamed about finding such a fantastical world, where women wore dresses covered in ostrich feathers, where music played and Fred Astaire danced. The mythic pair of Fred and Ginger swirled through a brightly-lit dream, while around Vancouver, men lived in cardboard encampments along the beaches, and lumber mills churned the stench of pulp through downtown. The city was a wild and strange place, with mud where roads later were, and in that harsh last year of the Depression, anything was possible—even a girl winning at cards, day after day, winning every game for a whole month that March.

That was the month a man actually managed to kill himself by jumping off the Burrard Bridge. A number of enterprising depressives had tried, but despite their enthusiastic leaps from the bridge, they were dredged still-breathing from the water by fishermen, who wrapped them in blankets and gave them warm toddies. The fishermen had better things to do than fish for men who'd failed to kill themselves, but what else could they do? There was practically a traffic jam of people waiting to throw themselves from that bridge.

The men who didn't want to kill themselves came down to drink and gamble in Gastown, the rough old part of the city near the port, where Dermot had his beer hall. It wasn't a glamorous establishment. From the sawdust-covered floor to the old pressed-tin ceiling, the room's atmosphere consisted of smoke and beer fumes, but there were fewer fights under Dermot's watch than in other bars. His beady Irish eyes kept even the meanest men in line, and if patrons didn't obey his dark glare, there was always his vast beard, bristling off his chin like his very own bear. Dermot managed to keep the bar going despite the general downward slide of the neighbourhood. Some months, the backroom games kept him afloat.

I put my two cards face-down on the table; I knew what I had. Face-up on the table, to complete my hand, were two eights (Clubs and Hearts), the Queen of Spades, and the ten of Hearts. Not a pretty show, such cards added up to nothing on their own, except that I was holding both the Queen and

Jack of Hearts. I had played the game tight, folding often, but my opponents at Dermot's weren't very good at paying attention. So now they overlooked the fact that I was betting hard—I could use the pair of Queens, if nothing else. The remaining player glanced at Kevin, who shrugged as he raised me. A man who worked for the railway was dealing, he'd been cleaned out a little while back. He burned the top card by turning it over and putting it to the side, as one does, and turned up the next card. To my delight, it was the nine of Hearts. That was that.

The more games that went through my hands, the more fascinating poker seemed. It was a kind of love affair, an infatuation that grew into a more serious emotion. Instead of being one-sided, this love seemed mutual. I knew even as a child that I was a plain girl, and men would never fall in love with me for my looks. I had squared myself with that. But the cards liked me, and Dermot was surprisingly honest with the cash he won when I played for him, splitting our winnings 20/80 exactly, keeping the greater part for himself. This was fair—I was learning, and that backroom was my apprenticeship. The good grace in playing was mine, but I'd never have gotten to play at all without Dermot. Because of his belief in me, I'd moved up from merely dealing the game to running the table for him. I played in the back while he ran the bar, a division of labour based on skill.

At Dermot's I learned about tells, the series of motions and notions betrayed by men's gestures. Tells reveal what you need to know about anyone's game. There are simple tells—you should always call a man who has a hand to his mouth when he places a bet. You'll be right more often than not. I always watched the way a man reacted, after I'd placed my bet—if he had a strong hand, his shoulders would invariably relax, just the tiniest bit, seeing that I was still in the game. Of course it's not that easy with life in general. Get me away from a table and I make mistakes. But I'm convinced that even in real life, there's always a telltale, giveaway moment. The trick is finding the tell.

As Kevin cleared out, a woman came in from the street, looking for a man she knew, or looking for someone to buy her a drink, or maybe looking for someone to buy her, quite directly. Dermot was up at the front of the bar within seconds, taking her politely by the elbow and escorting her out, assuring his patrons that there were no women allowed. "Keeps the bar clean," he said, and the men drinking his watery beer laughed.

When he returned to the doorway of the backroom, I said, "Don't you think that you're lying?"

"What would I be lying about? "

"That there aren't any women in your bar. There's me. "

"You're only a kid, Millard. And you're not in the bar, so to speak. "

I frowned at him. "I'll be eighteen next year. "

"If it'll please the lady, I'll call you Miss Millard. "

I rolled my eyes and put away my take.

"I wish your mother could spare you the whole night. "

He meant nothing unseemly. It was just the occasional midnight game, when a gambler passed through town or when someone had gotten lucky at something else. The stakes played at night were larger than the ones at his afternoon games.

"You know I'd like to. " Oh, I wanted to try my hand at a different kind of game, to look around the table and study the hands and watch new faces give themselves away. But I didn't see how I'd ever get out of the house—even asleep, my mother had razor-sharp hearing, probably because her men always left her sudden-like. I didn't need to explain this to Dermot. He seemed preoccupied.

"What is it? "

"If I call you Miss Millard and up your share to half, will you do it? "

"Half? Truly fifty-fifty? " I narrowed my eyes at Dermot, who looked at the stained ceiling. "Are you short this month? "

"Joycie's upping his fees. "

Joyce worked for the police force; he made a nice sideline off the bar owners, turning a blind eye to their misdemeanours in return for a bit of pocket money. I rested my hands on the oilcloth and spread out my long fingers. Each of my knuckles was chafed, every nail broken down to the quick. I didn't care. I turned my palms over, the skin crisscrossed by innumerable lines; my hands looked old enough to be reliable when I held a hand of cards.

"Fifty-fifty, " said Dermot, reading my pause as a near-acceptance. "Joycie's gone and recommended our game here to a man from Seattle that I don't rightly know and I don't rightly trust. He's coming tonight. I think you'd be a pretty distraction. "

"Mr. McMann, I'm not anything like.... "

"We're starting at ten o'clock. "

"Dermot, " I said, using his Christian name as I never did, to make him look at me. I even put the right sort of Irish tilt to it. The surprise fixed his eyes on my face. "I'm nothing like a pretty distraction. "

"You can play cards against him. That's pretty. Fifty-fifty, just for tonight. "

I thought about the money. The only kind of accounting I've ever been good at is the kind you do with cash when it's in front of you on the table. I could visualize it there. I could do any kind of sum at all with cash on the table. I did this sort of accounting for a little while as Dermot waited, but then I shook my head. Dermot wrinkled his forehead; he must have wondered how he was going to pay off Joyce and I felt badly for him. He was a sort of father to me, I never had any other to speak of. Playing this nighttime game wasn't really much to ask of me—I would gain from it, I'd be able to play a more difficult, more challenging game. My heart, as the expression goes, ought to leap at the chance. I stood up and brushed my hands as if I were dusting them off.

"I'll see what I can do, " I said.

From the very beginning, my mother disapproved of my poker-playing. When I was fourteen, in an effort to keep me away from Dermot's, she got me an after-school job in the hotel where she worked—a shift in the laundry. So I spent the afternoons at Dermot's, when I was supposed to be at school, and I worked evenings at the basement laundry. Then the chief laundress took sick, everyone in the laundry moved up a rung, and I washed up in a morning shift, which left me time for Dermot's, but I could no longer go to school at all.

My mother made no protest about my education; by then I was nearly sixteen, and the better wage of the longer morning shift was worth it. I gave my mother all my laundry earnings. No one at the school missed me and I didn't miss them. I had taken what I wanted. I could add, subtract, do percentages, I could read and write. No one felt it necessary for me to stay in school, not even Dermot, who'd at least taken some pride in my occasional good grade. So I worked full-time at the hotel laundry. The smell of bleach made me nauseous, every shift leaving the taste of bile in my mouth. I don't mean that as a metaphor. We used so much bleach, I really did feel sick to my stomach from it. Towels, sheets, pillowcases, tablecloths, napkins, aprons, all boiled white. Just thinking about those sheets, now, the smell drifts towards me and I feel queasy. I don't like white things around, it's such a false cleanliness—you can be clean and not bleached white. And you can be filthy and covered up with some ghostly white sheet, blue-white, it's so clean.

I laundered from five in the morning until four in the afternoon, Monday through Saturday. Then I departed the Hotel Vancouver basement, I took off my damp white apron and left it hanging in the basement staff room, and I walked down the street to join whoever was playing in Dermot McMann's backroom. I played poker until my mother finished her shift at the hotel; I made sure I always got home before she did.

My mother worked every day of the week in the Hotel Vancouver as a cook. She was never a chef, simply a cook. Only men were allowed to be chefs. My mother cooked the hotel guests' lunch and then she cooked them dinner. She worked until eight at night. Her favourite menu was the huge roast beef done up on Sundays, because the meat was carved in the dining room and she had fewer things to do in the kitchen. A good thing, because by Sunday night she was usually exhausted; on weekends she worked breakfast as well and sleep was a figment she imagined. No wonder she was right irritable if I woke her up.

I didn't see how I could slip back to Dermot's by ten at night without my mother suspecting there was a poker game involved. My mother was a decent woman, not God-fearing; intelligent, not educated; a brooder not a drinker. Well, not exactly. She had black hair and dark eyes and about all that made us look related was a certain similar intensity to our expression. When she was in her darkest moods, I used to make her tea, very strong. She would sit in the only armchair in our living room, wrapped in a red and black mohair afghan. I used to think it was the afghan that cajoled her into a better mood—I knew it wasn't my loyal company. Eventually I decided tea was the essential element.

If I went out for the night, maybe I could convince the boy who lived upstairs from us to lie for me. Teddy was my best friend, and when he smiled just the right way, my mother believed anything he told her. If I bought him a chocolate bar, Teddy would say anything. From the backroom, I went out into the alley. A guy was going through the rubbish outside the building. He was the colour of the empty tins he'd lined up around his feet—who knows what he planned to build with them. I was practiced in slipping around these rag-pickers, skilled at dodging the rest of the flotsam-jetsam that washed in from the port, the ex-sailors, injured loggers, idlers and rare family men who populated the tangle of streets that led up from the docks.

Coming onto Cambie Street, I skirted around a man delivering seltzer bottles, the glass necks clanking against one another as he brought the dolly over the curb. Main Street clamoured with people coming home from work. Hawkers and peddlers elbowed through the crowd, trying to interest passers-by with shiny buttons and shoelaces, bits of lace and scavenged hardware. I traipsed through the mob to Oppenheimer Park. All along the far side of the baseball diamond, herb sellers and fishmongers weighed out their wares. I passed the Japanese market on Powell that offered five types of bean curd in cakes, lined up in tidy rows—not my chosen treat. No, I stopped at the ice-cream cart on the far corner.

Money made a difference for the smallest of things. The cash I earned from my usual cut of winnings at Dermot's gave me the freedom to eat ice cream every day of the week, if I wanted. I spent some of those coins on socks and stockings—eventually I wanted to buy a new pair of shoes. I spent the coins I earned and stored the bills away, neatly filed in the pages of the novels I read. I only owned a few books, but they served me well, storing my money for the future. I hadn't quite decided what that future was going to be.

The rain was starting by the time I chose my ice cream flavour. The vendor scooped the vanilla I'd selected as large blops of water splattered down. The rain made everyone look polka-dotted but the weather didn't change how much I liked the walk, ice cream on my tongue, cone in my hand. The shops here had their old outfitter signboards alongside new neon signs, three different colours of blinking green-pink-white right next door to carefully-cut letters advertising brands of food and cigarettes. I couldn't read the varnished boards painted with hand-brushed calligraphy, written for the Chinese who lived on the far side of Hastings Street. The Chinese had come to Canada to work on the railway and hadn't ever gone home. Maybe they couldn't get home. Maybe they were stuck here, same as me, planning an escape but not quite clear how to do it. Somehow I imagined that China must be very much like the interior of British Columbia—mountains and lakes and dry cool landscape. I passed the Chinese boy selling firecrackers. He stood on the lid of the box and yelled as you passed his corner, and if you gave him a penny for a firecracker, he'd jump off his box, open the lid, and fish out a thin stick wrapped in red paper.

I turned onto my block of East Pender Street, all off-kilter houses and ill-kept gardens. I don't think East Pender was ever an elegant road. It sprang up fully-formed and crooked, with a ditch running in front of some of the stoops and nothing good to be said for some of its inhabitants. Our house was more or less identical to all the others, nothing to be proud of, though my mother was. Our house was painted a middling shade of blue, with peeling white trim and a verandah that gave straight out onto the sidewalk in three sharp steps, no intervening flowers or decoration.

We rented the ground floor, two and a half rooms, my bedroom being the half. It was designed as a pantry, cold as stink in winter, but it was private, it had a door and a window, so from the moment we moved in, I adopted it as my private room while my mother took over the real bedroom. The main room, the biggest part of the ground floor, served as living room, kitchen, homework room, dining room and bath, all at once and with serviceable furnishings.

As I approached the house, I wondered if Teddy was likely to be home. He was the most reliable person I knew. I didn't know then how he would change, I still believed in him, partly because he'd kindly kept the school bullies from breaking my skull, during the uneven years of my education—I was a small and solitary girl, and what's more, I liked to read, which made me entirely too attractive a target. I used to read aloud to Teddy before we went to sleep. I was indiscriminate—newspapers, advertisements for hair oil, any kind of book appealed to me—but Teddy preferred adventures like *Treasure Island*. I read to him while our mothers were out working. I tried to teach him cards, but he hadn't the patience to read them, so I went back to telling him stories.

Teddy was three years younger than me, but he was tall for his age. He could charm his way out of most arguments, but he always had a handy fist to back up his smile. Teddy looked older than he was, and he looked darn good. Something smooth and charming in his walk, an indefinable quality that made everyone turn and stare when he went by. I suppose we were the Mutt and Jeff of friendships. We grew up together in that crooked blue house.

As I got closer to our house, I saw him lying across our front steps, poking something with a twig. I finished the last of my ice cream cone as I reached our stoop, and kicked Teddy's leg with my shoe.

"Look't this," he said. He glanced up at me, pushing his black hair out of his eyes. He poked two beetles with the twig—he was trying to get them to fight, I suppose.

I stepped over the bugs. "Do you have a shirt you can lend me?"

He rolled onto his side. "Why?"

"And can I borrow your jacket?"

Teddy sat up, his brown eyes cagey. "What d'you want with my clothes?"

"I want to walk to Gastown at ten tonight with no one bothering me. Do you mind helping me, please."

"Why're you going out? You got a boyfriend?"

"Why would I want your castoff clothes for a date?"

"Oh, it's a card game...." He laid off torturing the beetles and threw himself through the door that led upstairs to his mother's apartment.

I went straight into my mother's part of the house, the screen door clattering behind me. My plan wasn't very original—if I didn't look like a girl, no one would be able to say they'd seen me walking through the neighbourhood late at night, on my way to Dermot's. And for the game itself, it didn't matter what I wore. I didn't care what the poker players thought of my appearance. No one ever looked at me and thought *isn't she easy on the eyes*. When a man looked at me in those days, he probably thought *isn't she a strange little shifty-eyed thing*. Fortunately, cards don't give a darn what you look like.

The only trick with the game tonight was keeping my mother in the dark. If she believed that I had gone to bed in a bad mood, she might leave me alone until the morning. She sympathized with bad moods, being queen of such things herself.

Teddy's steps tumbled on the stairs, then he pushed open the screen door of our part of the house, holding a jacket and a shirt for me, along with an old pair of shoes.

"Is Mary Ellen home?" I asked.

"Ma's out."

An even-featured woman with abnormally long eyelashes, her face polished by the sun, she spent hours outside, finding the right ingredients for her remedies. I could have trusted Mary Ellen with the truth of where I was going. She was good with secrets, and she knew truth could be complicated. Teddy was her spitting image. I've never understood that expression: did it mean they were so alike they might spit at each other? Though that wasn't quite true—where Mary Ellen's face was even-featured, Teddy's had a hint of unease. His eyebrows were ever so slightly crooked, his upper lip a bit too full, curved too much to one side, with a just-so tilt to his cheek— his features were the same as Mary Ellen's, same eyes, eyelashes, nose, yet rakishly set the tiniest bit off-balance. You felt trust, looking at Mary Ellen. You felt something different, looking at Teddy.

If Mary Ellen was out, it was because she was birthing a baby, or collecting plants to perform the kind of miracles people needed in those days. The kind of miracles we've come to believe only happen in doctors' offices and hospitals, which back then seemed to happen upstairs in Mary Ellen's very clean front room, where there was a table that wasn't used for dinner and where the curtains were kept closed. Everyone knew what Mary Ellen did in her house and no one thought less of her for it. Every woman in the district had gone up those stairs one time or another.

"Your mother would understand," I said, taking the clothes from Teddy and retreating into my pantry-bedroom to change.

My bedroom had once been painted an ill-chosen medicinal shade of blue that had faded to a more personable pale turquoise. There was space only for my neatly-made bed, with a well-organized bookshelf above my pillow and a row of hooks for my clothes, below the window. I sloughed off my usual dress and sweater, folding them and squaring them to the edge of the bed so they hid the hole in my beige blanket. I hated that hole, but I didn't have the skill to mend it properly, or the nerve to tell my mother that I'd torn it—a nail caught the blanket as I made the bed one morning, too carelessly, too quickly. So now I was stuck with the hole, ugly as it was. I reminded myself that summer was coming and soon I wouldn't need the blanket.

Teddy's clothes were too big for me, but I rolled up the trousers and hitched in the belt he'd brought me. The shoes were much too wide. I tried lacing them up with extra socks, sitting in the living room, but it was no use. I put on my mud boots instead. Teddy watched me silently.

"You have to tell my mother I've gone to bed in a mood," I said. "Be convincing so she won't bother checking on me."

"What do I get out of it?"

"A Snickers bar."

Teddy smiled. "One Snickers bar for lying to your ma, another for lying to mine."

"You don't have to tell Mary Ellen anything one way or the other, and you certainly don't have to lie to her," I said. "One Snickers bar, that's the offer."

He tilted his head to consider my outfit. "You look like that sorry git Plotznick at school."

Teddy was suspended, for the third time, forbidden now to finish the school year, for he had broken another boy's nose. The boy was the local bully, Gerald

Avison, who was picking on sorry git Plotznick. Teddy never liked an uneven fight. He respected other people's physical frailties. Intellectual frailty, well, he figured he was born to take you in any con available. He stomped across the schoolyard and stood in front of sniveling poor git Plotznick, careful not to step on the broken shards of the boy's knocked-off eyeglasses. He picked bullying Gerald Avison up by the hair, broke his nose with a clean punch of a loosely-balled fist, and left him bawling in the schoolyard. Plotznick didn't know what had happened. His glasses smashed on the ground, he couldn't see past his own unharmed nose. I easily imagined Teddy sauntering from the schoolyard, leaving a grateful Plotznick to retrieve the pieces of his broken spectacles.

I had my own reasons for disliking Gerald Avison—when I was fifteen, he'd cornered me at school, beside the janitorial closet. "Are you even a girl?" he'd said. "You don't look like a girl. Let's see." He rammed a mop handle between my legs and forced me into the cupboard. But before he could close the door, the recess bell rang and a torrent of children swarmed into the hallway. Teddy's class rushed past, and Teddy stopped. He took hold of Gerald Avison—before he'd even seen for sure that it was me, trapped there—and in the resulting tussle, he kicked Gerald in the head. Which meant I caused Teddy's first suspension. And Gerald's ear wasn't the same afterwards.

I adjusted the jacket and tried to look fierce. Teddy collapsed in laughter.

"I don't look convincing?"

"I hope the game's at Dermot's."

"None of your business."

"What am I supposed to tell your mother again?"

"Bad mood. I've gone to bed in a bad mood and don't want to be disturbed. If she believes you, I'll buy you a Snickers bar, but if she doesn't, no candy," I bartered. "Of course the game's at Dermot's, where else would I play cards?"

"Give it time, Mill. You'll play against the best of them. How about I get a cut for helping you get out to play?" That was Teddy all over—fourteen years old and working the angles.

"Fat chance."

"Then I want a dollar. No, two dollars. As well as the candy bar."

"You're a rat."

He grinned. And I agreed to his terms—he was too old to bribe with chocolate. I wished I had some other friend I could lure into helping me, but Teddy was my only ally—the neighbourhood girls my age had crummy jobs and worse boyfriends, and they had no time for me. Our interests were too different.

I believed that cards offered me everything I needed to understand the world. My mother was at fault for this conviction—first, because she offered no alternate beliefs, and second, because it was through her I discovered cards. Not directly. But I came to cards through Teddy's father, a soft-spoken man who spent too much time in my mother's company. Teddy's father was a gambler, the first I ever knew. He kept a pack of cards in his satchel, which is how I discovered those bits of cardboard that have made such a life for me. And make no mistake, I am forever grateful to him.

When we first arrived in Vancouver, my mother chose to play around with the only person we knew in the city—a gambling man who lived on East Pender Street, in Mary Ellen's house. We came down from the Interior, and my mother looked him up, for she was practical in affairs of the heart. We came to Vancouver and moved into the ground floor apartment of Mary Ellen's house.

My mother spent a few weeks in bed, when we first arrived. She was unwell, and despite whatever history lingered with Teddy's father, Mary Ellen looked after her. That's what Mary Ellen did, as a midwife—she looked after people, and sometimes she brought babies into the world. Other times, she sent babies away.

I'd seen Mary Ellen, a few months before Teddy's birth, helping a woman who'd come to her big with a child. I went upstairs after, to see the baby. No one was there, but a wrapped package sat at the top of the stairs. I know I shouldn't have opened it, but that's how I found out what happened to babies Mary Ellen didn't want around. I know I cried out—maybe in horror, but probably only in surprise. Children aren't naturally squeamish, or at least, I wasn't. The dead child in that package, wrapped up, curled as it was, poor thing, obviously the tiny bloody body had come out of the pregnant woman who'd been at the house—I knew that much about where babies came from. Such things weren't so mysterious back then. By the time I got to Vancouver, I'd seen a dead rabbit's stomach full of tiny unborn rabbits, which didn't scare me so much as surprise me, how they were packed up in there.

It must have been a terrible job for Mary Ellen, herself well into her sixth month, to help someone else lose a child—knowing as I do now, how losing things isn't easy. But that dead baby was a tiny bloody thing, wrapped in a piece of cloth. I suppose Mary Ellen was planning to bury it later, after helping the woman home. I wrapped the aborted child up as it had been before, not horrified by its squashed shape, only disturbed that it was so obviously dead. I hadn't expected it to be dead—I thought maybe it would be waiting for Mary Ellen to breathe life into it. Mind you, it looked more like a kitten than a baby and I'd seen kittens born dead; all that licking did nothing for them.

It must have been about the same time, one of those evenings, that Teddy's card-playing father came downstairs to talk with my mother. I used to think that's what they did in her room, they talked, while I was sent out to play on the veranda. On one of those evenings, while Teddy's father sat in the living room, smoking, waiting for my mother to come back from work, I crouched on the floor, looking through his bag. I discovered a patterned box with pretty pieces of paper flattened inside. I liked these cards immediately, I took them out without any trouble at all and laid them on the floor in front of me. Teddy's father noticed what I was doing. But instead of telling me to put the cards back, instead of scolding me for snooping, he explained the suits, the symbols, the face cards. What he noticed was my dexterity.

"You've not played with cards before?" he said after a bit.

I shook my head and shuffled the deck.

"Like this?" I asked him.

He demonstrated a more elaborate waterfall shuffle and I imitated him. He tried the same thing left-handed, a little awkward, and I smoothly did the same.

"Dear God," he said. I remember wondering what it was that concerned him religiously at that moment. I generally only heard the Lord's name used at times of mystery, upstairs at Mary Ellen's.

I was immediately taken with this new pretty toy, the wonderful sound of the cards rustling through my small hands. I was much seized with the colours, blue-patterned on one side and a firm red or black against white on the other. The medieval face cards, double-headed, always partly upside-down, I understood instinctively. Isn't something always turned over or hidden or peering at the world from another angle?

Teddy's father spent that afternoon teaching me Go Fish. When he put the cards away, he explained that they were fragile, these paper things, and expensive, and I wasn't to touch them without permission.

"Yes, sir," I said. One of the few times I listened quite seriously and didn't think of disobeying.

I wouldn't say I knew my future was in those cards, but I had seen something that filled me with awe. Something that was not of the Interior, not part of the bush, not a tomboy's toy, not a dead rabbit's bloodied belly. I hadn't thought about being a girl—I was satisfied with being a tiny tomboy—but I wasn't sure how to get on in this new city. All the children seemed so much bigger than I was. So I recognized those cards. I saw they could explain the world to me, they could offer a bigger future than I had understood before, from the moment I held those pieces of coloured paper and felt the way they fit in my hands.

"Your daughter's got a funny skill with cards," he said to my mother when she came home from work.

She prepared some dinner for me, and I didn't think she was going to deign to answer him. Often she didn't speak to me, I was used to it—better to have silence than shouting. But when the soup was in the bowl and set in front of me, she looked at him quite specifically.

"At cards," she said, "and how would you know that?"

He ran a finger along his mustache.

"I'd rather you didn't teach her your gaming trade," she said.

He shook his head fast. "Not at all, I wasn't...."

"Games?" I said, "You play games?"

My mother looked severe. "Most men," she said, "play games. And this one plays particular ones."

"With cards?" I said, delighted.

To his credit, Teddy's father lied. From experience, I can say that no one found it easy to lie when my mother was in the room, yet I think he must have loved both my mother and possibly me, for he said, "No. Nothing to do with cards. You should eat your dinner." That evening, he went directly upstairs and I wasn't sent out to play on the veranda.

It wasn't long after that Teddy got himself born. We heard him crying. His father was away, I don't know where. Teddy was born on the first of May and he was born a colicky baby, which means he cried without stopping, for months unending. He was a horrible ugly infant with a thicket of black hair cowlicking all over his head and black eyes glaring at the world. He took a quick look around as soon as he was born and screamed for five months nonstop. It's bruising to the ego, to have a child react in such a way, and his father, despite his generosity with cards and kindness to me, well, he proved to be our neighbourhood's usual temporary type. He took one look at Teddy and packed his bags. Bad enough to have a baby in the house, especially bad if the damn thing is so ugly, and impossibly bad if it screams all the time and a man can't get any rest. Neither could anyone else on our street.

"That man was no good anyhow," said Mary Ellen.

Then she turned her face to the wall and didn't move for two days. Theodore, for he was already named by then if not baptized, howled worse than ever. I couldn't blame his father for leaving—the noise was something amazing. But I was too little to abandon ship, and anyhow I was curious about the screaming ugly critter. When I heard him crying upstairs, I didn't want Mary Ellen to dispatch him like a squashed kitten, the way she'd done with that other woman's baby. So I went upstairs. The baby was wrapped up in a pale blanket, face up, squirming, and Mary Ellen was sleeping, drop dead exhausted despite Teddy's squawls.

I brought him downstairs, a heavy task for me, tiny though he was. I carried him down to our main room and my mother fed him lukewarm powdered milk, which didn't impress him at all. Mary Ellen lay upstairs as if she were dead. Of course she wasn't, but she was mourning herself, so to speak. Finally, now I suspect her breasts hurt too much to keep ignoring him, but back then I thought she had forgiven Teddy for what he'd done, getting himself born and so on, but Mary Ellen decided to turn her face away from the wall and feed Teddy again. Good thing too, I don't know if he'd have survived otherwise. He certainly wasn't impressed with the goo my mother tried to stuff into his screaming tiny self. I think maybe Teddy's height was because of all his fussiness as a baby—all that screaming served to stretch him out.

My mother took one look at Teddy, the shrieking child from upstairs, horrible as he was, and he moved into a place in her heart I didn't know was there. She fell in love with that baby. We'd gotten to Vancouver as a tiny team of two, the woman with long black hair and her small silent daughter. When I brought Teddy down from upstairs, the balance was shifted, though I didn't know at first. I learned my mother could be passionate—just not towards me. Sometimes Teddy seemed to be our only bond.

Teddy and I were from that one small house and we were allies; we had different fathers and different mothers, we had different faces and our hair and eyes did not match in any way, but I once believed we held the same view of the world. It made sense that Teddy's father was the one who first taught me cards, who noticed how perfectly those pieces of lacquered paper fit into my hands. And when he abandoned the household, Mary Ellen mourned for her husband, my mother missed her lover, Teddy screamed for his father, and I was left with two amazing gifts: a pack of cards and a bright new best friend.

I barely understood cards myself, but as soon as Teddy could sit unassisted, I demonstrated a waterfall shuffle for him. Between stories I read him, I taught him cards. Later, every game that Dermot taught me, I brought home and showed to Teddy. I made poker real for myself by teaching him how to play. I spread out the red and black afghan on the floor and we sat on the red and black squares, playing Crazy Eights and War and five stud, betting with licorice candies. I taught Teddy to hold a proper fan of cards by the time he could walk. I thought it was quite the accomplishment.

No wonder he now felt entitled to a cut of my profits. I sighed and shook his hand, very formally, as if we were partners.

2

The city smelled different at night, less lushly green. I wasn't usually in Gastown at night so I wasn't used to the quiet. The occasional car streaking by seemed like a bad omen, leaving the smell of gas and wet asphalt, metallic, hanging in the dark. I imagined I was completely invisible in my hasty disguise, I imagined I was part of the night, an appropriate street urchin. I glanced at the steam clock as I went into Dermot's—exactly ten minutes before ten, perfectly on time for the game. It was most satisfying to walk in the front door of the bar for a change. I stepped over the accumulated sawdust and ash and peanut shells that formed a kind of ridge at the threshold, and I bellied up to the heavy bar. It was so high I could practically rest my chin on it.

I said to Dermot, "Sir, can I speak to you for a minute?"

Dermot put down the whiskey bottle he was holding. Then he carefully set down the empty glass in his other hand. He pressed his lips together but he couldn't keep his beard from shaking with laughter.

To stave off his unavoidable remark, I said, "I'm Teddy Ahern's cousin. From Kitimat."

He got his beard under control and smiled at me. "They mustn't be feeding you much up there."

"My name's Mason."

"Mason?" said Dermot, raising one thin black eyebrow at me. "I think wee Billy might be better."

"Look," I said, "you want a mechanic, you've got one, just give me a beer for show. I'll spill it and not drink it, don't worry."

"A small beer for the lad? I think not."

"When's it starting?"

"A little while. Come."

He went around the bar and headed through the door that led to the backroom. It was empty. I chose the seat closest to the alley exit, as Dermot closed the bar door behind us. "That's a fool get-up you've got on, Millard."

"Mason."

"Have it your way."

"You want every neighbour on East Pender telling my mother they saw me walking the streets like a child harlot?"

Dermot snorted. The door swung open and Betsch, one of Dermot's better regulars, came in, drunk as usual. The drinking didn't affect his game—Betsch was a dreadful player, but enthusiastic, always with money of some kind. He worked on the railroads as a conductor or ticket-taker, and the job gave him certain opportunities, I believe.

"So when's it startin'?" He squinted at me. "Why in hell you wearin' that outfit, Millard?"

I exhaled in disgust. "I'm Mason Ildritch, Teddy Ahern's cousin. From Kitimat."

Betsch laughed so hard he leaned on the dirty wall nearest the door for support, his wide fat hand against the substantially faded red velour wallpaper that covered that corner of the room. Gradually he caught his breath.

"You tired of bein' a girl amongst all us men? You're a sorry lookin' boy, Millard."

"The girl has feelings," said Dermot softly. "You could be more polite."

Betsch sat down heavily at the round table. "You want to be a boy tonight, fine with me. Be whoever you want, long as you get Joycie off our backs."

Dermot shook his head sharply, as if Betsch had spoken too frankly.

Winch, another regular who drank his way through his hands, bad or good, came in and paused to hold on to the nearest chair. He wavered, as usual. "Who've we got here?" he said, and I swear he hiccupped.

Betsch shook his head.

"I'm just trying to get rid of this pup," said Dermot.

"Hello pup," said Winch.

Which is when Betsch stood and made an elaborate bow, sweeping out a hand towards me in mock ceremony. "Mason, Teddy Ahern's cousin, friend of Millard's," said Betsch.

Winch didn't seem to notice that Betsch was pulling his leg. "Can the pup play cards like Millard, is the question?"

"I'll do my best, sir," I said.

Before heading back to the bar, Dermot set me up at the table to shuffle the deck. Winch watched me a little too carefully, so I muffed up one of the shuffles just to distract him.

"You don't have your cousin's touch, for sure," he said.

I gathered up the few cards I'd let tumble onto the table, evened them up to shuffle once more when the door swung open. We all stared at the man beside Dermot in the doorway. The stranger wasn't as tall as Dermot, but his clothes made him more imposing—he wore a green three-piece suit, a slight stripe through the fabric, with a perfectly white shirt that made my nose itch with bleach. His tie was knotted in some peculiar way that gave him the edge over Winch, who was usually the best-dressed drunk in all of Gastown. This clean-shaven new mark looked so spit-polished and immaculately pressed, I wondered why he'd chosen to turn up here. I placed the pack down neatly and nodded as Dermot introduced us all and each. The mark's name was Roberts.

"Can't find enough men to play? We're reduced to cleaning out kids, now?" he said when I was introduced.

I narrowed my eyes and tried to imitate Teddy's schoolyard glare. The man smiled.

I'm not a skeptic; I'm suspicious, depending on the evidence. I didn't smile back at Roberts, though his calm face gleamed. I sized him up as a healthy thing for my ambitions. He looked like a real competitor, in those expensive clothes that he wore well, a new fish in my very small pond. I admired my opponent, secretly and to myself, while loyal Dermot made soothing comments about my abilities as opposed to my half-pint size. While they chatted, Betsch polished off another drink and eventually a fifth player arrived, someone I only saw occasionally at Dermot's, a man from high-class-on-the-hill Shaunessey, who enjoyed slumming every now and then. He wasn't a bad player, and with his bottomless wallet, he furnished a nice game.

The game of choice that night was seven-card stud, my personal favourite. A good memory is useful for stud because as you play, up to twenty-four cards get turned up and sent on their route, and even if they're gone, they keep influencing the game. It's easy to remember what they are, if you can be bothered to keep track. You'd be surprised how many people don't bother. In seven-card stud, two cards are dealt face down and one card face up, in front of each player. After the first round of betting, a new card is turned up in front of each player. This is Fourth Street. Later, there will be Fifth Street, Sixth Street, Seventh Street, and the river.

Doesn't all that sound like a mining town far into the Interior, up in the mountains? I wasn't born in Vancouver. My mother brought me into the world up in the mountains, in a ruined mining town towards Nelson, in a little house on Fifth Street, near the river. No wonder I took to the language of the seven-card game the way an orange-crested wood duck takes to water.

I understood within one raise why Dermot had asked me in. The stranger could play. He alone of the men at the table knew what he was doing and didn't allow his face to rush away with him. He played his hand and though I read him enough to know if he had something or was just bluffing, I couldn't dismiss his skill. And what surprised me even more was that he recognized straight off that I knew what I was doing. It was an understanding reached almost immediately—he looked at me without seeming to, a strange expression lurking in the corner of his mouth, maybe wondering if I was a cheating thing, if that was my role in the game, some strange trick child Dermot had dredged up in this rainy terminal town. I was careful to keep my hands very obviously aboveground for the next round. Which was tight, he nearly got it, but I won that too, chance favouring me with a pair of Aces.

It wasn't that I ever won absurdly at Dermot's—I'm lucky, not blessed, and there's a certain realism to luck, a difference between being lucky and being struck by lightning. I'm a good player, but no one wins all the time, and that night, I just managed to keep the man controlled. It wasn't easy work— Winch was playing like an imbecile, Betsch the railway guy was drinking so heavily that he could barely remember his calls, and the Shaunessey lawyer wasn't up to scratch, though he seemed to be enjoying himself. Dermot came in from the bar every now and then, kept everyone's drinks topped up and, I liked to think, kept an eye on the fair play, so that I could work in peace. I was really playing against the one stranger; the others were just providing us a game.

Poker isn't any one thing, any specific ability; it's a combination of qualities. The cards are essential, and so is a certain grasp of mathematics. And yes, I'm good at math, not school sums so much, they bore me, but the numbers themselves, poker odds aren't too difficult. I knew how to calculate how many outs there were, or how many cards might help my hand. Even at the simplest game at Dermot's, there were pot odds to be calculated—how much I could win, against how much money I had to put in to stay in the game. But poker isn't math—the most useful qualities to hold in a game aren't cards or odds. What's more crucial is basic human observation. With that, if the cards are in my favour, I'm as close to unbeatable as any one person can be.

A person can't have only one way of playing cards. You have to shift your style according to what's going on at the table, the feeling that the game gives you. And gradually, the feeling I got was that Roberts was going to give me trouble—in this business, feelings are as important as numbers. Winning a pot when you're holding a royal flush, that isn't proof you're a good player. That's simply the cards playing for you. What proves your worth is a sense of guile, of knowing how much your opponent is willing to lose, and figuring out how they'll play while they're losing it. The best players fold more often than the worst ones. The railway man, drunk with no sense of consequence, consistently raised before the flop, betting like a sea otter, greasy and bluffing so obviously that I nearly had to avert my eyes.

I'm a good bluffer. That means I'm a liar, a good one, unfortunately. What I'm telling you is that you shouldn't trust me. Dermot's bar was my introduction to the myriad uses of dishonesty: I lied to my mother about where I was, I lied to fellow-gamblers about my age and skills, and that night, I lied about the fact that I was a girl. I didn't lie to Dermot. And I didn't lie to Teddy, not back then, Teddy who was still my best friend, who was lying for me even as I sat there playing.

There should always be someone you're honest with, especially when you're a gambler. Then you know where safe ground is. Lies grow on a person, you see. My whole self, it might be argued, has become a series of inventions completely at odds with the essential physical fact of my body. Because I'm not a man, which most poker players are. But the bluff isn't just my appearance or how I represent my hand at the card table; bluffing has come to define my life. When I called my friend Teddy a con man in the making, I didn't mean that I was any different.

About an hour into the game there was a sudden shift, so shocking that I didn't understand how it could be possible. In fact it took me a minute to understand. You see, my odds had been excellent, I was holding another pair of Aces, beautiful. And then I lost to Roberts, who put out three nines, an impossible three nines. I went over the odds in my head, the cards played, where they ought to be in the discard pile. Reviewed these details while he raked in what there was. His third nine simply wasn't possible. He had to be—I wouldn't let my hands consider the option, but I knew it was true, the way you know an earthquake is coming by the way a dog runs away down the street. A shift in the air. For all his beautiful clothes, for all his smile, for his lovely hands, ah, with his long well-manicured fingers and his signet ring and his expensive watch on his wrist, he had just started cheating. I couldn't exactly tell how he'd put the card into play, but the exact mechanics of the thing didn't matter.

"Don't like losing, kid?" said the man gently.

I wondered how much Dermot owed this Joycie character. Certainly Betsch seemed to think the bar was in danger—he was trying to drink all the excess stock. No surprise that Dermot walked in just then to serve yet another round of drinks at the final turn. Dermot paused to stare at me—not for losing a hand. He might be disappointed, worried, but he'd not stare like that, no, there must have been suddenly something wrong with my expression.

"Sorry," I mumbled, glancing away. I was dealing next, which gave me a chance to shuffle badly. I bent a card right in half, the Jack of Clubs. "Sorry McMann," I said. "We're going to need a new deck of cards."

The man across the table seemed intrigued by this, only for an instant of course, and no one else noticed the shift in his head. He knew I had found him out.

"Christ," said Winch, "where'd you learn to shuffle?" Dermot excused himself and went for a new pack of cards.

"Can you bring us a whiskey, McMann," I called after him. He muttered impolitely about my pup cheek and closed the door.

The man across the table from me lit a cigarette and stared at me, but I ignored him. I wondered what to do with a charlatan like this. Not just a cheap cheat, which was the type I was used to—the local guys who bothered to cheat could barely play, so their double-crossing was worse than obvious and rarely helped their hands much. Dermot would take them aside and point out that he liked them fine as neighbours, but they weren't going to continue long as customers if they didn't shape up. Dermot had a way, no one ever got angry enough to shoot him—he'd learned his trade in moonshine-fueled silver towns, and those manners served him well in illustrious Gastown.

But this stranger named Roberts, he cheated so smoothly, and I had no way to call him on it. I didn't understand why he was bothering. Was he bored? His job, whatever it was made him travel places, bored him, so while he was in town, this is what he did? I wondered suddenly if this was all he did, I mean, if this *was* his job. I tried to imagine if he came into town in order to fleece foolish people like the men here. A dull lucrative way to spend his nights, if he was usually playing against amiable idiots like Winch. Why even bother cheating?

Which is when I looked up and met the man's eyes. He had lovely eyes, hazel I think is the word for them. Later, I'd say there were sunflowers set into his eyes, much later, when I'd had a chance to study their variations. But that night I looked up and saw his eyes were on me. I realized that he wouldn't normally have bothered to cheat, it wasn't in any way necessary. He was only cheating, he had only decided it was worth cheating, because of me. If it were just Winch, the Shaunessey lawyer, and the twitchy Betsch, there would be no need. He brought out the artillery because he was too proud to lose to me. I couldn't help but feel it was a compliment. I was a girl who got precious few compliments.

Dermot returned with a new pack of cards and whiskeys for everyone but me. I fanned out the cards, happy to see the pattern was different, bicycles instead of bees—good for Dermot, he'd gotten the idea. I didn't win the next hand. It went to Winch, minor miracle that I was happy to see, as if even Winch was trying his damnedest to save Dermot's bottom line.

Roberts seemed content, unbothered. Winding up to the last game, the air tightened, but it was important not to get distracted. Listen to the cards only, I thought, feel the numbers moving across the table. I had the King and Queen of Spades. I calculated my odds; the flop had two Spades in it already. Very nicely, the river card was the Ace of Spades. Inwardly, I smiled, though I had the requisite blank expression. I couldn't have a better hand, and I hadn't cheated to get it, either. Roberts was only somewhat ahead, and if I won the hand it wouldn't ruin anyone, it would just clear the man from Shaunessy out a little. I couldn't let myself think too much about what was on the line with this game: if you think too much about the outside world, you won't be able to hear the cards shift. I cleared my thoughts of whose money it might be, how those dollars would help Dermot, how they would help me, how this was my first serious nighttime game and look how gloriously... I set my teeth hard and concentrated. I knew I had the nuts, I mean, I was holding the cards needed to win. When I put the hand on the table, I allowed myself a sharp-toothed smile.

The man from Seattle nodded as I swept the pot towards me. "For a kid, you're lucky."

"For anyone, she's lucky," said Dermot. And then he blushed, a sudden red on the bit of his face that wasn't covered by beard. "I'm thinking of Millard."

Winch looked at me. He polished off his whiskey and topped it up with his always-available flask. "He doesn't look so ratty as Millard. Shame about that cousin a yours, pup."

"Did she pass away?" said the man across the table.

"No," said Betsch.

"No," I said at the same time, "she disappeared into the basement of the Hotel Vancouver. She washes sheets."

Roberts shook hands with Winch and with Betsch the railway man and with Dermot, and lastly with me. His firm handshake, dry, calm. Which is when I recognized how red and chapped and bleached-out my own fingers looked. Whatever my skill with cards, I had washerwoman hands. Not a boy's hands. The nails were torn and permanently cleaned by the sheets at the Hotel Vancouver. I sat down again while the various players left.

When it was just Dermot and me alone in the room, I put my head on the table, eyes level so I could gaze at the money I'd won. More than I'd ever had before. What would I do with it? An entire year's salary from the Hotel Vancouver, that's what was stacked on the table, twelve months of working in the bleach-stinking laundry, and here it was on the table in front of me. Half of it mine, half of it Dermot's, to pay Joycie. We'd won. But I was exhausted— I thought it would be exhilarating, taking this much money, but even though I was elated, inside, the effort of winning had felt like building a mountain by hand, with spadefuls of dirt. The delight at being finished didn't change the fact that I was dog-tired.

Dermot put a hand on my shoulder. "You okay, Millard?"

I nodded my head, not moving it off the table.

"You're tired is all. Work well done." He pulled out a chair and sat beside me to sort the bills and coins of the take. "Better even than I hoped. Under trying circumstances. How'd you know?" he said.

"There's only the one nine of Spades in the deck. Saw the discards, had already gone past."

He patted my pile of bills. "I don't like letting you walk home with this in your pocket. I'll put your cut in the safe if you want. Up to you, as you like."

"Better leave it here. What time is it?"

Dermot rolled up the money in a green felt cloth. He ruffled my hair, the way he used to when I was a child. "Too late for you. Go home Millard. Get some sleep."

They say the King of Hearts was inspired by Alexander the Great, him with his dancing girls and his dancing boys, that's why he was the leader of Hearts, the player of games. And the King of Spades is supposedly based on the story of David, King of the Hebrews—in the card, look, there's the slingshot he used in killing the giant. The King of Clubs is Charlemagne, he's holding the orb of Christendom, the round thing in his hand, that's the orb. It's important, I suppose, though it doesn't look very useful. And I've been told that the King of Diamonds is Julius Caesar, though no one's ever been able to tell me why. The king who gets murdered by his best friend. I am not sure what that means about the suit of Diamonds in general. Apart from the Ace, which is a handsome card, Diamonds are the suit I like least. Perhaps it's also the one I most resemble.

My mother was the Queen of Diamonds, all sharp ears and a firm hand. Before being hired as a cook for the Hotel Vancouver, she'd worked as the cook for mining operations—if nothing else, that's an environment that cultivates discipline in the midst of chaos—after the madness of those mining camps, the shouting and jostling of the hotel kitchen was relatively peaceful for her. But it tired her out good and plenty. Thank goodness she was sleeping soundly when I snuck back into our house. I put the clothes I'd borrowed from Teddy under my narrow bed and lay down in my little blue room feeling pleased with myself.

Dermot had told me, some time back, "You're a card whisperer. All those soothing noises you make if you're playing a particularly difficult game."

"I do?" I'd have to cut that out, if I was going to get better at the game—I couldn't go muttering about my hands, I'd give the game away.

"It's not what anyone'd hear. But you do it, just the same."

Tonight, I'd almost understood what he meant. I talked to the cards silently, they were like horses, fidgeting under our touch. It was as good an explanation as any. Maybe it was a sort of magic, a trick of fortune brought with me from the Interior. When someone in Vancouver said *the Interior*, they always sounded a bit dubious, a bit unsure, because from this damp exterior surface of the country, it was hard to believe that the Interior existed. But I knew it was there. I believed in the real country inside, protected by the mountains the way your heart is protected by the cage of your ribs. The Interior is hidden far from the city's buildings and machinations, and it is a place filled with luck.

Not that luck is straightforward. The Interior shudders with tremors from earthquakes and little mining towns shiver as fortune comes and goes. I was born during an earthquake, a very minor one. My mother didn't notice, childbirth being a good distraction from other natural disasters, or so she said. My father ran back to the house to save us, I was told, but I was already born, tiny fists held up. From the beginning, my hands were filled with luck. At least, that's what I remember—unprovable, memory being about as reliable as a drunkard's promise to pay when he gets up from the table. There are only three facts that I know for certain about my father, my mother's first husband. I know my father was a pretty man; I know he made my mother laugh; I know he walked away and never returned.

That was why we came out of the Interior, a black-haired woman and her scowling little daughter, a slip of a girl who fidgeted all the time. My fortune's always been in my hands, even before I met the cards. Whereas Teddy's fortune was in his face.

"Don't you see," Teddy had complained once, "your dad musta been hiding out up there in the woods with you lot. Not like my washout dad. Yours needed a place to lie low, like a pirate."

"I don't think so."

"What would you know about it? You weren't even three years old when he left."

In the Interior, I was a pretty little girl, that's what I remember. My mother must have only looked at me properly when we got into the city—that's when I realized that I was plain. Looking back, I feel curiosity more than anything— was I really such an odd girl, able to steer my future? How could anyone so young have made such clear decisions? I could argue my life has been at the whim of Fate, the word arranged in capitals, but a person can be complicit with fate. I was as determined a girl as ever has stood on this earth. Any decisions made? They were mine.

Picture me as a seventeen-year-old girl, wearing worn-out shoes and a strangely disinterested expression, a poker face I practiced carefully. Imagine my sharp mouth as quiet, controlled, to hide how incredibly interested I was in the world. Make the image of that girl plainer, and younger, for I looked much younger than I was. And even plainer, again. My mother had to admit this when I confronted her on the issue. "You're unusual looking, is all," is what she said. When I realized I wasn't simply a very short tomboy, that I was in fact just a girl with no looks, I stared at myself in a shop window and took stock. I had a face made up of funny angles, narrow eyes of no discernible colour, neither brown nor green nor anything else. I had hard cheekbones, a chin that broadened out oddly as if trying to give me a boy's jawline, and beyond the jaw, I had ears that stuck out.

I didn't get prettier when I hit puberty, exactly, though I grew into my ears a little. I had sallow skin. My nose was small and did nothing for my face except allow a pimple to sprout on its tip occasionally—though once I stopped sweating bleach at the laundry, my skin improved. My forehead remained too long for my face, or else my hair started too far back on my head, until I learned how to do my hair properly. And when I smiled at my reflection, I recognized that my thin lips framed small, very pointed crooked teeth. The only good thing that could be said was my teeth were at least my own and white, not rotten. I was thin enough to be practically concave, with no figure to speak of. My fingers were unusually long, especially since they appeared at the end of squarely-serviceable hands and rather short arms. And I had big feet, as a final blow to any possible elegance of movement.

"Beauty doesn't matter," my mother said. "Character is what counts."

But beauty does matter. My mother, for example, was beautiful. Teddy, rough-and-tumble boy though he was, was beautiful. I told myself that I was uninterested in beauty, that I cared only about being neat. I was very neat. But I knew I was lying: I cared desperately about beauty. After all, what else did I remember from the Interior, except that it was beautiful? The way the light moved across the green of the mountains opposite the gorge, or the way my mother used to walk down the pine-needle path from our house, singing to herself, singing to me. The twisting trees around and above us. These things were beautiful, and I never would be. If I wasn't going to be beautiful, I would turn my back on beauty. I would focus my attention on something else, and what came into my hands was money.

What I didn't realize was that, in turning my hands to money, the passage of cards through my long strange fingers made me something close to beautiful in other people's eyes. It would take me a very long time to discover this, that my narrow eyes, the peculiar angles of my face made me memorable. I was difficult to forget, once someone took the trouble to look at me properly.

It was difficult to fall asleep after that night-time game at Dermot's; I lay on my bed, eyes closed, going over the details. I thought about the man who seemed to play cards as a business endeavour, a way to get on in the world, who'd cheated and lost. The last card I saw in my mind's eye, my mind's shuffle, before I finally fell far into sleep, was the six of Hearts. A card that means luck and a helping hand. That's the card for me, I thought dreamily, I was determined to win by my own hand, thank you very much. I was born pig-headed, my mother would say. No doubt she was right.

All too soon the grey of early daylight seeped into the window and into my eyes and my mother was banging on the door.

"You're running late," she said, when I creaked open the door and blinked out. "Your mood better?"

She gave me a bread roll spread with crabapple jelly to eat on the way. I hadn't slept nearly enough, but I kissed my mother and went out into the drizzle of the morning. The clouds were heavy in the sky, pushing against the roofs of the houses, whose colours washed away in the grey light. The streets were quiet—only the earliest shift-workers were out, forcing themselves through the city to work in laundries, like me, or to file as clerks, or to work construction at the Marine Building site.

Vancouver was pinned between the water and the mountains, and in the morning, especially a wet morning like this, the city smelled like a lumberyard. The unlikely smell came from the downtown sawmills tucked into False Creek harbour, just a few blocks away. If you knew how, you could walk all the way across False Creek to the better side of town, balancing every step on the logs floating there. But I did not know how, and I never tried it, because even with skill, you could disappear, slipping down between the logs, the wood closing over your head. You'd be drowned slow like a trapped rat. Gerald Avison's older brother had died that way, and I was truly sorry it hadn't been him.

As I walked to work through the grey city, Vancouver seemed trapped like a rat, stuck between modern city and end-of-the-line train terminal, caught between an American past and a Canadian future. But Vancouver didn't drown, no, it turned itself into a proper little sea rat, stinking to high heaven while it paraded its fine manners. Walking through the early morning, it wasn't unusual for me to see rats walking calm as could be in the alleys and gutters. I saw a whole family of them once, leaving a ruined building on one side of the street, clearly moving to the cleaner building across the street. Vancouver was like a rat, prospering in unlikely circumstances. It was a city spawned by the Wild West and the Exotic Orient, two clichés hard to reconcile, two conflicting myths that had only one thing in common—the desire to gamble. Maybe Vancouver wasn't such a bad place for me to be.

I went down Granville Street, past the Orpheum cinema. 'Til we moved to the city, my mother had never seen such a thing as a moving picture, but she became a big fan of the vaudeville at the Orpheum. When I was too young to stay home by myself, she would take me with her when she met her men friends there. I liked the Orpheum, its velvety dark theatre and the crush of people, dressed up for their evening out.

A few blocks later, I reached the looming Gothic monster of the Hotel Vancouver, the dark shadow in our downtown, stuck all over with turrets and staircases, with the immense white kitchen where my mother worked. As I waited at the corner to head into the gloomy basement of the hotel, a streetcar screeched up, its trolley pole coming unstuck from the wires, the car trailing to a halt. Passengers got out, cursing. I crossed in front of the stuck streetcar.

The street was slippery, making the soles of my boots damp. Not that it mattered—my boots would be well soaked by the end of my shift. The laundry floor was always wet and I constantly splashed hot water onto my clothes. I already felt warm—soon I'd be roasting in the heat of the basement laundry. I'd recently convinced my mother to let me shingle my hair, thank God, really short so that it wasn't on my neck all day long. Before I cut it, my too-fine hair stood up on my head or hung down in my eyes depending on its mood, so no one might say that cutting my hair ruined any crowning glory.

I knew why my mother had chosen the laundry job for me, rather than have me work as a chambermaid. She knew quite well what those upstairs girls did with themselves. It wasn't that she judged them harshly; she was simply aware of their activities and most likely felt I was ill-suited for such work. I was such a small ruffian of a girl. If anything, cutting my hair improved my appearance. That was the only advantage the laundry gave me—short hair.

Whoever worked in the laundry had raw fingers and reddened blotchy skin from the bleach. It was a clean kind of hell, but hell just the same. The heat of the laundry seeped up towards me as I went in the back door and down the stairs. There were no windows in the laundry, only ventilation shafts. I glanced over my shoulder, taking my leave of the daylight.

Sometimes, while I worked, Teddy would turn up. He had the run of the hotel's backrooms and basement—everyone assumed he was somehow related to my mother, since he was pretty like she was, and as he went by, he'd have his dark hair ruffled by a breath of sweet outside air that followed him like perfume.

"You're gonna be a lady-killer, Teddy-bear," the porters would tell him. Teddy's appearance was our only distraction—no one else ever came to visit the girls in the laundry. Why would anyone go down there unless they had to? As I arrived for work, I coughed. The usual pile of bleached sheets waited to be ironed and folded and sent away. I put on my apron, feeling so tired that the bleach was like a drug, sending my head into an unnecessary spin. I set up the irons to heat and went through to the next room, where the girls I worked with were already scrubbing sheets, wringing them out through rollers and putting them to soak a second time. Sheets were hung to dry on long lines next-door to the hotel's hot water boilers, and once they were dry, we ironed them into neatly stacked squares of folded linen. We rotated tasks, Helen, Vera and me, it was all so boring and sweaty, it scraped our skin raw. Our fingers stung with bleach, our forearms chafed where we'd burned them, and we were chapped, all up and down, from the scalding water. I felt sick, even though Vera leaned over and tried to make me laugh by pinching my cheek.

"You're wiped out today, my girl. Up late?"

I shook my head. Much as I liked the girls, I had never mentioned the card games, I didn't think they'd understand. Vera and Helen had clear ideas of what was possible for girls, and what was foolish. So I lied. "Full moon, I couldn't sleep."

"My crazy neighbour Asunta was planting tomatoes all night long," said Helen, "I couldn't sleep neither. She sings to her plants. Her husband doesn't talk at all, no wonder she talks to the tomatoes."

"Helps them grow," said Vera. "She's not crazy, she's right."

I ironed. I kept singeing my forearm against the edge of the iron as I leaned to fold the sheet. It was difficult to reach the edges of the sheet, fold it, there, once, iron it again, fold it width-wise, press it again. It sounds simple, I suppose, but it wasn't. If I hadn't been so darned tired, I wouldn't have kept flinching as the iron touched my skin. I'd have remembered to lift my arm. But I was too busy thinking about playing cards. What if I arranged to play more games? Nighttime ones, where the pots were bigger, and even if the fifty-fifty cut at Dermot's was an anomaly, just to lure me into the one game, just the same, I could make more money at poker than I ever would here in the sweaty basement. I slipped on my next step across the floor, caught my arm against the hard metal of a shelf. If I hadn't been tired out by the night's poker game, I might have had the energy to be really elated, I might have even told Vera and Helen that I was thinking of leaving—but then I'd have to explain why.

I pulled another clean wrinkled sheet onto the wide ironing board. Pressed the square iron down upon it. The steam rose up and I coughed at the damp bleach smell as I reopened the iron, folded, pressed the iron down again. Really, there was a way out of this ironing and washing and bleaching. There were big card games in my future, it was going to be great, I thought, I would be rich. The money I'd won at Dermot's was waiting for me; what would I do with it? I nearly scorched one of the sheets, daydreaming about my options.

"You all right Mill? Lookin' peaky, you are," said Helen, coming out of the drying room with a fresh stack of tablecloths. "We'll be alright if you need to sit down for a bit."

I shook my head. They tried to look out for me, Helen and Vera did. I was younger, and far less experienced in the ways of the world, that's how they saw it, and in anything but cards, they were right. I didn't even have the menses yet; when Vera groaned about such things, I pretended to nod knowledgeably. Probably that was what Helen thought was wrong with me.

My mother would be furious if I left this decent laundry job, even if I could make better money from my hands. I could feel her disapproval already, and it made me flinch more than the searing edge of the iron. I had no idea of games beyond Dermot's, how to convince other tables to open their circle to include me. Roberts last night made it seem possible—he had obviously heard of the game at Dermot's, and maybe he had known the Shaunessey man would be there to provide him with a pot. Roberts was wearing such nice clothes, he oozed confidence. Was that what I wanted? To look as if I knew what I was doing? To at least dress like a lady, even if I wasn't? But then to cheat—that was a fly in the ointment. What a vile expression. A bug in the bleach. An ant in the pie. No, I couldn't cheat.

I smoothed another white sheet, folded it, ironed the top fold, carried it to the shelf, and started on the pillowcases. I arranged the monogram of the hotel so it was perfectly centred by the fold. Of course I wouldn't cheat at my games. What was the point of being a card whisperer if I cheated? The cards would stop speaking to me if I abused their trust in such a way. And yet—I thought about Roberts' clothes. He had money. Confidence. I wanted those things. Surely there was a way to play cards for a living without being a cheat, a way to work honestly, respect the cards so they respected me. Yes, I realize I'm speaking of cards as if they are a living entity. Who says they aren't?

For three hours, I ironed sheets and thought about playing cards, until my share of the pile was finished. By the last hour, I was sweating so much, I'm sure I ironed a goodly amount of perspiration into the pillowcases and white restaurant linen. That's what the bleach was for, wasn't it, to hide the smell of our sweat from the nice hotel patrons? Think of that the next time you lay your head in a room at the Ritz—though of course, they have better irons now, a girl wouldn't need to burn herself quite so much.

I returned to the washroom and took over from Vera, who went to collect the dry sheets from next door—the one job I found impossible because you needed to reach up and across, repeatedly, and I was too short. I stayed behind and poured dirty white linen into vats of boiling water. I was reaching uncomfortably far into one of the vats to loosen a sheet that was tangled, when I heard a sharp, "Yes, sir?" from Helen.

"I was hoping to speak with your associate here," said the sir in question. And I knew before turning around who it was. My hands soaking wet. No cards.

I dried my hands on my skirt and wiped my face, twice, a futile delay, before turning around.

"No rest for the wicked," he said.

He was wearing a different suit today, tweed, with a blue shirt. I concentrated on the edges of his face, unable to meet his eyes.

"I'm sorry sir, I don't think we've met."

He smiled. This time the smile was really for me, and it was superb, it changed what was otherwise an ordinary face into something entirely memorable. I would have stopped breathing were we in normal air. As it was, I inhaled the steam and bleach too quickly, burning my nostrils.

"Will you excuse us?" he said, charming, to Helen, and he held open the door, gesturing for me to step out into the corridor. I wondered how he'd managed to find me in the hotel laundry, how he'd gotten into the basement.

But before I could ask, he said. "You have great skill. How much of a cut did you get?"

"I'm sorry?"

"It was a fine performance. Perhaps we could go to dinner. When do you finish?"

"I can't go to dinner, I have plans." I had never been out to dinner anywhere. He made me catch my breath. I didn't understand then how obvious that could be, poker-faced or not.

"What about six o'clock? At the restaurant upstairs. It's very good."

Of course it was good, I thought—my mother's a fine cook. But I couldn't eat dinner there, however flattering it was to have this man turn up to talk to me. I shook my head. Was he looking to get his money back? Surely he hadn't lost that much, he must have some reserves to his bank-roll. I was annoyed by his eyes, how they shifted colour in the basement's murky light.

"Employees can't eat in the restaurant of the hotel? Is that the problem?"

I blinked. "My mother's the cook at the restaurant."

"Can't think of a better chaperone."

I repeated that I had plans already.

"Mmhm? You're wasting your talents in a laundry."

"I'm not planning to stay in the laundry."

"Smart girl. I'll see you later."

I was still shaking my head when he turned and walked down the hall. It took all my small discipline to watch him go away. Dinner in the hotel restaurant, a feat I'd never dreamed of. Imagining the meats, vegetables, desserts—my mouth filled with desire. He disappeared up the stairs and I had to blink a few times to force myself to turn around, not chase after him. He was a card cheat, I reminded myself, not a man to be trusted.

Back in the laundry room, Helen made an effort to look involved in her sheets and Vera pretended she had just stopped folding, but they weren't very convincing.

"Are you going to go?"

"Go?"

"Silly, it'll be a good dinner."

"Look at his clothes," said Helen. "Real good quality cloth."

Helen had an eye for such things; she was an Irish girl who'd washed clothes at a swank house in Shaunessy, 'til she got herself pregnant. As if a girl can get herself pregnant—even the Virgin Mary needed some help.

Vera rubbed her sweaty forehead. "You really going to quit on us?"

"How'd you figure that?"

"If you get a better offer, you should take it," said Helen. "And don't let him take no advantage neither."

"What's the job?" said Vera. "Is it with him? That would be...."

"No," I said.

Helen sniffed, as if I had offended her. "Don't want to tell the likes of us?"

"She's just not a talker, Helen, is all," said Vera. "Gets worried she'll make a mess of things."

Helen shook her head. "Does no good to be superstitious like that."

"Ah," said Vera, "she can't help it. She's a worrier, some girls do just worry."

"Well, there's no good in that," said Helen. Then she frowned, thinking of her own worries, no doubt.

If you're a gambler, worry and superstition come with the cards. I untangled the sheet from the roller and shoved it back into the water. I wondered if Vera was right, that I would quit, as if she'd read the thought in my mind before I'd even properly decided on it.

At the end of our shift, the two evening girls came in. Vera playfully swatted my shoulder as she left. "Go to dinner, silly. We have to seize the good things, we do, from down here."

I unwrapped the long strings of my apron, washed my face and went down the long basement hallway to the stairs up to street level. I wasn't even half a block down from the hotel, damp but more or less presentable, heading towards Dermot's as I always did after my shift, when he caught up with me, the man in the expensive clothes that I had fleeced. He must have been sitting in the lobby, watching the street, gazing out across to the law courts. The basement door led directly out onto that promenade—he couldn't miss me.

He fell into step beside me. I glanced for the briefest moment at him and I felt a rock slide down my throat, plunge through my chest and settle at my stomach. I was surely blushing. I swallowed and kept walking. I stared down at our feet as we walked, my boots cheap and worn, buttoned at my ankle, and his very shiny shoes, chestnut leather with handsome tooling along the edges. I disliked his shoes, I knew it was just jealousy but disliked them anyhow. I disliked the sharp clear sound of his footsteps, while my own soles squelched with damp on the pavement. I wanted to have shoes as nice. Just this detail made me want to cry. It was ridiculous.

"Wondered when you'd get off work," he said. "We haven't exactly met, have we? Stan Roberts." He paused in mid-step and put out his hand.

I didn't stop, but I thought it would be rude not to at least introduce myself, even if I didn't want to shake his hand—he'd seen enough of my chapped fingers last night. Without pausing or holding out my hand, I said, "Millard Lacouvy."

"So Miss Millard Lacouvy," he said, keeping up easily with my small gait, "you're willing to play cards with me in the backroom of a downtown bar but you don't want to dine with me in a hotel restaurant? Fair enough. There are men I feel similarly about."

We passed the clock tower on the Granville Block, and he continued to walk beside me. I was a proud girl, my mother had taught me by example, so I pretended to ignore him, even as from the corner of my eyes I watched him. What if I could do this? Walk through the daytime streets in my fine clothes, waiting for a nighttime game, trust the cards to bring me a living? Oh. I met his eyes for an instant.

"That clock's been wrong for three days," he said.

I glanced back at the Granville clock. "It's been wrong since before I was born."

"You were born here?"

"No. I was born during an earthquake up in the Interior."

"I was in Seattle during the last earthquake. Hell of a thing."

"Hasn't been one here in years. But the last one there was, stopped the clock."

We turned the corner and went down past the Dominion Building, where the manager had been killed in a sort of accident involving a pump shotgun. I'd told Teddy all sorts of ghost stories about the poor man and though I wasn't really convinced that the building was haunted, I rushed past it if I was by myself. I resisted telling Roberts the story, why would he be interested—and even thinking about it, I marvelled that I wanted to tell him the story. Why would I treat him as a friend? I didn't have any friends who cheated at cards.

"You have talent," he said.

I shuffled my soggy boots along the sidewalk. I saw that he had changed tactics, had left earthquakes behind and was focusing on cards. I changed direction too, more literally, turning back up Water Street because I didn't want to arrive at Dermot's with this man beside me. But even as I changed my route, I noticed that he kept pace with me, my short step against his longer stride. I slowed my steps even more, just to test his patience.

"Great hands and a quick head," he said, walking more slowly even than I. "Brilliant game."

"I can shuffle cards, doesn't make me a genius."

He laughed, and the lovely soft sound floated over the streetcar coming around the corner. It cut through the damp of the day. Had I let it, the sound might even have cooled my sweat.

"I make a living from my hands, Miss Lacouvy. I'm not someone to heap praise where it isn't due. But your hands'll soon be better than mine if you put your mind to them."

"I have put my mind to them, thank you."

I stared hard at the grey sidewalk as we walked, as if its uneven surface might occupy my entire attention.

"I'm not talking about last night's game. I'm talking about future games. We could be a great pair. You'd learn a lot."

"I've finished my schooling, Mr. Roberts."

"I'm going about this wrong," he said. "Please come to dinner with me. I'll be able to... Look, I haven't rehearsed this. I've never taken on a partner. Especially not...."

"I'm not a child."

"I wasn't going to call you a child."

"Then not a girl, is what you're thinking. You're right, there's no way you can play cards with a girl."

"Mmhm. What I was going to say, if you'd be so kind as to let me finish my sentence, is I've never been tempted to take on a partner before. Especially not someone I've seen play only once."

"And I was shuffling poorly."

The man had tried to cheat me at Dermot's game, and now he wanted to be my partner. Didn't he think I might have some sense of loyalty? McMann was more than just a friend, he was practically family. And what's more, Dermot would never cheat me at cards.

He should have had the decency to blush. I glanced at him to see, but he smiled and said, "Who taught you to play?"

I shrugged, I couldn't trust my voice.

"You could make a lot of money."

"You mean, I could make *you* a lot of money," I retorted.

"Absolutely. You could manage my games on the coast when I travel for the wire. We'd be working together. The numbers would be bigger than anything you'll ever dream of making for that McMann."

"Dermot McMann's a friend, that's different."

"You're way out of McMann's league. I mean this, Miss Lacouvy. I want you to be my partner. I've never taken anyone on to work with, but we would be unbeatable. It's an uncertain time, there's a war coming, certainly, but you're a phenomenon I would like on my side."

"A phenomenon?" I looked up at him, sideways-like. He was as good a man to look at as there could be. I looked away. I couldn't picture myself across from him again at a poker table.

"Think about it. Surely you don't mean to stay in that hotel basement. Laundry's a criminal waste of your hands."

"You think I don't know that?"

"Well, it bears mentioning. I don't make an offer like this idly. Mmhm. In fact, never. But you're...."

I stopped walking and so did he. And I admired him for another long moment—his suit, the way the cloth fit around his shoulders, how he didn't look warm even in the hot evening. I admired his eyes, steady, and the way he stood there, expecting... well, he wasn't expecting me to refuse him, I suppose. Girls didn't refuse him much, I was pretty sure that was the undecorated truth. Why would we? But I set my heart against the suggestion of working with him. Something in my expression must have warned him I was going to refuse, for he held out his left hand.

"Don't answer right away," he said, "You can think about it, I'm in town until tomorrow morning. If dinner at the hotel is wrong for you, perhaps there's somewhere else?"

I took a step backwards. I couldn't imagine asking the cards to speak to me for his hands, not for a man who could cheat cavalierly at a low table like Dermot's. It was that detail, specifically, that rankled. I smiled at Roberts politely, because all gamblers can lie with the shape of their mouths if not with their hearts.

"It's a very kind offer. But I can't see myself working with a man who cheats at cards."

His expression didn't falter even for an instant. He dropped his hand, but not in dismay, no, he simply let his arm return to his side. He stood stock still as I walked away. I didn't dare look back, for I knew I'd regret leaving him there—how often would I have a chance to seize such a good thing, as Vera said? I left him standing there, him and his handsome smile and the sparkling games he offered.

I expected he would stay there. I mean, I thought he would disappear and I would never see him again, never get tempted by whatever it was he offered. It was foolish to think such a thing, considering how small this world is for people who make their living with cards. I wanted him to disappear, so I would never be tempted again to work for a card cheat. Because the possibility was so very tempting.

3

I would find real card games myself, I didn't need any cheater's help to do so. Or anyone's help, apart from Dermot's. I walked away from Roberts' offer, but I carried his suggestion with me like a new shining jewel, though the afternoon air smelled insistent and rotten. Kind of a healthy smell, really, the way the city always was after too many days of rain, as if the ground was coming up through the streets to claim us all back into the earth. I thought about Roberts and his fine clothes. I was right in refusing him, but I couldn't quite go directly to Dermot's, that offer so recent in my head, my eyes filled with the idea of nice clothes and expensive shoes, the idea of power that money must bring to its holder.

With the money from last night's game, I could buy shoes as nice as any Roberts wore. Well, ladies' shoes, I mean. And I could dress well. More to the point, I could leave the laundry. I turned at Main Street, glanced at the mountains, then continued uphill past the underhanded gin joint. I wondered if I'd run into Teddy, because these were his favourite streets, but I knew he wouldn't give me any useful advice. I passed the junk dealers and the horse stables, the smell of hay and manure competing with the old used mothball smell of broken furniture. You could smell these streets on a person, if they spent long enough here, and Teddy smelled a bit like this, natural chameleon that he was.

I turned left at Hogan's Alley, an infamous little street never honoured with a place on the city's official map. The Italian grocery on the corner sold white balls of cheese, while around back there was a constant dice game going on. I paused and listened for the click of the falling dice, though Dermot had sternly warned me away from such distractions.

"Too easy to load," he'd said. "With your skill with the cards, you shouldn't mess with the dice." He wasn't joking—Dermot wasn't one to kid about games. I heeded his advice, but I liked listening to the voices and the falling sound of the little cubes just the same. The Alley, for all its notoriety, was a single block of two-storey wooden houses, apartments, and gin joints, with an occasional tumble-down square of plain earth strewn with struggling tomato vines. It was a hard-packed dirt alley, maybe eight feet wide, named in honour of its loudest resident, Harry Hogan, an Irish singer of sorts. Italian wine-makers with names like Macaroni Joe lived here, keeping books on the side. I knew Joe because Mary Ellen occasionally sent me up here to place a horse bet for her at Joe's. In winter, if I walked down the alley, I was likely to be shoved not-too-roughly aside by big sooty-faced guys who delivered sacks of coal all across the city. Through December and January, the Alley smelled of that strange sharp smell of coal, and in the winter grey, the cold rains smudged all our faces with smut. But in April there wasn't the same bustle in the Alley, at least not yet, with the late afternoon sun still in the sky.

I stood in Hogan's Alley listening to the clink of dice. I knew how little spare money was around for gambling, and I could see what a delicate line there was between men with nearly nothing and the man named Roberts. And Hogan's Alley was better than some of the places in our watery terminal city. The darkness of those years was more than just a name, outside of Vancouver, it was more than just a bad mood. The air really did turn black— men told me horrible stories, as I dealt cards at Dermot's. It rained earth. I am not lying. Dust storms, black blizzards, straight out of a Biblical plague.

"The wind came outta nowhere," a man from the prairies once told me, trying to explain how he'd come to Vancouver. I shuffled cards while he talked. "Clouds been on the horizon for two days, we was hopin' rain, but was the wind comin' in. Whipped a whole field of good dirt straight up in the air. I'm not makin' it up. I saw it. My own eyes."

He did okay at Dermot's. I didn't win too much money off him—don't think I have a soft heart. It was just the way the cards went, that day. He told me the dust blocked out the sun. Tumbleweeds mixed into the storm and collected in clumps against fences and houses and cemetery walls, like the skeletons of stillborn animals. Blow dirt, fine like flour, ground grit into people's teeth, blinded the cattle, coated every furled leaf, every dried-up bud. The men who got to Vancouver were refugees, that's all they were, people fleeing a terrible disaster. They didn't expect hope. The muddy shore on the lacy edges of Stanley Park and in the swampy rim of the city dump became their last desperate places of ill refuge—some scraps of land to lie down on, where they could sleep unmolested and salvage bits and pieces of garbage to keep themselves from the elements. And I had a job, at the laundry—only a fool would walk away from it. Fair enough that Roberts could make his way in this world with his fast fine smile and his cheating hands. But me? I was a pathetic stub of a girl. I sighed, stepping aside to let by a man carrying a dead pig. The hog sagged, its opaque eyes staring at the dirt of the road—and I was barely taller than the hog. But Roberts thought me old enough to manage his card games, old enough to smile at, in his slow way. If I was old enough for that, surely I was old enough to take the risk of leaving the laundry.

Poker was the first fair choice I'd ever encountered: unlike the rules in the rest of life, poker allowed me to walk away if things didn't look good. What else offered that kind of control over life? Where else would I be invited to play at life on the same level as any man, from any part of town?

I didn't need any accomplices apart from the cards. I flicked my fingers out and swung my arms as I walked downtown. No one noticed me. I put my right hand against my stomach like that painting of Napoleon that I'd seen reproduced in a history book—there, I did learn something in school. Unlike my schoolmates, the people in history books had real ambitions and hunger, they were impatient, like me. It's *British* Columbia, we're loyal to the Queen, so we mostly heard about the battles the British won, but I sympathized with Napoleon. I understood perfectly why Napoleon wanted to be Emperor—he was short and ugly, like me and I bet no one took him seriously until they were forced to. Napoleon won lots of other battles before Waterloo; he even got the beautiful Josephine to fall in love with him. He failed in the end, died alone on an island, but that's the risk you take in getting what you want.

I didn't expect anyone like Josephine to fall in love with me, and I had no use for conquering Europe. But I sure as heck wanted to play cards. Short and ugly and ambitious as Napoleon, yes, I suppose that was me.

I would allow myself one accomplice, I thought, crossing the street, and it wouldn't be Teddy, it would be Dermot. Because I could trust him, and he knew that at a gaming table, there are only two real things: the cards, and the money you've bet. My size and my looks and my girl self didn't matter a whit against the weight of the cards. Surely even Napoleon had an accomplice, didn't he? I would have to drop by the library and check.

Dermot had no family; he lived in a room somewhere in Gastown, but I had never seen him anywhere except his bar. Once a day, he stepped out onto the pavement and swept the sidewalk in front of his establishment. That was all. He went nowhere else. He had no need to, he had created his ideal universe, he drew in what he thought might benefit his bar and ignored the rest.

I first walked in as an envoy from Mary Ellen—she'd told me to find a man whose wife was having a baby. I was to find the man and fetch him home. She told me to start looking at Dermot McMann's bar on Water Street. Wasn't hard to find, the names of the different establishments were painted above the entrances. I came to a wide wooden frontage with "McMann" in big letters above the two plate windows. There was a pane of yellow leaded glass in the door but I was too short to see in. I pushed through the door and shouted the man's name, the one Mary Ellen wanted to find, as loudly as I could.

"He's in back, lass," said the big bearded man behind the bar. "What're you wanting him for?"

"I'm to deliver the message to him directly," I said.

Dermot, for that's who it was behind the bar, finished serving a beer, then came around from behind the bar and took me by the hand to lead me to the backroom.

"Well then," he said, and ushered me in.

That's how I first discovered the card room back there; the man I wanted was in the middle of a poker game. I delivered my message in strident tones, like a newsboy calling out the headlines: "Mary Ellen says get yourself up to the house, your daughter's born and your wife wants to see you."

When he got up from the table, I climbed into his empty chair, kneeling to see over the edge of the table. I picked up his hand of cards and no one stopped me, though one of them laughed. "She can't do any worse than Charlie."

Mary Ellen had taught me how to read fortunes with cards, but the only game I knew then was Go Fish. "What's this?" I said, holding out the hand. "I've never played this kind of Fish. What are the rules?"

Which made everyone laugh but Dermot, who put his big hand on my head. "Don't laugh at the lass," he said.

The other men threw over the game, but Dermot let me stay and play with the cards at the table. Eventually, he taught me to play poker. I think it started out as a lark, for he saw I had nowhere to go. But his lark bore unlikely fruit, and here I was seven years later, still playing for him.

When I got to Water Street, I went down the alley to the back entrance of the bar and banged the door heavily behind me, to be sure Dermot heard me come in. Kevin sat in the backroom playing a game of solitaire, cards laid out on the oilcloth in front of him.

"You're late," he said, not even looking up at me. "Wondered if you weren't coming."

"Dermot tell you that?"

"No. He promised you'd show up."

Dermot was smart in ways that schooling doesn't help with. He was good at reading people, maybe that's what we had in common. He grew up behind a bar up in the Lardeau, while the Silver Rush trailed out; nothing much went wrong in the streets of Gastown that he hadn't already seen. I think that's why he took a shine to me—I reminded him of himself as a child, an urchin growing up higgledy-piggledy in a wreck of a town. I knew he'd had a wife at some point, but she died in childbirth, the baby dead too, and after that, he wasn't much given to family life.

It seemed a long time ago, that I first picked up cards at Dermot's table. So many worthy cards had passed through my growing hands. When I got down to shuffling and dealing, I found myself reading the cards more carefully than ever. First round, I got the nine and ten of Diamonds, which made me think of prospectors—Dawson City's Gold Rush in capitals, our good B.C. Silver Rush, shining lines that magnetized hope for too brief a while. Lured men, and women too—which is how my mother's American mother ended up north of the 42nd parallel to begin with.

My mother was born in a tented-over cabin shell, in a prostitute's crib, but she was unwilling to follow the family trade, so she became a cook. There she was, Queen of Diamonds, the card appeared in my hand. There was always work for a cook in mining towns. Panning, rocking, all those men searching for a mineral that had about as much reliability as my friend Vera's affections. And even at that, I would put my money on a woman's heart long before I'd bet anything on a thread of silver disappearing into the centre of the earth. Sometimes I think the girls who ended up running those hotels, those dancing girls, they were smarter than the women who stayed home in shacks, waiting for another baby, sweeping rat turds out of the closet, brushing snow off the table where it blew in from between the wooden walls built of green wood that shrank worse every season. Married at fifteen some of them, and that wedding gown the only pretty dress they'd ever own, the rest of their clothes made out of flour sacks. No wonder girls ran away to Paradise Alley—at least they might laugh for a year or two.

I got a decent straight from those Diamonds. Poker's as strange a business as prospecting, maybe that's what the cards were telling me. Because after that one excellent hand, I had nothing tremendous for the rest of the afternoon. When the game was finished, I put away the cards as quickly as I could.

"She's got to get going," explained Kevin to the other men at the table. "So's her mother doesn't catch her."

The men nodded in sympathy. Before leaving, I paused in the doorway of the bar. Dermot took the dishrag off his shoulder and made as if to polish a glass. "What is it, Millard?"

"If I quit the laundry...."

"If you're smart enough," he said.

"If I do quit...."

"You could run any late night game here."

"Really?"

"But lass, forget the fool disguise. You looked right stupid last night."

I took his advice and I've never since tried to deny that I'm a short odd-looking girl at the poker table.

My fingers were beginning to touch everything like dirty laundry, harsh; I couldn't feel any other texture. Fruit, cards, skin, everything was bleached by my touch. So I had no regrets about leaving the laundry. I went in the following morning to the Hotel Vancouver and I told Vera and Helen I was quitting.

"You went to dinner didn't you?" said Vera happily. "Told you."

"Not exactly."

"But you're doing right by yourself, aren't you?" Helen paused, her arms filled with dripping white sheets.

I nodded and forced myself to work through the shift even though I'd given notice. I thought there was nothing about the basement that I would miss, but I was wrong, I missed Vera and Helen. I was going into a profession that offered very little by way of feminine companionship, and I didn't realize how I'd gotten used to their gentle ribbing. I told myself that being lonely was a fair balance—I was getting cards in return, I was being given a chance to play a good hand. The cards took the place of any other community. I took that hand, the cards' hand I was offered, and I haven't once regretted it. I haven't.

With Dermot's permission, I upped my cut and took thirty percent of everything I won. The rest went into Dermot's pocket, though he always set aside enough to guarantee our next game. It was a good way to improve my skill at calculating odds—I played with a titch more focus, knowing the game was my only living. On the second week that I ran the night table for Dermot, a man I'd never seen before came in and played the most illogical game I'd ever seen. We were playing seven stud, yet even with me studying every move he made, being shocked by every one of his foolish decisions, he won the game. I swore I'd never get smug—the worst player can take a pot through the intervention of fortune.

Dermot always managed to lure new fish to the bar; there weren't many open games in the city, especially if you were just travelling through, and Dermot guaranteed a polite game, unlike other dives.

"Sometimes I wonder how they find out about the game here," I said after a particularly fruitful night.

Dermot grunted. "You're something of an attraction, Millard. The word gets out."

"The card-playing dwarf? The girl poker maestro?"

I didn't imagine there were many polite words attached to whatever my reputation might be, and I didn't really think many people in the neighbourhood used the word maestro. Perhaps some other, less polite versions of the same thing.

Dermot squinted his small black eyes at me and scratched his beard. I shuffled the pack of cards under my hands and fanned them out to him, a neat wide arc of red-backed cards. He made a show of choosing first one card, then changing his mind, then selecting another. Finally he settled on a card far to the right in the fan. He turned it up so only he could see, looked at it and frowned and put it back into the fan. I shuffled the cards together, did a side shuffle and a waterfall, just for the show of it, to amuse Dermot, and then I turned the cards over one by one. When I got to the four of Spades, I stopped.

"That one?" I couldn't help being surprised. The black four means illness, not as dire as the eight of Spades, a death card. But just the same, the four gives a person pause.

"That's what I had, Millard."

We both looked at the four for a moment, then I drew it back into my shuffle and put the cards away. I tried not to put great stock on gypsy fortunes, whatever Mary Ellen believed. Cards play games for themselves when you don't give them strict rules to pay attention to. That's why they're better off in a proper game, poker or bridge or what-have-you, keeps them honest. But I touched Dermot's arm. "You should sleep more. You look tired."

"We have work to do, my girl. Go home yourself and give your mother a kiss for me."

He knew perfectly well what my mother thought of poker-playing, though I never mentioned the scene she made, the evening I quit the laundry—we worked for the same hotel, and staff gossip had her informed before I could break the news. So she greeted me that night by throwing her shoe at me. Walked in the door, took off her left shoe and threw it at my head. She was never one to waste conversation when action could be taken.

I dodged the shoe. "The money's better at Dermot's, you'll get more of...."

"As if I care about money. I was getting you a position, a life."

At which point she threw the other shoe. It hit my shoulder, not hard. I wasn't built big, but I was tougher than my scrawny shape suggested. I wished that I had a bottle of some kind in the house, I could have poured my mother a drink, taken the edge off her aim.

"Well, it's done now," I said, and with a feint to the left, managed to slip under her outstretched right arm, out and onto the veranda. She never liked shouting at me in the street—her rage was always enclosed politely by our limited walls. Knowing this, I didn't run, I stood my ground as she came furiously to the doorway. "Throw me out if you want, it's not going to change my choice any. I'll live upstairs with Mary Ellen."

She slammed the door hard, so the glass in our front window shimmered in its rotting wood frame. It was a good thing Teddy came along the street just at that moment, for if I'd stayed there alone on the veranda, I might have started to cry. I might have wasted time feeling sorry for my poor runt self, feeling sorry for my mother and her rage, which sizzled up in her at any trigger. Feeling sorry for the pair of us, trapped in that crooked half of a house. Fortunately there was no time for such pity, for Teddy came up the street smiling, with a black eye and a bloody nose, and he asked me upstairs for dinner. So instead of telling him about my day, I said, "What in the world happened to you?" as I followed him up to Mary Ellen's.

"Fault of the potatoes," he said.

His mother shook her head but didn't interrupt as Teddy told the story, beginning with the good upright citizens of Vancouver, their potatoes and their kind hearts. A row of church men went once a week to the beaten-down mud jungle at the end of Heatley Street, to hand out potatoes to the men collected there. Men who'd gotten caught the way leaves get caught at the narrow neck of a stream to rot, nowhere for them to go. Men who'd ended up on the edge of the city dump—their shacks were called a jungle. There were several jungles in Vancouver, in those days. But this was one of the biggest, right at the edge of our own falling-down neighbourhood. When the wind was wrong, you could smell the place—the reek of the garbage dump, accompanied by the smell of rot-gut pine sap liquor, which was what they drank, there in the jungle, so Teddy said.

He said that the St. Andrew's Protestant Relief Committee was loading potatoes into an automobile in front of their church—that makes it sound grand, but the Committee consisted of two men and a car. Teddy was wandering home after an unsuccessful loop through the Endowment Lands. "I was checking the traps for rabbits, but they'd been emptied before I got there. Like to get my hands on who did it...."

He was kicking a rock in the middle of the street when the churchman, wrestling a big bag of potatoes into the boot of a car, said, "Kid, a nickel for you to help me with this." He propped the potatoes on the bumper of the car, rummaged in his pocket and held out the nickel.

Teddy touched his cap, knew his way around a churchman, asked, "And unloadin' when you get there, sir? Wherever you're headed?" The guy sized up Teddy, a boy with the right smile for every occasion, a solid boy with looks that made men trust him. The church guy, maybe thinking of two hundred hungry men, dirty, often angry, sometimes drunk, under the Viaduct, in the mud, said, "Sure, kid, I could use a hand." A second, impeccably-dressed man came out of the church basement and took a seat inside the car, and Teddy's first introduction to the jungle was on a running board.

Once they got there, Teddy said he unloaded the potatoes, pocketed a second nickel, and slipped away. And then he strolled through the encampment, a place he'd never been before—he was wondering how such a place had escaped his notice when someone twice his age took a swing at him. Assumed he was an innocent church boy, probably with some money in his pocket.

Three mistakes, but only one serious error. For Teddy was not a church boy, and he had only those two new nickels in his pocket, and (here was the serious error) Teddy was an excellent dirty fighter, the very opposite of innocent. Looking for a clean fight? Don't go to a schoolyard or a squatters' camp.

Teddy said he wasn't expecting the swing, but he turned and punched the kid in the stomach. Not enough to hurt him meanly, only enough to have him double over. Then Teddy pounded him once, hard, with a closed fist on the back of the boy's head, and stepped back. He should have expected what happened next: the boy lunged back up and tried to plunge his forehead into Teddy's nose. Partly because Teddy was surprised, the boy didn't break his nose, only bloodied it, and hit his eye. The velocity of his leap threw them both to the ground, where Teddy rolled on top, clinging to the boy's hair and pulling his neck back, punched the boy, getting up as the other kid curled in pain. It was just brutal enough to impress the men watching. Because that's the only thing to do in such a place—watch whatever turns up. Two dogs screwing. Two boys fighting. Men too hungry to do much other than watch, no harm in it. The other boy skulked away quietly into the jungle's maze of shacks, and Teddy smoothed down his shirt—he was always fastidious, I suppose he got that from me. One of the men watching asked, "Where're you from, kid?"

"Here."

They convinced Teddy to fight for them. And Mary Ellen listened to his tale as she shook dried leaves into small jars, to give to her patients. I never learned what those plants were, what she collected and hung in bunches all along the hallway that led to her bedroom and to Teddy's, at the back of the house. But it made her apartment smell marvellous, that's what I remember most of all, even now—coming upstairs, the biggest difference between our part of the house and hers was that ours never smelled of anything other than the basic foods we'd been cooking. Whereas Mary Ellen's hallway smelled like a meadow was waiting around the corner, green and promising, and her kitchen smelled of preserves and tea and soup, no matter what time of year.

I suppose it wasn't surprising, brought up in a midwife's house as he was, that Teddy went looking elsewhere to learn how to become a man. Certainly I was no use to him—I had enough trouble with being a girl. But I was surprised how taken he was with the jungles. I wondered if he'd ever have hit anyone, if he hadn't started out by defending me.

I wanted to tell Mary Ellen about having quit the laundry, about playing nights for Dermot, but Teddy's fight took up all our talk at dinner. I didn't like to think of him in the jungle. I knew where it was—off Prior Street, there was a path, if a person stepped down onto the mud and flattened cardboard that led to the middle of the camp. A whole miniature city there, a city of unemployed men, living in a mudflat that began at the corners of Prior Street and Heatley. I wasn't afraid exactly, I knew the men living there weren't necessarily mean, but I knew it was no place for girls. No matter how mean I might be at a poker game, the jungle was something different and fierce; I knew better than to go there.

With the late-night games at Dermot's, I found myself walking home more and more often in the pre-dawn city, and I began to like ambling up through the empty streets from Gastown, too early for the shift-workers to be about, just the metallic nighttime smell of the city, with its undertone of sulfur from the pulp mill. More often than not, Teddy waited for me on the stoop of our house.

"Good night?"

"Fine." Boasting would bring bad luck down on me. Sometimes I said, "The cards were thoughtful."

"I made good on some bets myself." He stood up and puffed out his chest. He was so much taller than me, he hardly needed to puff, but he was pleased with himself. I think he felt invincible. He seemed shinier, somehow, more defined. I looked carefully at his face. He seemed okay, no new bruises, but it was difficult to be sure—the street was dark.

"You skipped school again?"

"I got suspended, remember."

"The jungle's no place for you, you should be in school." Though really, he didn't look like a schoolboy anymore, he looked grown up already, or nearly.

He sat back down on the stoop, suddenly all elbows and knees. "You're one to talk."

I rubbed my itchy eyes. "You shouldn't be brawling."

"It's not brawlin', it's boxin'. There's good money in it."

"There's money in a lot of things." I sat down on the step beside him. "If you don't want to be in school, why don't you get a job? Some kind of real job."

"You want me to be working in a laundry, now you're free of it?"

He laughed and I saw that his lower lip was swollen, a dark short line where the skin had split hitting his teeth. I looked away.

"There are other jobs."

"Not a helluva lot, Mill. You haven't been to the jungle. You should see who all's not working these days. Come with me sometime, see what I mean."

"I don't see any reason to go there."

"An' I don't see any reason to get a job. I'm doing good on the bets, with the fights. Come see."

I had seen enough of Teddy's schoolyard fights, I didn't need to see more. At my silence, Teddy elbowed me. I was going to nudge him back, but I felt awkward. I stood up.

"I'm going to bed."

He stood too. "You're a whiz at cards, doesn't mean you couldn't do something else if you wanted. You just don't want to."

I turned my back on him and crept into the house. What had Roberts called me? A genius with cards. I wasn't sure that I could do something else if I wanted. All I knew was that my mother's expectations for me, of working in a hotel basement, bleaching sheets, couldn't compare with my gambling ambitions. Surely my mother was a gambler too, in her own way—she chose to make her own living by putting food on men's plates, whether it was the metal dishes of the mining camp or the porcelain plates of the Hotel Vancouver. She had refused to marry three or four men who'd asked, right off the bat, when my father disappeared. And for a woman to choose any kind of independent life, sure it was a gamble, same as any other spin of the roulette wheel.

I played cards afternoons and most nights, except for Sundays—not out of religious respect, no, but Sunday was the one day of the week that I stayed home, cleaned our apartment and made dinner for my mother—I suppose I was trying to please her, same as any of her admiring men friends. And on the last Sunday of each month, I added up my numbers, carefully keeping each column straight, recording my earnings, admired how I was progressing. Keeping track of the numbers was important, otherwise it was too easy to get distracted by a momentary good or bad run. I didn't win every game; nobody does. But my numbers were as neat as any accountant's.

On the last Sunday of May, I sat at the kitchen table, my papers spread out in front of me; Teddy sat across from me, grinning crookedly—he'd just had his eyetooth broken in a fight, sheared off like a miniature iceberg.

He licked his tooth—it was probably sore. "Rich, aren't you? So whatcha doin' with it?"

"Doing with it?"

"Savin' the cash for what?"

I was saving money, that was true. I gave a portion to my mother to help pay for our small household, and the rest, I added to my bankroll, in the safe at Dermot's; one day I'd be able to play bigger games, not backed by Dermot, but on my own. I just wasn't sure how to do it, not yet.

"Hey," said Teddy, kicking my shin. "You could bet on me, I've got a...."

Before I had a chance to argue, my mother came in from work. I quickly folded my notes away and shoved them into the book, *A Farewell to Arms*, which I was reading in my spare time, an excellently depressing book that Teddy had stolen from the bookshop on Granville Street. He was light-fingered, and though I didn't approve, I couldn't help liking the books he pilfered for me.

My mother said, "What do you know of Harold Avison?"

"Harold Avison?"

"Yes."

Teddy looked uncomfortable. "There's the Avison kid," he said.

"Mr. Avison's brother's son," I explained. I wasn't sure my mother would follow otherwise. "Something of a bully."

"Has he bullied you?"

I shrugged.

Teddy said, "Not since I whacked him upside the head."

"That was nearly two years ago," I said. And the Avison kid deserved it—best if a bully has at least one cauliflower ear, that way people know he's a bruiser and steer clear of him.

"Harold will have to overlook the past," said my mother.

"Mr. Avison is no doubt aware of his nephew's displeasing personality," I said.

"Yes. No doubt." She looked at me thoughtfully. "Harold has asked me to marry him."

"Marry him?" we echoed, like a trained chorus.

Then Teddy asked, "Harold Avison?" as if he wasn't sure he'd heard correctly.

I said, "Do you want to marry him?"

We were unaware that my mother knew Harold Avison more than simply to say hello, so this was news. He was a white-shirted clerk type who worked in the courthouse across from the Hotel Vancouver. He'd said hello to me once or twice, which in retrospect should have surprised me. He seemed proper and upright and church-going. And though Teddy had gotten into a fight with Avison's brother's son, I suspected Avison would agree that his nephew deserved to be beaten up, probably on a weekly basis. The boy was one of the nastiest children I had ever met, the kind that pushes needles into cats' paws.

I wasn't so sure what Harold thought of me, and I wondered silently what my mother might have told him about her difficult daughter. Teddy took my lead and didn't speak either. Maybe my mother was hurt that we weren't more enthusiastic, for she frowned and went into her bedroom, kicking the door closed.

"Congratulations," I called after her. "That's wonderful."

"We better get her a real nice present," muttered Teddy.

"You could stay away from the jungles, that would be a present."

"Your ma doesn't care about that."

"I do."

He shrugged, held out his hand.

"What?"

"Money for her present. Give me what you wanna spend. I'll find some-thin' nice for her."

I took twenty dollars from the flyleaf of my book and held it out to him.

"That's a lot."

"Find something nice."

Teddy smiled too widely, his broken eyetooth so obvious that I suddenly felt uneasy about giving him the money, as if I shouldn't quite trust him. He looked like a man about to cheat at cards, not like the boy he was. "You should find some real work," I said sharply.

"What does that have to do with anything?"

"You're old enough to get a job."

"Mill, there's a thousand guys with no jobs in the jungle. Told you that already." He stood and leaned his forearms on the table. "Come see me box an' I'll look for a job. How's that?"

I recognized my own trick turned back on me. I sighed. "Ask someone else."

"Like who? Jenny's mad at me again, Sung broke his leg. Well, his dad broke it for him, and... who else would I ask?" He leaned closer and rested his forehead against mine. "Come on."

I sat back, but I nodded.

4

I kept to the bargain; I got up earlier than usual and put on my old boots, the worn and squelchy ones. Teddy held my hand until we arrived at the jungle, and then he disappeared into a crush of men jostling and pounding him on the back—he was the favourite to win. All too soon, I found myself on the edge of a dirt ring, in the middle of the camp beyond Prior Street, unable to see over the heads of the men in front of me. I felt some of them turn to stare at me as Teddy went off to his corner of the ring.

I felt smaller and younger than I was. It was one thing to be surrounded by men at Dermot's, it was quite another thing to be here, in this stinking camp—and it stank. The jungle smelled of dirt, of the ground itself, of pine sap and booze and the plain stink of men. Half the men standing around coughed and spat as if they had consumption or something worse. And even the clean-shaven, non-coughing types eyed me with a combination of suspicion and speculation. My guts suddenly stabbed me, as if I'd eaten a rock. Surprised, I curved my shoulders inwards and looked for somewhere to sit. Maybe if I could slump down I'd feel better. It was a cramp, same as you get in your leg; I thought, I'll live. But I felt really unwell.

There was a shout as the fight started. A guy whistled. I could almost see the top of Teddy's head, then a glimpse of his opponent's blond dusty hair. There was a shout, and then both fighters disappeared behind the closing ring of men betting and watching and cheering for their chosen boy. I took a step back, then another, hunching my shoulders. The men were focused on the fight. There was a hard thud—someone must have fallen, and there was cheering. The top of Teddy's head appeared again. I turned away and spotted a tree stump, left to itself in the mud and cardboard of the jungle, and I crept over and sat down. In a moment, when I felt better, I thought I'd stand on the stump, I'd be able to see Teddy. After what seemed like a long while, the cramp receded. A man whistled again from near the ad hoc boxing ring, perhaps a round finishing. Curious, I stood up, and I realized what was wrong with me. I couldn't believe it—I hadn't gotten my period when the other girls did, at school. Mary Ellen had told me not to worry. "Everyone's different," she said. Just there, in the jungle, I wished I'd stayed different. I was not at all happy to join the ranks of bleeding women.

"You should put this on, yeah?"

An old guy, with the distinctive stoop that men seemed to get if they lived long enough in the jungle, was suddenly beside me at the edge of the crowd. He held out his jacket. It was about as filthy as everyone else's, that good shine that comes from use, which at the time I thought simply came from travelling the rail lines, as if somehow the grease came from the trains. I was unimpressed with myself, but I took the jacket, slipped it on. The arms hung way past my hands, but the hem came down to my knees, a good cover for the mess I'd made of my dress. I was so embarrassed, I couldn't say anything.

"One o' my daughters is a bit like you," he said. "Little stick of a thing, lotsa energy."

The noise of the fight rose and I glanced towards the cleared space, but all I could see were men's backs. Too many people crowded between me and whatever Teddy was doing.

"How old are you?"

"Fourteen." I lied because I was embarrassed that the blood had to hit just then, in a cardboard jungle, on a warm day.

He nodded. "My daughter's your age..." he trailed off, then pulled his focus back. "You have a home, don't you?"

When I nodded, he looked over my head, purposefully. A cheer, quickly squashed by some new attack, went up from the front of the crowd. The man shook his head.

"Well, you should be there. At your home. I'll walk you to the edge of the jungle."

He waited for me to go ahead of him along the narrow part of the path. Back through the beaten-down mud, past some shacks, snaking along the edge of the dump, until the path widened enough that we walked side-by-side. We heard another roar from the men behind us, the fight still going on. I was abandoning Teddy, but I didn't care. I hadn't felt anything different until that sudden cramp—that worried me. Surely a girl was supposed to notice there was blood coming away from her? I'd been too focused on Teddy, too worried that he'd get another bloody nose. And here I was, covered in blood. I sighed. My back hurt.

"What's your name?"

"Millard."

"Well, Millard, your brother Ted's a good fighter, but..."

I didn't bother to explain that he wasn't my brother. I was too busy wondering if my guts were going to ooze out between my legs before I had time to walk home.

"Young Ted, if he's got his place to be, he shouldn't be here with us. Isn't a pretty place," persisted the man.

"Teddy goes where there are new things to learn."

"Not get much outta school then?"

"He's been kicked out."

"An' you? Stick with the schooling, you'll be a smart wee thing."

I didn't have the heart to tell him what I generally did with my time. We reached Heatley Street. No cardboard shacks here. The street was paved and there were small houses, only the one storey, most of them, just neat enough to distance themselves from the jungle's chaos. The air was bad because of the dump behind us, the sawmill down river throwing in its aromatic two cents as well, but this was where the city began and the jungle left off, right at this unprepossessing corner. We stood at the edge of what was considered civilized, then I stepped onto the split pavement of the sidewalk.

"I'll send your coat back with Teddy," I said, holding out my hand, pushing the jacket cuff back over my wrist.

The man shook my hand, surprised by my gesture. His fingernails yellow and shattered at the edges, the skin of his hand solid. He reached to the lapel of the jacket, undid the tag looped there. "You don't need this on."

United for Democracy, it read, a little cardboard tag on string, same as a baggage tag—everything ran like a railway station in those days. He slipped it through the buttonless buttonhole of his shirt's breast pocket. It fluttered there for an instant, and I thought of flags, because of the blood on my dress—a lousy girl flag. I'd rather be United for Democracy than be a girl. Nothing to be done about that, so I walked out along Heatley, past the houses gradually bigger, their windows gradually less dirty, until I reached my own plain street.

I heated a tubful of water, tore the slip I kept for medium good into strips, put the jacket aside to be cleaned later on, after I'd dealt with the dark blood that had dried blackish brown on my dress. I wondered why it wasn't proper blood-colour, something especially unwanted about this sort of blood, that's why the body got rid of it every month? I wondered why Mary Ellen hadn't told me what to expect. Maybe she assumed my mother had said what was necessary.

When the water was good and hot, I carried it to the bath and scrubbed myself, every part, using more soap than probably I ought, even if it did come from the Hotel. Considering the price of white soap and everything else, we were blessed with my mother's job. I got out of the bath, layers of folded rag in my underclothes, bunchy and uncomfortable. I was washing the man's jacket when the screen door banged; I didn't even need to turn around, I knew it would be Teddy.

"You didn't keep your end of the bargain."

I turned to glare at him; he had a reddened eye, again. It wasn't yet black, but perhaps it would soon be all colours of the rainbow. "How are you going to grow up to be a lady-killer if you let people hit you in the face?"

"Funny." He had the common sense to wash his face and hands before he came home, so his swollen eye was the only trace of his adventures. His shirt clean, he'd taken it off for the fight, like the well-brought-up child he'd never been.

"I didn't realize I had to stay 'til the end," I said. "I felt uncomfortable."

"You see any of the fight? I did good."

"You're worrying your mother, brawling all the time."

He laughed. "She say that?"

I didn't answer, because of course she hadn't said anything of the kind. When he went upstairs, she would silently make a poultice for his bruises—I'd watched her, on other evenings, steam herbs and wrap them into a clean cloth and hand them to him. Once I asked her what magic was in those weeds she picked, but she only winked at me.

Teddy opened the tin breadbox on the kitchen counter and tore off a piece of bread. "Ma's got other people to worry about, Mill. Wanna get a milkshake? I'm hungry."

I realized he couldn't go upstairs right then, because there was a woman in Mary Ellen's front room. Honestly, Teddy's mother didn't have much to say about his whereabouts because she was too busy. The only house that gained clients on our street during those black years was ours, because Mary Ellen lived upstairs. Married women with three children already, you think they needed another baby to feed, things so hard already? No wonder Mary Ellen had customers. And if occasionally a car appeared in front of our house and a woman from up-on-the-hill Shaunessy stepped discreetly up the worn front steps, careful in her expensive shoes, and knocked on our door, I explained it was upstairs she wanted. Perhaps it was simply to remind us that everyone, all across the layers of the city, everyone was finding themselves with problems.

I left the jacket to soak and pulled myself up to my entire and full-grown height of four feet eleven inches. "We'll get milkshakes. And then you're looking for a job, mister."

"Mill...."

"I'm not fooling. You work, or you get back into school. You want to be a boxer? You want to hurt people for a living? That's an honourable thing to want. Wonderful."

"There's decent money in it."

"That's not decent money. There's blood on that money."

"And what you...."

"There's no blood in a poker game." I believed that, then.

"I thought you'd be proud of me. I won. I always win. Like you with cards. I won."

"You know what happens to men who get hit in the head too much? They get soft in the brain."

"But I'm good, Mill. I'm good at this. Dontcha see?"

"You just can't think straight because you've gotten yourself hit in the head already. Boys like you can't think. They turn into men who lumber around, who don't have their lives anymore. Hands like yours are only going to land you in jail."

"You'd bail me out."

"No I wouldn't."

"Forget it," he said, going out and slamming the door behind him. A real-life Jack of Spades, all dark edges. I finished washing the man's jacket and hung it out on the back laundry line.

The next day, Teddy and I didn't argue about the boxing match because he was desperate to give me the latest news from the jungle: the men were marching downtown, to show their displeasure with the government.

"Hundreds an' hundreds of 'em, Mill, you wouldn't believe. They're occupyin' the Post Office an' the Art Gallery an' the Georgia Hotel, an'...."

"They're occupying the Georgia?" That was just across the street from the gloomy Hotel Vancouver. I wondered if the news had filtered down to Vera and Helen, sweating in the basement.

"They say they ain't leavin' 'til the government gets 'em jobs. Police can come an' arrest 'em if they want, they ain't leavin.'"

"Don't say *ain't*." Then I looked at him. "What were you doing there?"

Teddy looked disappointed. "I missed it mostly. You wanna go downtown an' take another look?"

"No."

"You're no fun, Mill."

I didn't argue with that. I made Teddy a cheese sandwich and we played cards—I skipped Dermot's because the streets were so restless. And below the window, on one of the bedroom hooks, I hung the coat that the man in the jungle had so kindly lent me.

The day after that was Sunday. I cleaned house and made dinner for my mother, who reported that all the lights were off in the Georgia Hotel and the men were apparently being very respectful of the furnishings. On Monday, I started to feel anxious for news, so I went down to McMann's beer hall, to see how Dermot was doing. I went past the front; the establishment was packed, men spilling out onto the sidewalk. I went around to the back and banged on the door that separated the backroom from the bar. Dermot opened the door. He looked tired but pleased, his eyes even smaller than usual and his shirt less than clean, and he nodded to himself when he saw me—always a sign of his good humour.

"How are things keeping down here?" I asked him.

He shrugged. "You heard they left the Georgia?"

"Today?"

"Late last night. The hotel beer parlour undermined discipline a wee bit. Some of 'em here now, not sure where they got money for beer, but here they are. And paying, too."

"So they're still occupying the Post Office?"

Dermot was about to answer me, but behind him, Betsch, the railway man, veered towards us. He was at that midpoint in his drink where he was no longer shaking but comfortably tight, enunciating carefully.

"What'd they want with the P.O.? Nothing to drink there." He spotted me and said, "You playing tonight?"

"If there's a game, Mister Betsch."

That night, Betsch the railway man played well. He came into a slew of two-pair hands, twice with Aces up. One of the managers of the Georgia Hotel joined the game late; he looked like he hadn't slept in days and he was carrying an overfilled wallet.

"No point in bribes," he said. "Might as well spend it."

Dermot didn't ask the hotel manager who he'd been planning to bribe, or whose money it was, while I dealt him into the game. I had a nice few hands that night, especially as twice in the evening I started out with a set. I fought hard against being pleased with that—statistically speaking, a set only turns up every four hundred and twenty-five hands, so two in one night is pretty darn unusual. Sometimes the cards have a sense of humour, toying with us, toying with luck.

When Dermot had finished counting the night's take, rolling my cut into its own pouch to put in his safe, he said, "So you'll be needing some seed money, to move house when your mother's married?"

I hadn't thought about it and I hesitated a long while before answering. "I can hardly go with her," I said finally.

He nodded.

"I haven't quite decided...."

"You'll be independent," he said. "It'll be a fine thing for you, Millard."

"I barely know Harold Avison," I said.

I knew only the external markers of his life which so impressed my mother—his house, his job at the law courts, and his chocolate-coloured Buick coupe. I had spent an afternoon lurking outside the courthouse where he worked, to get a better look at him. He paused only for a moment, long enough for me to shake his limp white hand and congratulate him. I searched his greenish eyes for some sign of personality. A spark. There must be some passion there, I thought, or he would hardly marry my difficult mother.

"Not that he isn't friendly enough," I added, not quite truthfully—when I'd seen him outside the courthouse, he had gotten into his beautiful car without offering me a ride, and he had driven away.

Dermot said nothing. So I started, the very next day, to look for accommodation. I paused at every window advertising rooms to let, I lingered outside the downtown hotels that had rooms by the month, I even tried a boardinghouse a few blocks from our East Pender home. The woman who answered the door was skinny like me, but not natural-like, more as if she'd been left in a window in the sun too long, so her life had gradually evaporated and all that was left was a pile of bones arranged in layers of cardigans and men's trousers. She grudgingly led me up to the second floor. The brown runners on the stairs were worn and there was a nasty stain on the landing. The hall smelled of burned cheese that had been grilled shortly before the Great War was declared. We passed four closed doors, then she put her hand on a greasy brass doorknob and said, "Why are you looking for a room?"

"To live in," I answered, though I realized even as I spoke the words that there was no way I wanted to live in this woman's house. The air felt heavy with dust and disappointment, not at all an environment conducive to good gambling.

"And you work?" She still hadn't actually turned the doorknob to show me the room.

"Yes, I work."

She waited, and I panicked. I didn't want to lie to her. I just couldn't see myself traipsing through her house with money from playing poker. "I have to go," I said, and I turned tail, tripping down the stairs and out across the worn front porch. I slowed only when I reached the corner. As I slunk back to our own street, I wondered what poor souls lived behind the closed doors. A purse full of money, I thought, if I start playing really good games, that's what I'd be carrying around with me. And then? I could rent myself a better room, a better address, a better life. I wanted to look as if I were a lady. There was no way I could pretend such a thing, living in that horrid grey house on this side of Main Street.

That evening, Teddy came downstairs and announced that Mary Ellen wanted me to stay on, after my mother left.

"You could take over the place, have the big bedroom for yourself." Teddy leaned against the door. "You've got the money to pay the whole rent. Ma won't raise it on you. It's a good idea, huh?"

"That's true."

"Fine, I'll...."

"No, Teddy, that's not what I mean. Yes, it's a nice idea, but I'm not staying here."

"Why not?"

I was washing dishes, finishing up with my fork and knife from dinner. I thought about the colourless woman in that grey house I visited. I opened the single kitchen drawer and put the cutlery in its place and jiggled the drawer back so it would close, as much as it ever did.

Silence was never useful with Teddy. He rolled back on his heels to make the door screech on its sprung hinge. "We're not posh enough for you now? Is that it?"

"No, I just...." I wanted to tell him that I was modelling myself on the sophistication of the seven of Clubs, no tricks, no unnecessary decoration. It wasn't about being posh. But before I could explain such a thing to Teddy, his expression had grown dark and he tumbled out the door, letting it bang closed behind him.

🐭

All through the month of June, the men from the jungle occupied the Post Office and the Art Gallery. Seven hundred men in a couple of downtown buildings, trying to get food and work and places to live—because the government had stopped paying out relief and they had no choice. A whole month, they were there. I promised my mother I wouldn't go near the buildings and I stuck to that promise. I didn't see Teddy at all. Finally, I heard his jumbled footsteps on the stairs coming down from his mother's, and when I got to our front door, he was already on the sidewalk.

"Where've you been?" I said. When he turned, I must have gasped. He had a terrible bruise on his jaw. "What happened?"

He shrugged. The bruise flowered across his face, dark burgundy-blue along the jawline, yellow up into his cheek, red across his ear. I stopped on the step just above the sidewalk and put my hands on my hips.

"You gonna get all disapprovin' on me?" he said. "Ma didn't."

"You...."

"A copper hit me. K.O.'d an' all. Felt incredible Mill."

"What do you mean?"

"Hit me with a billy-club, knocked me out. Mill, you just fall right into this blackness, it must be what dyin's like. It's amazin'," he said.

I hit him, with my small and completely pointless balled-up fist. I hit him in the chest. "Idiot," I said as forcefully as I could. "You were over at the Post Office."

"Close," he said.

"I don't want to know."

"Won't tell you anyway, you'll jus' hit me again. Which is pretty funny."

"Funny yourself." I curled my angry hands into balls, wrapping my arms around my ribs, hiding my fists underneath my armpits as if I were cold.

"They're gonna end the demonstration. The cops are. They're massin' up."

"And you're going too...." I turned and went back into the house. So there it was. At the end of six weeks, the Vancouver police were finally going to end the demonstration, and all Teddy wanted to do was get hit in the head. Because it felt good, like dying. I wanted to hit him in the head myself, bash some sense into his obviously battered brain.

When I went back outside, Teddy was gone, and I spent the day looking for a room to live in, so I didn't see the police with their clubs and tear gas. That's how it started, Dermot told me later. When the riot started, I was on the far side of downtown. I saw men running towards the noise, it sounded like a train, almost, the way those wheels screeched and the wind went by. But this wind was a shouting human sound with no rails to follow. As men ran past me, I leaned against the wall of an apartment building, felt the rough bricks through the fabric of my dress. The police began barricading Burrard Street and I wanted only to get away from whatever was going on—I was a coward, thinking of that mob. All I could see was Teddy's face, that bruise, where he'd been clubbed.

The streets were suddenly blocked, as if it was all carefully planned in advance. Police cars parked sideways, choreographed, as if the entire city had converged on the few blocks around the granite building of the post office. I backed up, dodged around the people trying to get through the barriers—I had no desire to see what was happening. I rushed west, away from the shouting, towards the park.

Within a few blocks, the noise of the riot disappeared. I mean, it was gone completely. Late afternoon sunlight filtered down through tall trees, the wooden houses boasted flowers in their window boxes, and children played on the front lawns. It was strange. I paused in front of a four-storey rooming house, wooden siding, peaked roof, with the usual Rooms For Let sign in the window. Something about the elegance of the street made me linger—maybe I was searching for a good hiding place, an escape from the chaos downtown. The house was probably too expensive for me, but I went up to the door anyhow and rang the bell.

After a brief delay, a faint snuffling, shuffling sound came from the far side of the door and a shadow appeared against the glass. The door opened.

"Yes?" The man in the doorway was the size and shape of an ancient sea turtle. His hands were so bent up with arthritis, they moved like flippers.

"About the room to let…." I started.

"You respectable? Only respectable girls in this house. Young ladies only."

He stared at me. We were exactly at eye-level to one another, something that had to be as rare for him as it was for me. I smiled with all the youthful naïveté I could muster but I don't imagine it was all that convincing—such things look better at a poker table than in natural light. Just the same, the hunchback nodded at me.

"The room's upstairs," he said. "Right at the top, end of the hallway. I won't go up myself, the legs, y'know."

He shuffled back so I could come into the small hallway of the house, with its very clean linoleum floor and white walls. There was a small alcove furnished with a wooden chair and a ledge, where a half-finished beer was balanced. "Go on up," said the hunchback, toddling slowly back to his chair. I watched as he maneuvered the glass of beer into his crushed flipper of a hand.

Up two flights of stairs, what I noticed was the scent of the place—the mildew of Vancouver's park-like West End mixed with floor wax and yeast, as if someone was baking bread downstairs. I reached the top floor, the stairs turning onto a narrow landing where there was the shared bathroom. I walked down the hall and paused on the threshold of the one open door. Though the gabled window faced north, the room was bright, papered in white and cream stripes. The bed had a plain wooden headboard and white sheets. The floor had a pale blue rag rug. Against the wall, beside the window, there was a bureau with a tilted square mirror. I walked over and adjusted the mirror, slanting it low enough to reflect my face. My reflection seemed at ease in this room—a safe place, I thought, thinking of what was surely happening downtown. I pictured Teddy's bruise in the mirror and turned my head away.

Opposite the bed, there was a large closet, practically the size of my current pantry-bedroom; though I had nothing to put in such a closet, the idea of it impressed me. The closet door had a glass doorknob, elegant as crystal. I ran my fingers across the prim corner of the clean white bed. This room would be too expensive for me, but it was nice to pretend that I lived here, as I went back down the well-waxed stairs, tightly holding the handrail.

The hunchback watched me return. "A dollar an' a half a week," he said before I could open my mouth. "You pay Miss Jones. Her office is back there. She's not in, right at the moment." He nodded towards the hall that led off into the main floor. "I'm the watchman for the house. Nothing much happens here without my say. I'm Max."

I couldn't believe the room was within my price range—I had enough money for the first week, right there in my pocket. I resisted getting the dollar and coins out right then, there, to prove that I could pay for it. "I'll take the room," I said, trying to sound calm and reliable. "It is nice to meet you, Max," I added, remembering my manners. "My name's Millard. Millard Lacouvy."

He tilted his head back to get a slightly better look at me. "Move in tomorrow morning. Pay Miss Jones when you get here."

I nodded, but Max was already dozing off, his beer carefully balanced in what was left of his hands.

Making my way home through the eerily calm city, I kept my head down, as did anyone I passed, as if we were sneaking past something ugly, none of us quite sure what it was. At the corner of Pender, waiting while a car drove by, I glanced at a small group of men standing well back from the streetlight—three men holding a fourth upright, trying to help him walk. He was covered in blood.

"Girl, don't I know you?" called out one of the men.

I saw that the man who'd spoken was the same person who had lent me his jacket in the jungle. He crossed part of the way across the street, and I met him there. He wasn't as stooped as I remembered, but he looked dirtier than he had been. Not only the blood from his friend, I mean, but his shirt too was dirtier. Maybe it was just that he was in shirtsleeves now, he no longer had a jacket to sleep in.

His friends meanwhile leaned the injured man against the lamppost while the blood ran from his head, gruesome.

"He's going to bleed to death," I said, "You should do something."

"We know that, girl."

"There's a woman lives on this street, I'll take you there."

Mary Ellen took one look at the men standing on our veranda and ushered them upstairs, not hurried, just practical, moving the injured man as little as possible, evaluating what could be done. Glancing over her shoulder, she said, "You go on home, Millard."

I went down and got the jacket hanging on the hook in my bedroom. When I walked upstairs, two of the injured man's buddies had gone into the main room with Mary Ellen. The man I knew was standing at the top of the stairs, having some trouble lighting a cigarette. I put the jacket on the banister beside him.

He nodded. "You washed it."

"Least I could do."

He took a final stab at lighting the cigarette, this time managing, inhaling the smoke hard, swallowing. He leaned one shoulder against the wall and looked down at me. "Good thing I saw you t'other day, yeah?"

"Good luck," I said.

"Ah, luck." He exhaled some smoke through his nose and nodded towards the closed door. "I'll best be goin' inside, girl."

I remembered that he'd said he had a daughter. I wondered what she looked like, and where she was. If my father were alive, would he look so old, standing there? Luck would never tell me.

I was in my bedroom when Teddy slammed our downstairs door. I heard the loose floorboard creak where he always tripped against it, and I came into the living room just as he threw himself into our lone armchair.

"Your ma home yet?"

I shook my head. "She'll be back around six, it's Sunday."

"Hotel let the staff go home early. Avison'll probably pick her up, keep her outta trouble."

"And you?"

He smiled, making the yellow of his fading bruise streak into green and black along his cheek and up into his hairline. "In the middle of it, Mill. 'Course. Trouble and me." He held up two intertwined fingers, the way you'd cross your fingers for good luck. "Nah, I was getting somethin' for your ma."

He fished two fingers into his pocket and slowly pulled out a fragile rope of white beads. I moved closer to have a better look. Pearls.

"Proper wedding present, dontcha think?"

The pearls had a silver clasp, a tiny diamond chip set into the filigree. Each pearl was knotted separately from its neighbour. They weren't exactly white, more like bone-colour, they were iridescent, cloudy, a few slightly yellowish. I'd never seen pearls anywhere but in the Birks display window.

"Where'd they come from?"

Teddy dropped the necklace into my hand and I closed it into my fist instinctively. The pearls were warm.

"They're the real thing," he said. "From the pawn shop, the one on Water Street. Got a good price."

"Where'd you get such fine taste in necklaces?"

I put the pearls on the table, stopped myself from counting each bead, each knot. I looked back at Teddy, who was silent. Usually he boasted of his conquests, so I knew his odd look had nothing to do with the neighbourhood girls. I was suspicious. "There's no box. How are we supposed to give them to her like that, looking like you stole them?"

He laughed. "You want a box? I'll pinch one from Birks."

I wondered what had happened to that twenty dollars I gave him, but I knew my mother was going to love the pearls. "They're perfect."

As I went to put them on the windowsill of my room, Teddy hauled himself out of the armchair, lazily stomping upstairs to Mary Ellen's. Which is when I realized I hadn't told him about my new room, that I was moving.

I had bought a new cardboard suitcase a few days earlier, knowing I would need it. I dragged it out from under the bed and began packing my things. Really there wasn't much, a few books, some clothes. I need different clothes, I thought, folding what I had. My face would be the same, my size wouldn't change, but I could make myself better, surely. I picked up the pearls from Teddy. They were cool now, from the windowsill. I coiled them inside a clean handkerchief and set them on the dining room table.

I wasn't sure how I was going to tell my mother that I'd found a room. With the aftermath of the riot downtown, maybe she wouldn't be home until late, perhaps I could go to Dermot's, see if there was a game after all the unrest. I was kneeling on the floor of my bedroom, trying to fit the filled suitcase under my bed, when my mother came home.

"Downtown's back to normal," she said, standing in the doorway of my room. "Some of those poor boys, no older than Teddy, you know." Then she stopped and put her hands on her hips. "What in the world are you doing?"

"I've found a room. You can come see it if you like, near Stanley Park."

"You're running away."

I stood up. "You're getting married."

"I gave up on you a long while back, Millard."

I looked at my Queen of Diamonds, there in the doorway. I wondered if I could get past her, out into the living room.

"What have you done now?" persisted my mother.

"Nothing."

"You haven't taken a high road. Harold worries about you."

"I like Harold Avison. I'm glad you're marrying him. Teddy and I have your wedding present and everything," I said slyly, hoping to distract her. "Look...."

"Teddy can give it to me. If you're going to leave, then leave."

She turned on her heel, a few long strides and she was in her bedroom, the door firmly slammed behind her. Then the door handle was wrenched open again. "I said, get out. If you're leaving, get. Now." And the door went back on its hinges with a resounding smack.

It wasn't the departure I'd hoped for. That white and cream striped room in the West End seemed awfully empty, now that I was really going there.

"Mother," I said, not too loudly, "I'd like to take the afghan with me, may I?" When I heard nothing from the bedroom, I gathered the black and red blanket up from the armchair. Folded, it fit easily into my suitcase. I set the suitcase down by the door, so I could put on my coat—it wasn't raining, but wearing a coat is easier than carrying one. As I pulled at the sleeves, my mother came out of her bedroom to stare at me. "Is Teddy helping you move your things?"

"I haven't got many things. I have my books."

She came over to me and I steeled myself for a slap, but she put her hand under my chin and stared at my face for a long time, then released me. "You take after your father."

She had never said that before. I wondered what she'd seen in my face, as I forced myself to kiss her cool cheek. With me gone, who would make her tea if she got one of her black moods? Teddy, perhaps, would understand. And then Harold Avison could make tea, of course. The reason I was moving—I had forgotten Harold entirely, just then.

5

On Main Street, nearly at Hogan's Alley, there was an Italian tailor's shop. In summer, the corner smelled of beer with the strong underwhiff of outhouse, for nothing so elaborate as a sewer serviced the street. I stopped at the well-kept little shop front for the first time that new day, after I'd settled my suitcase at the boardinghouse. I had on my best dress, such as it was, a two-year-old brown serge, absolutely free of style, not exactly too small, but not doing any favours to my slightly improving shape. My left hand scrunched protectively in my pocket, fingers curled around my winnings. The door of the Italian tailor's shop swung smoothly closed behind me as I darted inside. The room smelled strongly of lemons. Oak shelves rose up to the ceiling, bolts of dark suit fabric on one side, light patterned cottons on the other. I didn't have a particular pattern or material, I was only determined that the tailor would make me a new woman—or at the very least, a new dress.

Behind the counter, there were satins, I learned later these were for lining the clothes—none of my clothes until that moment had been so rarified as to have proper satin linings. At first, I thought I was alone in the shop, I could see no one, and then there was a slight movement in the far corner as the tailor straightened and got up from his sewing machine. He was taller than me, but not by much, with smooth skin, round gold-framed spectacles, and shellacked black hair that made the whole shop smell of lemony hair oil. He listened to my request for a plain dress and jacket, and drew a quick outline on a piece of cutting paper. I watched his slightly chapped hands, his gold wedding ring glinting in the light. He held out the page and I squinted at his drawing. It looked more or less like a dress. I wondered if he had any daughters, if this is what they wore.

"No pockets," I said, "it's very important, not having pockets." I pointed to a green fabric but he shook his head and brought out a blue cotton. "Less expensive," he said, "But less wrinkling, better line." He talked some more about line, waving his hands. I didn't see what line might do for me, but I paid him what seemed like a lot of money to do what he could.

As I made my way to the West End, I studied the clothes on people around me—as the streets moved towards the better part of town, the fabrics became cleaner, more expensive, less busy, too, less fussy. I had no ambitions of dressing so well as the fancy ladies of Shaunessy, but as I walked past the stores on Granville, I thought I might aspire to look as sharp as the shop girls, almost glamorous in their clean collars and wide white cuffs. I hoped the tailor would do well by my money. When I reached the boardinghouse, I went upstairs and locked myself in the shared bathroom and washed in the real built-in bathtub so thoroughly, I sloughed off a whole layer of skin.

When I went back at the end of the week, I saw that the tailor knew his business; he made clothes simply and didn't fool around with special effects. The dress was neat, plain blue cotton with two small pleats in the skirt and a removable white collar and cuffs. He'd made a matching blue collarless jacket to wear over the dress, with close-fitting sleeves and no pockets.

I put on that new dress for my mother's wedding. The ceremony was a simple thing in the church around the corner from Avison's house. She and Harold Avison swore fidelity and honesty and obedience, and I tried not to wince. I imagined her slapping Harold Avison and throwing her shoes at him, and I shook my head, there in the church during the ceremony.

My mother wore a pale yellow suit bought specially for the occasion, with the string of pearls at her neck. Teddy told her the necklace was from Birks, which was true in a roundabout sort of way—there was the shop's recognizable little lion crest on the underside of the clasp. In the front pew, Mary Ellen was in her best dress, Teddy beside her in a borrowed grey suit, only slightly worn at the sleeves, pulling a bit at the shoulders where the jacket was clearly too small. I tried not to be surprised at how grown-up Teddy looked. Trailing into the church behind our small parade were the various Avisons, fatter and better-fed than we were, but I thought overall, what with Mary Ellen's and Teddy's good looks, my mother's glowing intensity, and even my really very nice new dress, our side of the family was more comely than Avison's.

The church was a bit too hot, and it seemed to get still hotter as the minister droned on and on about fidelity. The stained glass behind him was blue-green, like my earliest memories of the water's edge. I found myself remembering the cabin I'd been born in, near the lake, and I held that image in my head, trying to feel cool. A remembered colour, a breeze, as if I were still three years old in the back of the canoe, paddling though not getting anywhere much. The water ruffled green, waves going out to the other side of the lake, black shore becoming mountains, their triangles comforting white at the top. I pushed the paddle into the water again, looked down along its wood into the water, how it was a surface and yet transparent, how below, beyond, there were shapes of weeds. I looked up, my father watching, possibly he smiled at me, or was he just smoking, difficult to tell, squinting against the sun. West of the Rockies, West of the Law, he said to me, like a fairy tale book, east of the sun, west of the moon. The ladies in those drawings wore such colourful gowns, I remembered tracing them against my mother's fingers, cool glossy paper. My mother's effort at lady-fying me, for my father's great ambition was for me to be as good as any boy, even if I was small for my age, even if I was a scrawny child. I could swim underwater with my eyes open. And skip a flat stone five times, easy.

"Great tricks you've taught her," said my mother in the middle of an argument that had nothing to do with me. I knew this from the very first time I heard them argue, but still I fled the house and spent the night up a tree, angry at them both. The pine scraggy but perfect for my skinny arms, short legs; in all my memories before Vancouver, I am always either naked or in practical boy's clothes. Pine scratches didn't bother me. I remembered spending the dark hours in the middle of the tree, the back of my head against the trunk, legs akimbo on the branches, watching the light of the moon. Did my mother really leave me in a tree all night? I think she did. Even now, I think I am remembering this quite correctly.

In the morning she came out and asked, "Are you coming down or did the ravens make off with you?"

I did come in and eat breakfast and didn't sulk anymore. I was very small but I was not anyone's pawn. My father left after shaking my hand formally and swinging me up and around and combing my hair out of my eyes. My mother let him leave and didn't get swung up or around or hair-combed. I was eating porridge with wild honey and reconstituted milk when my mother rushed out of the main room and through the door and along the path where my father had gone. I thought while I finished my breakfast that my mother wasn't obliged to come back for me, that both my father and mother might walk off right then, leave me alone. It made me respect my black-eyed mother, that she came back some hours later, even if her hair was undone and her eyes vicious as lynx eyes. It was to the good that before my mother's return, I stood on the stool and did the dishes, counted them carefully and lined them up neatly below the shelf where they belonged. I wasn't tall enough to reach the shelf so I arranged the dishes by size in a small stack.

"That's that," said my mother.

Now she was marrying somebody else. With a start, I focused again on the church. I wondered if she'd really been married to my father at all. She had never worn a wedding ring; she had only an unframed photograph of my father's face, slightly blurred, sandy-haired, possibly smiling, though the photo was so creased, I couldn't be sure. He was wearing mill clothes, as if he'd just finished work. I looked at Harold Avison up at the altar in his grey striped morning trousers. Outside, a photographer was waiting, booked especially to take pictures of us all, after the wedding. There would be no blur to Harold Avison's face, it would be clearly etched and ever-so-slightly disapproving every time he looked in my direction.

We posed on the steps of the church. Then my mother kissed Mary Ellen and Teddy, and she took me to the Avison clan's formal lunch, at Harold's brother's house. The bully Gerald Avison sat at the far end of the table shovelling food into himself, while I didn't say much except "thank you" when a plate was passed to me. I wished Teddy had stayed for lunch; at least I'd have had someone to talk to.

Harold didn't speak to me. I imagine my mother had admitted that her daughter was morally destitute, or whatever a churchgoer like Harold might think appropriate to say of a gambler. He eyed me sidelong—I was an unfortunate reality, but at least I wasn't going to live with him. My mother was remote at the end of the table, her black hair piled up on her head and her dark eyes flashing on the rare occasions that our gazes crossed. Maybe she was stewing at the effort of being polite to Harold's conservative relatives. Or maybe it was no effort at all. I don't know why I expected her to give me some kind of advice, to head out into the world with some words of wisdom. I was on my own. Doesn't poker give everyone that chance, that moment to take control, to make clear decisions, choose which hands to use and which to toss away?

I didn't change from my wedding clothes before going to Dermot's. In the backroom, the cards were loyal as ever, always changing yet reliably present in my hands. Towards midnight, I got the six of Diamonds. I stared hard at its pattern and thought of Harold Avison, how that sharp-edged six meant trouble in a second marriage, and though it was a strong hand, I folded. However lynx-eyed my mother might be, I didn't want that card for her.

What I wanted was a better game, but I was uncertain how to find it. If I could just find the right game, the right table, I would make sense, I would have a spot in the world where I could put all my affections, where the cards would read my fortune easily. Meanwhile, I counted games, hands. I tried to invent new strategies for poker, there in the backroom, wearing my old clothes, meeting Dermot's eyes at the end of each night's game, waiting for his approval, satisfied when he nodded. Then I walked through Gastown, the wet pavement slick under my new boots, through downtown in the West End, to sleep in the white boardinghouse room. I murmured goodnight to the hunchback doorman in his niche and walked upstairs through the baked bread and clean wax smell of the house. Each night, I shut the door to my room and walked barefoot across the rag rug to look in the closet at my new blue dress hanging there, waiting, as I was.

My new chance came in the unlikely form of Betsch, the twitchy Canadian Pacific man. One night he did not badly for a while, but when he went all in on a very dicey proposition, I cleaned him out and he groaned. "Don't you think, McMann, the girl should start breaking down other men's pocketbooks, instead of being always at mine?"

"What are you on about?" said Dermot.

"You should getonnatrain." Betsch waved at me as if he were indeed going somewhere.

I glanced at Dermot to see if he took offense, but Dermot looked thoughtful. "It's true," he said, "there's probably card games on trains."

"Always a card game on a train. Jus' a question of what game you want to play, shrimp." Betsch stood up. He weaved even before he took a step away from the table—his view of the world was so obviously fuzzy at the edges, I found it difficult to take him seriously.

"You think I can play cards on a train?"

"Always games...." he repeated heavily, fussing with his pocket and giving up.

"I don't see how anyone would open a game to me," I said. "You play with me because you trust the house."

"On my word, the guys would play with you," said Betsch, with perfect enunciation, then he coughed wetly and spat, which rather ruined the effect. "The passengers, they would." Dermot held the door steady and we watched Betsch teeter towards the carved wooden bar and place one hand on the firm wooden edge. Then he got his other hand onto the bar's edge, and hand over hand, as if climbing a rope, with his legs listing out from under him, onboard a storm-tossed ship, he managed to get himself through the room and out the front door.

Dermot turned back to meet my eyes. "You should think on it, Millard. You have to move up some time." He sat down at the table and began counting the take, dividing out my portion.

I watched him sort coins and dollar bills. When he'd finished, I took my portion and put it in the purse I'd taken to carrying everywhere. I'd bought it at Woodward's, just around the corner from Dermot's, it was navy blue leather, very smart, with a pretty clasp. "Trains?" I pressed the stiff leather strap of my purse in my hands. "Do you mean you're booting me out?"

Dermot snorted. "I'm proud of you, and you're a right ambitious lass. Can't expect you to stay put at this table all your days."

I put the purse on my lap and fidgeted with the clasp, staring at the brass-coloured metal. Click it was closed, turn the toggle, now it was opened, click, now it was closed.

Dermot leaned over and rumpled my hair. "I'm expecting you to take your training and your wise hands and get yourself some fine games, lass. Betsch is no fool." When I glanced up dubiously, he added, "His word's worth something to his fellows. You've been bankrolling the money, Millard, you should go. It's a fine chance."

I held onto my purse as if it were the most solid thing in the room. But Dermot stood and pulled me to my feet and wrapped me in a bony Irish hug. "I don't mean for you never to get back here my girl. But you're going to try your hand at the bigger tables. You may as well get started. The games'll still be here if you're back only on Tuesdays 'stead of every day of the week."

I nodded, but I didn't trust myself to say anything; for once I walked out through the bar, through the front door, not caring if the few remaining patrons caught sight of me. I wasn't at all sure my hands would bring me through. I knew Harry Betsch respected my skills only because I had repeatedly taken his money—maybe it even amused him, to boast to his CPR colleagues about a little girl card shark he knew. Betsch was like most of the men at Dermot's—he didn't mind losing to a girl. The men at Dermot's had watched me grow up. Sensible gambling men, husbands and fathers all, they kept a paternal eye on my evolution, which left me ill-prepared for men's behaviour in the real world. Only later did I learn that even if no one is threatening you, it's best to keep one eye on your way out. A back door. A waiting car. You should always keep a key in your pocket and enough money for a ticket to someplace else. Since leaving my mother's house, I've spent an entire life in carefully-timed departures. Nothing shameful about departure—I learned that when my father left, and I confirmed it when my mother decamped from the Interior.

Not everyone has a kind personality, a character that sits solid like a six of Clubs. No, players can be downright unfriendly, some even imply you have been cheating. I'll say one thing straight: I have never cheated at cards. Any such accusations are entirely false. But men don't like to lose to a lady. To a slip of a girl. To a bitch. To a witch. To a whore. All the words never leveled at me when I played at Dermot's but that I came to hear once I stepped out on my own. Walking home that night, going to the boardinghouse, I should have been steeling myself for every bad word a man could find for me.

Vancouver had its first real card clubs by then. The classiest was the Railway Men's Club on Dunsmuir, upstairs from the bus terminal—those buses meant the street was always crowded with passengers and waiting families. I walked past the building every day on my way to Dermot's, and I admired the neon script announcing the destinations of the buses outside. Montreal, New York, Seattle, San Francisco—Las Vegas wasn't even listed yet, though one day it would feature large on my list of itineraries. Much as I admired the building, with its dreamy destinations, I couldn't walk in the club's door, let alone play there. That word Men in its title, it was quite accurate. The Railway Men's Club was strictly for the middle managers of the Canadian Pacific and Great Pacific Railways, some so wealthy they were ferried from the Hotel Vancouver to the card club in the very grandest of big black limousines. The tables of the Railway Club weren't available to the gentler sex, not for cards, not for anything. Which is why Harry Betsch's suggestion of the trains was such an inspired idea. I might not be welcome at the Railway Club, but I could play the very same men, on their very own turf, on the trains that clanged in and out of the station on West Cordova Street.

I had been on a train only once, with my mother, coming to Vancouver from the Interior. We sat in a freight car with seven or eight mill workers, all men who'd known my father. I remember only the open door of the car, the way the landscape went by, so many trees, striped flashes of light, and how I was forbidden to move. I sat beside my mother and chewed the knuckle of my index finger. I knew this trip would be different from that experience: I'd be travelling on a proper passenger train, for one thing. And I was my own person now, taller, with clearer talents.

The train station stood importantly just on the edge of Gastown, only three blocks from Dermot's bar. The building was built importantly at the edge of the water, facing the mountains and North Vancouver. Twenty tall white pillars stretched up three storeys high across the brick façade of the station. Wide awnings protected the entrance, just like the entrance of a grand hotel, and its wide stretch of sidewalk on West Cordova Street was swept clean twice a day by boys in uniform. Canadian Pacific porters stood ready to help with baggage on either side of the wide front doors. I walked past on the far side of the street a few times, studying the main door. The white pillars and the elaborate white stone made the brick building look like a mansion, as if all the passengers were honoured guests. I tried to believe that I was absolutely invited.

On the appointed day, I bought a small alligator-skin bag specifically for the trip. I took my blue dress from its hanger in the closet, and as I did up the buttons and straightened my cuffs, I tried to feel confident. I carefully packed the small alligator-skin bag with necessities; I liked this new ritual of getting ready for a wholly different kind of game, a table where Dermot wasn't watching over me. My hands were going to be fine. I took a deep breath,, touching each object carefully—I had bought myself a tortoiseshell hairbrush and manicure set which I placed in the bag along with all my money from Dermot's, for my bankroll. The bills were wrapped in a cotton envelope. I put a sweater on top of the money. The alligator bag was brown, with gold-coloured clasps that made a satisfying click when I closed them. I smoothed my hair and stared in the mirror. Yes, I would do. I walked purposefully out of the house and through the West End, the same route as I took to Dermot's every day.

It was just beginning to rain when I walked down West Cordova. A taxi splashed past me and as I stepped away from its wake of surging puddles, it screeched to a stop and deposited a man in a tweed suit in front of the station. He went in without holding the door for me and I caught its swing back towards me, pulling it open with difficulty. Going through the doors, I remembered suddenly how I'd last walked out of here, a three-year-old girl dragged along by a determined black-haired mother. I'd been so overwhelmed by the journey, I didn't remember the clean pillared interior, the beautiful polished benches in the waiting area. I paused under the coffered ceiling and tried to believe I was up to the job, as the man in the tweed suit strode past purposefully. I had to believe I could play poker against a man like that, I had to be sure in my heart that I could win. I watched him disappear through the doors leading to the platform. I looked down at my shoes. The complicated marble floor tiles echoed with women's heels, the softer tread of men's shoes—a mingling counterpoint with voices and clanging of the trains outside. I forced myself to look up, as if I knew exactly what I was doing; the departures board showed lots of time before my train left.

To the right, there was a soda fountain coffee shop. Oh, I was tempted to just stop there for a milkshake, but I resisted, I knew if I stopped at all, I might never get on the train. So I looked firmly to my left, where a barber was shaving a fat man in the shiny single chair of the shop. I watched the barber neatly cover the customer's chin with lather—that was simple, useful: the man needed a shave, this was the barber's profession. But me? I wanted to have a purpose, I wanted to have a profession. I was so unsure, uncertain the cards would be true to my hands—or my hands, true to the cards.

I went cautiously to the ticket counter, where I bought a coach seat on the train to Calgary, exactly as Betsch had instructed. I slid the bills under the glass wicket and the woman counted the one dollar bills, her long red nails clicking against the counter. When she finished, she pushed the ticket back to me and smiled. "Have a good trip, lovey," she said.

I turned back to the elegant waiting area. There were small vignettes of scenery, painted below the ceiling. There were gold swags of plaster and two elaborate gold and ivory clocks, and a great deal of pink and cream molding. A kind of dance hall for the waiting passengers. I wouldn't have been surprised if everyone had paired off and begun a Lindy Hop all across the floor, a carefully choreographed musical number that didn't include me. It was too nerve-wracking to stay under the coffered ceiling, so I went out through the swinging doors to the platforms. Beyond the doors was a different world, filled with steam and smoke and noise, grey and damp. The engines were enormous, groaning, puffing, stomping their hooves, impatient horses in their stables. The glass roof barely seemed able to contain them. The platforms were like sidewalks, crowded, porters with bags, people reached for their tickets, newsboys ran up and down with the evening's paper, tramps begged for change. I found myself standing with my back against one of the iron pillars near the door. I watched the movement of people back and forth, looked up at the huge trains. I thought of the cards, relying on my hands to bring us both to a good game. My train was at platform number three, a number that signaled caution in every suit. All right then.

I stepped through the crowd to the correct platform, clutching my alligator bag so the handle cut into my fingers. The train Betsch recommended was a real trans-continental, winding through the mountains and way across the country, though I took a ticket only to Calgary. I memorized my coach number, the train, and the platform—it was hardly memorizing, I suppose, I couldn't help remembering numbers. They comforted my nerves. So when I found the platform, the number three, I threw back my shoulders, I stepped up the giant metal tread into the train car. No porter helped me look for my seat. They were busy helping wealthier, more important customers, with more luggage and more confidence than I. The car was crowded and warm, the burgundy leatherette seats worn. But the frosted light fixtures gleamed and the glass of the window was clean, so I sat down, bag at my feet, and stared nervously out the window, waiting for the train to leave, trying not to watch the other passengers. I didn't want to speculate about the marks I'd be likely to find. I wanted to go into this first game with a clear head, undistracted by expectations. I was too aware of being out of my depth, I was too aware of the train. I stared at my feet, at my beautiful alligator-skin bag. Wasn't it the mark of a lady? I stared at its brass clasps until I heard a scuffle of last-minute passengers and a sharp whistle. The train shuddered, there was another whistle, and we were underway.

No chance of backing out now. The train lurched, swayed. I sat in my seat and felt increasingly ill. At least there was no one in the seat beside me. I'm here, I thought, I'll get used to the train's slithering movement, so unstable, even sitting down. Imagine standing, imagine playing cards, the shaking surface of the table—I closed my eyes. I had paid my rent for the rest of the month. I'd brought all the rest of my cash from Dermot's, a total of four hundred dollars. I opened my eyes. The streets of Vancouver unfurled on the far side of the window, unravelling into landscape, into evening. I glimpsed the sudden flares of hobo fires, and then the train slipped out of town. Further on, there was an Indian village, small houses fading into black woods, no moon visible. There were a few stars in the sky, but mostly only the outline of trees, dark shadows of mountains.

A toffee-haired porter passed by, old enough to be my father, his uniform so starched, he could barely lower his chin to meet my eyes. But when he did take my measure, he winked at me. Imagine a freckled customs guard, winking at you. That sort of unnerving certainty. He paused carefully, his brown hand on the seat behind my head.

"Aren't you the girl Betsch told me to look out for?"

The contact made, I smiled as sweetly as I knew how, no matter that my heart was beating loudly enough that he might have heard its pulse over the noise of the train. "My daddy taught me to play cards," I said.

"He did, did he?"

He looked back at the people in the rest of the car.

"Later on," he said, very quiet-like, "there'll be a game with some boys in compartment D, car seventeen. Harry said you 'n me might come to some kind of agreement. There's a Yank that owes me a few dollars. My name's Karmel."

"Pleased to meet you, Mister Karmel."

His expression changed to something very close to a smile. "Jus' Karmel's fine. You wait for my word, Missy."

Then he made a peculiar bow, a kind of nod but starting in the chest, folding from the shoulders, before continuing down the aisle. The train whistled, brakes scraped metal against metal, and we stopped at a tiny station. Doors banged open and from the window, I watched men drag a pile of white Canada Post bags off a cart on the single short platform and into a car further up, behind the engine. Then the whistle again, steam from the engine clouding the little station platform.

I decided I should at least explore the train, get my bearings. Know the playing ground, so to speak. I would find the dining car and order a cup of tea. Yes, surely that's what a lady would do, if she were travelling to Calgary by train, she would have tea. That's what I decided, anyhow—I had no idea what a lady would do, under any circumstances, train or not. I stood awkwardly and held the back of my seat to get my sea-legs. It took a bit of getting used to, the swaying and lunges of the train as the wheels rolled along the tracks, dragging us forwards through the landscape. I walked holding the top edges of the coach seats with my right hand, balancing along the aisle with my alligator bag. It took a little bit of doing to get through the compartment door and into the next car. The black shaking metal platform worried me, you could see glimpses of the dark rails going by, the clanging iron of the train beneath. But I willed myself through the shaking metal plates, I was going to be fine, oh, I tried to believe that the more risks I survived, the better a player I would become, the more invincible I would be. The train lurched through a short tunnel and the darkness startled me. When we came through into twilight again, I pushed on through the next coach car and pulled open another compartment door. A man coming the other way helped me negotiate the double doors on the far side.

Through yet another set of heavy car doors, I found myself in an entirely different world. An etched glass panel divided the more casual smoking and drinking parlour space from the formal dining area of the car—men and women sat down for supper on the train as white-coated waiters handed them small white cardboard menus. I walked down the aisle between the tables, trying to look as if I belonged there. I tried not to knock into the white tablecloths clamped to the edges of the tables with little silver clips. Trying to walk smoothly through the dining car—ah, a difficult trick to master, the way the train swayed along on its track. I wondered if trains ever fell off their iron road, swinging so far one way or the other that they landed flat in the ditch.

On the far side of an etched glass panel in the bar area, I saw only one woman, chatting to a man in a brown suit, a derby on the little table beside him. He blew cigarette smoke at the ceiling as I passed, and his companion gesticulated to make some point—I noticed her elaborate diamond gold rings. In the other seats, men read newspapers, shaking the pages straight as I walked by. I wondered if I'd find myself playing cards against any of them. I sat down in the one remaining empty chair, at the furthest corner of the car, and when the tall barman came over, I said, "I'm a friend of Karmel's, may I have a cup of tea?"

The barman was tanned as if he'd lived a long life in the sun of the prairies, black hair cut like a military man's, skin crinkled around his brown eyes. He smiled at me as if I were his daughter. I knew the look—it's being small, people assume you're in need of being mothered. Just then, I didn't mind at all.

"Karmel is a good man," he said. "You all on your own on this big train?"

I shrugged and the bartender, this I had not expected, he shrugged right back at me, as if to say, *Oh well, that's the way the world goes, we do the best we can.* And he brought me a shortbread cookie with my tea, for no reason save sympathy.

It was a funny kind of contrast, these people sitting so appropriately inside the dining car, as if they were sitting in the gold and red lounge of the

Hotel Vancouver, while outside, the night grew black and wild, framed in rectangles of window. The barman brought the passengers whiskeys, coffees, hot toddies. The train was coming into the mountains, and I glimpsed the rare station, a flash of lights coming up, the train rattling, shaking, settling to a stop at an isolated platform, then lurching out, leaving the tiny town behind, the steam puffing from our engine and along the length of the snaking cars, past our windows, white. When my tea arrived, I concentrated very hard on not spilling it. I would learn to keep my hands steady by practicing with the teacup, holding the saucer just so.

Karmel found me after another hour, and escorted me further along the train into a first class sleeping car—a narrow hall with metal and wood doors, all closed. Clean white curtains hung at the windows as I brushed along the corridor. Karmel knocked on the door of compartment D. Inside, four men hunched expectantly at a tiny folded-down table. There was one empty seat, perfectly placed, waiting for me. The blind was drawn over the window, the little compartment's bed was tucked away. Those five seats arranged at the small oblong table should have been all I needed to feel at ease. I waited for my worries to slide away onto the railway tracks below and disappear into the night, but they didn't. The rocking movement of the train made my hands feel disconnected, not exactly queasy, but wrong.

As he introduced me, Karmel smiled in a servile way. "I promised her father before he died, I'd keep an eye on her," he said.

I was intrigued—he'd made that story up on the spot. The men at the table looked puzzled—I was a circus trick they'd never seen before. Three stood politely to shake my hand. The fourth nodded to me, he was dark and a bit older than the others, and when he spoke, he had a pronounced New York accent. "So this is how you're keeping an eye out, is it?"

Karmel smiled, revealing a gold tooth, bottom left. "I thought it might give you all a chuckle, to play against a wee slip of a girl from Edmonton. Since her daddy was someone I knew when he went off to the War, an' all... those days, promises you made, you keep 'em."

Another good card, I thought, these men are just young enough to have missed the Great War, and for all their obvious wealth, the one thing they could envy of Karmel's would be that experience—whether or not Karmel had really been there.

"The War," murmured the man who hadn't stood, impressed despite himself by the trenches of Europe. Big guys like that, they were all sorry they'd missed the chance to be proper soldiers—fools, I would say now, they didn't know what they were regretting, and they would have a fresh chance soon enough. The New York man pushed himself up from the table and gestured for me to sit in the empty seat beside him. One of the other men stepped aside so I could pass, and we all took our places at the table. The room smelled of tobacco and men's hair oil. I thought of the Italian tailor on Main Street and I tried to smile a little.

Karmel brought four clean glasses for whiskey and a cup of coffee for me, which I set beneath my chair, beside my alligator bag, there was so little room on that train table. We each cut the deck to decide who would begin. It was that easy, to begin playing with them, and once underway, the game shouldn't have been any different from playing at Dermot's, except that we were enclosed in a train compartment. But there was no one I could rely on. I was by myself, hurtling through the darkness. Karmel came by from time to time, so I had someone to watch over me, but he didn't believe in my cards. I had to conjure up my own faith. And perhaps my faith couldn't keep up with the train, its lurching around every corner—my hands shook with the constant movement, the stops and starts at every station. I could barely remember what cards had been put into play and my heart trembled, not because of the other players— they confused me, but they weren't threatening. No, it was the cards, they just weren't coming to me. I folded hand after hand. I tried to have steady fingers, I rested my wrists on the tabletop to keep them sure, but the cards I wanted didn't come to me. I stayed quietly in the game, watching the New Yorker that Karmel disliked battle another wealthy man, the pots getting bigger as they out-bluffed each other. Three of the players were subtler by far than anyone I'd seen at Dermot's; the fourth man, directly across from me, had signet rings on almost every finger and his yellow and white checked suit clashed virulently with his green shirt.

I tried to focus on the game. I had an occasional big card, but at random, so I could do nothing with it, a lone Queen of Clubs, a solitary Ace. It saddened me to fold a handsome card like the Ace of Diamonds, a card that was tough as nails. I listened hard but I couldn't hear the cards' message over the rattling wheels, the screeching of the brakes as we paused at tiny mountain stations. I took increasing amounts from my bankroll, and folded, kept folding, watching that money disappear, round by round. The man directly opposite me smiled encouragingly. I didn't know what to do with his expression, how to read it with meaning for his cards. He was twitchy, rubbing his eyes, scratching his ears, making all kinds of faces at his different hands—so many tells that none of them helped me.

The chair was too high. I had my alligator bag underneath my feet and I took to leaning forward against the table, resting the tips of my toes on the bag, trying to gain some purchase. I was dealt a series of small pairs over several hands, two fives, two threes. As if the cards were trying to tell me I was too small for this game, giving me tiny numbers. Finally I got two sevens, Hearts and Diamonds, and because I didn't want to fold all the time, foolish pride, I forced myself to bet in.

What the cards were trying to tell me with all those small pairs was: You're not ready yet. Because I lost. Two sevens don't hold up against much. The Yank looked pityingly at me as he turned over his hand, "A full boat, gentlemen. And, excuse me, miss."

Some players called a full house a "boat" or a "full boat" or even a "tight." Which is how my throat felt as I slid to the edge of my seat and put my feet on the swaying floor of the train compartment. I stood up and forced myself to smile, I managed this feat, I stood steadily. I picked up my bag and said, "Thank you for your patience, gentlemen. You've shown me how the game is played. I'm grateful."

I didn't look at their expressions as I left. They were already shuffling a new game out onto the table. Maybe one of them cracked a joke about my size, the cheek of me at their table, and they'd taught me a lesson hadn't they—no, I heard nothing of the sort. My imaginings came from wounded pride. Alone in the corridor, I stood dully in front of the door that led into the lounge car. I must have stood there, numb, all through a fresh round of cards, maybe several, because suddenly the man in the yellow and white checked suit came out of the compartment and chuckled to see me.

"Where are you going to, little lady?"

He twitched just as much away from the table as he did playing cards. He wasn't a big man but he loomed towards me, peering, as if he were trying to identify a new breed of bird, taking note of colouring, behaviour, flight pattern, for future reference. I smiled warily as he pulled open the door that led out of the car and gestured me ahead of him. I went past quickly, across the shaking black platform connector, and pushed hard on the door to the lounge car. I didn't want to be trapped between cars in the rumbling guts of the train.

"I have a lot to learn," I said.

"Why don't we have a drink? Watch the scenery, you can tell me where you learned to play cards."

"My father taught me." It seemed the easiest lie available. I wondered why this man was bothering to talk with me. Perhaps he saw me as a fellow eccentric.

"He must have known his players."

The parlour car was practically empty. The man offered me a seat and lit a pipe. "I'm from Edmonton. Which is where you're from?"

I made a noncommittal murmur, which soon became a cough—I wasn't used to the strong tobacco he was smoking. Before I could answer properly, the black-haired barman came over and stood silently waiting for our order.

"Now, you want a coffee? A cocktail? Little young for that maybe. Myself, I always take a Manhattan, so you choose whatever you like, a little girl who can play cards probably knows what she wants to drink."

I ordered tea with lemon, and the barman caught my eye for an instant, out of sight from my companion, a swift sharp glance to let me know that if there was any problem, I had only to say the word. I held my head up a tiny bit higher.

"I'm in the bridge business," said the man across from me. "Beck's the name. George Mackenzie Beck. Edmonton's been good to me. Good for bridges." The trace of a frown sketched across his face. "Not good for much else." He tapped the bowl of his pipe with his hand. "Was in Vancouver working on that Burrard Street Bridge, y'know, with Sharpe. A concrete man. That bridge is too heavy. I'm a girder man, myself, I like the engineering of the thing, don't muck it up with prettiness, that's my opinion. I'd like to get my hands on that Granville Bridge of yours. That truss they've got, completely outdated. I could do something really spectacular there. But it takes time. Money."

"As everything does," I said.

"Too true. But keep your eyes on Granville, one day, I'm going to be the man that rebuilds that bridge. Before I die." He paused. "You're from Vancouver, aren't you?" As if reading my mind, he added, "The way you speak, my dear. My wife's from Vancouver. She has just the same way with the vowels."

I put a slice of lemon in my tea and stirred it with a spoon.

"So where did you really learn to play cards?"

"Clearly, I have more to learn."

George Mackenzie Beck shrugged. "You know my dear, I can give you some advice."

I took a sip of my tea.

"Simple advice, my dear. When you have doubts, find eight outs. Else you must fold."

"Why eight?"

"Eight ways to win the pot, depending on what card comes up on the River. If you can't see eight ways to win, you fold."

"Eight," I said politely. It was too simplistic a formula, but maybe it worked for him.

Perhaps sensing I was dubious, he said, "Believe me, eight's the magic number. I can't begin to tell you why, but I can tell you, it does work. And why mess around with questions when you've got something that works? Course, if I'm building a bridge, I ask the questions. But you don't have to drive a car over a hand of cards. You just have to win the pot, don't you agree?"

And then, thank goodness, he stopped talking about cards, and began telling me about his most-perfect dreamed-of bridge, what he wanted to build in Vancouver, if he ever got the chance. He told me all about girders and I pretended to be interested. I tried to imagine the bridge, thinking, what else can I do? If not cards, I'll be back at the hotel laundry, horrible thought. Maybe I could get work washing dishes upstairs, instead, except I was too short for the sinks. My mother couldn't help me at the hotel—she had quit her position when she married Harold.

My eyes must have become so round with fear that the man said, "You're looking a little bit under the weather. Don't let a little loss stop you now."

I nodded, unable to speak, I had worked myself into such a frenzy. The conductor walked by, announcing the next station.

The man nodded, put money on the table to pay for his drink and my tea. He smiled at me. "A pleasure to meet you, little lady. And remember the eights."

"Thank you sir." The eccentric eights wouldn't help me. The man half-bowed and left me with my thoughts and my half-finished tea.

When Karmel came by, I told him I'd lost. His expression revealed how much of a fool he thought he'd been, to have believed Betsch, to think someone like me could actually play cards. And to prove him wrong, I said, out of the depths of my panic, "I am sorry. But I can do better. Is there a game on one of the returning trains? I could settle our score en route back to Vancouver." My fingers gripped my alligator bag—my hands were independently minded and shocked I'd made such a foolish claim.

Karmel didn't notice my terror. "You don't beat easy, I like that. See what I can find."

After an anxious two hours, during which I tried to doze but couldn't, I got off at Calgary, and Karmel switched me over to a train that went through Jasper. He gave me the name of one of his friends working the new train. I boarded and found Karmel's friend, a weasel-faced man whose tea-coloured skin reminded me of boys I'd seen in the jungles.

He stared at me unsympathetically. "Cards? You?"

I nodded, clutching my alligator bag. I had almost two hundred dollars left; I hoped it would be enough to see me through a fresh game.

"What the hell," he said, "Karmel's funeral, not mine."

He led me through first class, past the sleeping compartments, through another connecting door, into an even more luxurious car where there were only two unmarked doors giving onto the corridor. "Wait here," he said, knocking on the nearest door. He went inside, closing the door behind him. I leaned forward but could hear nothing.

The door opened again and the man came out, frowning. "They'll allow you to play. But I am tellin' Karmel this is the one and only time I do him a favour...."

"Of course," I said, and went past him into the compartment. It was a kind of living room, much larger than the compartment on the previous train. A young man lounged on a green sofa, while two older men sat at a small round table. Cards lay scattered between two cut crystal glasses filled with ruby-coloured alcohol. The table had a slight raised metal lip, to keep the glasses from sliding off.

"Lovely to meet you," I said.

"So you're the entertainment, a bit of sport with cards. Are you really a magician?" said the young man, stretching his arms idly.

"No, I thought...."

"Oh he's just teasing you, girl." The older man nearest me turned and wearily eyed me, from my shoes to my unimpressive hair. "So you play cards. You up to a game? I could use some distraction." He turned to his heavily-bearded companion, nodded to the glasses, the cards, "You in, Stetham? Get your mind off your losses."

The bearded man snorted but gestured towards the empty seat at the round table. I didn't know who these men were, but I didn't care; it couldn't be worse than the game I had lost, getting to Calgary. I sat down politely and rested my wrists on the raised metal lip of the table.

It wouldn't take them long to ruin me if the cards so chose—I tried not to flinch when the first ante was fifty dollars. The young man on the sofa watched my gestures carefully for the first two rounds, I think he was disgusted that a girl as small and, yes, compared with their extravagance, shabby as I was, that such a girl even knew the rules of poker. But the man who'd initially invited me to play seemed more and more amused as my hands improved. I was down to my last fifty dollars when I got a handsome flush—all Hearts, three, ten, and the Queen. And by wink of fortune, the seven and the King appeared on the porch. I went all in. I had no choice if I was to stay in the game. When I won the pot, the man opposite me laughed with pleasure.

"What do you know," he said, "someone who's up to my standards."

Which I thought was a tad impolite to his companions, but they didn't seem bothered. I was starting to hear the cards again, even with the noise of the train, the distractions of pulling into tiny stations. Another round, the whistle blowing. A new porter knocked and stepped into the compartment to say, "Everything alright gentlemen? Miss?" I glanced up and I stared, surprised—his skin was the blackest I had ever seen. But I had no time to contemplate his face, he disappeared out the door, and I had cards to watch. I blinked and went back to my hand. I played a ten of Clubs, dark card of good fortune.

I don't know why the cards allowed me to perform alongside them on that train. There in the elaborate sitting room, lurching through the mountains, the cards recognized me as a fellow acrobat. Maybe they were testing me on that first trip, to see how easily I would give up. Their answer was in my presence on this second train: I do not give up easily. Small and dogged, the cards might say of me.

Far into the night, there was a knock on the door.

"Town of Hope, sir," called the porter without opening the door.

The young man on the sofa sighed. "Middle of nowhere, here we are."

"How fortuitous," said the man opposite me, folding his hand.

His bearded colleague studied his hand, gazed at the cards in front of me, then back at his own fanned possibilities, and he folded too. As I raked in the pot, the young man stood up and sauntered to the table to rudely pick up my discarded hand.

"She bluffed you. Thought as much."

"Albert," said the bearded man, standing. His voice was low and severe—he had barely spoken through our game. "That is reprehensible. No gentleman touches another's cards."

"She's hardly a...."

I carefully put my newly-earned six hundred dollars into my alligator bag, snapped the clasps closed and stood up. I was a good foot shorter than the young man.

The bearded man glowered. "An apology is in order, Albert."

"Not at all," I said, "it was generous of you all to play a game with me."

Albert turned away lazily. The still-seated man watched him leave. His gaze travelled back to me. "The pleasure was entirely mine. Rare to have a decent card game."

"You play very well, young lady, and I apologize for my nephew." The bearded man shot the closed connecting door a searing look. "My late sister spoiled the boy. He is likely jealous of your skill."

The seated man laughed. "Boy can't play his way out of a barrel. No excuse for him."

"But he was quite right," I joked, "I'm hardly a gentleman." I shook their hands as the train slowed, brakes screeching. "Have an enjoyable stay in Hope."

The bearded man snorted in some kind of amusement.

I was amazed to walk out, down the corridor, out of the elegant car, across the clattering connector, the metal plates shifting under my feet, then through the first class carriage, and finally to the parlour car. This is how it feels, I thought, to win properly in the world. But all I felt was tired. The train lurched as it came into the station and I staggered against the etched glass divider that separated the bar from the reading area. An empty leatherette armchair was just beside me and I sank into it, dropping the alligator bag on my lap. Awkward. I put my exhausted hands on the green armrests and stared at the bag, willing my head to clear, my eyes to stop burning.

I looked up to find a barman watching me. I gave him as fine a smile as I could and ordered a pot of black tea, good and strong, to put life back into my hands. There was a large elderly man snoring in the chair at the far corner of the lounge, and two couples involved in a game of whist, but otherwise the lounge was quiet. No one paid attention to me as I flexed my hands. They had done it, my cards and my fingers, and so what if the effort made me so tired I could barely move my bag to the floor, so what if my hands shook pouring my tea. This was the nature of the world I wanted. The train got underway once more, and I watched the sunrise come in over the mountains, the rattling wheels of the train underneath my feet. Brown velvet curtains framed the gradual colouring sky.

I resolved to earn enough money to always travel first class; as the sun appeared, I began to feel better, surer of myself. I would have to learn to go without sleep. I needed to memorize the train schedules to and from Vancouver, as far as Winnipeg and Seattle, to know when to get off a train, when to catch a return. The unsympathetic porter came through the compartment and glared at me.

"Your introduction was very kind," I said. "Here's something for your trouble, of course." I folded a ten and a twenty together into a neatly-palmed thirty dollars—a fair percentage of my winnings. I would give Karmel the same, when I next saw him, for getting me onto this train after his earlier disappointment.

The man's expression improved. "Look forward to seeing you this way again," he said, and passed on without checking my ticket.

I put my head back and watched the landscape go by, as if it were something I was dreaming, a rewinding of the path I'd taken the night before, but this time in brightening daylight, and with the blinds open, and with new money in the alligator bag.

My mother's new house was white with grey trim, on a quietly residential street above False Creek, just past Granville—not the toniest part of town, but dignified, middle class, as if to prove that my mother had washed East Pender Street off her hands just the same as me. When I went to dinner, the Sunday after that successful train trip, pretty well the first thing she said was, "You haven't seen Teddy have you?"

"I don't see Teddy very often." It was true, he was past me, like a train without a set schedule. He got himself into and out of brawls that were none of my business, or so I imagined. There was no reason to see Teddy. He was my friend, wasn't he? Shouldn't I have looked after him a little? I forced myself to look at my mother's new kitchen, the shiny refrigerator and stove, counter gleaming clean, a thin band of metal around its edges. Sharp and clean like a knife, this kitchen. There was no reason to think of Teddy.

My mother said, "And you're still at Dermot's?"

"Some of the time."

"I don't want to know what else you're up to until you have a real job and I'm not ashamed to see you in my house."

"This is...."

Harold came to the kitchen doorway and gave me a welcoming nod—from him, the equivalent of a rousing hail-fellow-well-met. I changed my sentence mid-stream. "... a lovely meal you've got roasting. The chicken smells wonderful." There's nothing like roast chicken for improving a conversation.

"Your mother is a talented homemaker," said Harold.

I nodded.

"Skills you could profit from, young Millard."

I picked up the plates and went past him to set the table in the dining room. If my mother expected me to learn homemaking skills, she might have demonstrated some when I was growing up.

Sometimes when I walked down the hill from seeing my mother at Harold Avison's house, I took the tram over to visit Mary Ellen. If the meal wasn't too long, if my mother spoke cheerfully to me once or twice, if Harold Avison deigned to smile, then I went across to East Pender. I told Mary Ellen about the night trains through the mountains, all those wonderful views which I never saw, travelling through the darkness so much of the time. "You're comin' into your own, aren't you," she said encouragingly. She recognized the skill in my hands; she knew from experience there was nothing a person could do about natural skill. I told her everything I couldn't say at my mother's table.

"Abilities will come out whatever you do, may as well profit by your hands," she said. "What I've told Garcia downstairs. He's a wonder with machines. He's gotten himself a job in a garage."

When I looked confused, she added, "My new tenant, Garcia, lives downstairs. I'd hoped... well, it was silly. There's no reason for Teddy to be interested."

And I knew, I recognized a bluff. "He'll find something," I said. To distract her, I told her about the first class dining car, the food that was served there, how nice it was.

At Christmas, I bought her a perfect present—a lynx-fur collar for her coat. An Indian man was selling them at the Edmonton train station, very beautiful furs they were. He had them laid out neatly on a bench in the waiting room, and I went through his wares while waiting for my next game, my next train. He showed me the mittens made of rabbit, the collars of weasel, and when he described what kind of animal a lynx was, I told him I'd seen that fierce cat, once, in the Interior, when I was little. "Mean but handsome," the man agreed. So of course I chose the lynx, very pretty silver fur with a reddish under-tinge.

"Don't I look posh," Mary Ellen said, trying it on. She kissed me and gave me a seed-cake and a big jar of herb tea, the kind that's good against cramps.

"What's Teddy up to these days?"

The wrinkle just past Mary Ellen's smile deepened. "You haven't seen him for a while, have you?"

I couldn't meet her eyes.

She put her hands through her hair, as if shaking off her mood. "You've put on some weight," she said, "You look happy."

I don't know whether I was happy exactly, but I was no longer the scrawniest kid on the street. I wondered how Teddy was doing, really. And if, when I next saw him, he'd notice that I looked different, because of my increasingly-confident hands.

"You stay disciplined, you can do this right," said Mary Ellen. "Stay good and clear and listen to your cards. You're a strong little thing."

I explained to her that, if I did the job correctly, I could keep playing the same people for quite a while, even if they aren't part of a regular game like a Dermot's. "They'll get used to you," she said.

Some of the men travelled by train consistently. We became familiar to one another and I learned their names. Their friends began introducing themselves to me. As I learned their playing habits, their ticks and styles of play, I suspected they began to regard me as a challenge, a run of fortune they wanted to break. I made the trains into my own special boxing ring, my own private circus acrobatic display. I turned eighteen on a train between Calgary and Regina, I ordered fresh orange juice and a piece of angel food cake in the dining car and for the first time, I looked with pleasure at my reflection in the dark train window.

I longed to play the best poker games in the country, to be at tables with big pots and serious players, but the only route I could see forward was through these trains, these closed compartments. I wanted to be older, to be taken more seriously. I got myself a safety deposit box at a bank on Granville Street to store my bankroll. The bank's plain long metal box was perfect, it looked like a library catalogue card holder, secure, discrete. After a game, I got into the routine of settling my money inside this blank box, then walking home to the boardinghouse.

When I reached the boardinghouse, I let myself in—Max the doorman always greeted me, no matter what time of day or night. I don't think he ever left his alcove by the front door, reliably dozing there, waiting for us residents to buy him a beer.

"How're you doing, honey?" he always said when I came home. It was alright for Max, an antediluvian turtle, to call me honey—he didn't mean anything by it. I paused in the entrance hall, long enough for Max to say, "Buy us a nightcap?"

Though it was eleven in the morning, I knew the drill—back outside, across the lawn to the Abbotsford Hotel, where the barman knew Max. How could anyone refuse an antique reptile a single glass of beer? Especially when he was one of the only people I saw, week after week, who wasn't somehow connected to a poker game. Dermot, the men on the trains, even the grizzled lady who sold me tickets at the station and called me "lovey," every single person with whom I was acquainted, I knew from playing poker. Max was different. To him, I was just a girl who lived in his building.

What's more, Max believed in fortune with as much conviction as I did. He read palms, and rumour was that he was always, I mean, always, right. I didn't let him read my palms. I didn't want him looking at my fortunate hands. I didn't even want him knowing about my card-playing, but when I came back with his beer, he smiled.

"Cards come your way, honey?"

I stared at him. I hadn't told anyone at the house what I did for a living, nor had I mentioned the trains. "Why cards?"

Max drank a bit of his beer. "Recognize you as one of fortune's fellow-players, honey. 'Course it's cards, what else would it be?"

I should have been startled, but somehow his knowing made me real, a real girl, with a real life, however strange that life might be. "They weren't bad," I said.

"You have to be polite to cards, is all." He eyed his beer and gradually dozed off again in the sun, while I went quietly upstairs feeling a little less solitary than usual.

Max could see fortunes in beer foam, much the way ladies used to read tea leaves. I once watched him smack his drool-spattered lips and squint into a beer on behalf of a girl who lived on the ground floor. She had fallen in love with a young man at work, so she bought Max a beer and stood by, twisting her ringless fingers.

But Max shook his trembling head. "No good, honey," he said, "Ill-suited, I'm real sorry." Her face turned bleak. "But someone better'll come along, you wait," he added, looking back at the glass. He shook his head over the beer and took a sip. The girl broke off with the poor guy she was considering, on account of Max's warning.

I didn't ask Max about my prospects for marriage. I already knew what my choice was going to be—I wasn't interested in marriage or children. I had fallen for poker. It wasn't the money that seduced me, it was the game itself. The money I won wasn't spent on clothes or jewelry—it was strictly the way to keep playing. Which meant that money had a great deal of importance, but very little meaning. It never occurred to me that there might be another game to want.

I became an expert on train schedules, I learned which lines attracted better fish—what wealthy men are called, when they're targets in a poker game. There were professional sharks, which I aspired to be, and there were fish and flounders. Some trains had no fish at all, and I consoled myself by sitting in the dining car. Every train was differently decorated—the Argyle was my favourite, carpeted in dark blue and paneled in black walnut.

"Miss?" asked the waiter. He no longer seemed surprised to see me travelling alone.

"The steak in pepper sauce, medium-rare please." Because that's how the lady at the table next to mine had ordered hers. "With the green beans." I smiled when the meal arrived—so many foods I had never tried before, not only a steak in sauce, but new kinds of fish and vegetables and fruit—like the pink grapefruit half, offered at breakfast, each segment carefully delineated, in a china bowl with ice nestled around the outside to keep it cool.

I ate, watching the handsome men travelling with their girls. Then I turned my gaze back to my book. I worked my way through all of Charles Dickens that way. Lonely, sure, but I liked sitting at that beautifully set table, the silverware heavy and with the train company's initials. The bleach smell of the white tablecloth was barely present underneath the scents of food and perfume, alongside the odour of the train—metal, sweat and energy. The waiters treated me as if I were important; perhaps they felt sorry for me, a young girl dining alone, travelling through the mountains. Eventually they all learned why I was there, I learned their names, every waiter, every porter—I refused to call everyone George, as some passengers did, the too-general name taken from George Pullman porters. Those men kept me informed of where I should be playing, who to keep an eye out for, and I tipped them for the information. I made sure we all gained from my profits.

One evening, I ate roast beef while reading a biography of Queen Victoria—whom I liked, she seemed nearly as fierce as Napoleon and just as short. I looked up as the dining car suddenly went silent. A tall thin man walked through, the porter rushing forward to open the door at the end of the carriage. I took a sip of water as the thin man passed my table, and I couldn't go back to concentrating on Victoria. That man was the reason I was on this train, he was my target. The porter returned and paused by my table.

"Car five, compartment seven, it'll be," he said, his lips barely moving.
"Thank you."

I hadn't yet met the well-dressed thin man, but Martin, the porter, had filled my head with stories about him—Solomon Lazarovitch was from Montreal, as was Martin. Well, Lazarovitch had grown up in Montreal—he'd been born back in Romania, before his parents decided Europe wasn't all it was cut out to be. He'd arrived in Montreal as a babe in arms, and the city, more specifically a few streets within its core, became his hometown. When he turned twelve, he reinvented himself as Sam Lazar, saying he wasn't ashamed of being Jewish, it was being unpronounceably Jewish that bothered him. As a self-invented man, Sam Lazar had a reputation, a Montreal history that involved the usual thing that reputations do, as to where his money had come from, what exactly he was running into America, over our untidy border through those profitable prohibition years. So even walking by, Lazar carried with him a series of unproven rumours that ruffled the dining car's white tablecloths.

When I walked into compartment seven, four players sat at the oblong table already, two of whom I knew. A small fat man stood by the window and greeted me like an old friend—he was going to deal for us and he managed the introductions for the men I didn't know. A wide man in stripes barely acknowledged me, but Lazar's expression was pleasantly neutral; he stood and bowed ever so slightly in my direction, removing his hat before sitting down again. I already knew the weasel-nosed man to my left. He always wore a checkered suit—he fidgeted with his pockets when he had good cards, and blinked frequently when he bluffed. Men blink more when they're lying. Women don't. Accustomed as we are to wearing mascara, we learn early how to control our blinking. I had just started wearing make-up, hoping it made me appear older, or at least more respectable. No doubt I looked like a waif playing dress-up, but at least it kept me from blinking.

I took my place between weasel-nose and the wide man in stripes, who hardly deigned to acknowledge me. To make conversation, I said, "I'm en route to Regina. And you?"

"I don't need to tell you anything," said the fat man, "you'll be out of this game so fast you won't know where you got off the train. D'you even know how to play seven card stud, little girl?"

Sam Lazar cleared his throat. The aggressive tone in the fat man's voice didn't worry me, though the blowhard was lucky at first. I held relatively steady, folding most of my hands but staying in the game—sometimes it was necessary to wait, to toss away eighty percent of my hands, gradually luring the fish into a false sense of superiority. In this case, I changed my aim—first, gut the fat man. Then hook Lazar.

When the fat man was thoroughly trapped by his own foolish bets, I started playing to win, and in the process, Lazar lost a stupendous amount of money, despite his solid playing skills. Huge bets, taken on a whim I supposed. More money than I was used to seeing move across the unsteady table of a train compartment. Yet Lazar accepted his losses with suave aplomb. Now, a man who isn't ashamed of losing and who can pay his own debts is the kind of person I liked to see. Not like that—Lazar's angular face didn't move my eighteen-year-old heart, nothing like that. No, I admired his game and his suave manners, that was all.

My hands came into their own when I was blessed with an Ace of Clubs and a seven of Spades. After a while, the seven of Clubs and then the seven of Hearts appeared in front of me, face-up. I waited for the River with a kind of serene pleasure. I had a great affection for this particular kind of hand— filled with potential and risk. The dealer burned the top card and put an Ace of Diamonds in front of me. I smiled with all my sharp crooked teeth. From that round on, I bluffed calmly and won pot after pot from the fat man, who ordered more whiskey. Lazar, sober, with some quietly spoken calls and some nicely-timed decisions, won about half of his money back from the fat man, while I took the rest. By the end of the game, I liked Lazar's indifference in the face of good news just as much as I liked his calm during shipwreck. He had a sense of inner quiet, the kind of stillness that's written around a person's shadow, a quality that dealers appreciate. And he played left-handed—he wasn't the type to change a personal habit just to seem normal. I admired him for that.

I left the game when the fat man was finished. I had no interest in breaking anyone else. I could feel the deck on my side, in harmony, a kind of athletic grace, like a perfect baseball pitch, maybe, or an Olympic dive.

❧

If playing at Dermot's was my schooling for cards, then the trains were my university. Along with five and seven-card stud, which I was used to, there were hold'em games and Omaha eight-or-better, and all kinds of bizarre variants invented in late-night kitchen games across North America, that men brought out to see if changing the rules of play might improve their luck. Double stud, Johnny One-Nut, Wild Cards, Scungilli, I learned to play them all. It wasn't enough to be a great five- and seven-card player; if men knew I was good at one particular game, they'd avoid it just to stump me. When a new rule baffled me, I learned to hide my surprise. I hid all my emotions—on the trains, I tried to teach myself to *have* no emotions.

By early March, the cherry trees were out. It was a rare sunny Sunday in the city, the newsboys gleeful in the warmth, shouting the latest headlines about Europe and the coming war. A military marching band was slated to parade along Main Street, not far from my old house on East Pender. I walked down Main, past Hogan's Alley, the pavement slick with earlier rain, drying out in the sun. A perfect spring day in Vancouver—the air conflicted with fruit blossoms in the trees and rotting vegetables in the gutter.

I thought I might drop by Mary Ellen's in case she wanted to see the parade with me. At the corner of East Pender, I paused, standing in the crowd, waiting to cross the street. A too-big black-haired man stepped in front of me. Despite the new height, I recognized Teddy, filled out from when I'd last seen him, muscles underneath his shirt, which made me think he must still be boxing. I put my hand on his back and he turned around. Handsome as ever, though his cheek had the faintest trace of a bruise. Dark smudges shadowed his eyes, the coal of sleepless nights.

He frowned. "Left your boyfriend and come back to the old neighbourhood?"

"What boyfriend?"

He blew a raspberry at me, took my hand in his fist and pushed us out past the crowds, so I didn't get to see the marching band after all. Teddy stopped in front of the ice cream cart and bought us each a cone. We walked away from the hordes, through the too-familiar Strathcona streets. A few children played jacks on the sidewalk. I stepped around them.

"Come back to see how the place was gettin' on without you?" said Teddy, when I hopped back onto the uneven sidewalk.

"I'm downtown, it's not like I've gone away."

"Your ma says you're always on a train or in the mountains or someplace…."

"You've got to stop getting hit in the head, can't be good for you."

"This? Was nothin'." He brushed my cheek with his thumb and licked it. "Ice cream. You're lookin' almost pretty these days."

I shivered up in goosebumps. I told myself it was the ice cream. But to be called almost pretty was more delightful to me than being beautiful every other day of the week—it was more believable.

"How's your ma holding up?" he asked.

I stared at my ice cream. "You should go see her sometime, she'd be happy." I hadn't seen her for over a month; I'd skipped dinner to play cards.

"She sees me often enough."

"She thinks of you as a kind of half-son."

"Which makes me your half-brother, you half-wit."

"I'm not...."

He smiled, teeth very white, his broken eyetooth as pointed as ever.

"How's Mary Ellen?" I said, to change the subject.

He didn't say anything for a moment. "You didn't hear?"

"What?"

"Ma's dead. Figured you heard about it."

"What?"

"Yeah, a month ago. You missed the funeral. You were away."

The air flattened and roared, a train engine toppling through my chest. I struggled to breathe. "A month ago?" My voice tiny, buried in the noise of my head. My feet stopped moving. "My God, Teddy, what happened?"

He walked on without me, past a burned-out corner store, dirty planks thrown outside—a smell like wet newspaper, as I tore my feet from the sidewalk and rushed to keep pace with him.

"I wasn't... I'm so sorry I wasn't...."

"Are you, now? You not going to eat that? Give me that." He took what was left of my ice cream.

"What happened? Why didn't anyone tell me?"

Teddy finished the ice cream in silence. Had Mary Ellen been sick when I last saw her, it must have been the end of January? She didn't look sick. She'd seemed sunny as ever. I hadn't visited her since. I hadn't known. My right hand pressed against my throat, as if my breath were caught there. We turned onto Princess Street, passing rows of houses a little taller maybe but otherwise just the same as our old house. An old woman sat on a veranda and stared suspiciously at people in the street. I looked away, while Teddy kept on walking, so fast I was nearly running to keep up with him. I pressed my hand against his arm, trying to slow him down.

Finally he said, "One of those women Ma was helpin', the boyfriend wasn't so kind. Came into the house and stabbed the pair of them. Ma was tough. She made it out to the sidewalk and named the guy before she went. There was nothin' to do."

All I could think of was Mary Ellen in her front room at Christmas, laughing at herself in the fur collar I'd given her. "Don't I look posh, sweetheart?" she'd said, kissing me on the forehead. She wasn't afraid of blood, I thought. What did that have to do with anything? I closed my eyes, still running forward to keep up with Teddy, and I stumbled on a bit of uneven concrete. My eyes blinked open, a blue metal taste in my mouth as I touched the sidewalk with my hand and regained my balance.

"I should've been home," said Teddy. "They've got him in jail. Which is a big fat waste if you ask me."

"I'm sorry."

"Thought you'd come to the funeral."

We reached the end of Princess Street. "I didn't know."

"Your ma came. She said you weren't in town."

"She might have called me." We passed the tall lopsided houses that face out onto the railyards, and started walking along the rails. A train pulled slowly out of the roundhouse some ways from us. The grinding noise made it impossible to speak.

When it had passed, Teddy said, "I figured you were in town and didn't come for some reason. I dunno."

He seemed so big and so lost, I stopped on the railroad ties and put my arms around him and held onto him as if there was a rainstorm about to wash me away. My face against the fabric of his shirt, the smell of bleach and bread. I could feel his heart beating.

"I would have been there."

He rubbed his eyes and I let him go. He said, "You ever been up in the roundhouse?"

"No."

"Lots of mountains."

"I don't...."

Teddy stepped off the rail and onto the gravel on the far side of the tracks. He held my forearm as if I might need help balancing, as we made our way along the rocks, avoiding bent rail spikes and broken hinges still attached to chipped-off slivers of wood from the trains. I let him help me. He held my arm as if I might disappear if he didn't keep his grip. He didn't know how his hand felt there, his fingers could have baked through my dress to leave a scar on my skin. I wouldn't have even been surprised. Nothing will surprise me ever again, I thought, as he pulled me forward.

There was no one outside the roundhouse; any workmen were no doubt at the far end of the yards, waiting for the military parade. We went in one of the side doors—the roundhouse was the train turnaround, I'd walked past it often enough. A round building, the brick stained from grease and steam. We walked past two huge steam engines, waiting for repair alongside a pile of massive rail sections. Sun coming in the tall windows caught heavy dust and grit in the air. A long staircase wound tightly against one curved wall, thin metal banisters all that kept us from falling into the vast open space of the turnaround. We went up and up. Teddy was moving fast and I was out of breath, the spiraled flights of metal stairs echoing with our feet. Then a wooden door that Teddy kicked open. He pulled me through and we stood in some kind of office, there wasn't much in it, only an empty wooden counter stretched out below a low long window. But the view—he was right, it was all I saw, a vast swath of hard blue sky above the mountains. The Lions still very much covered in snow, Crown Mountain, jagged Grouse, Mont Fromme.

He put his hand on my shoulder to turn me away from the view, bringing his head down to kiss me. His mouth was hard and soft, the cigarette with ice cream taste of his breath. I leaned away but opened my lips, I could have moved further back but I didn't. I should have. We'd grown up in the same house. I loved Mary Ellen, maybe more than my real mother, but I breathed him in. His hands slid along my back and against my ribs. When he lifted me against the counter, I put my arms around his neck.

The rest was messy and clumsy. If you want specific details you'll have to use your imagination. There was nothing gentle about it. Neither of us had any finesse, we hadn't learned it yet. I imagine I'm not the only girl to think *what a fuss people make about nothing*, at least at first. It was awkward. I wrapped my legs around his hips and pulled him as close into me as seemed possible, even as the edge of the counter cut into my tailbone. And then for a moment it wasn't nothing, for an instant I felt something much better. Then it disappeared and I yearned for it to come back.

Teddy opened his eyes and blushed to see that I was watching his face. I put my hand over his mouth to keep him from speaking and his lips parted beneath my fingers. We peeled ourselves apart, most of our clothes still on, just a question of arranging—for once I was grateful for all those under-clothes, even my stockings, fussy as they were. Clothes gave me something to do, to adjust, to layer on top of whatever we'd just done. It was all messed together, being in the roundhouse and the taste of vanilla in Teddy's breath and the news about Mary Ellen, and the military band, which was going by just then, the tubas and thumping drums coming across the railyards to find us, up in a room we weren't supposed to be in, the mountains anchoring us against the sky.

7

Mary Ellen taught me that cards tell people's fortunes, that the fortune in your cards can be the one in your stars or in your pocket. Emotions had no place in that handful. "You have to learn Fortune has no heart," she said.

"But there are Hearts," I argued, "with Spades and Diamonds and Clubs...."

"Just don't rely on the hearts."

When I sat down at my next game on the train to Bellingham, I thought of Mary Ellen. I didn't think of Teddy. Strange, I guess. But my mind tangled her into the way her son made love with me. I looked at my cards and folded that night whenever Hearts showed in my hand, I couldn't help it. I didn't see how I could have missed Mary Ellen's death, her funeral. I blinked and cut the deck for the next game; I drew an Ace of Spades.

When I was little, I kept my eyes open for the cards men threw away after a particularly unsuccessful game. Bad hands thrown out a door into the alley, or out a window, or torn in half and left in the gutter. I looked at them; I never kept them. Even before I met Dermot, I knew by instinct that tossed-away cards must be disliked, unlucky, discarded for valid reason. The Ace of Spades was the only Ace I ever saw tossed away. Mary Ellen told me that the Ace of Spades was *knowledge gained*, "good to remember," she said. "Always gain what knowledge you can."

But everyone knows, the Ace of Spades is the card of death. Maybe that's what Mary Ellen meant, I don't know. She was the one who told me how cards were invented by the Chinese, after they invented paper for money and for writing on. Cards grew logically out of such a combination—you layer paper with glue until it's thick enough to endure the play of money. There: cards.

I folded one more hand, then for my last game got a straight with the Ace of Spades. I gathered the money and wondered what that meant, if winning could be considered a kind of knowledge. Probably not.

When my train got back into Vancouver, it was mid-morning. My tired mind wandered over towards Teddy and then moved away like a gun-shy horse. I shuffled off the train and along the platform into the station. I don't know what made me glance into the coffee shop, I didn't ever stop there, it wasn't my routine. I intended to walk over to the bank, as always. But I looked at the counter that morning by instinct and there was Teddy, sitting on a stool in front of a cup of coffee. He was talking with the woman behind the counter. She was blond, built like a fire engine, all clanging bells and spinning lights. I was going to look away, really, but Teddy shifted his eyes to the mirror behind the counter and saw me. He spun around on the stool and gave me a thousand-watt smile as he stood up. The smile drew me into the coffee shop, as if I had no will of my own. Hearts, I thought, as if Mary Ellen was right there, frowning.

When the blond woman picked up the coffee pot to pour me a cup of coffee, he said, "She'll have a cup of tea."

We sat down and I set my alligator bag on the empty stool next to me.

"Long trip? Where'd you get to?"

"There and back."

The blond woman brought me a metal teapot and white teacup. The teapot was so shiny it hurt my eyes.

"You here on Friday?"

"It's Tuesday," I said. "I'm here to play at Dermot's."

"Yeah, but are you here Friday?"

"What happens Friday?"

"Friday, you're goin' with me to the Cave Cabaret."

I was too surprised to even pour my tea. I just stared at him. He'd lost the smudges underneath his eyes, he looked radiant.

"It's like a cave," he said, "with stalactites and pirate stuff. You'll like it."

"Stalactites?"

"Yeah, those pointy things.... Like in *Treasure Island* you used to read. But it's a dancehall. I'll pick you up."

"Don't pick me up," I said too fast.

He leaned over and brushed his mouth against my forehead, quickly, I don't think the blond woman behind the counter even noticed. "Ashamed of me, or what?"

"No." I picked up the teapot and poured my tea with great care.

"You avoided me all last year. You can't get away from me anymore."

I sipped my tea, keeping my eyes glued to the cup in my hands.

"You don't have to weigh it out like a bet. How 'bout I meet you at the Sylvia Hotel, you live near there, right? That okay?" He took out a gold-coloured case from his breast pocket, opened it and flipped a cigarette up to his lips, then struck a match on the edge of the counter. I watched him slip the metal case smoothly back into his pocket. It seemed an unlikely gesture, an unreal accessory for him. He exhaled. "I won it off a guy. I didn't lift it, if that's what you're thinkin'."

"Of course that's what I'm thinking."

He grinned, all teeth and genuine good humour. "So, the Cave. Friday. I'll meet you at the Sylvia. Wear dancin' shoes."

"Since when do you dance?"

"Trust me."

"I can't dance."

"You just have to follow," he said.

I fumbled through my alligator bag, searching for a coin to pay for my tea. Instead, I dropped the bag, the contents sliding out into Teddy's lap and onto the floor. The money I'd won on the train and my emergency bankroll, each wrapped separately in cloth, and then my change purse, handkerchief, powder compact, spilling onto the floor. I leapt up.

Teddy picked up the two envelopes of money, put them back into the alligator bag and whistled. "You're doin' okay."

He leaned down on the floor beside me, helping to gather the coins, the compact, the key to my room and the key to my safety deposit box, tied together with a piece of red string. I had no keychain. He touched my hand, putting these things back into the bag.

"Friday at six, at the Sylvia," he said.

"Fine."

At Dermot's that night I could barely focus on the cards. I played as if my eyes were shut, even Betsch managed to win a few pots. On Wednesday, I sat on the train, studying the women around me. A woman with a fox-fur collar ready for the mountains talked to her companion, who stared past her, thinking of his business propositions, I imagined. She might say anything at all, he wouldn't hear her. Further down the car, a pretty face like a coin to be rubbed for luck travelled with a mother who looked nothing like her. I studied the girl's make-up, the cloche hat she wore. When she walked from the dining room, I watched the way she stepped, lightly, as if she were barely on the train. I liked walking solidly where I was, and coins, however pretty, get dirty, soiled by bets and losses, concern and confusion—no wonder there's such a need for bleach in the world, we strive so hard to seem clean.

Yet when I went to play, I worried about dancing shoes. I didn't fold in time, I bet on hopeless small pairs, I played for flushes when there was no way in heaven I was going to make them. I took an unscheduled break in Calgary, sat in the train station for three hours waiting for a return train. Which did I want? A good game, or a pair of dancing shoes? I tried closing my eyes and opening them again, but the light green walls of the train station didn't change. A porter called hello to me as he wheeled a luggage wagon past me. A pale pink hatbox balanced precariously on top of a brass-trimmed trunk.

I left the train station and walked over to the big Hudson's Bay Department Store. I ignored the imitation gold jewelry, the perfume; I bought the first pair of shoes that fit, black T-straps with heels.

"Very fine for dancing," said the salesclerk, holding out his arms as if holding a partner.

"I hope so," I said, and ducked my head as if I were shy. I wanted to be a girl, for once, to see what it was like to have a date and a dance to go to. The man wrapped up my shoes, gave me a special cloth to polish them and wished me a wonderful evening. I didn't bother playing cards on the route home.

That evening I changed into my new shoes, checked my navy dress in the hall mirror and went out to the Sylvia. The hotel was just across from the beach. The evening was clear, the sky silver-gold with sunset, tingeing the hotel's ivy-covered facade. I struggled with the heavy carved door. Across the empty lobby, Teddy stood talking to the girl behind the registration desk. He leaned in and she laughed. He half-turned as I walked towards him.

"Julie here tells me we're gonna see the best band in all of Vancouver. If not the entire west coast of North America."

"Oh."

I had put my overcoat on top of my dress, which was a bit too long for the coat and I was sure I didn't look right. My left foot hurt already from the new shoes. I tried to wiggle my toes and scuffed one foot against the other. But Teddy put his arm around me and led me out through the side door of the hotel. He seemed very pleased with himself. I shrugged my shoulders so his arm fell to my waist.

"What are you smiling about?"

Teddy laughed. "You showed up. I told that Julie girl that you might not turn up, you might leave me in the lurch. I told her, here I am, all dressed up, tryin' to lure you away from your first love. Dunno if you're gonna show."

"My first love? What are you...."

"If there'd been a sudden good game, you'd have forgotten all about me, Mill. Left me flat. But I reserved us a table anyway."

I felt suddenly warm, as if the setting sun reached straight into my lungs, as if I could breathe out all the fear I'd felt on the way to meeting him. The Cave was very red. White candles dripped wax across red stalactites and stalagmites, a cave-like ceiling arched overhead, and the walls and the furniture were all dark red. The stalagmites created odd unsteady tables and we sat at one of these, a stalactite behind my head. I remember Teddy laughed at this, and when the waiter arrived at our table, we ordered punch, as red as the darkness of the club. I drank it too quickly and shook my head when Teddy asked if I was having fun.

"You aren't?" He looked so suddenly concerned that I ordered another glass of punch.

I should have asked what was in the stuff. It tasted like fruit juice but packed enough of a wallop to obscure any memory of music or dancing. What I do remember is opening my eyes against the fabric of a shirt. White shirt, in near-darkness, a slight smell of bleach, of bread and honey, and I shifted so I could breathe. The air was cool. We were outside.

"So, you're awake now are you?"

I straightened, turned against Teddy and looked at my stocking feet.

"You took your shoes off. Said your feet hurt."

I strained to see if I'd managed to lose my purse as well.

"Shoes, purse, coat, I'm workin' as your personal manservant here. Got all your things. Unless you had earrings. Mighta lost those 'cause you're not wearing any now."

I shook my head, and the night swirled, the texture of the dark shifted forwards, filling my head with noise. I leaned my forehead against his shoulder. "Sorry," I said.

Teddy laughed. "Sorry? God, I wouldn't have missed it for the world. You were great. Until you fell off the dance floor. I've never seen you go from awake to asleep so fast."

I closed my eyes in humiliation, felt Teddy's fingers against my ear, in my hair, then his mouth against the sharp angle of my cheek.

"You're awake now, right? I'm gonna take you home. If you tell me where you live, be easier."

"I can get home all right." I reached down to find my shoes.

"We're in the park. It's midnight." He helped me put my shoes on, but kept one hand against my waist so I wouldn't move from his lap. "If anyone's gonna take advantage of you, I want to be sure it's me. So I'll walk you home." He pushed me up onto my feet and I leaned against the log bench we'd been sitting on. My heels immediately sank into the moss and mud of the dark path. Though I'd played in the park when I was little, I hadn't been anywhere but the seawall for a long time and now I wasn't sure which direction I was facing. Teddy was right, even if I managed to keep my balance in my heels, it would take me at least an hour to figure out which way was downtown, especially the way I felt. On fire. Sick. I hauled my heels out of the mud, balancing with one hand against his shoulder. He stood up. "So?"

"Next door to the Abbotsford Hotel, I live in the boarding house there."

He held out my coat and I managed to get my arms into the sleeves. It was a bright night, but with the trees looming over us I couldn't see Teddy's expression as we walked—which meant he couldn't see mine, either. I don't know what my face would have looked like, afraid, I guess, confused. He held my arm until we reached the sidewalk outside the park, then we walked along side by side without touching. When we reached the corner of my street I paused to brush my hands through my hair. There was a light on in Max's alcove, but otherwise the house was dark, like every other house on the street. Even the Abbotsford Hotel was quiet.

Teddy cleared his throat. "You look okay. Not like you've spent a night in the woods with a hooligan."

"Thank you for the evening. It was very kind of you."

"God, Mill, don't be so formal. You know me. You've always known me." He grabbed my shoulders and kissed me hard on the mouth, lips closed, then let go of me. "We'll go for breakfast after your game at Dermot's. Wednesday morning. Granville Street. Eggs and bacon. You can tell me about your game." He tapped me in the arm, like a punch with no backing to it, and walked away. He didn't look like anyone had hit him recently, but he had paid for our table at the Cave, I imagine he paid for our drinks. He had to be making money somewhere. I sighed. I listened to the sound of my breath as if it was from someone else, sighing down the street after him, then I went inside to tiptoe past Max.

The next day, and the one after that, all through the weekend, I travelled miles of mountains I didn't see except as silhouettes in the dark, the occasional metal gleam of a river as the train came round a curve of a cliff, the light of the engine ahead for an instant, visible and then dark again. The Interior, glimpsed from the inside of train compartments. I imagined how the train looked to people whose towns we passed through—a brightly-lit snake coiling past, moving steadily, clanking as if armoured, forward and then gone, light spilling from the windows where our card game was in progress, three of Hearts, three of Clubs, four of Diamonds, red and black and red. Singing. The Jack of Spades. I blushed, for no cause other than that card, appearing in my hand.

I didn't hesitate on Wednesday morning. I stepped onto a train instead of meeting Teddy for breakfast. To prove that I didn't care. I was trying to be such an expert in departures, in leaving everyone behind—if you leave first, you're not the one that gets hurt. Wasn't I supposed to take after my father? Leave first and you don't end up like my mother, standing alone at a whistle stop on the railway line with everything you own packed into a single satchel and a little girl you never asked for crying at your side. I stared angrily out at the unspooling landscape beyond the train window and pressed my index fingers against the corners of my eyes.

Every time I walked by the coffee shop in the train station, I hoped to see Teddy there. For three weeks, I glanced and looked away, ashamed, and when I had finally taught myself not to look, he called my bluff by falling into step with me as I passed beneath the coffered ceiling of the station's waiting room.

"How's tricks, Mill? Good game? So good you couldn't stop an' meet me for breakfast?"

I must have winced at how good he looked. He laughed at my expression and walked with me, along the hall and out past the front pillars of the station.

"I was thinkin' maybe you could do me a favour."

"A favour?"

"Yeah, a game."

My heart turned into mere air in my throat and I thought I might choke on its absence. "I don't feel like it."

"Or lend me some cash."

"Why would I do that?"

"See, it'll be more fun if you play the guys. Win the money off them for me."

"I don't want to hear about it." There were no taxis in front of the station, no simple escape.

Teddy nudged my arm. "You could get the money back, easy."

"Why would I do that?"

"I dunno. To make me happy." He put his hand against my back, his fingers catching at the belt of my skirt. "But I'll think of somethin'. Forget it. Nice day, huh?"

We walked up Granville. A girl herded her younger siblings out of a bakery; boys played tag on the street—a car squealed its tires to avoid them.

After a while, Teddy said, "I work with these guys, they're… mainly it's the guy what runs the boxing over on Dunsmuir."

"The boxing?"

"I've been helpin' him set up the games."

I shivered, wondering how much money he'd lost for the boxing boss.

"Play them for me and I'll buy you a Snickers bar." He laughed, but I couldn't, thinking of all the bribes I'd offered him in the past. "Come on Mill, you're the one who taught me to play cards."

He touched his four fingers and thumb to my hand, like a starfish, and pressed my palm flat against his. My hand looked like a child's—no one would ever look at Teddy and treat him as a child. I folded my palm away from his.

He caught my fingers. "You're jealous of cards, is all. Other girls are jealous of girls."

"I don't care what you get up to."

"So take on a game for me."

It must have been the warmth of the day, or the lazy way he walked beside me, that made me even consider doing what he asked. "It'll be the last favour I do for you."

He laughed again.

I won back the money he needed, easily—the three men I played weren't very skilled. They were sports bettors, that was how Teddy met them. Their conversation was entirely focused on boxing and baseball. They didn't know I was playing on Teddy's behalf—I had myself introduced by a guy I knew from Dermot's, it was no trouble. The game itself was dull, though I won more than Teddy had lost.

I thought it would be fine, but afterwards, I didn't like what I had done. Somehow the money smelled like the rags Mary Ellen used to burn in the backyard. I couldn't bring myself to give Teddy the bills in person. Instead I counted out the money in that circular room up in the roundhouse, overlooking the mountains. A pier had caught fire the evening before, while I was playing cards—maybe the strange smell came from the pier, not from the money at all. The CPR guys had worked like mad to get the boxcars out of the way, moving freight trains out so firemen could get to the pier, but by the time the final trains pulled out, the last boxcars were on fire. The roundhouse had a good view of the smoke spiralling up from the ruins. My stomach turned over, watching the smoke fade out into the white sky. I laid the money I'd won for Teddy out as a bank cashier might, in a neat fan pattern, all the bills facing one way. I looked down towards the tracks and watched Teddy make his way across the railway ties, expecting to meet me. I ran down the stairs and left by the side door before he'd made it into the building. I hoped he would be sorry I wasn't there to see him.

They say gambling is addictive, and I won't say that's wrong. But people think the thrill of winning money is the root of the addiction. It's not. Winning is merely what you need to stay in the game. Dollars are just necessary grease, an excuse to play. I mean, playing had nothing to do with money; the cards had chosen me, and I wasn't going to misuse them by bailing someone out just because he had some fool claim to my affection. Love was a warmth I could do without, a fire I was not going to get burned by—any one of those blazing comparisons, the way those boxcars burned and afterwards nothing remained except some twisted metal.

I marked my weeks by Tuesdays, my night at Dermot's, where the men I played wore expressions so obvious, they may as well have written their hands on a blackboard for everyone to see. Tuesday's game was like family. Which probably explained why I was upset when Teddy came in, very late, through Dermot's bar. I didn't see him, but I recognized his voice, seeping through the slightly opened door to the back room. I heard him ask Dermot if I was still playing. He waited until I was finished the game, then he swung the door fully open and leaned on the doorframe.

I barely glanced at him. His lower lip seemed swollen again. I looked away. "What? You need another bet paid off? Lose a fight?"

Dermot looked from me to Teddy, shook his head and went back to mopping the bar floor.

"Don't be like that, Mill. I'm here to thank you. I'm in everyone's good books now, figured I should come by, thank you in person."

"You're welcome. Now go away, I have a train to catch."

He shook his head. "No you don't."

"How would you know?"

He made a show of looking around the backroom. "I don't see your bag. Nice bag, alligator, right?"

"Oh, for goodness sake." I shoved my winnings into my purse, got up from the table and went out the back door into the alley, giving the door a hard swing closed behind me.

On Water Street, he caught up with me, put his hand on my shoulder. "Don't do that," he said, and when I turned to brush his hand off, he kissed me, his mouth tasting like coffee and honey and sharp metal. His lower lip had a deeper groove in it, where he'd been punched—his teeth had cut open his old scar and the skin wasn't yet healed. But he kissed me anyhow, holding his hands against my neck, my chin, to keep me from moving away.

I had never thought the body, with all its flaws and insignificance, could be something so powerful. Not romance—I don't see how anyone can think sex is romantic. No, more like recognition, standing there, kissing him on the rain-wet sidewalk. He gave me back to myself, nothing to do with cards, no relying on numbers. He believed in the body. Maybe it was something he learned from boxing, or maybe it was something he knew by instinct, the ability to be fully present, aware of every movement, every muscle, every touch. Teddy gave me this secret and if it was in return for the poker game I won for him, so be it.

Maybe he thought I'd give him my heart, that temporary playing card, but it wasn't like that. Making love with him wasn't about hearts. What I wanted was the shininess that made him glow with being alive. As if he understood my desire, he gave me this spark, handed it over in full, with his own earnest wanting as well. I wish I'd known what to do with that. If I'd trusted him, or kept it for him, safe, maybe I could have given it back to him, when he needed it, after the war. Maybe we'd have turned out differently later on. Afterwards, I mean.

All that spring, I kept working on the trains. Coming back to Vancouver, I would make a new resolution; as the train went through Port Moody, I swore on any card I held that I'd avoid Teddy. If I didn't see him, then I wouldn't find my hands distracted by his skin. But back in Vancouver, I was distracted all over again. I ruined my second-best dress, making love with Teddy in the woods of Stanley Park, I may as well have had no shame. The smell of pine lingered in my hair for a week.

I hadn't taken much notice of the war. That seems terrible, but the war was way over on the other side of the world, in Europe, in countries whose borders kept changing. I knew there were boys over there who were Canadian, yes. But I read the newspapers mostly to keep conversation going at the game table. The war wasn't immediate or real, at least not until Kevin came into Dermot's backroom one Tuesday heavy but proud. His son had joined up.

"Very brave of him," I said.

After Kevin had gone, Dermot grumbled about how if the politicians were so gung-ho on war they should send their own darn sons to die, not boys like Kevin's, who'd never harmed anyone in their lives. I murmured agreement, not really understanding what he meant. I could recite train schedules from Vancouver to San Francisco, from Hope to Winnipeg, but I had only the mildest grasp of Europe's reality. I noticed the uniforms, that was all, soldiers and officers in the stations, waiting for trains to take them away.

Recruitment drives began to appear in the city like parties. It was June, the city grew green with summer, damp with rain, the West End streets proud with rhododendrons in every ridiculous shade of peach and pink. School wound down for the year and children ran along the wet sidewalk, chasing each other, the lucky few with bicycles roaring full speed through puddles.

I came home from a game that took me across the prairies to find recruiters setting up shop in all the downtown hotels—the Hotel Vancouver, the Sylvia, even the Abbotsford. There were lots of boys interested. A war in Europe sounded pretty exciting compared to the tumble-down mildewed streets of Vancouver. The uniforms looked colourful and new—it was hard to believe that people were actually dying, far away. What with the posters, the marching bands, what with so many people out of work, small wonder that boys lied about their age to enlist. At least they'd get decent meals in training. Wars come around convenient-like, as make-work projects to keep young men busy, cut their numbers down a little. All those notions of justice, saving the world from fascism—when have politicians ever made a moral choice? When have they ever been kept awake by nightmares?

Do I sound bitter? I probably am. Because on the twelfth day of the month, Teddy signed a piece of paper that stated he was eighteen, exaggerating his age by two years. He wanted to be a pilot, very dashing, but was told he was too tall and didn't have the education. If he was lucky, he'd become an aero-engine mechanic. For training, he'd be paid 70 cents a day. Right after signing his name on that piece of military paper, he got a new pair of boots.

"D'you like soldiers?" he said, joking, showing off the boots when he met me that evening, and then he took me dancing at the Commodore. He wasn't the only boy in such boots on the sprung horsehair dancefloor, and surely I wasn't the only girl who didn't think too much about what that meant. But after an hour at the Commodore he moved his hand from my waist and said, "Let's go. This band ain't so hot."

So we left the splendour of the dance floor, while the band still played, and we spent the night in a half-empty house Teddy knew of, not far from our old street. That sounds curiously romantic. It wasn't. We couldn't go to my boardinghouse, no gentleman callers allowed, and Teddy was no gentleman, at that. He was only a boy, living in a half-empty house much like the one we'd grown up in. I never found out what the arrangement was, and I didn't care. I was too busy undoing the latches of his clothing. It was all connected, his soon-to-be departure and my sudden craving for the way his body folded and unfolded around me. He was being sent to Lethbridge, Alberta, for training. I knew the place as a whistle stop along a route that I played. As we lay in the dark, I curled my knees up to lean against the line of his left hipbone.

"What will I do with you out there?"

"Keep the home fires burning. Let me know where to find you when I get back."

I had the impression that the fabric of the dark around us shivered.

The day he left for Alberta, I didn't see him off because I woke up alone in my boardinghouse room in the early hours of the morning with the sheet beneath me soaked in blood. A sharp stabbing pain to the right of my stomach, and the wetness of the blood, seeping along my legs, woke me. It's a fairly awful way to come out of being asleep, though I suppose not so horrible for a girl as it might be for a man. I sometimes doubt there's a woman in existence who hasn't at least once woken up in bloody sheets. There's nothing original about it. I knew, waking up, what had happened was clear, though a baby at seven weeks is what, not much bigger than a silver quarter, is it? I got up and untangled my nightclothes and went slowly down the hall to the shared bathroom, where I sponged myself off. I sat there for a long time, but eventually, I got a bucket of water and put the bedclothes to soak. Then I scrubbed the spots off the mattress.

Maybe a foolish girl would have sat and cried. But I was practical, I washed my hands, I found two pairs of clean underwear, and I vowed to pay more attention in the future. That Wednesday, I paid a lot of attention. I folded myself onto the part of the mattress that was still dry, I wrapped that old red and black afghan around me, and I looked out the window. I pretended the afghan had been made by my mother, but I don't think it was—I had never seen her knit anything. The afghan had simply been with us, always. The miscarriage went on for four days—you wouldn't think something so tiny would create so much blood. What a mess. I paid attention to every twist of my guts.

Mary Ellen could have told us this was utterly predictable, but she was gone and Teddy never listened to anyone's advice unless it pleased him. The body is like that, it takes away what you know and fills your hands with want. I stayed in my plain white room, curled on my side, looking out at the blue-grey mountains. The weather had nothing to say to me, no information to impart. You might think that I was waiting for Teddy to come and save me, but if I didn't show up to see him off, Teddy would assume I was in a game, why shouldn't he think so?

I forced myself to eat soda biscuits. I made endless cups of tea. On Tuesday evening, I dressed and I went down to play a few rounds of poker at Dermot's. No one asked me how I was, though I caught Dermot looking at me strangely. I was too tired to concentrate on the cards.

After counting out my take at the end of the game, Dermot fixed his eyes on me. "You're looking peaky, Millard."

I silently folded the sixty-two dollars that was my portion and put the money into my purse.

"Ahern's training in Lethbridge, is he?"

"I suppose."

"You think I'm that much of a fool, my girl?"

"I don't want to talk about it."

Dermot snorted.

I forced myself to stand up very straight when I went out the alley door, but before closing the door behind me, I said, "Thank you for asking, Dermot."

I felt too unwell to walk far, and I took a cab back to the West End. I asked the driver to stop at the beach below the Sylvia Hotel, I paid him and walked down unsteadily to the sand's edge, my heels sinking. The sun was coming through layers of grey cloud, like chimney smoke blocking the distant view. I remember how the sand stuck to my green shoes. The water ate away at the grey beach, coming closer and closer, right up to my toes until a rogue wave came up and soaked the soles of my shoes, ruining them.

I grew very cold. I knew I wouldn't tell Teddy about any of it, there was no kind of letter to write about what had happened. Even distracted as I was by his body, I wasn't the right girl to be anyone's wife, let alone anyone's mother. No one arrives at a poker table with a babe on the hip. If I hadn't lost it, I'd have had to find a woman to do what Mary Ellen used to. I closed my eyes against the sunrise, pale smoke though it was.

That first week after Teddy left, I shivered whenever I saw a uniform, came up in goosebumps when I remembered how Teddy felt or tasted. I wasn't wounded, that wasn't how I felt. More like I'd been ill for the spring and I was getting healthy again. When my colour came back, I got a nice little winning streak on a train. I went all the way to Winnipeg and back. When I felt back to my real self, I visited my mother and Harold Avison's house for Sunday dinner. I hadn't seen them since Teddy left; I knew he'd gone by their house to show off his uniform, he'd told me about it, gleaming.

My mother served chicken over rice. The only food Harold enjoyed was chicken.

"Did you hear? They're converting the old Coal Harbour yards to produce minesweepers for the Atlantic," said Harold. "Exciting times, yes indeed."

I thought it was exciting that Harold had spoken. Normally we ate in pristine silence broken only by our knives squeaking against the too-new gold-rimmed china plates.

"Teddy looked very handsome in his uniform," said my mother. "I'm going to be very worried about him, of course."

"Of course," I echoed, wondering if she ever worried about me.

When my mother went into the kitchen to prepare dessert, Harold said, "What you need is to marry that nice young man and settle down."

I coughed, mildly, but the gesture took on a life of its own and I couldn't stop coughing. Finally I saw that Harold was holding out a glass of water, which I gratefully drank. As I did so, he said, "Very proud of young Ted. We received a postcard from him, where did I put it...."

I got my breath back. "You got a card?" I hadn't heard a word from Teddy. It didn't occur to me that he might write to anyone, though I knew he could—I had forced him to write out what little homework he'd done, through school.

"Yes," Harold said, getting up from the table to fetch it. He returned with the postcard and passed it to me before sitting down again. I recognized the building on the front of the card: the train station in Calgary. I couldn't help but think Teddy had chosen the card with me in mind. On the back, he'd printed in crooked pencil letters, "Camp Kenyon (Lethbridge) nice + sunny, lodes of good guys here. Food good too. Best to Harold + Mill. Love Ted".

Best, I thought, that's what I get? A single word, lumped in with Harold? I didn't expect much, but he might at least have sent me a postcard of my own. He knew where I lived. I stayed angry with him all through dessert, even though it was a butterscotch layer cake, one of my mother's old Hotel favourites for summer weather. We finished the meal in silence and I washed the dishes alone, Harold insisting my mother listen to the radio with him in the living room.

Maybe it was the postcard, maybe it was the taste of sweet butterscotch which inspired me to go to Lethbridge. Because when I got onto a train on Wednesday morning, heading south, I thought, *Why not see how he's doing, say hello.* I played a dull but passable game, distracted, I guess, though my bluffs were as solid as ever. As I gave the porter his usual ten percent tip, Martin said, "There's a fatter purse coming down this line on Friday. I can find you a seat if you want." I think there was a taste of sugar in my mouth as I said no. "I can't be here on Friday, I'm going to be in Lethbridge."

"Those Montreal types don't play so often these days...."

"Next time," I said, "next time, save a seat for me."

I had no one to give me good advice. Dermot had never liked Teddy, he was hardly going to encourage me to visit the boy. I could have asked Max to read a beer for me, but I didn't want to know what he'd see in the foam. Nothing good, I suspected. I didn't even shuffle a pack of cards and read myself a fortune. No, I sent a telegram to Camp Kenyon addressed to Theodore Ahern. He could sign himself "love Ted" all he wanted, I wasn't going to call him that. My telegram read: "IN LETHBRIDGE FRIDAY FROM VANCOUVER STOP".

It was raining when I left Vancouver. The porter helped put my umbrella and bag on the overhead rack. I took a moment to admire the sheen of the first-class car, the way everything was polished just so and how suavely the passengers took their seats. I sat by the window and opened the newspaper I'd bought in the station. I had started paying more attention to the papers, I wanted to know what the war was about. So I read all about the sinking of the German Bismarck, and then I read about horse racing, how they were going to introduce evening races at the track.

I'd never bet on horses. Aside from the sheer unpleasant size of them, horses are both more and less predictable than cards. I didn't like the idea of putting my money into a game I wasn't playing, but the horses only barely covered what I was really thinking. The Bismarck reminded me that Teddy was going to an actual, real, war, that he was going to leave Canada and go to some new dangerous place, to live inside a real battle, not a news report. While I kept playing some game or other, on this train or another. I looked out the window as night came on, until all I could see was my own reflection. When it was time, I went down the corridor to play cards.

It was hot that night on the train. I considered asking the porter to open a window for us, but I didn't want the smuts from the engine to mess up the deck, and none of the men complained of the heat, they just removed their jackets and loosened their ties. I didn't loosen anything. I ordered a cola with ice instead of my usual cup of tea, and I laughed politely at the inane jokes made by an English officer en route to Camp Kenyon. I won his money and when the game finished, I sat in the dining car and watched the mountains' striations of violet and greenish mauve underneath a sky burned white from the sun. The light hurt my eyes after all the grey cloud of Vancouver. I very nearly got off the train at a whistle stop before Lethbridge, I very nearly lost my nerve.

The English officer looked at me strangely when we both got out at the Lethbridge station. There was no one waiting for either of us on the platform. I picked up my alligator-skin suitcase and followed the officer through the one-room station to the curb. He looked down the dusty street in disgust; I suppose his ride was late. Teddy was nowhere in sight. It was sunny, already so bright I felt I'd gone through the looking glass, from the rain-filled Vancouver streets to the dry red dust foothills of Lethbridge.

"Visiting someone are you?" the officer said. "Or just passing through long enough to wipe out the other men while you're at it?" His accent made his sentences go up in the middle.

"My fiancé's training here," I said. God knows why I said that. It was the first story that came into my head and it seemed as good a lie as any. Teddy wasn't the kind of boy to resent a lie.

"I'll give you a lift, if my ride turns up."

"Very kind of you."

"If I play my cards right, I'll get back to a table with you and win my...."

"You played very well, sir. I was surprised by my...."

"You're not going to say beginner's luck now are you?" This time his voice went up so high it cracked with effort.

I turned to look down the street again.

"Where are you going?" he persisted.

"The hotel," I said confidently. I couldn't imagine a town like Lethbridge had more than one.

An army jeep veered around the corner, the driver, its sole occupant, honking the horn. The tarpaulin covering the back was askew and torn on one side.

"Can't they get anything right in this godforsaken country?" said the English officer, which made me glad to have taken his money. The jeep lurched to a stop in front of us and the grunt driving leapt out at attention, saluting us sharply. The officer ignored him and waved me towards the front passenger seat as he flung himself with great disdain into the back.

The driver looked fourteen, pale skin and pale eyes and a fine down of reddish hair visible on his scalp below his peaked cap. He was about to say something when the officer shouted, "Get on with it private. We don't have all day. Take this lady to the hotel. Wherever in hell it might be. Now."

We took off and immediately went over an incredible bump in the road. I yelped and the army grunt whispered, low enough that officer wouldn't hear, "Sorry miss, road's been torn up by our maneuvers."

"It's all right. I'm grateful for the lift."

"Hope it's not impolite to ask, but you are here for Ahern? He told me...."

"What, he's in a card game?" I muttered, "can't get out to meet me?"

Clearly puzzled, the boy said, "No miss, he's marching around in the dust 'til sunset. He said if I saw his fiancée, I mean you, miss, if there was any way to drop you at the hotel, he'll meet you there for dinner."

I marvelled that Teddy had actually made plans, amused he'd used the same obvious lie about our being engaged. We went over another colossal bump in the road and the officer cursed with gusto.

"Sorry sir," shouted the grunt.

I felt badly for the driver, he was no doubt Teddy's age, but he didn't have Teddy's bulk or confidence. "Where are you from?"

"Gimli, miss."

The officer made a spitting noise from the back. "Would you shut up soldier, the lady doesn't need your...."

"The officer's not in the best of moods," I whispered. There was no need to explain that his grouchiness was partly my fault. I raised my voice slightly, to reach the officer's ears. "It's very kind of you to take me to the hotel, sir, I really appreciate the lift."

The boy from Lake Winnipeg flushed as we veered around a corner and pulled up in front of a building that looked like a vestige from my Silver Rush childhood. Three wooden storeys tilted unevenly with age and dust, the hotel sign crooked and a big half-dead cottonwood tree in the empty lot next door. The hotel had been grand once, with its crenellated metal cornice and tall old letters on the faded red sign. The boy hopped out, ran around the jeep and gave me his hand to the sidewalk.

"Don't look like much, but it's the best in town, miss. Hot water'n all."

Hot water, I thought, will wonders never cease. But I thanked the boy, suppressing an instinct to tip him for his trouble as if we were on a train. He stood at attention as the officer unfolded from the rough back storage area of the jeep and settled into the front seat, and they drove away, taking the corner at the end of the street in a cloud of reddish dust. Behind me, I heard the door of the hotel swing open and I turned. Teddy stood in the doorway in uniform. I forgave him for not meeting me at the station, I was barely on the stairs before he picked me up and wrapped me in a hug. His uniform smelled of tar and oil, not at all like him, and his hair was shorn almost to the scalp. I touched his ear for an instant, the edges of his hairline sunburned, his face tanned. He looked almost sheepish.

"I'm lyin' low, couldn't come out 'til they'd gone. Is the new one a Brit? All we get out here is jackass Brits."

"I took him at cards last night, if it makes you feel any better."

"That's my girl."

We went into the hotel together, as if we really were engaged.

"My wife's here," he said to the hotel clerk. I didn't have time to even gasp. "Her train was on time, the men picked her up. I'm thinking she'll need breakfast and then a nap. What do you think?"

The hotel clerk was plump and dark and no doubt suspicious by nature, yet he beamed at Teddy like a benevolent uncle. "We'll get you breakfast, Catherine will, and show you upstairs...."

I hoped he was nearsighted—I had no wedding ring to play wife with. Teddy laughed and smiled and hauled me fast up the stairs to my room. At the end of the second-floor hallway, he opened the door to an enormous pale rose room that ought to have been haunted by Miss Havisham. Far too many white eyelet curtains hung around the bay window, little scraps of lace draped every horizontal surface, doilies and tablecloths festooned various chairs and night stands. Overwrought pink fringes shaded the lamps. The bed was enormous and covered in white piles of this and that, fabrics with long names and elaborate weaves. A small porcelain sink stood in the corner, and I slipped out from Teddy's arm, took off my hat, and washed my hands and face gratefully. I was drying my face on a towel when Teddy came up behind me and began kissing my neck. He had too many hands all of a sudden.

"I missed you," he said. "Didn't think I'd have missed you like this."

With him pressed against me, I thought of telling him about the miscarriage, but I didn't know what to say. I looked at my hard eyes in the mirror and folded that story away into the box of myself. He lifted his head up from my hair and met my eyes in the mirror.

"Goddamn it."

"What?" The cool porcelain through my cotton dress was reassuring compared to the heat of Teddy's skin.

"Guard duty."

"Now?"

He ran his fingers along the seams of my dress, trying to find the zipper. I shifted so he wouldn't.

"You're supposed to be doing what?"

"Patrollin'. Two guys per shift. No one in his right mind is gonna haul ass out to sabotage a bunch of Harvard trainin' aircraft. And we don't get ammunition, just a ruddy bayonet. So we'll what, wrestle intruders to the ground and pin 'em with a bayonet? Bullshit." He kissed me again. "Mostly we just stay in the aircraft hangars, outta the sun. My craps game's getting better."

I nearly laughed, not from good humour, more the kind of laughter that comes from sorrow and nerves. "That's what you're doing out here? Playing craps?"

"Yep. Wanderin' around inside a fence. Shooting dice. Every now and then we practice putting fuses into bombs."

"More use than craps."

"Yeah, well, I'm a free man this evenin' after guard duty." He picked me up and dumped me on the white-layered bed, where I sank as into a bowl of cream. "So don't go nowhere."

As I struggled to get off the bed, he smiled and then he was out the door. I listened to his boots on the stairs and then the quieter steps of the hotelkeeper's wife, coming up to see if I wanted breakfast. I smoothed my hair. I wondered if there was a train to get me out of town as quickly as I'd arrived, I felt actually sick, I wanted him so badly. I wanted to fold my hand, but I found myself slowly walking downstairs to breakfast. The hotel staircase smelled of dust and singed wood, its carpeting worn in spots. The rug had once been expensive, a Persian-type red and blue paisley affair swirling across every step. I held onto the wooden banister, smooth and solid, while Catherine, the hotelkeeper's wife, walked ahead of me, talking, leading me into the dining room, sitting me down and fussing with tea and a local newspaper. The lead story had a picture of a grinning army boy and an airplane, Lethbridge dust in the background.

"Let me cook you up something," said the woman. "I won't be a moment. You must be just exhausted. I know what those trains are like, not a whit of sleep you can get on them...."

"That's true." Especially if a body is sitting up playing cards all night. As she left, I looked around. With cheap wood and optimism, a homemade wall cut the hotel's old elegant dining room roughly in half. A slight smell of burning tinged the air—I wondered if that was me, if my dress was scorched by Teddy's touch.

Catherine came back from the kitchen with a great round tray. Seeing me looking at the makeshift wall, she said, "From the fire. Last fall. Kitchen burned, there wasn't much we could do with the far side, so we put that up meantime. You know, 'til things pick up."

"Hasn't the army helped business?"

Catherine was a skinny woman with long arms and cowlicked brown hair that failed to braid quite right. She balanced the tray on her hip, ran her other hand against her hair. "Good for business?" She considered. "Sometimes an officer wants a real bath. We have lots of hot water if you want. Tub's down the hall, third floor."

"Thank you."

She set out orange juice and coffee, a plate of brown toast that was burned on one side, a pat of butter and a bowl of greenish-yellow jam. "Gooseberries," she said. "I get 'em myself. You take the eggs over easy or what? That's how they ended up, hope you like 'em. The butter's real, we got a decent butter supply still. Bet you don't see that in the city."

My plate had two messy eggs, bacon, and a huge pile of potatoes. At least I was hungry. When Catherine had all the plates and cutlery on the table, she sat down in the empty place across from me, as if I were the most interesting thing that had happened in a week.

I put jam on my toast. "You've eaten?"

"Oh, hours ago, the husband, He's been up since six, you know. Running a hotel is an all-hours job, He sleeps on his feet half the time, I come downstairs to get the fires going in the winter, you know, five in the morning, and He's fallen asleep at the front desk wrapped in that bearskin rug. He works too hard. You're terrible young, with your boy in the army, but you'll see as you go on, the way I have, the good men work too hard, He certainly always has. Always wanted to run a hotel, He did. Last year, it's amazing we didn't lose the whole place, the fire started in, He was beside himself, He was...."

Her hunger for female company gave me a running commentary to accompany my breakfast. I learned more than I necessarily wanted about the trials and tribulations of the Lethbridge Hotel and the impact of Camp Kenyon on the town's moral fibre. Poker's a lonesome job—I wouldn't have thought the same would be said for an innkeeper's wife, but Catherine talked as if she hadn't had a sympathetic ear in months. "He's always up and at 'em, you know how that goes, and He's not looking after himself, I have to force Him to eat in the evening, otherwise He's...."

I had nothing to say to Catherine, but no matter, she talked enough for both sides of a conversation. I was exhausted by the end of breakfast, maybe from making so many appropriate sounds of agreement.

"I'm a bit tired," I finally said, interrupting Catherine's extended analysis of the innkeeper's bunions, or perhaps his mother's, I had lost track. I never did notice how sleepy I was until a good five or six hours after a game, which made this about the right time for a nap.

"Oh Lord, of course you are, dropping, no doubt and here I am going on, boring you silly. I'll get you into a hot bath, that's what you need. A good hot bath and then into bed with you, feel right as rain by this afternoon, trust me."

"I have enough rain in Vancouver, thanks."

"Can't say the same here, hasn't rained in three weeks and two days, or is it three days, no, today's Friday, there you go. No wonder the hot bath is such a rare good thing, in these parts."

While the water filled the huge white tub, she beetled back and forth fetching bath salts and soap and two big towels, reasonably white though they didn't stink of bleach. She resolutely did not look at my ring-less hands but treated me like the very best guest in the world, which made me think she had as few girl friends as I did.

I closed the door and got into the bath, wondering where I'd be if I didn't play poker. If I had no calling. Would I marry a hotelkeeper and concern myself with town gossip? I could marry Teddy. And? My pulse raced unhappily. The last thing I wanted was to become the equivalent of an innkeeper's wife. I closed my eyes and sank down under the hot water, blowing bubbles as I submerged.

The day slipped away as I napped in the mitten-soft bed. When I finally clambered out, it was three in the afternoon. I dressed and slipped downstairs without being seen by Catherine, though her husband glanced up from his newspaper as I went past.

"Good thing you've got a decent hat, this sun."

I adjusted my narrow straw hat more securely on my head. It wasn't exactly practical—I'd bought it because I liked its red ribbon. "Is there anywhere nice to walk?"

"There're the shops," he said. Which was no help, but I thanked him and pushed through the front door. A man loaded boxes of empty soda bottles into the trunk of his car on the otherwise empty main street. I browsed through the aforementioned shops, of which there were a total of five, finishing with a drug store that smelled of old eggs. There were a couple of wan-faced girls at the soda fountain who all but stopped breathing when I walked in. I could feel the soda clerk eyeing me—tourists weren't exactly common in a town like this one. I left without buying anything, expecting their disapproval to find voice the moment I got to the sidewalk. I tried very hard not to shudder. I reminded myself that my hat, at least, was very nice and while a little dressy for a town such as Lethbridge, perfectly respectable.

I walked up through the residential streets for a few blocks, each house perfectly aligned with its neighbour, spindly shrubs neatly set back from the sidewalk, each one so nicely kept and looked after. So quiet, no sign of life. Those streets seemed a constant admonition—there was no room for a woman like me here, no place for my hands or my ambitions. I had a paranoid feeling that the deserted-feeling houses really were empty, that no one was alive here at all, no one except the army boys, marching around in the dust outside town. The empty sidewalk led down to the edge of a wide, shallow river. I walked along the narrow dirt path that followed the riverbank—no one was fishing, and I saw only one duck, bobbing along in the water. I envied the complacency of the duck; I felt dusty and tired by the effort of keeping my head up. The path gradually looped back downtown.

Back in my lace-draped hotel room, I lay on the bed, first on my back, then on my stomach. The later it got, the more I began to wonder if Teddy had been caught sneaking back to his patrol shift. I imagined military punishments for breaking orders. I was here because I'd missed the weight of him, the way he smelled when he made love. I missed the smoothness of his shoulders, the muscles in his face that clenched when I took him in my hands. I missed touching him, which wasn't the same as missing him, exactly. I was trapped in my Dickensian hotel room. I watched the main street from the bay window of my room and there was nobody about, not even one solitary soul taking an evening promenade through town. If I went downstairs, I would be stuck in the lobby with Catherine, who would worry over Teddy's absence the way a dog licks a scratch. I found myself longing for the game I might have played on the train.

At ten o'clock, I cursed myself for having missed dinner—I was hungry, but I'd waited, thinking Teddy might show up, after all. I wondered what ordinary girls did with their evenings, waiting for their men to turn up. Ordinary girls became mothers, which gave them ample occupation. I undressed and caught sight of myself in the mirror, skinny, pale, slouched with regret. I put on my nightdress. I didn't look much like a married woman, but I didn't look much like a scarlet lady, either; I looked like what I was, a scrawny girl, caught in the too-bright light of an oncoming train. I got into bed and convinced myself there was no humiliation in being here alone, simply the way the hand had played out. Obviously Teddy was caught in the routine of the army base. I would leave in the morning, I pictured myself checking out of the hotel and escaping from Lethbridge, shuffling a deck hard and coming up with all the wrong cards. I turned out the light.

Somewhere in the hotel, there were voices, footsteps. There was a mild knock on the door. I didn't answer, but the door creaked open anyhow.

"You're in bed? Don't you want dinner?" Teddy pushed the door shut and turned on the lamp.

"I gave up on you."

"You shouldn't have done that, Mill. I always come through."

"Eventually."

"I'll make it up to you," he said, in a movie idol kind of voice, but I didn't really forgive him, even as I put out my hands in welcome. He took off his jacket and started undoing his shirt. As he leaned down I smelled the dust and underlying tar from his patrol, but when he kissed me, his mouth tasted of whiskey. I sighed into his kiss, I opened my mouth.

"No dinner then," he said, pushing me back against the bed, unbuttoning, unbuckling, undoing. I wanted to be undone, done over. The dust made his skin gritty against my fingers. I dug my short nails past his waist onto his hips, sat up against him. "Christ," he said, as if there was no way to get far enough into me. My hipbones might break against him, and that would be fine, that would be good. I wanted to be lifted right out of myself.

Later, I realized he never explained why he turned up so late. Instead, he shrugged off the rest of his clothes, switched off the lamp and lay down beside me in the dark. He slowly trawled a hand across my back as I lay face down, his fingers up and then down, as if I were a cat, as if I might purr, but I was quiet.

When he reached the triangular flat of the small of my back, he said, "Why don't you marry me, when this is over?"

I pressed my lips against the pillow, trying not to cough. In the warm dark, stroking my back, Teddy waited. "Your mother wouldn't mind. She's near adopted me already."

I tried to sink further into the bed and finally sighed and rolled over, away from him, but he turned with me, pulled my nightdress off my shoulder and pressed his big head against my skin. I could smell the honey and sweat of his scalp. I missed his hair, put my hand across the dark stubble. Maybe he knew I wasn't going to answer him.

After a long time, he moved so he could see my eyes in the darkness, said, "Don't worry about it now. We'll get it official-like when I get back."

He slid his hand across the fabric of my nightdress and ran his fingers along the pushed-up hem, let his index finger trace the wet slide into me. He touched me, insistent, two fingers suddenly inside me until I gasped and tightened my thighs against his arm. His gaze so intent on mine, so dark and shiny even in the dark of the room that I had to blink, close my eyes, to come back into myself. He moved his hand to my hip and shifted my legs to curl against him. I must have fallen asleep, because I was startled when he pushed himself away from me.

"What?"

"Have to get back. I'm not supposed to be here, Mill."

"You've only been here a little while."

"It's almost four."

It took him no time at all to get dressed. I wondered what a properly-raised girl would do, as the man who wasn't her fiancé dressed and headed back to a training base. Not fair to blame any of this on the way my mother had raised me. I tried to get my nightdress back on.

"You have a craps game or something?"

That wasn't what I meant to say, but he laughed. "No."

"Well. Try to stay away from...."

"Craps? Trust me, I'm better at craps than at marchin' around." He came over to the bed, pulled the sheet up to my chin, and leaned across me.

"Well. Look after yourself."

Teddy was more alive than anyone I'd ever met, he was filled with energy and brightness, that was what he gave me, maybe the only thing he could give me. That shine and the smell of him on my skin. He grinned, his teeth were the brightest thing in the room's dim light. "Don't worry, Mill. Have yourself a fine time at those train games, get rich as stink. When I get back, I'll help you spend all that money."

He kissed me, tongue along my teeth. He brought his scarred lips together against mine and put his hand across my eyes to close my eyelids. When I opened my eyes, the dark room was worse than empty.

On the train home to Vancouver, I didn't play poker. I sat in the sunroom and looked at the view. All I could smell was Teddy, with the tar and dust that soldiering had added to him. The sun came through the windows half as strong as it must have beat down on him, walking around the inside of the fence, on patrol. I squinted out at the foothills and wondered if he was in the shade, throwing dice. It wasn't fair for me to disapprove. What was fair, anyhow? Rich as stink, I thought, good, let him come back and help me spend the money. I should have thought it through a little better than I did, I should have wondered what Teddy thought, what he might hope for.

Shortly before Halloween, 1941, Teddy left Canada on the troop transport *Awatea*—a boat named for some word in Maori, they said in the newspaper. Which didn't make much sense to me, since the ship was heading to Hong Kong. While he left, I played hold'em, which made my opponents show off like pigeons, puffing themselves up over their cards. I didn't much enjoy hold'em, but I teased out every hand, bluffed through the ones that didn't give me solid percentages. Unlike my usual willingness to fold, at that game I stood my ground. I was getting better at judging my opponents— how they would behave, under which circumstances. Like waging a battle.

Poker is risky, like going to war, or making love. Every move you make has to be carefully weighed against what you stand to lose. Maybe that explained why I wasn't in Vancouver, Teddy's last night on shore. Five stud, seven stud, hold'em, it didn't matter—poker was better than being made love to, the game really mine, really in my hands, a game of skill and knowledge and luck. I could walk away with a purse full of money, and still have some self-respect, which a girl can't really say about a tumble across the sheets, however enjoyable it might be at the time. Gambling's more romantic than romance.

My last hand was a pair of nines, Spades and Clubs; the flop consisted of an Ace, the nine of Hearts, and a six. I bet hard for Fourth Street and Fifth, because I knew I could. My opponents went for the bait—there were still lots of high cards in the deck, they had decent hands that made them think they could beat me. But my luck held. I swept the pot towards me. The nine of Hearts is a wish card, making dreams come true, though I didn't like to express my dreams, or even think about what they might be, in case they made the gods of fortune look askance. Anyhow, the nine of Clubs was a pig-headed card, the nine of Spades even worse.

The train slowed, approaching Bellingham. "You ever find yourself up in Banff, little lady, you should look me up," said the tallest man in the room, a man built to sit on top of a horse and hand down the law. He passed me a card that read *Philip Forres, Barrister, Sausalito 9175 California;* I smiled that I'd pegged him correctly for a legal type. He said, "You should come on up and play with us sometime."

Banff. I thought of the little ski town in the Rockies, on my favourite route between Vancouver and Calgary. Forres held open the door for me and I went past him, out into the corridor. I never got off at Banff, but I knew the Swiss chalet-style train station—promising fish often boarded the train there.

"I stay at the Banff Springs. Give me a call there." He shook my hand and prepared to leave the train.

I stood in the corridor as Karmel helped him off. When he'd flipped up the step, the train lurching, the porter turned. He looked tired.

"Do you know anyone who plays cards in Banff, Karmel?"

"Sure I know a guy in Banff." He opened the connecting door for me and followed me through to the next car. "Name's One Shot. Lemme know when, I'll get you his phone number."

If I was going to get rich as stink, as Teddy had said, Banff was perfect. I wasn't over-reaching, I was just trying to go forward. I thought about the idea for weeks and then, at the beginning of December, I called the man named One Shot. He gave me a date, and on the appointed day, I packed an extra sweater for Banff's cold mountain air. As I came down the stairs, Max waved an envelope at me.

"You never pick up your mail, honey. Those other girls ask for their mail twice a day, hoping for a letter, and here you have one sitting all by itself for a week."

"I don't know anyone who'd write to me," I lied, knowing full well who had written. My name was printed in pencil, crookedly, across an envelope postmarked from Honolulu. I didn't open it until I was on the train en route to Banff. I sat in my first class seat, the letter an illicit weight in my alligator bag. I dreaded and looked forward to it and finally I brought it out and held it as we passed Port Hope, the mountains rising up sudden-like all around the tracks, blue-green in the evening light. I looked at the envelope for a long time before I got around to opening it, as if the letters of my own name might tell me something about Teddy.

The handwriting was easy to read, thin words across a single sheet of paper. He spent most of the page describing flying fish he'd seen. They sounded big as dolphins. Flying fish and the lousy food they ate on the boat, while I headed into the mountains to play a far less magical kind of fish. He didn't put in any endearments, but I wasn't expecting them. I wasn't sure what to do with the letter, except to fold it up and put it in my purse, while I looked out the window at the snow, blue snow in the grey early twilight as we came into the mountains. What I was hungry for, I would learn to do without.

I checked myself into the Banff Springs Hotel, because that was what One Shot suggested and because it was the best hotel in town. A special car waited to pick up hotel guests from the train station. I had only my alligator bag, no suitcase with brass tags, no trunks, no mountaineering equipment. The car drove us past skiers carrying their skis, and little chalets with snowshoes stuck in snowbanks near the door. We crossed a little bridge over a frozen river, huge peaks looming above. After another bend in the road, the hotel rose up like a great stone French palace.

I checked in and a bellboy showed me to my room, which had wide windows looking into the jagged mountains, a disturbing view in the deepening evening. I lay on the bed and thought about Teddy, in the middle of an ocean, just water as far as the eye could see in every direction. Blue. His letter about the flying fish folded at the bottom of my purse.

The game was in a suite on the immense second floor of the hotel; the halls were patrolled by white-jacketed butlers who bowed as I passed. Huge vases of flowers adorned the narrow hallway. I marvelled at the fresh gardenias and orchids so late in the season, their heavy perfumes strange in the thin mountain air.

"Millard Lacouvy, I couldn't be happier to see you," said Philip Forres when he met me at the door. He looked honestly glad. "Some very tough eggs here, Miss Millard... let me introduce you. But first, our dealer. One Shot, meet a lady who plays a good game."

We played a short game of five-stud, to warm up, during which one of Forres' friends was knocked out. The friend didn't seem perturbed; he buttoned a brown striped jacket on top of his lilac-coloured vest, adjusted his tie, and shook everyone's hand except for mine. For me, he bowed low and kissed my wrist. For once, it was impossible for me to keep a poker face, I was quite astonished and I am sure looked it. After he left, we played hold 'em, at Forres' request.

The final hand, I held the Jack and ten of Spades, and the initial flop stood me beautifully: the seven, eight and Queen of Spades. One Shot picked up the deck and burned the top card automatically. I saw it was a three of Diamonds. Then very slowly, it seemed to me, he brought up the next card, the River; he set the nine of Spades in the centre of the table.

"I'll be damned," said Philip Forres, tossing his cards into the muck. "But I don't regret inviting you."

I smiled, an honest wide grin that I rarely allowed myself at a gaming table, all sharp teeth and triumph. I couldn't help it, I had succeeded at this new level of game, I was good, I really was, even if I had to involve the Queen of Spades to do it—a card that represents an unscrupulous woman. I wondered if the card was supposed to represent me? I wanted to tell someone, but that would have to wait until I returned to Vancouver, at least then I could boast to Dermot. Well, maybe not. No point in boasting.

I went to my room to change clothes and wash my face—I was too excited to sleep, though it was seven in the morning. So there, I told the mountains outside my window, you just try crushing me. Then I went down to the dining room and watched the expensive wives at breakfast, women who knew how to coordinate the colour of their dresses to best complement their lives, to arrange their decorative hands in their laps—their hands only useful for applying rouge to their painted lips or for rearing their soft children. They relied on their husbands for their livelihoods, their husbands who weren't on a ship in any foreign sea. I glanced at their polite plates of toast and fruit salad and I ordered an enormous breakfast with sausages and potatoes and creamed spinach too. I wondered how spinach managed to grow in the mountains.

On the train home, I thought about how cards were honest. An honest exchange, I mean: I extracted money from those women's husbands in return for a game of cards. No flirtation, no sex, no promises of marriage or affection or friendship—none of the questions that confused me when I last saw Theodore Ahern. I glared out at the mountains as the train wound towards Vancouver.

At the waterfront station, the newsboys were shouting about an attack in the Pacific. I bought the paper on the platform and read about Pearl Harbour as I stood under the echoing coffered ceiling. The noise of voices and foot-steps and the creaking screech of the trains—I can't think of Pearl Harbour without that cacophony filling my head. I wondered if Teddy was in Hong Kong. The papers predicted a battle there, though while I read those head-lines, the fight had already begun. It started the morning after Pearl Harbour; somebody must have planned it that way.

I didn't even properly know where Hong Kong was, just that it lay some-where on the edge of China, but I stared at the maps printed in the news-papers, trying to understand the geography, and I bought a reddish Bakelite radio for my room. The Canadian regiments fought and every day, I followed the news, sitting on my bed, my shoes off, knees tucked up under my chin. Eighteen days after the battle began, Mr. Churchill made a formal statement that Britain and Japan were at war. There were rumours in the newspapers that they were using Hong Kong as some kind of diversionary tactic. The Brits allowed the Japs to slaughter our troops as a diversion, which isn't a way I had ever thought of using the word—men dying as a tactic in a game.

I heard the real news at Dermot's when I walked into the backroom from the alley. Three men I vaguely knew were there and Dermot was setting out glasses of beer for them. I'd just sat down when Betsch came in looking haggard rather than drunk.

"Have you heard? It's all over."

Dermot snorted, expecting one of Harry's usual grandiose statements about the world, but I said, "What's over?"

"Hong Kong's fallen. The Japs have them."

I looked at Dermot, but he'd turned to watch his bar through the open door. Teddy, in Hong Kong—that's it, what now, I thought. I took the cards from the middle of the table and cut the deck and dealt one down, the next three facing up. My upturned cards were the seven, eight, and ten of Spades, a suite of trouble and imprisonment—not death. I swirled the three cards back into the deck and shuffled again.

Soon after, the Japanese in Vancouver were rounded up and sent away—to the Interior, which seemed a very strange choice of prison, to me. And their boats were confiscated. That's a sorry sight, a pile of boats chained to a dock and no one looking after them. It should have made me feel better, that someone over here was paying for Hong Kong, suffering alongside, but seeing the boats didn't make me feel better at all. The empty boats made the war real, they were afloat and there wasn't any purpose to them. Which is how I felt, afloat and empty, while the seasons kept right on falling past me.

I played cards and gathered hands up and played them again, folded, played again, won, waited for another hand. Rain wiped the day clean or left me covered in mud, depending on how the games played out. The months went past as train stations while I played poker, focused on the immediate numbers, not on the long-term implications, not looking at anyone except the men directly across the table, studying their personal ticks and refusing to think of who else might have made a similar gesture. I was good at it. My game got better, I won higher pots. My God it was three years, even now, if you asked me, I can list the names of every whistle stop station, and some of those towns don't exist anymore except in my mind. Fancy that.

Whenever the trains brought me back home to Vancouver, I walked through the station in my wood-soled shoes and paused in the ladies' room. I slowly grew out my hair, wore it coiled onto my head in any number of elaborate up-dos—I thought it made me look taller. I learned to smile more often, I began to wear lipstick; it didn't mean I was happier, only better at bluffing. I studied my expressions in the bathroom mirror at the train station. I adjusted my blush, repainted my lips, re-twisted my hair, re-pinned my hat at a sharper angle. I made sure the seam on my last pair of real stockings was straight. I walked across the echoing marble, past the benches filled with waiting families or with soldiers. Since all the men had been sent to war, women now worked on the trains, not as porters, but on the engines, maintaining the locomotives. I walked past and bought a newspaper to read in the cab, on my way to the bank, where I put my bankroll away. So on the steps of the bank, sometimes, I read about forced marches in China. I read about war camps and men starving. I read about executions. No wonder I usually threw the newspaper away and walked home severely to my same plain room in the West End.

If I came home in the morning, I walked around the seawall before going to bed. The waves rolling in from the Pacific helped my head. If the news hadn't entirely shaken me, I went over the cards I'd played. I kept studying the game—much as I loved Dermot, loyally returning most weeks to play at his backroom on Tuesdays, he hadn't taught me anything new in years. I lit a cigarette, cupping my lighter against the breeze coming off the water. I stood at the promontory above Third Beach, exhaling smoke. Yes, I learned to smoke, a convenient excuse to fill my hands when I wasn't playing cards—compared to playing poker for a living, a little thing like smoking hardly mattered.

One day I heard someone cough and say, "Mill-ard?" There was a low catch in the voice that I recognized from school. I turned around to see a thin man in uniform, wearing glasses, with a bandaged face. He came slowly over to where I was standing. His white-blond hair shored up in a sudden gust of wind and I recognized Adam Plotznick, who'd been in my class when I was a kid, before I quit school for the laundry. Last time I'd seen him, he was barely bigger than me, a glasses-wearing runt, favoured target for bullies. He'd grown at least a foot since I'd seen him and he'd filled out through the shoulders. His uniform glinted with ribbons and crosses. He walked stiffly, as if there was something wrong with his back, forcing him to stand at attention all the time, even when out for a stroll.

"Thought you looked familiar," he said.

Despite the strips of bandage across the right side of his face, setting his thin gold spectacles off-balance, he still had an aristocrat's nose. Plotznick had taken to adulthood rather better than to being a kid: even with the bandages, his face was honest, reassuring. I suddenly imagined him leading men into battle. He had that kind of nose.

"It's nice to see you, Adam."

"Come up here for the view?"

"Walking clears my head." A new layer of clouds was coming in, but even so, we could see the far line of mountains on Vancouver Island. They looked like a mirage.

"I came up for some quiet," he said.

I looked back at the road on the far side of the promontory; I could see a taxi waiting. "Where were you stationed?"

"You mean, where'd I get this?" He touched the edge of one of the bandages, three strips of white against the pale skin of his face. "Nothing. Flying glass in London. Shoulder's the problem. Do you have time for a coffee? Promise I won't bore you with the details."

I said okay, because I had nothing else to do. The wind was shifting the rain-clouds closer. Adam hailed the cab and asked the driver to take us to a Davie Street coffeehouse. He paid the driver while I hurried inside out of the rain.

Adam joined me and fitted himself awkwardly into the booth I'd chosen. "Only got back three days ago. Helluva trip. The boat kept taking detours because of the submarines. And the train was packed with the saddest cases you can imagine." Adam folded his hands together and cracked his knuckles. "My mum's been lovely, but she's stone deaf now. I feel like I'm shouting all the time." He cut his eyes to the other tables nearby. "Am I shouting?"

"No."

"Good. So, how are you? How's your mother?"

A few raindrops started to splatter against the window. "Mother's well," I said. "She married a clerk, Harold Avison. I think you'd already left for Winnipeg when she got married. It was Winnipeg wasn't it?"

"Yup."

"And she's living on West 10th. I'm living not far from here. And Teddy Ahern's in a Jap POW camp. We think. That's about...."

Adam put his left hand over mine. "I'm sorry, Millard."

I nodded, accepting his sorrow, though I had no clear claim upon it.

"I'm sure he'll come through," he said.

The waitress brought the coffee and a pitcher of milk and asked if I minded having a vanilla milkshake, they were all out of strawberry. When she went away, I said, "Why were you in London?"

"I managed to get half my shoulder blown off in Normandy." He took a sip of the coffee, frowned at its bitterness and added some milk. I watched the white bloom in the coffee. "They more or less patched me together again, but now I'm declared unfit. Got a two day holiday in London before I came home. Buildings are half falling down over there, Millard. You wouldn't believe the place, like a bad dream. I was standing on the street. A window came down on me when a bus went by, cut up my face. Not even the Blitz, just a bus an' a window. But it's the shoulder sent me home, can't shoot anybody for a while, I'm too twitchy, doctors say. Might shoot the wrong man." He attempted to laugh. His uniform jacket was buttoned loosely, but only his face and his odd posture hinted at any wounds at all.

I wondered at the heroic-looking crosses and metal bars on his uniform. "Surely everyone gets twitchy," I said.

"Some take it better than others."

I thought how, at a card game, no matter how calm you play, enough hours without sleep and anything might happen. It felt like that, suddenly, at the diner, the table between us.

"My platoon was full of Yanks. They volunteered in Canada, crazy buggers. Right at the beginning of the war. They hauled themselves up here to sign up and get blown to bits. Some of 'em even got sewn up again, nearly into one piece. Normandy's the flattest damn hellhole you've ever seen, pardon my French. Worse'n Winnipeg, an' that's saying something."

The waitress plonked my vanilla milkshake onto the table.

"Tell me to shut up if I start talking about that again," he said. "Don't want to talk about that. Tell me what you're up to. Or, lemme guess... you're working as, hmm, as an engine wiper. I can see you doing something like that."

I pursed my mouth around the straw of the milkshake, not knowing what to say about my career of choice. He wasn't as far off as he could have been—the engine wipers worked in the railyards, and what with the boys in uniform, Canadian Pacific had started hiring girls for the job. "I spend a lot of time on trains, that's true."

Adam laughed and said, "No, I'm off base. You're still taking money away from the boys at school, aren't you...."

"You remember that?"

"I was one of the ones you took money from. I guess you don't remember." The skin on the right side of his face rutched around the bandages as he smiled.

"Pretty much so," I said.

"Get out much?"

"I work a few nights a week."

"Have you seen Dal Richards, you know, at the Roof?"

"At the top of the Hotel Vancouver? No."

"Didn't you work in that hotel once upon a time?" He didn't give me time to answer. "You should go. We should go. I'll take you. We'll go see this famous Richards and his eleven-piece band. You won't even have to dance with me—with all the stitches they've stuck in my shoulder, I can't move more than to the bar and back. Leave you free to dance with whomever you like. I'll just pay for your drinks and try to be witty."

I said I'd go, because it felt good to talk to Adam. He'd been away, he'd seen the war, he'd seen the world beyond the watery green edges of Vancouver.

On Thursday night, Adam looked pretty fine, dressed for the Rooftop. But after a while he said, "You're not dancing. I don't expect you to sit here all night with me, being bored."

"You're not that boring."

He laughed. "Don't you like dancing?"

"I was never too much in demand."

"Fascinating girl like yourself? Sure you could get a dancing partner."

"I'm plain and short and I don't dance." Honestly, I didn't want to dance—I'd only ever had one dance partner, and he had gone to Hong Kong.

Adam leaned forward, awkward because of his shoulder. "You don't really believe you're plain, do you?" He put his index finger against the point of my chin. "You're not, you know. You're wonderful, someone no one can forget. I would recognize you fifty years from now, if I'd only ever seen you the once. You don't look like anybody else."

I moved my face away from his hand, embarrassed. "I don't see much wonderful about that."

"It's a compliment, Millard. Just say thank you."

On the dance floor, couples arranged themselves for the next song. Adam laughed. "You are short, though, that's the unvarnished truth. If you aren't dancing, I'm going to pretend you're sitting with me 'cause you want to."

At the end of the evening, when Adam dropped me off at my boarding house in a cab, he asked if I'd go out again, the following Thursday.

"I won't be any taller."

"And it'll be two months or more before I can dance. We're a good match."

I played cards through the weekend and into the following week and only remembered on Wednesday afternoon that I needed to get home to meet Adam for our date.

"Think of me at all during the week?" he asked.

"I try to keep my attention on the cards, I didn't think about you...." I trailed off, realizing that didn't sound very complimentary.

"Wouldn't want to clutter up your head."

"No," I said, trying to explain. "I... never go out. This is a treat, Adam, to be out with you, I just don't think about going out, is what I meant."

Adam waved to the waitress to bring us another round of drinks. "What do you do at night then?"

"My only date is with cards, Adam, I work at night. Gamblers avoid daylight."

"So you're a vampire?"

I shook my head.

"Pity. I've always liked vampires. I might have invited you home with me."

"To watch me turn into a bat?"

"You'd have to watch out for the cross over my bed, of course. It is my mother's house."

"Is she really very deaf?"

"As a post." He grinned, which turned the fact into an invitation. I laughed, but after one more date, I did go home with him, not to erase anyone, that's not what I meant to do.

Adam could only lie on his back because his shoulder was a carefully-reconstructed Meccano set, held together with stitches and pins and sticking plasters. That first time in his bed, I touched him cautiously, as if one of us might shatter.

He murmured, "Millard, either you make love to me like you mean it or you can pretend to be a nurse, I'll get you a little Red Cross hat, and you can go upstairs and shout at mother."

❧

Adam took me to the vaudeville show at the Stanley Theatre, to see jugglers and top-hatted tap dancers, trumpet players and child magicians. We sat on plush seats worn thin in different coloured patches, trying to keep our shoes from sticking permanently to the floor of spilled candy and drinks. After our first visit, I made sure to arrive late—every evening began with a slew of newsreels, even as the battles slowly ground to a halt in Europe, even as the war was running to the end of its tether. I didn't want to watch the war reels, even the triumphant ones about liberating prisoners. Especially if the reels were triumphant. The camp liberations were the worst reels yet. I'd already read too much in the newspapers; maybe I was afraid of who I'd see if I looked too carefully at the faces.

At intermission one night, Adam said, "It was your birthday last week, wasn't it?"

I shrugged. "I don't really celebrate them."

He put his hand in his breast pocket and brought out a slim wrapped box. "I got you a present."

I took the flat little box reluctantly, hoping it would be a fountain pen, something useful, practical, but the narrow blue velvet box held a gold bracelet, spread out on white silk.

"I can't accept this," I said.

"Because you're waiting for him, aren't you."

"No, that's not what I mean." I held up the bracelet. "It's very nice, don't get me wrong, but I can't wear it at a game, it'll distract me."

"So wear it when you're not at a game, Millard. Your whole life isn't spent at a poker game, you know. You're good at other things. You'd be a great mother." He blushed so deeply that his hair nearly got blonder.

"You've got to be kidding."

"I'm not. You've been putting up with me, my shoulder and all. You're very patient, and at the same time you don't tolerate any nonsense."

I tried very hard not to roll my eyes and I succeeded, but Adam noticed the effort I was putting into it.

"It's just a bracelet, you know," he said. "You don't have to give me any answer."

I shook my head.

"If you don't take it, what I am supposed to do with it?"

I kissed him on his searingly hot cheek and and put the bracelet in its box. He pushed the box back at me.

"Just take it, doesn't mean anything. I'll feel like a right idiot taking it back."

I didn't want to marry Adam, but not for the reason he thought. The ringing in my head, sure, that was worry for Teddy, but it wasn't a church bell—I was only hoping the war would end.

I fidgeted with the bracelet. I wore it for a few days but finally took it off, setting the frail gold chain on the table of the dining car in the train while I ate. The waiter, a round man named Jacques whose Canadian Pacific uniform was an unfortunate size too small, followed me when I left, saying, "Mad'moiselle? Your bracelet?"

The fact is, I lost the darn bracelet in less than a month, it wasn't even exactly intentional. But Adam came around to realizing I wasn't going to settle into anything resembling the traditional girl next door. He didn't ask how I'd lost the bracelet, though occasionally he'd hold my bare wrist against his teeth and bite my skin.

"What's it like?" I asked him one night. His shoulder had healed enough for him to lie on his side.

"What's what like?"

"Being in the war."

Adam narrowed his pale eyes. "You don't want to ask me that, Millard. It's still going on."

"But we're winning, now."

"I mean, it's still going on, in here." He ran his fingers over the healing cuts on his face. "I don't want to tell you about it. There's enough noise as it is." He nudged me over and lay flat with his eyes closed.

The room was absolutely quiet apart from our breathing. I tried to hear the noise in his head, but I couldn't. I brought my mouth close to his ear. "There's a band from San Francisco at the Roof next Saturday, can we go?"

He exhaled and opened his eyes. "I've been meaning to tell you...."

"What?"

"Weekends, you're always playing poker."

"And?"

"So on Saturday, I have, I mean...."

"You're busy?"

"It's, uh, more complicated than that."

I suddenly realized what he was getting at. "You're going to the Roof with someone else."

He looked doleful.

"Lucky guess?"

"I'm sorry, Millard."

I found that I was getting out of bed and getting dressed, faster than I had time to think. "You might have told me," I said, when I'd struggled success-fully into my slip.

"I didn't want to hurt your feelings."

"My feelings?" I searched for my second wool stocking. "But does she, I mean do you...."

"I don't know her very well, Millard. As yet."

"Not as yet?" I found the stocking and stood on one leg to get it on.

"The problem is, she says I have to stop spending time with hoodlums."

"Hoodlums?"

Adam coloured, his fair skin going red in a flash right up to his pale hairline. He sat up carefully and leaned against the bedstead. "She thinks I'm out playing poker whenever I meet you."

"So I'm a hoodlum?" I buttoned my shirt over my breasts. "That's better than having another woman?" I clipped the stockings to my garter belt and stepped into my skirt. The zipper was stuck. "We both knew it was coming. That it was just...."

"One of those crazy things? One of those bells that now and then rings? Come on, you could sing with me." Adam leaned out of bed and put a hand to my waist, as if we might finally dance together.

"I can't sing. Never learned."

He put his face against my shirt for a moment. "It's what you want, isn't it?" After a moment, he said, "You might know her, she works at the Hotel Vancouver. You used to work there, right? Vera."

"Vera? Vera Pierce?" I tried to imagine her now, freed from the laundry, with a bracelet on one arm and Adam on the other. They would both be laughing. I liked the idea of Adam laughing. "I like Vera," I said.

He smiled and the scars on his face only made his expression nicer. "So you do know her?"

"We worked in the awful basement laundry together."

"She runs housekeeping now."

"If there's an opportunity, tell her hello from me. From the hoodlum." I paused. "I can't imagine there'll be an opportunity."

Adam made a funny face, a kind of shrug that only involved his mouth. "I don't know, Millard. I wish...."

"Don't," I said. "Don't wish for anything that hasn't happened."

As good a motto as any. Adam had never been a bell, that clear church sound; he was more like a welcome distraction from the Tin Pan Alley ringing in my head. There was never any level playing field, no amount of skill I could acquire, that would help me be someone's bride. That's what I should have told Teddy in Lethbridge, except I didn't quite get around to it. The heart's a funny animal living in our chests, isn't it? Either forgotten in its place or it's in our mouths, brimming with pleasure or chewed up in pain. Which made me think of Teddy. Pain and something else. The nine of Hearts, that card for dreams come true. A card freshly peeled off a well-worn deck, a card for Teddy, to get him out of that place wherever he was, to get him out alive.

Not long after, I sat eating breakfast in the dining car, reading the day-old Vancouver newspaper. A new law was coming into effect, to limit the froth on beer glasses to half an inch. There were rules for everything, I thought, wondering how the skinny froth would affect Max's fortune telling. As we neared the city, I finished my tea and looked out the window at the rain. I pictured Dermot measuring the froth on a glass of beer. When the train reached the station, I decided I would go down to Gastown.

On the platform, the newsboys were shouting something about a bomb. I didn't know what they meant until I bought a *Sun*. The Americans had dropped a bomb on Hiroshima. I read the newspaper without moving from the platform and when I'd finished, I looked past the train to the mountains, trying to remember which direction I'd been heading in. The ringing in my ears was worse than ever.

9

At the end of August, I was about to sit down for dinner at Harold Avison's house when my mother said, "We've received a telegram."

I was about to pull out my chair, but I stopped, my hands frozen to the wooden chair back. There were only two kinds of telegrams.

"Yes," said Harold, "Young Ted is coming home."

I inhaled, as if I'd forgotten to breathe. My mother took the lid off the casserole and sat down across from me.

I tried to sit down calmly but my limbs wouldn't fold properly, I gripped the edge of the table. "Why didn't you tell me when I first walked in?"

My mother crossed her hands. "You were late. Another minute, we were going to sit down without you."

Harold began a rapid grace, throwing in some thanksgiving for good measure.

Teddy was alive. After all of this. He had survived the internment camp. The chicken casserole in the middle of the table smelled of cream and nutmeg and I swallowed hard against a sudden nausea.

"When?" I said, as soon as Harold finished praying. I should have said, I knew Teddy was alive, all this time, I knew he'd come home. But I had tried very hard not to think about where he was, only that he wasn't here. How that had been hard enough to hold onto.

"October," said Harold. "They're sending a ship. When he arrives, young Ted will stay here. Until he's on his feet and he's gotten himself established." Established as what, Harold didn't specify.

I moved the chicken around on my plate and I don't know how I got through to the end of dinner. Afterwards, I found an indifferent game that kept my head busy until I could get on a train. The weeks that followed, I was always in motion, I stopped in Vancouver only to change clothes. I felt Max's puzzled turtle eyes on me one evening as I ran down the boardinghouse stairs.

"I'm going to miss my train," I called to him, and I rushed through the rain.

But eventually Max managed to position himself between me and the staircase. He tilted his reptilian head to one side, trying to size me up with his heavy-lidded eyes. "Fortune treating you meanly, Missy? You sure are on the go."

I bought him a beer—the froth neatly measured by the Abbotsford bartender. I carried it across the lawn, through the Vancouver drizzle, and placed it on the ledge of his alcove. "My fortune's fine," I said.

He stretched his neck up to stare into my face. "Seems to me," he said, "fortune isn't the problem. It's yourself you're giving all kinds of trouble to." With his crippled hands, he torturously brought the beer over to his mouth and took a slurp.

"I didn't—" but I stopped myself before I said anything rude to Max. He was right, even if I hadn't asked for his opinion.

I needed the landscape moving past me outside the window because I couldn't spend six weeks standing still, waiting for a ship to come in. I sat on those trains, playing cards, knowing it was not my ship coming in. I thought if I wasn't in Vancouver, I wouldn't be plagued with thinking about him. Vancouver to Calgary, to Edmonton, to Saskatoon, down to Regina, back through the States, to Seattle, up into the mountains again.

Trains carrying returning troops crossed in front of us on the rails, delaying my regular routes. I wondered what the soldiers glimpsed from their converted boxcars, what they saw of us in our first class coaches, in our clean clothes. Soldiers who needed jobs, and new houses to live in, and wives and children to go with their new homes. I wondered if Teddy remembered what he'd said in Lethbridge; I knew the idea of marrying me was only a passing whim. A good thing he hadn't—he'd have to come back and figure out what to do with me. Now he could come back and start afresh, a clean slate entirely.

The *Prince Robert* docked at Victoria, while everyone on the mainland held their breath. And a ferry brought the men across from Vancouver Island, to our very own downtown. I went to meet the ferry. Of course I did. The dock was terrifying, solid with people, so crowded you couldn't see where the land stopped and the water began. The whole rain-streaked downtown reeked of fear and hope, such a roll of the dice—we were all waiting for the boat to come in and tell us our fortune. I stood as far away from the gangplank as

I could. Being small is no advantage in a crowd; so many people all crushed together, I might be trampled before I ever managed to find Teddy.

I'd worn my highest heels, and I was wearing a new dress, fawn grey with red dots through it, and a red hat. It was a good way to welcome someone home, wasn't it, wearing a stylish hat with a turned-up brim? I tried not to think about how he might look, tried not to hope for anything. Everyone on the dock was surely having the same struggle. Who would he be, now? Three years ago, he had kissed me in that hotel in Lethbridge and told me to get on with my playing. I'd taken his advice.

The rain subsided to drizzle. We held our breath in a stench of wet wool and anticipation, people pushing forward to see if the boat had finally docked, was it tied yet, were the men on deck recognizable? A band played, brassy and out of key, but the crowd, murmuring, nearly covered the music. I climbed onto the square marble base of a pillar outside the Port Authority building, and I could just see the boat's gangplank was being properly anchored to the dock. The woman nearest me started to cry; the boy clutching her knees began to keen but she took no notice, enough tears running down her face to flood the downtown. I held my breath and didn't cry, I strained to see across the crowd, scanning the faces of soldiers as they disembarked, as they limped or were carried or managed to rush on their own legs down the gangplank into the arms of their women.

Mothers and wives surged like a solid mass back and forth across the gangplank, colourful hats now mingling with green army caps and shorn heads and bandages. All those men in uniform, some of them walking, some of them in casts, some on stretchers. Most looked skeletal. Most were crying, from happiness or another emotion. And then someone lifted me down from the base of the pillar and Teddy was back. I didn't untangle myself from his arms until he had pushed us through the crowd. Street traffic was stopped for the occasion, and families and soldiers spilled out in all directions into the city, ignoring the rain.

Teddy stood in the drizzle as if waking up. He was thin and bloated at the same time—his arms were sharper, his shoulders hard-edged, but his face was puffy, his nose sunburned. There was something like a razor in the way he moved his head, first staring at the buildings and then lowering his eyes to see the streets, how crowded with people. I put my hand on his shoulder, to make sure he was real. He was alive wasn't he? That was good enough.

"It's still here," he said.

"The city?"

He looked across the water, at the mountains just visible through the low November cloud. Did he think the Lions might have disappeared? He glanced down at me and stared for a moment, as if the cloud were behind his eyes. "Where are we going?"

"My mother's. Harold Avison's house."

"Christ everything is the same. Thank God."

"Almost," I said quietly.

"I didn't know I'd be back." He stood there, as if he didn't know which way he should walk. I couldn't expect him to notice my hat, under the circumstances. I took his hand awkwardly, and began walking up the hill, walking alongside all the other couples and mothers and sons and families, all caught in their own homecomings. At the end of the street, the traffic wasn't blocked anymore and we waited for a streetcar to take us over the bridge. Transit was all free that day, in honour of the troops; we crowded on with everyone else. Teddy looked out the window and kept repeating, "That's there... look, the yellow house is still there. And the hotel. And the bank there and the...." He smiled for an instant, but all I recognized in his expression was his broken eyetooth, sheared off in a fight so long ago. He let go of my hand and put his palm against the rain-speckled glass.

Harold's house looked especially neat and white, even in the grey rain; my mother had put up new lace curtains at each window. There was a pine tree on one side of the porch, and the lawn was immaculately mown, an unearthly bright green from the months of rain. Coming there with Teddy, the house seemed like a haven, exactly the hearth soldiers were supposed to long for.

We turned down the path and Harold swung open the front door. He said, "Welcome home, Theodore," in a prepared hearty way, as if he and Teddy really were related in some way or another. Teddy shook his hand. In the living room, my mother threw her arms around Teddy and kissed him.

"It's good to be back," he said.

Thin as he was, Teddy seemed too big for the house, a visitor in boots walking through a doll display. I waited for something to get broken, though he moved so carefully, as if his limbs hurt. Maybe it was his skin that made touching anything painful, even putting the soles of his feet on the ground. I think the living room filled with fog, the dining room too—there's no other explanation for the way we sat, over dinner, not talking about the war, as if we could pretend it hadn't happened. Teddy talked about things we'd done as kids. Describing to Harold how the front veranda on Pender Street leaked and how my mother had made him fix it, how he'd trapped rabbits in the Endowment Lands, how he'd learned to swim in False Creek, dodging the pulp mill's logging rafts, how the hallways of the Hotel Vancouver were perfect for hide and seek. He didn't mention Mary Ellen. I stared at him, trying to see the boy who had done all those things, trying to see him.

An electricity defined his edges, where he touched the table or the silverware, the way he moved his head. When he met my gaze, his eyes were blank dark pools. I couldn't think of any stories to add to Teddy's. He was the prodigal son, that was his role at dinner, even though he wasn't my mother's son, and what's more how could he be a prodigal when he didn't talk about where he'd been.

My mother kept saying, "It's very good to see you, Teddy."

He picked at his food. I leapt up to clear the roast chicken from the table. I brought out the trifle and set the dessert dishes. At least walking back and forth from the kitchen, I could surreptitiously study Teddy. It was really him—I don't mean he'd been replaced, impersonated. I just mean he was so different, not only that his spark of live beauty was drained from him—no wonder, that was no surprise. No, I'm not explaining this properly. Teddy formed a barrier in the room, he wasn't entirely there—that's not right. I mean the opposite: he was there, and nothing else was quite as real, as brutally present, as much of a cut through the air, as he was. If I had a house of my own, he could have gone there, we wouldn't have been at that table. Except I did not want a house of my own.

I cleared away the dessert, and my mother and I did the dishes, cautious not to clatter any of the pots or cutlery. I wanted no sudden noises. Teddy and Harold talked of who knows what in the living room, I could hear the radio, on briefly, then off again.

"He looks better than expected," said my mother, listening to his footsteps as he took his bag upstairs. I dried and put away the plates, counted the stack of clean dishes in the cupboard—seven salad plates, eight dessert plates. I wondered what had happened to the missing salad plate. I was counting things again, a bad sign. I was never going to be able to ask Teddy what had happened over there—hadn't Adam evaded the same question? I counted the dinner plates because I couldn't count the ghosts Teddy was carrying.

He came back down the stairs, heavy and delicate treads, and stood in the kitchen doorway. "You still livin' downtown?"

I nodded.

"I'll walk you back."

"You're surely too tired, Teddy. You should rest," said my mother, taking his arm and leading him into the living room as if he were an invalid.

"No, I'm...."

"Boy's probably restless, just off a boat and who knows what," said Harold, and I was grateful. I went to get my hat, trying to believe that Teddy would be fine here, it would be good for him to be looked after—my mother adored him and Harold would be a good influence. I kissed my mother formally as I always did, I shook Harold's hand, and I left the house with Mary Ellen's son.

Teddy strode silently through the drizzle and I tried to keep up with him. He turned at Burrard. The view of the mountains was entirely clouded in and suddenly, I don't know why then and not before, I stopped and put my arms around him. I didn't know I had started to cry until he said, "Shush, Mill. Shhh." But then he just let me cry, not asking what I was crying for—a good thing, since I wasn't sure if I was crying for him or selfishly, for myself, because I didn't know what to do. He rubbed my shaking shoulders distantly, until I realized I was only standing there, no longer crying, my face against the regulation green shirt that did not smell like him, not as I remembered. Every man must have been given a new uniform, a clean shirt as a reward for having survived.

"Don't you wish you'd married me when you had the chance? We could be home havin' a big scene about it."

"What?"

Teddy took me roughly by the shoulders and held me at arm's length. He searched my face, but I wasn't sure what he was looking for. He seemed so much the same and so completely different from the person he'd been before.

"Well that's the truth, isn't it? The guys're home findin' out their girls have screwed them around and their pals are dead and no one missed them anyways."

I tried to shift away from him but his grip was too strong. He stared through me, the misty rain falling between us like a veil. I put my hand against his chest; I had no answer to the terrible things he said.

He relaxed his arms but kept hold of my shoulders. "Is there a game tonight?"

"What?" I didn't think I had heard him correctly.

"Is there a game?" he repeated.

"A card game?"

"Yeah."

"No, of course I'm not going to a game."

He let go of my shoulders. "Not one of yours. A game for me, Mill. I'm not going to sleep. My dreams'll have me screamin' to wake the dead. I can't very well lie awake in that blue wallpapered room for twelve hours. I can't. I'm goin' on to Ontario, there's a... anyways, while I'm here, it's good to be at Harold's house. It's damn straight of him, but...."

"You've got to be kidding."

Teddy turned and walked away, fast. I chased after him.

When I was back at his side, he said, "I can't prowl around their house and I won't lie there alone all night. And I'm not walkin' around with you, cryin'. I want a game. I'll find one myself."

"You should get some sleep." He wasn't making any sense. "Go back to Harold's house and just go to bed, rest for a while. You'll feel...."

"Not likely."

"Well... we'll go for a drink or something, we'll...."

"I don't want to talk about this," he said, still walking. I was falling forward to keep up with him through the wet streets below Harold's house. So many of the houses lit up, I wondered how many other girls had been waiting for someone, for a moment this strange. The drizzle changed to a definite rain.

"I can't believe you only got home and...."

"You can believe anything you want. I don't care."

I didn't want to leave him alone, he seemed dangerous, I mean the way a bomb might be, a wrong touch and anything might happen. I fell back on safe ground, the calmest place I could think of. "We'll go to Dermot's." Yes, that backroom at McMann's bar, the safest place I could think of.

"You're still there? Christ."

"Only sometimes."

There was a streetcar on the corner and Teddy stepped on without even glancing at me. As we went downtown, Teddy watched the view as if it were a film reel, while I watched him. When we were close to Gastown, I pulled the cord for the stop. Getting off, he stumbled on the steps and caught himself against my shoulder. I don't think I'd ever seen him be clumsy before. It was nothing, that small stumble, but it worried me more than anything he'd said. Walking beside him, I felt his clothes at the far edges of my fingers, damp wool uniform grazing my fingers as we walked. I worried he'd stumble again.

We paused in the street outside Dermot's. A few patrons in various states of inebriation slumped at the bar, a couple of demobbed men drank at a table. I couldn't see Dermot. "We'll go around, I never go in through the bar," I explained, leading Teddy around the building, hoping maybe he'd change his mind and we could go somewhere else. But he walked ahead of me down the alley and held the door for me. In the empty backroom, I banged on the dividing door leading to the bar, hoping that Dermot would hear, wherever he was. Sure enough, he opened the door.

"Millard. What are you doing here?"

"That's no way to say hello."

"I thought you'd be...." He paused, looking past me to where Teddy was standing. "Ahern. Welcome home, good to see you." He clapped Teddy on the shoulder. "Very good to see you. Quiet night, here, though I expect Kevin and the boys in a bit."

"A drink would be fine in the meantime," said Teddy.

Dermot looked at him, and I wondered what the barman was thinking, if he was appalled I'd brought Teddy here. I wished I could explain, say it wasn't my idea, but Dermot said, "I wouldn't mind sitting down with you. Nothing much happening that I need to keep too close an eye on." He walked back through to the bar, leaving the door open. I watched him choose two short glasses and pour a healthy dose of Jameson's whiskey into each of them. Into one of the glasses, he added some water. When he came back to us, he gave the unwatered drink to Teddy, clinked glasses with him and nodded to me before drinking. "Good to see you, boy. Welcome home. You want a cup of tea, Millard?"

I shook my head and the three of us sat in silence. Teddy and Dermot seemed quite comfortable without conversation, and every question I wanted to ask was impossible to express. I ran my fingers gently along the edge of the oilskin on the table, counting the tacks that held it down. Before Teddy had even swigged back all his whiskey, Kevin showed up—he could play nights now, his wife was dead. She took sick when their son was killed in France, passed on a few months after that dreaded telegram appeared at their door. Cards were one of the few things Kevin had left; they were no kinder to him than before, but at least his losses at the table were a distraction from his life's real losses.

Soon, another two men showed up to play and they didn't blink at Teddy's being there, they probably didn't know him. Kevin did, surely, but said nothing about it—maybe he had forgotten, one more detail drowned out by other sad facts tumbling through his memory. When Dermot went back to the bar, I shuffled the deck and dealt us each a card. We played high-low, Kevin's choice.

I don't know how Teddy acquired the money in his pocket that night; there must have been dice onboard the boat that brought him home, that was all I could think of. He hadn't learned to listen to cards any better than before—I should have refused to bring him to a game, I should have insisted we go out dancing or to a bar or for a walk—anything at all other than this. I watched him, trying to find the boy he'd been; even the way he moved his hands was different. All of this in my head as I got a two-Ace hand, Spades and Hearts, unbeatable, a high hand that also played well low.

I silently willed Teddy to throw in the towel. *Fold the hand, darn it, just stop playing at this.* I couldn't bear to look at my own hand, knowing I would win, while he bet, while he stayed in the game, holding on. He didn't fold, no matter how much I stared meaningfully at him; he bet on Fourth Street, continued to Fifth. When I took the pot, I realized that I should have folded, at least I wouldn't have beaten him. He had been away more than three years. I could hardly bear to deal the next round.

After another loss, Teddy leaned towards me. "Don't get up, sugar. You're solid as ever. See you round." I dropped the cards in my hands and stood, my feet sinking into the treacle that replaced the floor. Teddy swung the door closed behind him and by the time I had laboriously made my way to the door and opened it, he was gone. I might have sunk to my knees. Perhaps he went to drink somewhere far away from me, or he went to find another game, one where the cards weren't only mine. I tried to believe everything was alright—he was alive, that's what mattered, he was in Vancouver, and the war was over, finished with, but it didn't help. I was still standing, and I knew I had to turn and go back to the table. I couldn't have cared less what cards I got.

When the game had finished and Kevin had tottered home, slightly more to the good than usual, Dermot came in and counted the take. But when he'd pushed my share towards me, he went into the bar and brought back two clean glasses with the bottle of whiskey. He set one in front of each of us, and pushed the water jug towards me. He poured a tot of whiskey into each glass, though ordinarily he never gave me liquor.

"Health," he said, holding the glass out as if for a toast. I picked up my glass and smelled the whiskey, then touched the edge of my glass to his. I tentatively tried the drink, but the first sip made me cough. I poured some water into my glass.

Dermot waited until I set the jug back on the table. "An' why are you here, tonight, Millard? You shouldn't be here tonight of all nights."

I pushed the whiskey glass back and forth along the oilskin tablecloth, watching the amber drink slosh back and forth.

Dermot coughed, as if I weren't paying enough attention. "The *Prince Robert* getting in, why come here with Ahern? Much as it's good to see him back in one piece, an' all."

"It wasn't my idea." The heavy foot of the glass contained a bubble, visible through the whiskey and water. The drink now had a pale sheen, like tea made on the prairies with hard well water. Looking through the bubble in the glass, I stared at the oilcloth. This table where I'd played with so many different kinds of fortune, where I'd learned to read cards along with men's faces—I wondered if Dermot could read me so easily. "He's only just back," I said.

"An' you here?"

"He's got a job lined up in Ontario somewhere."

Dermot was silent for a long time. What was I supposed to say? He downed his whiskey and set the glass beside the pack of cards on the table. "I'm thinking of leaving the business."

"What?"

"The bar. It's a good time to sell, all the boys coming home. One of them will want to run a bar. And I'm...."

"You can't retire." Teddy back, Dermot retiring—fortune was having a joke at my expense.

Dermot shook his head. "I want to move back to the hills, Millard. I'm tired of Gastown an' all. I could open something in Kamloops maybe. I like it up there. The world's going to change with the war over. The city'll change. You watch. I don't want to sit through another turn o' the wheel." He poured himself a fresh tot of whiskey and stared at it.

One of the few remaining patrons banged his fist on the bar. Dermot groaned, but he went and served the guy another beer, carefully swiping off the top foam with a wooden ladle. I wondered if Teddy was drinking beer, wondered what he might smooth out of himself by drinking, if it would help more than the cards. More than I could help. Maybe he had returned to Harold Avison's house. Maybe he was sleeping. I had a stern sip of the whiskey and it didn't help at all. I wondered when Teddy was leaving, if I would see him before he went. Fortune doesn't favour the heart. I leaned forward and picked up the deck of cards on the table, shuffled and fanned them, face down. When Dermot sat down opposite me again, I offered him the cards. He took one, looked at it, and hid it back in the fan. I shuffled and turned the cards slowly over until I reached the five of Diamonds.

"Success in business," I said. "Maybe you should sell." I shuffled the card back into the pack as he took another sip of his whiskey.

"You're like me, Millard," he said, turning the glass around in his hand. "There's no point trying to be what you're not. Learned that a long while back. You can work 'round to being what you're good at, best thing to do. Don't get yourself burdened down with something you don't really want. Isn't fair."

He meant someone, not something. Isn't fair to whom, I thought, and I put the pack of cards down between us. Dermot picked up the deck with his big hands, shuffled the cards easily and fanned them again. I pulled out a middle card and tossed it lightly onto the oilcloth. The four of Clubs shone up at us.

"Choices to be made, Millard," he said. "You should go on home."

The four of Clubs is a disaster card, he surely knew as well as I did. It means change for the worse, betrayal and lies. He gathered up the cards and shuffled them again. "Another card?"

I shook my head and stood up.

"Go on with you then," said Dermot. "Nothing a person can do to figure things out for 'nother person, Millard. Not the cards, neither."

His beard was more grey than black now, a grizzled Irish bear—maybe it was the four of Clubs, or Teddy being back, made me look more closely at everything familiar. The alley was slippery with rain and at the corner of Water Street, I hailed a cab. I wondered where Teddy had gotten to, just back in his hometown after God knows what nightmares. I closed my eyes so I wouldn't search the wet streets for a glimpse of him.

10

Guilt is a tricky thing. A person can't win money with cards and worry too much about the loser's feelings. Guilt was never a natural part of my makeup. But after that night at Dermot's, I stayed away from Teddy until he left. Whatever he had seen, whatever had taken the shine from his eyes, I was only going to make it worse. I stood in the lobby of the Sylvia Hotel and telephoned my mother.

"I won't be able to come for dinner," I said. "Could you tell Teddy...."

She interrupted me. "The poor man, back from hell he is, and you galli-vanting all over."

"I'm not galli...."

"You could at least be a better influence. I'm ashamed of you, leading him into...."

"Mother, before the war, Teddy wasn't exactly a paragon of...."

"Don't you dare say anything about Mary Ellen's boy."

Which is the closest she ever came to mentioning Mary Ellen at all. I said, "Tell him good luck, when he goes." Good luck. I hoped luck would serve him better than it had in the past.

I wasn't particularly interested in my life right then. The only time I felt honestly alive was at the table; the rest of the days merely passed by. I dressed, and ate, and spoke to the few people I knew. I ran into Vera on the street and she showed off a beautiful sapphire engagement ring. "Do you know Adam? He grew up on your street," she said.

"He's a wonderful man." I congratulated her and gave her a kiss. We met for lunch, once or twice; I couldn't tell her anything much about my games, but her company was a thin salve for my loneliness. In the spring, Max said there was a phone message for me, from a man in Ontario. His name—Max searched his pockets awkwardly—"I wrote it down," he said sadly.

"It's alright. It's better if you lose the message."

"You're a difficult one, aren't you?" he said, using his forearm to slide his beer closer. "Not sure what you're wanting, is that it?"

"No," I told him. "I know what I want."

Max coughed. "A bad influence, is he?"

I thought of Adam and Vera, how she had unknowingly called me a hooligan; I was the bad influence, not the other way round.

"You ever want me to do you a fortune, let me know," Max murmured.

I shook my head. I hoped Teddy was happy, out there wherever he was. I was afraid for him, afraid of the blankness in his eyes.

In September, an envelope arrived and Max insisted I open it in front of him. "Because if I don't, you'll just put it into a drawer and pretend you've forgotten it. No point doing that, ignoring fortune."

"It's not fortune." But I took the envelope—there was a curious bump in it. I tore along the edge and a blue stone rolled out into my hand, rough and unpolished. Blue like marble, like the sea. There was only a short note inside, "Home at Christmas. This is a Princess Sodalite." He hadn't bothered to sign the note, though there was a cross at the bottom of the scrap of paper—hard to say if it was a "t" for his name or the "x" of a kiss. His writing was as crooked as ever.

Max stared at the rough blue pebble in my hand. "And that is?"

"Sodalite," I said, as if I knew. "I don't think it's useful for anything."

"Might be lucky."

"Probably not." I set the pebble on the ledge, beside Max's beer.

No wonder I spent those next months far from Vancouver. Mostly I was in Calgary, playing a series of games with high-strung ex-military men—as long as I wasn't playing against Teddy, I didn't mind the demobbed guys. They were fair enough targets. Having survived the war, they knew exactly what they were gambling with, which made the game more interesting. Unfortunately some of the ones who were good at cards had also gotten themselves addicted to junk, which made them reckless at the table—something I took advantage of, I admit. They'd been home for at least a year or more, but I don't think they were any closer to putting down the things they'd seen.

I didn't compare Teddy with the junkies at that table—they were probably upright kids who'd been on a battlefield, and who was I to say what they needed to get them through what remained of their lives? Teddy had never been an upright kid, and I had no idea what was getting him through his days. I wasn't exactly looking forward to seeing him at Christmas dinner with my mother and Harold Avison, but I knew he would be there.

In Calgary, the hotel where we played was right above the train tracks; the coiling screech of the wheels ground beneath my windows whenever I went upstairs to sleep. When I finally checked out, one of my demobbed fish was waiting for me, loitering in the lobby.

"Miss Lacouvy." He twitched only a little as he spoke. "I wish I had better luck. I want to compliment you. Live up to your reputation, you do."

"My reputation? Oh dear."

He smiled. He wasn't a mean-looking man, strung out though he was. "Heard about you from Sam Lazar."

"I have great respect for Mr. Lazar."

"Bet you do. Was expecting to see him this evening at Banff. Thanks to you, I won't be making it."

"Is there a game?"

"What I thought is I might put a bee in your ear. Lazar playing, a couple of others, fatter wallets than I have, I can tell you that."

"Thank you."

He shrugged. "I'll see you another time, want to make sure your purse is good and healthy when I get back to it."

I could stop at Banff on my route home, play for a couple of days and still arrive back at Harold Avison's house in time for Christmas dinner. Too tempting to pass up, and more than likely One Shot would be running the Banff game. I telephoned him, straight from the Palisades lobby. His wife answered. I listened to her household, not so far away—static on the line, but I imagined her clicking heels, a shout for her husband, and somewhere in the house, the son they doted on. The kid had made an honest man of One Shot—I mean, his son's skiing accident had led him to the Lord. Didn't mean he didn't deal poker anymore, just meant he dealt honest, which was why I liked him. Then the receiver clanged and he was on the line, out of breath.

"Yeah?"

"It's Millard Lacouvy. Hear you're setting up a game with Mr. Lazar."

"How're you doing, Millard? Been a while."

"Is there a seat at the table for me?"

I heard him snort on the other end of the line. "Always a seat for you, Millard. Always."

"Starts Friday?"

"Yeah, back of the golf club. I'll leave you a note at the Springs. You'll be at the Springs?"

"Of course."

"See you then, Millard."

The train going up to Banff was delayed because of a bear on the tracks. I wondered what Teddy was doing. I tried to imagine him working at a job—doing what, I couldn't imagine. Perhaps Harold Avison had some useful advice for him, could steer him into, oh Lord, not a court job, that would never work. I put my head back against the seat and tried to think about anything other than how Teddy used to be and how he might be now.

Skiers and sightseers crowded the Banff train station, but I quickly spotted the chauffeur waiting for guests of the Springs. I shared the ride with a couple dressed entirely in fur, complete with raccoon hats. The hotel had a doorman wearing enough gold frogtags on his cloak to wait upon the Queen. But as must happen occasionally for even the Queen, my room wasn't ready. I went to the restaurant, a carved wood and stone mezzanine over the lobby with huge picture windows giving out onto mountains. I ordered a tea, which didn't really seem grand enough for the view. The Rockies were worryingly jagged, snow covering the uppermost parts of them, bare vertical stone below, sheered off and black. I didn't like the mountains, looming so close like that, so I moved to the opposite chair and put my back to the window. In changing seats, I could watch the lobby. A wide man in a camelhair coat came into my line of vision. He seemed not exactly familiar, but something about him bothered me. I drank a bit more of my tea, waiting to see his face, but he didn't turn in my direction. I had a definite feeling I didn't like him.

The game was in a log cabin overlooking the snowed-in golf course. Not a rustic shack—this was the Springs, and their version of a cabin had nothing in common with the tumbled-together houses of the Interior, not at all a rough slammed-together house like the one I'd been born in. At Banff, all was polished and wood-paneled. When I stepped into the entrance hall, I stood on a luxurious Persian rug to stamp my shoes clean of snow.

"Make sure the door's latched, sometimes get bears right up on the porch. Ya don't get that in Vancouver now do ya?" said One Shot, who'd gotten even fatter since I'd last seen him.

"If the men play badly, I'll invite the bears in for a game."

He laughed, his jowls jiggling. "Come on in, the gents are here already. Good of you to make a grand late entrance, eh?"

I wasn't late, I was exactly on the minute of eight o'clock. The curtains were drawn in the main room, a jolly fire was going in the hearth, and the air was already filling with cigar smoke. Sam Lazar turned from the fire as we came in.

"Miss Lacouvy! Now this is a pleasure. Gordon Hamovic, Vince Jones, Henry Klesser, do you know...."

They all wore expensive pullovers and sports trousers except for Lazar, who was in one of his usual striped suits. He waved a hand towards the door. "Avison'll be back in a minute."

"Avison?" I said.

The door on the far side of the room opened; it was the wide-shouldered man in the camelhair coat. He had one ruined ear, and a face pitted with acne scars. His glare was an all-too-familiar beady stare—the son of Harold Avison's brother. The ruined ear, that was Teddy's handiwork. Teddy, and the radiator.

"Mr. Gerald Avison," said our fat host, going forward, "this is...."

Avison ignored him, too busy giving me the once-over.

"Gerry," I said, "how nice to see you again."

"Who the hell are you?"

Lazar cleared his throat with a warning growl. "Where are your manners, Avison? Miss Lacouvy is a friend of mine."

One Shot made a very slight and rather apologetic little bow to the assembled company and went out to fetch the cards.

"Having a drink, Avison?" said Klesser, holding out a bottle of rye.

The grown-up nasty child said, "Oh yeah, the dwarf. You grew. Didn't recognize you."

I smiled as charmingly as I could, though I had trouble believing he hadn't recognized me. There was something specifically malevolent in his eyes. "Don't we all grow up," I said. "You're looking well."

Lazar caught my eye, as if he was trying to warn me of something, while Klesser poured me a drink from the seltzer bottle, added a few ice cubes.

"Shall we get down to...." One Shot came back with a bowling bag filled with packs of cards. We checked them for tampering, okay'd them, and he broke the first pack open.

"Five stud's my chosen game," said Lazar. "That acceptable to everyone?"

Once that was established, we got down to poker. In the second hand, I raised on a very nice pair of Aces, Clubs and Spades. Lazar folded. The other men followed suit, thinking perhaps that Lazar knew me and might know whether I was bluffing or not. But Avison didn't go for that line of reasoning. He wanted me out of his men's club and he bluffed right back at me, thinking that his aggressive playing would scare me off. He doubled the pot and squinted more fiercely when I met his raise. When I had won the hand, I made sure he saw my cards, to see I wasn't bluffing. So that in the rounds that followed, though I bluffed through most of them, Avison was so angry with me that he met every raise as the rounds piled up, trying to put me in my place, holding in with weak cards that I demolished. He was the kind of man who believed there was only one place for a little woman, and it was certainly not at his poker game in the lodge below the Banff Springs Hotel.

I wondered how he'd gotten out of serving; it seemed obvious he hadn't wasted a second of his life in uniform—he'd have been such perfect cannon fodder, too. Instead, Teddy had nightmares, while Avison gave people bad dreams. I closed my eyes to clear my head. Suddenly I had a strong personal goal. I wanted to enjoy myself, oh, more than that, let me be honest—I wanted revenge on the bully of my childhood, even though it was an old hurt. I watched every card, every move, hunting every detail about his game.

The next round, he tried to convince the table that he had a royal flush, which I knew wasn't true. The look he gave me when I raised and called him was a look of pure hatred. The cards seemed to dislike Avison as much as I did, for I pulled in high cards beautifully. I caught Avison glaring at me repeatedly. "Raise," he said, putting in more money.

Lazar quit early, saying he never played cards on the Sabbath. I'd never heard him pull out that excuse before. He dozed on the couch near the fire, so he was there when I closed Avison out at seven-thirty on Sunday morning. One Shot congratulated everyone, but Avison pushed away from the table in silent fury and stomped out without closing either of the doors. A gust of snow blew into the room as he left.

Lazar insisted on having his chauffeur drive me back to the Banff Springs. We were too exhausted to make small talk, but as the car pulled up at the Springs, he said, "I am always pleased to play across from you, Miss Lacouvy. I hope to see you again soon."

"I would like that," I said.

As I got out of the car, Lazar added, "I might advise you to watch your back, my dear. In this town, such as it is."

I wasn't sure what he meant, but before I could ask, he signaled the chauffeur and they drove away.

When the hotel's car dropped me at the station, there was already a crowd of people outside, wrestling with their bags, calling for porters, shoving to get to the platform. I had reserved a sleeping compartment for myself—the cards and I both deserved a holiday, and I planned to sleep all the way to Vancouver. I wasn't in any great hurry to get onto the train, so I crossed the street to buy a package of cigarettes. The shop had a gift shelf of delicately woven wool scarves and I chose two for my mother—it was Christmas, after all. Holding my purchases, I wove through the crowd to reach my wagonette.

On the wide seat, I set my alligator bag with most of my winnings. I stayed on my feet and looked out the window—I had a compartment facing away from the station. Beyond the window, rows of freight trains were stacked with tree trunks much too big to be called mere logs. The mountains glowered fiercely behind. I opened the window a smidgen, to freshen the air in my little room. I found my lighter in my purse and lit a cigarette, leaning my forehead against the metal window frame. Then I heard the metal-lined door of my compartment swing closed. I spun around.

A small-headed, flat-nosed man I didn't know stood there. If he hadn't been in my private compartment, he'd have been a very nondescript kind of man in a navy coat, but here, he took up too much room. His body was too big for his close-set eyes.

"Are you looking for someone?"

"Don't be a dope."

I pressed my back against the window frame, my purse looped over my arm. I didn't want to look at my alligator bag.

"We can do this two ways," he said. "You can give me what I want...."

"You're looking for someone else," I said. "I don't know you."

"Or I can make you very sorry, and then you'll give me what I want."

"I really think you're mistaken." I wondered if anyone would hear me if I called out. There was such a crowd in the station, the noise of luggage being loaded, but I cleared my throat, thinking that I would scream as he took a step closer. I could smell the grease he'd slicked into what there was of his hair.

Before I could make any sound, he said, "I don't like your attitude." He put out a hand and though I shied to the side, he caught me by the throat, the way you'd throttle a cat, if you were going to do such a thing. I coughed and hit at his arm with my lit cigarette. With just the one hand, he squeezed a little bit, pressing my head back against the edge of the window. I couldn't breathe. I kicked my knee up, to try to catch his crotch, but I missed.

"You want to play games?" he said. "Good."

He brought his flattened face very close to mine, the pores of his skin all I could see. I tried to push against the bulk of him. I was desperate for air, my arms and legs jerking like a marionette's, up, down. Somehow I got my purse jammed behind my body, between my back and the wall, and I left my wrist there, even as my hand bent backward. He leaned back and smiled, loosened his grip on my neck for an instant, long enough to pull me forward and throw me back against the wall, near the little sink. I gurgled, trying to shout, or even reason with him. With one hand he grabbed all the fabric of my skirt, the other hand squeezing my neck more and more tightly. A whistle blew as a bright redness filled my eyes. He was smiling, the ugly man, smiling, such pleasure in his face as he pulled my head forward by the neck and banged my skull against the corner of the wall. Then there was nothing but bright red light.

When I opened my eyes, I was on the floor and there was a tramcar wedged into my head. I tried moving my arms, to convince the tram driver to back up and give me some air, stop running me over. Then I realized it wasn't a tramcar; it was just the metal below the train seat, where I had fallen. There was a horrible pain around my neck, which meant my head was still attached. I pushed myself up, but my left wrist sank under my weight. I gasped and feebly wiggled a finger, then tried to bend my wrist. The pain was searing. I sat on the floor of my train compartment. There was another whistle—the sound that had brought me back to the land of the living. The train was leaving. I blinked my eyes. The floor was patterned with blue roses and they were rolling off the carpet and into my head, down my throat, making me gag. I staggered upright and spat, coughing, into the sink. I wiped my lips with my hand, my wrist throbbing as I turned away from the mirror. My alligator bag was gone. A torn brown paper lay on the seat, and when I moved it, the two scarves I had bought for my mother unfurled onto the floor, pretty blue fluttering things. I leaned down to pick them up and saw my purse, underneath the seat—it had fallen, unnoticed, the purse behind me and then rolling out of sight. The man hadn't bothered with it.

I scrambled through the contents and found the velour pouch of my compact case—fifty dimes. Five thousand dollars, barely a quarter of my earnings from two marvellously successful weeks of work. Lucky to have even that. I jammed the compact case back into my purse. The train lurched and I staggered into the corridor. The porter was a man named Harry, I remembered him from previous trips; I called his name as loudly as I could.

He came down the corridor from the furthest bedroom compartment. "Here, Miss."

"A man," I said, "did you see...." At the end of the hall, a woman passenger stood at the open door, staring at me. Harry reached me just as I was pushing the window down, but we were only in time to see the end of the platform, the parking lot. At the end of the lot, a black sedan was parked so its owner could watch us leave. The car had plates from British Columbia and the back windows were rolled down. There was a movement in the back seat, the sleeve of a camelhair coat appeared at the window—as if Avison were raising his hand to wave at the train. I knew absolutely that it was him, I don't know where my conviction came from, but I banged my injured wrist on the window frame and yelped in pain. Then the platform was gone, the train picked up speed, and we went over the river, already on our way.

I leaned my forehead against the window frame, cold air surging in—I tried not to cry. Harry put a hand on my shoulder. "I'll get you some ice, you've got a bad mark on your neck, Miss."

He brought me ice, wrapped neatly in a white CP napkin. I held it dutifully against my bruised neck, but all too soon, the red marks weltered up like huge fingerprints. Later, they would turn yellowish blue and grey against my unporcelain complexion.

Harry shook his head. "What happened?"

I held the ice against my neck. "There was a... I was playing...."

Harry frowned in sympathy. "You win a game and he didn't like it? He steal from you?"

I was too ashamed to continue. "Do you have a bandage, I need to wrap up my wrist, I think it's sprained."

He wrapped my wrist as gently as any nurse, leaving an unsightly bungle of bandaging under the sleeve of my blouse. I thanked him.

"You go have a nice hot tea in the lounge and I'll make the room up for you. And when you come back, you lock that door and don't open it for nobody." He held out my jacket, which I'd taken off to ice my neck. He helped me on with it, getting the sleeve over my bound wrist, and he arranged the collar high so the welts on my neck didn't show too badly. "You look fine, Miss. If you need anything, you ring. Right away. I wish I'd known."

As I was leaving, he muttered how much he hated white men like that. It was kind of him not to mention foolish gambling women in the same equation. I had been stupid, naïve, thinking the train made my game inviolable, that no one would ever touch me. I made my way along to the train's dining lounge, my purse tucked under my damaged arm, opening the doors awkwardly with my good hand. I knew the man who'd attacked me wasn't anywhere on the train, I knew he had stepped off, holding my alligator bag, he had gotten what he wanted. But I crept down the narrow train corridor, afraid of meeting him, and when I reached the dining car, I chose a seat at the far end, right beside the bartender's galley. It was early in the day, but the bartender didn't question my choice when I ordered a whiskey.

"With ice?"

"And water. Lots of water, please."

"Headin' home for Christmas?"

I nodded; pain shot through my neck. I hoped the liquor would dull the pain and do something for my fear and humiliation, too, though maybe that was too much to hope. I stared at the drink. I tried not to waste time hating Avison, but I've never been much of a churchgoer—I would have happily driven the train right over his bones.

The whiskey burned my throat. Medicinal, I thought, thinking of Dermot pouring me a drink. A bit of pain isn't going to kill me. Oh, but as the train gained speed, the mountains unfurled outside the windows and their shadows were the colour of bruises. I stayed in my seat near the bar and sneered out at the scenery as if it were responsible for my fall, my loss. I rested my sore wrist on the little counter beside my drink. My winnings gone, and no one to care, no one to even notice—small wonder that, as we got closer to Vancouver and the rain started in, my mood became so bleak I couldn't even pretend to sit calmly in the bar. I had never understood my mother's dark moods, when we lived together in that little house on East Pender Street, but now I saw how bad choices might dwell in one's head until there was nothing but cloud. I retreated to my sleeping compartment, locked the door and lay down fully dressed on the bed.

The train drew slowly closer to the wet city where I'd grown up, where Teddy was from, where Avison was from. I wondered if anyone ever changed, was it possible? I wished I'd taken more heed of Sam Lazar's words, when he dropped me off at the hotel. I shivered against the train's narrow bed, knowing I should have looked out for myself better. The train rolled steadily along its track, paying no attention to my regrets, I could leave them wherever I liked along the line. As we got closer to the city, I curled at the foot of the bed and pushed up the blind, pressing my sore hand against the window. New houses came into view, growing up the sides of the mountains, a puzzle of residences and construction sites where there had once been a clear green line against the white cloud that came down from the mountain top. Near my hand, there was a trace of water along the sill. Rain smudged the view as we pulled into the station.

Jack of Spades, Queen of Diamonds: there was no time to go back to my boardinghouse before going to Harold Avison's for Christmas dinner. I stopped in the station washroom to powder my face; I took one of the finely-woven scarves I'd bought for my mother and tied it around my neck. Its cream and blue pattern hid the bruises that had blossomed across my throat. As for the bandaged wrist, I didn't know what I would say about it. I wasn't sure I would be able to lie, to pretend I was fine. I was not fine. I had no luggage, only my navy purse and a book for Harold, pretty pictures of the mountains. I found myself staring at my reflection in the station bathroom.

When she worked at the Hotel, my mother cooked the guests' Christmas eve meal, and their midnight mass dinner, followed by their Christmas morning breakfast, and their celebratory lunch, and their roast turkey dinner. No wonder she used to spend Boxing Day at home with a cloth over her eyes. So I celebrated the holiday upstairs with Mary Ellen and Teddy, where there was stew and some kind of fruitcake from a neighbour, and a stocking for each of us—an orange, a candy cane, a pair of socks, a book. I blinked hard, unsure if I was crying for Mary Ellen or for myself. I ran hot water over my hands and dried them carefully, trying not to move the muscles in my swollen wrist.

The taxi let me off and I winced, paying the driver. At the door, I paused— Harold had pasted a neat label below the doorbell, "Avison," it read. The brute was Harold's nephew—just the kind of detail Lady Luck finds amusing.

"Very nice jacket you have there, Millard," said my mother when she let me in. "Nice to see you looking ladylike."

I followed her back to the kitchen, moving deeper into the smell of Christmas dinner, roasting turkey and an underlay of sticky sweetness, the pudding simmering on the back burner. I felt suddenly sick; I sat down suddenly, holding onto the table with my good hand, and the nausea passed. Just pain from my neck, I told myself, that's all. My mother had her back to me, as she cut giblets into a pot on the stove.

"Teddy's found his own place now," she said. "He'll be here shortly. He helped put up the tree, did you notice it?"

"I'll go take a look." I rested my arms on the table and tried not to slump.

"He comes by nearly every day, since he got back. He's a good boy."

I tried to miss the implication that I wasn't nearly as good. "That's nice," I said. "Is he staying then, not going back to Ontario?"

She looked at me over her shoulder. "You have an ungenerous heart, Millard." She focused on the left sleeve of my jacket. "What did you do to yourself?"

"What do you mean?"

"Your wrist, what's wrong with it?"

"Oh," I said, shifting my hands off the table and into my lap. "I slipped, there was an icy patch near the boarding house this morning. I fell right into the street, most embarrassing."

My mother turned back to the giblets. "I don't want to know what trouble you've gotten yourself into. I won't have you bringing trouble to Harold's house."

"I'm only here for dinner," I protested. Merry Christmas, I thought. She'd been cooking all day; she was allowed a rant or two, all the better if she got it out of her system before we sat down to dinner. At least she valued food too highly to fling a chicken heart at me.

The doorbell sounded, releasing us. I followed my mother out to the hall, feeling dizzy. Shape up, I told myself sternly, so my neck hurts, so what? The man might have killed me, and here I am, alive. I had trouble taking my next breath. I settled onto the living room's ungiving sofa and concentrated on the Christmas tree, sparkling with crystal stars and icicles; I felt just as likely to shatter at any sudden touch.

Kissing my mother on the cheek, Teddy stepped into the living room doorway. He had grown out his hair, and his face was broader, healthier. When he caught my eye, he frowned ever so slightly.

"I'll just finish with the gravy," said my mother, going back to the kitchen.

"You not gettin' my messages?" Teddy said, coming into the middle of the room. "I talked to the old guy at that house you used to live in."

"I still live there," I said, "but I was in Calgary."

"For months?"

I went to shrug and my neck hurt so much I almost cried. But Harold came into the living room and Teddy turned to shake his hand. Teddy had brought gifts, too, a new pipe for Harold, and gemstone bracelets for both me and my mother, the kind of silver bangles that have a hinge and a clasp, with an extra-delicate chain as a safety loop. There was a lot of enthusiasm from my mother, some appropriate noises from Harold—I didn't need to say anything. Teddy frowned, seeing me fumble with the bracelet, awkward because of my left wrist. My mother showed off her bracelet, unmarked silver with four yellow tourmalines around the band.

I leaned forward to admire it. "It's beautiful, Mother."

She went back out to the kitchen. Teddy sat beside me on the sofa and took the silver bangle from my hand. I looked at the fragile-looking filigree, three dark blue stones set around the edges, as he fitted it onto my right wrist. The colour of the stones shifted like oil in water—blue, then green, then silvering grey; the silver band was small enough to fit like a manacle. For all the size of Teddy's hands, he remembered exactly the smallness of my bones. Harold went out to help my mother move the turkey from the oven—it was that heavy a bird.

"Where did you get the bracelets?" I said.

"Pawn shop in Toronto. Polished up nice, huh?"

I looked carefully at the stones. "You like Toronto?"

"They're labradorite," he said, doing up the security clasp, fingers at my pulse. "Real fire to 'em, like opals. Bracelets didn't look like anything much when I bought 'em, believe me."

I adjusted the bracelet.

"Worried I nabbed them from somewhere?"

"No."

"Nah. These were too nice to pass up. Was tempted to get you a new set of pearls from 'round the neck of a girl I met at the Rooftop the other night, but I figured you'd be suspicious." He winked and made a delicate gesture in the air with his hand, as if tracing the line of someone's neck and unhooking the clasp. I wondered if Adam had been there with Vera—Saturday nights at the Roof.

Teddy took my left hand and ran his fingers over the loosened wrapping on my wrist. "I'll do that up better for you." He unwrapped the bandage and laid it out flat against my skin, retied it. "Too tight?"

I shook my head.

"What happened?"

"I fell."

He raised one eyebrow. I didn't remember him ever doing that before. The thin bloated look of his initial return had worn away. He'd recreated a surface kind of shininess with the new suit, his hair grown out a bit. He looked like a world-weary businessman. A consciously-created surface to hide whatever part of himself had been a prisoner of war, whatever damaged self might linger beneath the handsome shell.

Once Harold Avison had finished his extended grace, dinner was quiet. I managed to hold my fork and knife without wincing every time I used my sore wrist—a poker face has occasional practical use. We ate the enormous dinner my mother had prepared; she had taken to Christmas cooking and baking and even decorating with a vengeance I'd never seen before. Maybe she was happy playing the role of perfect homemaker for Harold Avison. Did she think I could make the same transition, that Teddy was the answer to the problem she thought I was? I noticed Harold beaming at Teddy and I wondered if Teddy had tried to dissuade them on the subject—he'd been clear enough, a year ago, that he was glad he hadn't married me.

But when I made motions towards going home, after dessert had been cleared away, Teddy said he'd take the cab downtown with me.

"Mind if we walk?" he said, when we were out of the house. He held the umbrella over my head, but the difference in our heights meant I got good and wet anyhow. The sidewalk was a smooth black reflection under our feet. The marks on my neck ached, as if everyone could see and reproach me for my bruises. Any problem that befell someone like me was surely my own fault. At least Teddy doesn't believe that, I thought, edging slightly closer to him, familiar and unfamiliar though he was.

Teddy walked with me silently until we reached Granville Street, when I asked, "Where are you staying? Are you staying?"

"I've got a room at the Ivanhoe."

"Quiet?"

He made a "boo" noise, whistling air.

"What?"

"I don't sleep, Mill. Noise is no problem."

"What do you mean, you don't sleep?"

Waiting for the light at the Burrard Street intersection, he put a hand out beyond the umbrella. "It's stopped raining." He closed the umbrella. It was still raining, but I was wet anyhow, the umbrella made no difference.

"At least I'm not screamin' anymore," he said. "Some of the guys, Christ, only thing helps is junk. Best thing out there. Makes a guy feel nothin'. And trust me sugar, feeling nothin' is exactly what the doctor ordered." When he saw my appalled expression, he ran a hand across my back to reassure me. "Not my thing," he said. "Don't really miss sleeping."

"You must be exhausted."

"Nightmares aren't worth it."

"Gin used to put Mother to sleep, you could try that."

"Nah, makes what you remember worse. I'm fine, not sleeping. Gives me more time to think on things."

"What things?"

"Nothin' special."

"So how is Ontario?" I said, cautiously. "You like it?"

Teddy interrupted me. "You have some boyfriend knockin' around?"

"What? No."

"No?" He put his arm closer around my shoulders, nudging my neck. I couldn't help wincing, I think I even gasped. I wasn't used to pain, I was bad at it.

"What?"

I closed my mouth against anything I might say. Maybe I gasped as much from pain as from something else, for I suddenly wanted the weight of him against me, I wanted him to reassure me after the terrible train ride, make me feel less alone. It was Christmas day; a person isn't supposed to be alone on such a holiday. Teddy hailed a cab, looked carefully at my face, then pulled me with him and told the cabbie to go to the Ivanhoe.

His room on the top floor was down a dim greenish hallway, many wooden doors, all closed. He got the door to his room unlocked and picked me up, I didn't care what the room looked like, it was dark, the walls close. He was rummaging through my clothes before we reached his bed. His hands on my ribs, the small of my back, I turned against him, trying to get my hat and coat free without hurting my wrist. His dark eyes glinted in what light there was from the window. He murmured something I couldn't quite hear, but there was enough pleasure in the sound that I let him take off my shoes, my coat, and when I gasped at the pain of my neck, he must have thought it was only my want for him.

He found the buttons of my dress and undid them, slowing down, his fingers exploring every strap on my slip and brassiere, lingering. When I wore only my stockings, my clothes in a pile on the floor, he stood me up on the bed, so that I was ever so slightly taller than he. With the city light coming in the window, I was nothing but a pale shape; I wouldn't have wanted to be stripped naked with the lamp on. Teddy ran his hands across my shoulders and down my bare breasts, around my nipples, hard against his palms, then along my hips. He caught my hands, gentle with my bandaged wrist, and brought my fingers against his chest, on the buttons of his shirt, his tie. "Now me," he said, "undress me."

I had trouble undoing his tie in the near-dark, but the buttons of the shirt were simple, I undid his cufflinks, untucked his shirt, shrugged it off him, put my hands beneath his undershirt and pulled it over his head. My fingers followed a slew of marks up his shoulder, Braille along the blade of his back, but when I tried to make him turn, to look more closely in the near-darkness, to see what it was, tattoo or scar, he pushed my hands lower.

Belt, two buttons, a hook, a zipper—men's clothing used to have as many complications as girls'. He barely moved to let me take off his clothes and I hesitated, my hands on the smooth skin of his hips. I remembered the last time I'd touched him and I wondered how many others there had been since I'd seen him in Lethbridge, thought about where I had been in the meantime. Not as if I'd been loyal to anyone in particular, I thought, but I couldn't budge my hands. It was cold in his room.

"Mill." He put his arms around my shoulders and I fell against him, shaking with the pain in my neck. He pressed himself into the bed, pulled me to him as if there had never been a space between the past and present, no space between us at all. But I knew more about what I wanted in this, from his body, how I wanted to move. When he put a hand against my shoulder blade and my bruises made me cry out, I put my teeth into his palm, pressed my face into his fingers.

Afterwards, I shifted, shivered—my neck hurt almost unbearably, my wrist, too. He muttered, "You're cold, get under the blanket."

He dragged the blanket over me and I slid my right hand under the pillow. My fingernails raked against a coil of beads, cool to touch—a necklace under my hand, which I pulled out from under the pillow. The beads glowed in the faint light from the window. A pearl necklace. I sat up and flicked Teddy with the clasp at the bottom of the pearls.

He turned to look at me and blinked, memory surfacing from a long way away, this necklace finally coming into focus for him. "Oh." He stretched out under the sheet. "I said I nearly gave you a necklace," he said. "Want it?" He rubbed his forehead, pushed his hair back as if he was trying to clear his head.

"Whose is it?"

"Well...."

I moved to get out of bed, appalled, but Teddy ran his hand across my arm. "No one lost them here, Mill, for God's sake. I put them there for safe-keeping, slipped my mind." Teddy sighed and lay flat against the sheets. "Why's it matter?"

I swung the necklace to and fro like a pendulum. I knew Teddy was a pick-pocket of fair talent—a delicate touch despite the size of him. He'd always stolen books for me and expensive ingredients for Mary Ellen's salves. I knew he'd stolen pocketbooks and watches, until he could easily have a conversation with a woman while stealing her husband's wallet. His joke about the Roof and the girl—I hadn't really thought he was joking. "Who?" I said.

"No one I'd want here. The diamond and sapphire doo-hickey, I couldn't help noticing."

He meant the clasp on the pearls—even in the dim room, I could see why he'd noticed its glitter. I coiled the necklace into a double spiral and dropped it on the bedside bureau. "How'd it get here?"

Teddy sighed and turned on the bedside lamp; the room was bigger than I thought, and neat. Apart from the bedside table, there was a sink and a mirror. No armoire or closet, nowhere to hide a necklace, perhaps why he'd put it under the pillow.

"No big thing," he said. "Loosed the clasp, slid it off her neck into my sleeve. I was barely thinkin'. She was thick like a post, wife of a banker." He told me that as they left the dance floor, he intentionally tripped another man who then bumped into the girl. "I took her home to her husband's house in a cab, dropped her off...." And when he leaned in to kiss her, he'd said in a shocked voice, "But your necklace! The clasp must be loose." She had put her hand to her neck with a soft gasp. Wondering, I imagine, how she was going to explain the necklace's disappearance to her husband. Teddy was solicitous; he searched the cab and promised her solemnly that he'd find the necklace for her, search the hotel's nightclub, its restaurant. Teddy had the decency to look embarrassed when he told me that she wanted to run away with him, leave her husband—she wanted to live a wild life like he did. No doubt he rumpled her hair and kissed her forehead.

"I told her I couldn't do that, she needed a soft life an' as for me, nah, I was no good for her."

I sat there in his bed, wrapped in the sheet, and I wondered why he was telling me this story, why he thought I'd want to hear about the girl who was his latest mark. Maybe I deserved whatever story he chose to tell me. "You're no good for anyone," I whispered.

"You think that?" He pulled me harshly down to lie against him. The white snake of pearls glowed beside the bedside lamp. The bruises on my neck throbbed. I was here because I didn't want to be alone, however terrible a reason that was, and Teddy smelled almost the way he used to, just then, like honey and pine needles and bread. I meant to explain, or take my words back. I pressed my head against his shoulder.

But instead of turning off the light, Teddy eased my head onto the pillow. "You say you fell?"

I pulled the sheet up to my nose.

"Here? And here?" He put his hand against the sheet to touch the marks on my neck, his fingers against the swellings, gently, very gently. As if measuring the size of the hand that had done it.

"I fell."

"Not buyin' it."

"I did. I fell."

"I'll find out who did it." He brought his face down until our noses were touching.

"There's no who." That wasn't what I wanted, much as it might please me to imagine Teddy pounding Gerald Avison into dust.

"Christ," he said, "what's been happening while I was away? Who does this? Where is he?"

"It never happened before, and it won't happen again. I'm fine." Thinking, no, I'm not fine, but I'll be alright here. "It's not what you think."

"What am I supposed to think?" he said, hoarse. "Some guy tries to throttle you after a game, what the hell else?"

When I didn't answer, he closed his eyes for a long minute, his dark eyelashes shadowing his cheek, so close I didn't breathe. When he opened his eyes again, he threw himself back against the bed and put his hands to his face, pushing his palms into his eyes. He exhaled hard and stared at the ceiling.

I followed his gaze; it wasn't an attractive ceiling, dingy with ancient stains from roof leaks. "Can I turn the light out?"

Instead of answering me, he got out of bed and grabbed his trousers, dressing, putting on his shirt, his jacket, with his back to me.

"Where are you going?"

He shook his head, as if shaking off water, and looked fiercely at me, maybe trying to pierce through my head to see what had really happened, to read my bruises and have the story made clear. Then he left, closing the door firmly, and I was alone in the room.

When he had been gone for an hour or more, I dressed, but I didn't want to leave. I lay back down on the bed and pulled up the blanket, covering even my bruised neck, covering even my head.

11

By the time I got back to my boardinghouse room on Boxing Day, I wanted nothing except to spend a week asleep, alone. I didn't want to hide in Teddy's room any longer—I had run out of ideas of what to say to him, if he did come back. The only person I might have asked for advice was Dermot, he would have asked about my wrist, wrapped up as it was, and he wouldn't have let me go until he'd heard the whole story. No. I had built myself a solitary gambling life, and here I was, solitary. If I wasn't gambling, there was nothing for me to do.

I locked my door and though I knew it was stupid, I wedged the back of the wooden chair underneath the doorknob, balanced the water pitcher on the chair—at least there would be noise of falling glass, if anyone came in. Realistically, I knew no one was going to come in, but I couldn't sleep any other way. I spent three days in bed, hiding like an animal. Max actually came up and knocked on the door, wheezing from exertion. It took some time for me to remove the barricade and open the door.

"Thought you were home," he said, bracing one of his arthritic hands against the doorframe. "Oh, those stairs."

"What is it?"

"Ah." He struggled to stand more upright. "Worried about you. You ill? All that runnin' about and now nothin'? You sick?"

"I'm tired out by the holidays."

He didn't comment on the fact that I hadn't washed my hair, and he didn't seem to notice my bruises. My neck hurt so much I could barely turn my head.

"Nearly the end of the year. Goin' out for New Year's?"

Which reminded me that I had a commitment to play on December 30th, not on a train, thank goodness, no, it was an occasional game in Vancouver run by a man named Murphy. I had played his games before. This time, he said he'd promised his clientele something a little different—which meant I was the entertainment, the dwarfish girl poker player, special for the holiday season. Murphy wasn't a bad fellow, he knew I'd profit from the guys' curiosity; even if I was the difference they were coming to see, I'd win enough money to make the circus act worth my time.

I thanked Max. "I'm fine, really." He peered at me crookedly, but he turned and painfully made his way back downstairs.

I washed my hair, stifling a cry each time I shifted my neck. And my wrist? I couldn't sit at a table with my wrist swathed in white bunting, so I unwrapped the bandage and wore a tight-sleeved sweater that came down low on my hands. I wouldn't move my left hand much; I wasn't going to be dealing and my wrist made no difference to my game. I tied the thin wool scarf loosely around my neck to hide the still-visible marks on my throat. Downstairs, I asked Max if he had an aspirin.

"So you've come down," he said. "You drink too much eggnog over Christmas dinner?" He squinted at my scarf.

"I think aspirin would help."

"So it was the eggnog. Fearsome stuff. I never touch it myself." He nodded at his beer. "Could try some hair of the dog. Beer's good." He waved one of his flippered hands towards the hallway. "Aspirin's in the cabinet over the sink. I know you don't use the downstairs loo, you wouldn't know, but there's a cabinet full. Whatever ails you, help yourself."

I doubted there was a cure for what ailed me, but at least the aspirin would dull the persistent throb when I swallowed. I treated myself to a taxi, which splashed through the rain across the Burrard Bridge to a classy-enough hotel. "Mr. Murphy's expecting me," I told the doorman.

The elevator whisked me to the sixth floor. Murphy let me into the suite. "Glad you made it, Miss Lacouvy."

And then I walked into the green hotel living room and stopped dead—Teddy stood near the curtained window, with his arms crossed on his chest. He wore a charcoal suit and he looked like he was worth a million dollars, not a penny less.

"Hello, sugar," he said, smiling as if we were in cahoots.

"You know each other. Good, good," said my host.

"More or less," I said, giving Teddy the very worst look I could. He folded away his smile but a glimmer lingered in his eyes.

"'This is David Heasel... over here, Montgomery....'"

Heasel was still in his uniform, which I thought strange. But what I truly cared about was that Teddy had shown up at one of my games. How dare he? I took the seat opposite him, wondering if he was checking up on me, following the possible source of the marks on my neck. Not likely, though. When my mother said I was a bad example, that Mary Ellen's son would have turned out pure as snow if I hadn't introduced him to cards, I wondered if she was right. I tried to force my mother's voice out of my head, but how could I play cards against Teddy when three days ago he had abandoned me in his bed? I tried to convince myself that the game was more important. I tore my eyes off his and set my purse beneath my chair.

We started, Murphy dealing. To my left, there was the first of the demobs, Montgomery, a basic player who understood the game and seemed to be playing for the hell of it—a healthy attitude, if you're not too attached to cards, because you won't ruin yourself. His pal, Heasel, was deadly serious, one of those players who fingered his money whenever he made a bet, nervously stroking his glass of rye. He drank a full shot for every round of cards dealt and still managed to be lucky for a while. For the first three hands, I folded; I had nothing of interest and I knew that over time my decisions would beat Heasel's nervous playing. I lost the next round, a full house, to Teddy's flush, and I thought, wildly, that Teddy might play well. But having him win wouldn't make me any happier—it wasn't the winning or losing, the plain fact that he was playing cards made my head ache. I picked up my hand again to check what my cards were, unable to even remember the suit. My wrist ached.

Teddy didn't listen to the cards any better than he had in the past, though he'd gotten good at being quiet, a differently useful ability. He had no give-away gestures, yet I read every hand he got, by the way he wouldn't meet my eyes. Only once did he meet my gaze full on, his eyes black as ever, the pupils enormous, and I looked away. I was no expert in emotions, not mine, certainly not Teddy's. My area of expertise only allowed me to predict the obvious—that Heasel wasn't a good-looking drunk and would be sloppy when the booze started to hit him.

Sometime in mid-morning, Murphy asked if we wanted to take a short rest, but when I said I was fine, the men all nodded in agreement, not willing to be out-played by a girl. By lunch, Teddy was nearly out of the game and though my heart flinched, I didn't stop myself from beating him in the next round.

Later, I took a decent pot with nothing more than a lowly pair, five of Diamonds and five of Spades. Everyone but Heasel took it in stride. Teddy poured a glass of rye off to the side where he couldn't see anyone's hand. Strange that he was still here, I thought, wondering if he was waiting for me. A new round was dealt. I folded immediately, and Heasel, foolishly, turned to Teddy and muttered, "You say you know this bitch?"

Teddy changed his grip on the bottle he held, though his expression of mild uninterest didn't falter. "What?"

Murphy intervened before Heasel could repeat the question. A brawl would do nothing for anyone's pocketbook. But even with Murphy's soothing noises, Teddy looked grim for the rest of the afternoon, and Heasel continued to mutter that good old Ted hadn't put up much of a fight at the poker table. Montgomery wasn't doing any better, but at least he shut up about it. That's what the game is, after all, a series of gains and losses; a person shouldn't play unless he understands this truth, has made peace with whatever the cards demand. And they will demand something—the question is only how much you're willing to give up.

Finally Heasel went all in and the game was over. "You're gonna need someone to walk you home," he said, standing, knocking his chair against the wall, staggering a little to get his legs untangled.

"She doesn't," said Teddy.

"Whaderyou know about it?"

I stepped around Heasel and shook hands with Montgomery, who had the decency to look uneasy about his pal's behaviour.

Murphy apologized, "Not my usual standard," he said. "I try to run an upright game, no drunks, no cheats, no slurs...."

I told him to think nothing of it. "Nature of the game," I said, "not your fault."

Teddy walked with me into the elevator and as the doors closed, he said, "I should've hit him."

"I can look after myself."

He gave me a disbelieving look, then stared resolutely at the steel doors of the elevator. "I might still hit him," he said. "I've got nothin' better to do with my night."

"The guy has nothing to do with anything, Teddy."

"Okay. I'll stand around while you get yourself strangled. Or mugged. Wait for you to turn up dead. Christ." He put his arms out on either side of the doors, impatient for them to open.

I glanced at myself in the long thin elevator mirror—did Napoleon ever doubt himself? I remembered the portrait of the French general—he wasn't handsome, with his pallid complexion and his lank hair, but I loved his worried, determined expression. Surely Napoleon had sometimes questioned his purpose, his ability, his love for his chosen game. I touched the scarf at my neck, as if I had tied it there with a particular flair for fashion, Teddy a dark cloud beside me.

"I didn't know you were going to be there," I said as the elevator came to a halt and the doors slid open.

On the far side of the lobby, the doorman swung open the door for us. A slight drizzle was all that remained from the drenching rains. We stood on the step. There was no taxi outside the hotel entrance, nor any car on the street in either direction. "Where is everybody?" I asked.

"Fireworks," said the doorman. "Everyone's down at the beach. If you wait an hour, the taxis'll be running again."

"Guess we're walkin'," said Teddy. He took my arm as we stepped out onto the sidewalk.

"You can wait, I'm fine." I held myself stiffly away from him, my arm rigid in his grasp.

"Don't be..." Teddy shifted his hand to lean me more intimately against him. "I'm not an idiot, Mill. I wouldn't choose to play against you. Heasel was *my* mark, I wasn't expectin' to lose him to you. If Murphy'd told me in advance, I'd have been outta there, I promise you. I had investment plans for Heasel. Now I just have to break his jaw."

I ignored that and focused on the word investment. "What do you mean, investment plans?"

"You don't understand, Mill. We're alike, you and me."

"We grew up in the same house. That's not...."

"Not that I'm good in poker for Chrissake. You can beat me with one hand tied behind your back. That's not what I'm talking about. You think you're fine without me, you're better off. You're wrong."

"I never thought I was better off. I was praying for you to come back, I was...."

"Oh, Christ, forget marrying me, that's not what I'm sayin' here. Does anyone else understand how good you are? Anyone in this town? Will anyone else back you up when you have a problem?"

"I don't have any problems I can't deal with."

"Yeah, I noticed."

I pulled my arm out from his and fished my cigarette case out of my purse, awkward with my sore wrist, but I clicked it open and managed to politely offer Teddy a cigarette. He took two and lit them, one for each of us, sheltering the flame from the drizzle with a cupped hand. "You learn to smoke while I was away?"

I frowned as I inhaled. "How much have you lost?"

He didn't answer, so I repeated the question.

After a while he shrugged. "Oh, it adds up, here and there."

"Have you been playing a lot? Honest games? Or what? What did Murphy mean back there?"

He laughed. "If I cheated, I'd be doin' better."

I tried to concentrate on my cigarette, but I was calculating—what he'd lost tonight, multiplied by how many games? How many weeks had he been playing? I wondered if he'd started as soon as he'd gotten back last year. My fault, hadn't I taken him back to cards first thing? He'd come back from the War and all I could tell him about was how good cards had been to me. I'd taken him to Dermot's the first night he was home, for goodness sake, yes, he'd asked me to, but I was the root cause. "You shouldn't touch cards, Teddy. They don't listen to you."

"Nah, my game's improved, you didn't notice? Mostly it's not cards. Stop worryin.'"

I exhaled. I could see the smoke hover in the drizzle, a visible sigh as we crossed the black street together. All the traffic lights were reflected in the puddles, shiny red. I wished on the lights, as a person might wish on the stars, that Teddy would change his plans, find a different use for his time. But the lights changed to green just the same.

"Who do you owe money to?" Maybe if I could pay off his debts, he'd find some kind of job, work a different con, anything to keep us separate. And I'd go back to playing the train games. I shivered and nearly chewed my cigarette.

Teddy put his arm around me. "Really. Don't worry. Just getting' some financing going."

"Who then?"

"Mill, stop. They can wait 'til I pay them."

"How much?"

"More than you're holdin'. Look, once I get 'em paid off, I'll swear off this stuff. Okay? Forget about it."

"Really? You'd stop playing cards?" We'd had this discussion a long time before, and he'd only lasted a week.

"Sure," he said, easily.

"I don't believe you." I dropped what was left of my cigarette and ground it into the sidewalk with the damp toe of my shoe. "You owe what, twenty thousand?"

He said nothing.

"More than twenty?"

"Stop. I need it for a mine. It's going to be good. So drop it."

"What mine? How much?"

"You're like a terrier with a rat, Mill. Jesus."

"That's one of my better qualities."

He laughed and put his arms around me, which wasn't fair—I was tired from the poker game, incapable of bluffing.

"I wonder how they'll look, what with the rain," he said.

"How what'll look?"

"The fireworks, idiot." He leaned down as if he was going to kiss me.

I had forgotten it was New Year's eve, had forgotten the fireworks. "Could you ask Harold's cousin to get you a job with the Parks? He said he could…"

"The Parks?" He started to laugh.

"I'm serious."

He shrugged his arms more loosely against my shoulders. "I'm not the competition, Mill. I'm on your side."

"I don't want you on my side."

"Sure you do."

"Harold's right."

"That's a first, saying Harold's right about somethin'. What's he been tellin' you?"

"That he could get you a job with the Parks."

"You sure you're not thinkin' up ways to keep me in Vancouver? You miss me, after all?"

Just then, the first of the fireworks began, the sky flickering with lights. At the first big bang, I felt Teddy's labored breath. He dropped his arm from my shoulders.

"What's wrong?"

He shook his head as brilliantly-coloured sparks rained through the sky in between the buildings, falling towards the water. "We can watch from the bridge," he said.

Other people had the same idea, but the earlier rain had thinned the crowd out some. Teddy led me past a clump of people at the entrance to the bridge. "What?" he said, though I hadn't spoken. He looked as if he were concentrating very hard on hearing a sound that wasn't there. He stopped at one of the little niches in the bridge railing, where you can stand and look at the view, except that night, the mist had smeared the lights of the freighters, the boats were far away in the darkness and there was nothing to be seen until another bang of fireworks lit up the sky. Teddy blinked and lowered his head as if he'd gone gun-shy, which was maybe the truth.

"Do you want another cigarette?" I said.

He shook his head and put his hands on the railing on either side of me, holding onto the metal bar as if we were on a boat listing in high waves. In between the fireworks, in the long pauses, the night seemed almost as dark as it had been during the War. He leaned us both towards the water.

"Kiss me." He pushed me against the wet railing.

I leaned into him, trying to keep the wet bars away from my coat. "Don't, Teddy."

He closed his eyes. There was another burst of fireworks; he opened his eyes again. "You're here," he said.

Where did he think I might have gone? His jacket smelled like the almost-rain around us—water and mist suited him. But when the next flare of fireworks illuminated his face, he stared at me, his eyes like black mirrors. Maybe that should have told me something different, I don't know, but I stood on my toes and kissed his closed mouth until he opened his lips. I ran my tongue along the healed groove in his lip that I knew too well. I poured everything I was thinking about into kissing him, all the years he had been gone, when I had missed him or not, every minute of his leaving, along with every reason for not marrying him. But I don't think he understood what I meant, because he sighed as if something in his blood had suddenly calmed down.

The last firework was an enormous explosion; I was facing the wrong way and turned my head as Teddy pressed his forehead against my hair. I watched the sparks falling everywhere into English Bay. I eased myself out from between his arms, moving away from the bridge railing.

"What?" he said.

"I'm going home."

"Come home with me."

"That didn't work out so well last...."

"You don't have a game do you?"

"No, the game finished, remember?"

He closed his eyes for a moment even though there were no more fireworks. I looked at his eyelashes, how the mist had gotten into them in the dim night.

"I just want to go home, that's all, I'm tired." I said.

He put his arm around me. "I want you with me tonight."

I went with him, even though his expression was unreadable, his eyes too far away and shuddering. He pushed us past the people who were crowding the sidewalk.

I woke up curled against Teddy's left side, grey light coming in from the window. We hadn't pulled the curtains closed, and I could see it was raining again. I rolled over to look at Teddy. Hadn't he said he never slept anymore? Well, he was sleeping now, with a face so calm it made my stomach hurt. The pearls were no longer on the nightstand. When I couldn't stand watching him anymore, I got up and started to dress, trying not to waken him. I pulled my sweater over my head and winced a little when the fabric caught at my wrist.

"Still hurts, huh?" Teddy watched me through his eyelashes.

"You were asleep."

"I woke up. We goin' to breakfast?"

"No."

He got out of bed and put on trousers, an undershirt, but not before I'd seen that the marks across his shoulder and back weren't a tattoo, they were some kind of scar. Shrapnel, maybe, like Adam's healing skin. I blushed, remembering that, but Teddy didn't notice. While he shaved, lather and bristles on the porcelain lip of the room's chipped sink, I sat on the bed, opened my purse and took out the money I'd made at Murphy's game, stacking the bills on the rumpled sheets. The total was twenty-one dollars over $13,000. I looked at the money and pulled one thousand out from the pile for myself, taking the unlucky thirteen out of the equation, leaving twelve thousand on the bed.

"What are you doing?" said Teddy, drying his face.

I stood up and found my hat, adjusted it on my head, repositioning the hatpin without looking in the mirror.

"I said, what are you doing?"

"Lending you some money."

Teddy put on his shirt, fidgeted with the buttons, then gave up on them. "Christ, you're difficult. An' to think I could've fallen for a normal girl, who kept normal hours, who worked, oh, I dunno, at Woodward's in the dress department, something nice an' dull. Where I wouldn't be worryin' every time I look at you...." He stopped, let his hands hang by his sides, as if forcing himself to be still. "So where d'you want to have breakfast?"

"I don't."

"I'm going to sort things out myself, Mill. I don't need this."

"I'm doing you a favour," I said.

"That's not what you're trying to do."

"You can use the money."

Teddy looked me steadily. He very carefully did up the buttons on his shirt. "What you're up to is no favour to me."

"I'm getting you out of this business."

"Why don't you get yourself out of the business? If you're so keen on the getting out aspect of things."

"Cards are all I have, Teddy."

"Christ, just leave well enough alone." He closed his eyes and I went past him, quickly. I don't know if he felt me go, but as I opened the door, he brought his fingers up to his face for an instant, then slammed his hand flat into the wall above the sink. It sounded like a door banging shut. The shaving mirror shimmered on its wire. I winced, but his eyes were still closed, as if he was trying to steady his temper, his hand still flat against the wall. I left the money where it was, on the bed, and I ran along the Ivanhoe's dim hallway and down its three flights of stairs.

On the walk home, I remembered it was New Year's day. Main Street was shuttered, the bars dark all down the block, and when I turned onto Georgia, none of the cheek-by-jowl Chinatown grocery shops were open. One solitary vegetable vendor stood sadly beside his cart of wilted lettuce, not even bothering to call for my attention. Maybe I looked as dejected as his produce. I walked past the narrowest building in the city—its red and green paint had grown dingy. A broken gutter leaked torrents of rain down the front, gushing straight across the sidewalk. Strings at eye-level dangled down from the upper storeys—strings leading to small ship bells, which served as doorbells for the inhabitants. As a kid, Teddy used to pull every one of them to hear the bells ring. I winced again and of course it was the cold wind, hurting my neck.

Up the slight hill to Granville, past the small hotels, the few people about were dressed in Sunday best, which made me feel wrung through a wringer in comparison. I was still wearing the impractical cork-soled shoes I'd worn to Murphy's game and I squelched at every step. December had been too much for me, everything about it was foul, from Vancouver's weather to the bruises on my neck, from Teddy's gambling debts to the way my hands suddenly felt. My fingers were tired, my wrist still throbbed, and my palms felt dirty, as if I'd dealt fortune wrong.

I stopped in front of the Hotel Vancouver, gazing up at the stonework, all those elaborate windows. I held my hands out in front of me, up in the rain. They looked no different. I glanced at the wide glass doors that led into the lobby and the figure reflected there was still me, in a bedraggled hat, my damp coat marked down the front from being pressed against the railing of the Burrard Bridge. The mark seemed appropriate—I felt scarred. Not by Teddy, but by my own stupidity. I turned from the hotel with a shudder and the bruises on my neck sent shooting pains down into my throat.

When I walked into the boardinghouse, Max looked up from his little alcove and said, "What is it, honey?"

"Happy New Year."

"Some games are like that," he said. "But you get a fresh chance, New Year and all." His head swayed towards the door, indicating that he wanted a beer. Why not? The first day of the year, surely he deserved a beer before noon. I went back out the front door and across the lawn to the Abbotsford Hotel, leaving muddy shoeprints as I went into the bar. I bought a pint of lager for

Max and a lemonade for myself. The bartender wished me happy New Year and he didn't wipe the top of the beer glass to measure the foam—he knew Max's predictive qualities. I took a sip of the too-full glass of lemonade before going back across the lawn.

In Max's alcove, I put my lemonade on his shelf and held out the beer in both hands. He studied me, then squinted into the beer foam. "Huh," he said. "Lookit that." He nodded at the foam. "See there, you've got a bird, pelican or some damn thing."

"A bird?"

He took the beer from me in his awkward hands and peered into the glass, close enough that his nose nearly ruined whatever pattern there was in the beer foam. "Yep, some damn tropical-like bird. Let's look at your hands." He set the beer alongside my lemonade. I had never let him read my palms before, my sore hands were my business. But now I held them out. As Max studied the lines, he gradually bent over so low I could feel him breathing, his old beer breath snuffling across my right palm, then my left. He nodded.

"Yep, you've gotta make a move, you've got a split in the line there. You're better off makin' the change yourself. Otherwise someone'll do it for ya. Choices to be made, honey. You have to go. Follow that bird to where it's at. Best thing to do, go soon. An' give the old man a kiss."

I patted his bent-up shoulder and kissed him on the cheek. "I wouldn't go anywhere without your blessing."

He picked up his beer and huddled over it. I was dismissed; in a few minutes he'd be asleep. He had long ago mastered the art of dozing while holding a glass steady in his flippered paw. I took my lemonade and went upstairs.

12

Roulette is a game that keeps no history. Unless the wheel is fixed by the house, each spin is completely new, past events have no relevance. But poker relies on history—the dead cards point to the next play and there's no fix on this earth to change this basic principle. That's why poker is consistently interesting—it's closer to real life than roulette. Our acrobatics are haunted by history.

Come January, I couldn't get back on a train. There was my history—the trains held all my best games, my most reliable source of income, but Banff lingered in my fingers. I cradled my injured wrist longer than I should have, and I dragged my feet going back to work. Finally I could wait no longer. Without the train games, I was quickly pricing myself out of decent-sized bets. So I forced myself to put on my luckiest dress, a high-collared red affair, a bull's-eye flag against my gloom. I pulled open the curtains—it was, of course, raining, the mountains invisible. I dragged on my overcoat. The mark from that night on the bridge had dried and a stern brushing made the coat look alright. I put what was left of my bankroll, my solitary thousand dollars, into my purse, I snapped the clasp shut, I picked up my gloves, I pinned my red felt hat onto my head, and I went out. Max was dozing in his alcove as I went by.

I hailed a taxi to take me through the soaking streets, down to the train station. The paltry light remaining in the day disappeared as the car splashed through the streets' deepening puddles. Outside one of the Granville hotel bars, there was a group of men, some kind of fight, there in the rain. And then the taxi was approaching the train station, taking the curve past the plane trees, stopping in front of the entrance awnings. My hands were frozen onto the strap of my purse. "Miss?" said the taxi driver, "the station, Miss, here we are."

"Yes," I said, and stared down at my fingers, uncurled them, opened the clasp of my purse and managed to pull out the fare. But I couldn't budge from the back seat. Finally the cabbie sighed, got out, came around the cab, and opened the rear passenger door. I placed my gloved hand in his and allowed myself to be pulled out of the taxi.

"Thank you," I whispered.

He shook his head and closed the door. I didn't notice him drive away, because I was staring at the entrance. I had walked across that speckled marble so many times, why was I paralysed now? I forced myself forward but I tripped on the brass grill that led into the station. At the ticket counter, I asked for a ticket to Edmonton, I knew the route—through Jasper, not Banff, I would have no grief from that. I paid her the necessary money and walked towards the train platforms. The barber was closed; the magazine vendor was packing up; the little coffee counter was still open, shiny, the same brassy blond who had always been there, chatting to the salesman types.

Through the doors, the big trains waited, engines stoking. Porters wheeled baggage past me as more passengers arrived, but I couldn't walk forward. My fellow passengers presented their tickets to the conductor, asked for advice, and boarded the train. There in front of the main doors, I was very much in the way, and finally a porter yelled out, "Miss Lacouvy, get yourself onboard, whatcha doin' there...."

The first warning whistle blew: three minutes. I stood perfectly still. The conductor stepped on board, a porter pulled a greyish laundry bag onto the train, then leaned down to fold up the iron step. Another whistle. He flipped the temporary shelf inward and glanced over, catching my eye. Then he swung the lower half of the metal door. It was too late; the final whistle blew sharply three times and the great iron wheels lurched into motion, the huge beast of the train pulling forward, very slowly, and then it was definitely moving, the Express to Edmonton, leaving without me.

I slowly unclenched my fingers from my purse, let the strap slide down my uninjured wrist until my arms hung limp by my sides. I went sadly back into the lobby, past the benches of waiting passengers—their trains late, family delayed, connections missed. And me, with a ticket in my hand, unable to step onto the train. My hands felt strange—my fingertips tingled, a failed barometer. I had let my hands down.

I walked slowly to the far side of the station where the washrooms were and gave a dime to the attendant. I closed the door behind me. No one saw me crying. After a very long time, I flushed the toilet and came out and went home, and I'm sure my eyes were as red as my lucky dress.

I stayed in bed all the next day, and that evening, I didn't bother dressing up. I chose a safer bet and went down to Dermot's, walking, not bothering with a taxi. I tried to remind my hands to stay limber, clutching the umbrella's slippery wooden handle, the sidewalk slick with rain under my feet. I went around to the alley and pushed open the back door, but there was no game. I shouldn't have been surprised—Dermot had found a buyer for his bar. The deal was going through at the end of the month and while his regulars still showed up on Tuesdays, most other nights the backroom was quiet.

"Wasn't expectin' you, lass," said Dermot. "It's a fine surprise, you bein' here, but there's no cards tonight, Millard. Busy night out front, can't stick back here too long."

I nodded. "Thought it was worth dropping by, there's no train games for me at the moment."

Dermot frowned. "A bit under the weather?"

I sat down and leaned my elbows on the table.

"Millard?"

I focused back on Dermot.

"Any little thing you're wanting to tell me about?"

"No."

He coughed and looked back towards the bar. "I'll see you Tuesday, lass."

"Of course."

When he left, closing the connecting door behind him, I dropped my head into my hands. I was soaked with rain by the time I got home again. On Monday, I tried a different kind of train: the day trip to Seattle. I didn't even give myself the luxury of a taxi; I walked to the station in the rain and started coughing as I went down Granville Street. My hands began to ache as I reached Cordova, my fingers going completely numb, my palms like cold glass. I peeled off my gloves, shook my hands like wet rags despite my sore wrist. I folded my hands across my chest like an offering and went no closer to the station.

On Tuesday, I was back to Dermot's, and even though there were only regulars there, and Winch was playing like a monkey, I lost.

"Now that's a rare present," said Kevin, pocketing his winnings.

Over the next week, I played two desultory games for Murphy and lost both of them. I was unable to bluff, I couldn't concentrate even when the cards were kind—a two-Ace hand, a King-high straight, even with those gifts, my bad decisions weighed on me and my hands ignored the cards.

I skipped the following Tuesday's game at Dermot's; I knew he'd ask me how I was, and I didn't want to lie. The city did nothing to help my mood—Vancouver should have been booming, but it felt shabby as ever, veterans holed up in vacant buildings, sitting on city benches in their leftover grey-green uniforms, trying to fit the wreckage of their shell-shocked lives back together. Others wandered the streets, better dressed than they'd been before the war, but looking for work, just the same. When one asked if I had any odd jobs he might do, I stared at him.

"Me?" I sounded so surprised, the man took a step backwards.

"Not bothering you, Miss, just curious. No work that needs doing around the home?"

I shook my head. "I'm down on my luck too, soldier."

My landlady hired one of these men to repaint the trim of the boardinghouse. He was afflicted with some kind of tremors, I wasn't sure if it was caused by drink or the absence of same, or if it was some after effect of battle. He managed to polka dot the entire front garden with peach-coloured paint while I admired his handiwork from the comparative safety of the curb. The spots were almost cheerful until the rain wore them away.

I went for long stupid walks in the rain, trying to tire myself out enough to get onto a train. It didn't work. I could have walked halfway to Seattle, I still wouldn't have been able to get back on a train to play cards. It was ridiculous. My fingers itched as soon as I thought about playing. My bank account went nowhere except down. I paid my weekly rent and tried not to ask myself what Teddy might be doing with the money I'd left on his bed, out there in the city. I cursed myself for even wondering.

Every morning, I slunk past the beginning of the park and forced myself to eat breakfast at the Sylvia Hotel, up in the Dine in the Sky restaurant. The brown brick hotel was the tallest thing in the West End, looming over the beach. It comforted me to go up the stone steps and take the elevator to the restaurant, it felt safe. No one I knew would find me here—certainly not Teddy, nor any of Dermot's regulars, and I didn't think I'd see anyone from the trains. Over time, as I turned up so frequently that long month of January, the waiters learned to bring me a pot of tea without being asked. Usually, I picked at some eggs and stared over the rim of my teacup, focusing on the elevator doors, watching the little green light flick on, the arrow move down to L and then back up to ding-a-ling a new arrival. As if despite my conviction that I'd never be found here, I was making sure no one snuck up on me.

After breakfast, I walked on the path that snaked alongside the beach. The dark trees of the park seemed eternal, unchanged, as if I'd never gone anywhere, as if there had never been a war, as if I hadn't worked my way to some of the best games in the country, to the Banff game—I glared at the trees. It was too grey, too cold, for anyone to linger by the edge of the water, but I walked there routinely, hunched against the wind. When I tired of criticizing the trees for their endurance, I sneered at the grey-brown sand. I didn't see any change coming—not in the weather, not in my luck, not in my bleakly-chosen solitude. I could say I was remembering those nights before the War, when Teddy's dark eyes were as soft as his skin, but that wouldn't have been true. I mean, I did remember, but there was no connection between the two moments, only time that had gone past me.

On the last Tuesday of January, I went up to the dining room for breakfast, chose my usual table, and the pot of tea arrived, as it always did. I stirred the tea leaves inside the pot, wishing fortune could be affected by such a simple gesture. I didn't have enough money to risk playing Dermot's that night; I considered ordering just toast instead of a full breakfast, to save myself the extra dollar, as if a single dollar might make a difference to my bankroll. I stared across the room and noticed the elevator arrow moving up. Before I had a chance to order my meal, the elevator dinged, the gold doors opened, and Sam Lazar stepped out. It shook me out of my stupor. He saw me immediately, avoided the maitre-d' and came over to say hello.

"Miss Lacouvy, unexpected pleasure." He paused, took off his hat, and shook my hand with an elegance that should have seemed exaggerated, but wasn't. He didn't comment on my icy fingers.

The maitre-d' followed him, saying, "Sir?", wanting to lead him to a clean and empty table.

Lazar ignored him. "May I join you?"

"Of course."

He shrugged himself out of his wet coat and sat down across from me. "Haven't been out to the coast in winter for years. I forget how much rain there is."

The waiter brought coffee for Lazar.

"What do you usually order?"

"Eggs Benedict."

"We'll have that then. And orange juice, don't you think?"

The waiter nodded.

Lazar leaned back, surveying the room, and as if the tables of the Dine in the Sky inspired him, he said, "Have you ever been to Nevada?"

I shook my head. The maitre-d' came rushing back and asked if we would like to move, there was a window table available. Lazar shrugged. "I suppose so. Miss Lacouvy, do you have any particular preference for this table?"

"Not really."

We moved to sit by the window at a table for four, an immaculate white tablecloth freshly unfurled for us; I could smell the bleach when I sat down. I forced myself to sit straighter, to fight off that laundry memory.

"I'm talking about serious desert," Lazar said, contemplating the rainy view out the window for a long moment. "A place out there. The Flamingo."

"I've heard of it," I said, though it was only a rumour, what I'd heard.

"On the lookout for good dealers, down there."

"Really?"

"Dick Chappell runs the place. Keeps changing the table guys, can't get the balance right as yet."

I waited while the waiter poured fresh tea into my empty cup. I wondered why Lazar was telling me this.

Lazar added sugar to his coffee. "You might get along with Chappell. Good man."

Had he heard about what had happened to me after the game in Banff? I supposed it was possible—maybe Avison hadn't been able to resist boasting. But I didn't see Lazar as a man to do people unnecessary favours.

"It's going to be quite the place," he said.

I took a sip of my tea. I had nothing to lose, anymore. "Are you're saying this Nevada place needs me?"

"All five feet and ten fingers of you, indeed, Miss Lacouvy. No one out there's got a mechanic that's anywhere near touching you. If you don't mind my saying so."

I might have blushed. I didn't like being called a mechanic, it wasn't flattering—I was an honest player, and mechanics tended to cheat. But he'd called me five feet tall, that was nice, since on a good day, which I hadn't had for a while, I was barely four foot eleven. Finally I said, "I'm not really a...."

Lazar looked out the window again. "Of course I don't know if you'd consider dealing. But the Flamingo could use you."

"Is it pink?"

"You're thinking it's a silly name for a casino, but in fact it's got style. The Flamingo's gorgeous, an oasis being run by low-class types like myself. It's not necessarily popular in all quarters but it's full of aspirations, Miss Lacouvy. A bit like Vancouver used to be, before your time of course. I think you might find the place interesting."

"Kind of a big move."

"Change can be a good thing, inspiring. It's going to be the place to play, maybe not quite yet but it's coming. Las Vegas is the place to get into. It's going to be the best game on this whole spinning earth, I promise you."

I tried to imagine the tablecloth as a map of America, tried to locate Nevada upon its smooth surface. "To be honest, I hardly know where Las Vegas...."

"Sunshine, that's where it is. In the desert, where it's nice and warm and dry. Think about it." He waved his hand towards the outside windows, where a new downpour slapped rain against the glass as if on cue. "There's a six-day law, raised pay, you name it, if the Local's asked for it, the Flamingo's doing it. Only company in Nevada to comply with everything on the list. Do you like cats?"

"About the same as I like people. Depends on the individual."

Lazar smiled and drank his coffee. The waiter brought our breakfast, and for the first time in weeks, I actually enjoyed the food.

"Benny Siegel didn't invent the idea of a Vegas casino," said Lazar. "That's just part of the legend and we're not going against the story. Really, it was Meyer's idea. Lansky, you've heard of him?" he asked.

I nodded, my mouth full. I wasn't sure how I'd phrase what little I knew about the crime boss—I didn't know Sam Lazar worked with him. I thought Sam was strictly a Canadian big shot.

Lazar leaned back in his chair, holding his glass of orange juice as if it were vintage wine in cut crystal. "Siegel launched the Flamingo December 26th. Unlucky day after Christmas, not that I celebrate the day, myself. Staffed the tables with dealers who had no clue they were supposed to make the players lose money. God knows where Benny found these guys. The place lost $300,000 the first week. Three hundred thousand! He closed up shop this month. He's rethinking, doing some *hard* rethinking."

"Who ever heard of a casino losing money?"

Lazar shrugged, clearly unwilling to tell me more. He polished off the first of the eggs, took a slice of toast from the silver toast holder. "You have to love the dreamers. The charmers. But you've got to have enough common sense to hire practical guys, dealers with talent, with a touch for cards. Dealers like you."

"Dreamers are too unpredictable?"

"Yes. Benny's added all kinds of attractions, a gymnasium, a pool, a steam room, tennis courts. He's got forty horses for the stables, there's a nine-hole golf course to go with the hotel rooms and the little bungalows. It's classy, Miss Lacouvy. Reopening this week, and Siegel's got the magic. And a hair-trigger temper. You should never play a game with him. I certainly wouldn't. His twenty-thousand buy-in, that game, runs in his suite? Avoid it."

"It sounds too rich for me, don't worry."

"He's got it fixed in his favour. Don't waste your time. But for all that, Benny's charming, inspiring." Lazar paused, considering. "Psychotic," he added, "but charming."

"The two can go hand in hand." I finished my eggs Benedict; it was suddenly all delicious, the food, the conversation, the possibilities.

"He's determined to have the Flamingo make money this time. You could help."

Across the table from me in that grey morning light, across the dirty breakfast plates, yes, Sam Lazar looked like a hazy kind of angel sent down to rescue my skills before I lost all taste for the game. I had something like a vision, there in the Dine in the Sky, even as I wondered about Siegel's tilted table, up in his private Flamingo suite.

When we finished eating, Lazar signed for our breakfast. He held out his hand as we left the table. "I hope you take my advice. A lady like you might take a shine to the Flamingo, pretty place that it is. I put my money on the place being a success, Miss Lacouvy. Please consider it." He let my hand go and stepped aside to let me into the elevator.

"I will think about it," I said.

When the elevator reached the lobby, Lazar tipped his hat. "Give my best regards to Chappell, if you go."

I walked out into the rain. A way to play within the safe confines of a casino, where the thugs would be on my side—it was tempting. I hadn't thought of leaving Vancouver, but if I did, no one would miss me. Dermot had sold his bar, and my mother noticed me so rarely, if I moved to a different kind of poker game, in a different kind of city, she would like pay little attention. The only person who might notice was Teddy, and from him, I was already doing my best to be absent. I walked up and down the beach, across from the Sylvia. The rain curled down my hair and dripped underneath my collar as I walked. I stopped and watched a woman chase a dog, far at the edge of the waves. Her small daughter ran back and forth, waving a stick for the dog to fetch. So simple, the mother in a grey raincoat and her girl in rubber boots, the dog and the beach—even in the rain they were happy.

If I left Vancouver, I'd be leaving Teddy. There was nothing to leave, I reminded myself, but just the same, I couldn't pack my suitcase without calling him. I pulled my coat closer against the rain and walked back into the Sylvia. From the hotel payphone, I called the Ivanhoe and left a message, asking him to meet me at a Granville Street diner, tomorrow, for lunch. A fool gesture of fare thee well. I couldn't help it, I couldn't leave the city without at least telling him I was going, to clear my plate of any leftover stories, leftover hopes—his or mine, I wasn't sure whose.

Back at the boardinghouse, I gave notice and pulled out the old cardboard suitcase from underneath the bed. I had thought the suitcase was elegant enough, back when I moved from my mother's house, but now it seemed cheap-looking and unfashionable. I regretted my well-used alligator bag.

That night, I went to play at Dermot's and somehow, the fact of having packed my bag influenced the cards. My cut from the night totaled two hundred dollars—enough for a bus ticket and a room in Las Vegas, when I got there. After the other players left, I stood in the doorway that led to the bar.

"I'm taking a job down south," I told Dermot.

He picked up another glass to polish. "You're not yourself these days. A change might be a good thing, lass. What's the job?"

"Working for a casino."

Dermot gave me a searching look, his black eyebrows creased together. "Good offer?"

"I think so."

"That's my girl. Don't let anyone take advantage of your hands, now."

If I wanted a blessing, this was the best I was likely to get. "I promise, Dermot."

"Where is it?"

"A casino called the Flamingo, in a town called Las Vegas. They need dealers, and I'm told I'm highly recommended."

"You are highly recommended, Millard."

"I wouldn't play here without you, anyway. Wouldn't be the same."

Dermot set the clean glass precisely into position in the stack of waiting pint glasses, tossed the dishcloth over his shoulder, and leaned over to embrace me, awkward through want of practice. I hugged him back, despite the sharp bruise that remained on my neck.

"You be a good, lucky girl, now."

"I'll do my best," I said.

"Your best is darn good, lass."

When I went out the following day to the diner on Granville Street, it was still raining. Thirty-seven days, non-stop—I couldn't help but keep track. As I came in, shaking my umbrella, I saw Teddy sitting at a booth near the window. He stood up and kissed me on the cheek. As I slid awkwardly into the booth, he said, "So, d'you miss me?"

"Well...."

"I was back in Ontario for a month, Mill," he said. "Was fantastic. Look at these things." Teddy reached into the breast pocket of his grey suit jacket, held out his hand, fingers curled around something in his palm. When I leaned forward, he unfurled his fingers. A half dozen tiny stones sparkled in his palm, purplish, dove-pink, they would have been pebbles except they were too small, too polished.

"Some kind of gemstone?"

Teddy laughed. "This is amethyst, Mill, from a town called Pearl. Go figure. But this mine's gonna to make me rich. Then I can have some fun."

A mine of pretty purple stones? I wanted to trust his gleaming belief in good fortune, and the stones shone in his palm as if, inanimate though they were, they might believe in him too. I picked up the darkest one, deep purple, a pebble the size of the fingernail on my smallest finger. I held it up, to look at the way light came through the stone: a tiny purple cloud between my fingers.

"You should keep it," he said. "Matches my eyes, dontcha think? Make you think of me, get it made into a brooch or somethin'. Not a ring."

It was nothing like his brown eyes, even when they were bright and laughing at me. But an amethyst from a town called Pearl seemed about right for a gift from Teddy—a tall tale made real. He put the rest of the stones back in his breast pocket and said, "Really, keep it. You ever wear that bracelet?"

I put the tiny purple stone in the velvet pouch of my powder compact and thought of the silver bangle, now packed in my suitcase. The opportunity was perfect for me to bring up the Flamingo, but instead, I ordered a milkshake from the waitress. I wished I'd taken the time to buy myself a new package of cigarettes.

Teddy guessed what I was missing and lit me one, handing the burning cigarette to me across the table. I thought up different gambits about going to Vegas, while blowing smoke towards the ceiling. I watched it spiral up above Teddy's head.

"I have a job, I think."

"A job?" Teddy stretched his arms along the back of the booth.

"In Nevada." The milkshake arrived and I poked the straw further into the ice cream.

"Hell of a train ride." He waved one hand towards the window, imagining the station right there, the train just leaving, now, for Nevada, as if he were waving farewell. He smiled.

The fingers in my left hand began trembling. I pressed my nails against the handle of Teddy's hot coffee until the shivering passed. "No, a real job. Dealing cards, not a single game. A job."

"It's hot in Nevada, Mill. You won't like it."

With the burning tip of my cigarette, I pointed out the window at the rain, as if to say, wouldn't hot be a nice change?

"And it's far away."

I nodded, waiting. But he didn't say anything else, just drank his coffee and lit himself a fresh cigarette. He stared at the cigarette for a while. "The mine's gonna take a lot of time for the next few months. Lot of travelling. Thinking of getting myself a car. You can help me choose it."

Which is how I found myself standing in a car lot on Granville and Broadway, rows of cars like giant candies, shiny with rain, blue and white and green and yellow. Cars so fresh, they seemed to grow fully-formed in this grey parking lot, unlikely treats. I stood in the drizzle, smoking. Beyond the cars, heavy clouds weighed upon the blue-black mountains. No amount of hard candy could relieve that gloom.

Behind me, Teddy kicked white-walled tires and talked engines with one of the car salesmen, who perhaps wondered how I fit into the picture. I wasn't sure why I was standing there; I had no opinion about cars, but it seemed easier to stand here in the car lot, in the rain, than talk with Teddy about Nevada. I didn't want him to argue with me, but I was surprised, maybe disappointed, that he had merely warned me about the weather. I threw my cigarette away and frowned fiercely at the clouds. I turned and frowned at Teddy, too, handsome though he was, standing there in the rain, laughing with the salesman. I couldn't hear the joke.

"How 'bout this one, you like this one?" asked Teddy, coming over to me.

Beside me was a white sedanette with chrome on its front that sparkled like teeth. I looked at it and shrugged, not out of nonchalance or even ill-humour—I really knew nothing of cars. He popped the white hood and stared at the guts of the machine while I watched; the salesman trailed over as well, metaphorically rolling up his sleeves to sell Teddy this sedanette. No doubt he'd been hoping to sell something a little more substantial.

"Okay then," said Teddy. "We'll take this one."

When the salesman went off to start on the papers, Teddy closed the hood and said, "You ever drive before?"

"No."

"I'll teach you. Be fun." He went inside to sign the paperwork, leaving me beside the car and I wondered for an instant if he expected me to help him pay for it. My ungenerous heart, I chided myself, as the rain began to fall in earnest. I opened the door of the white car and slipped into the driver's seat. The red interior was cozy. I set my hands on the steering wheel, surprised to see out the windshield—cars usually made me feel like a child, unable to see over the dash, but this was low enough that I might be able to drive it, though I immediately scooted over to the passenger seat when Teddy came out of the office with the keys in his hand.

"We'll go down to the tracks near the port. Lots of straight empty space. No one for you to run down," he said.

"Now?" I said, but Teddy started the car and we were out of the lot and onto Granville. He paused at the red light, played with the windshield wipers, the emergency brake, the radio—which gave him loud blasts of static until he got it set to a jive station. "This is a nice car," he said, over the music. "Good choice, Mill."

"You're really going to teach me to drive?"

"Sure, why not?" When I didn't answer, he said, "Haven't missed me at all, have you, this month I've been outta town? Now you're moving to where in Nevada, exactly, where're you going? Heading outta town like the devil's after you."

"You sound like Mother."

"Bet you haven't told her yet. She'd have let me know."

He drove towards the tracks near the port, the wipers going back and forth across the windshield, wiping the view clean and then not—the mountains, the bridge, False Creek below, with the closed pulp mill, one of its roofs starting to fall in. And then the road turned, twisting across the train tracks, and the windshield wipers trailed water across the view; there was the roundhouse, and the bridge, and a train. I glanced at Teddy.

"*Is* the devil after you? Am I the devil?" He bent his arm along the back of the seat to rest on my neck. Cool hand, reminding me how he'd measured the marks on my neck.

He swerved off the wide street and followed the railway tracks a ways down to the port, along past the sugar factory, until we reached a long straight road with no traffic to speak of—just the tracks, no trains now in sight, the wet road, and the rain leveling off to a mere mist.

"I'm gonna pull over here so you can drive. It's easy." He stopped the car, got out and I slid over. But when he got back into the car, instead of giving me instructions on how to drive, he said, "Let's drive to Vegas. You an' me. It'll be a trip. Whatcha think?" When I didn't answer, mostly because I was trying to figure out how to shift out of park, he said, "Come on, Mill. Take me to Vegas."

"You don't need Vegas," I said, and the car suddenly lurched forward going much too fast. At least the road was straight, and there was nothing on it except the sedanette, devouring wet pavement as fast as could be.

Teddy whistled. "Try it a little slower, okay darlin'?" He leaned over and turned off the windshield wipers. As we faltered in leaps to a crawl, he said serenely, "The brakes work. That's good."

I drove past the sugar refinery while Teddy lit another cigarette. "No," he said speculatively, "I don't need Vegas, you're right. The mine's gonna be busy when it gets going. I've got some remarkable guys interested."

The road curved into the port's loading dock. I braked, and stalled, and started the car again, attempting to turn the vehicle around. I finally located the R and we reversed rather faster than I'd expected. Teddy reached over, popped the shift into drive and pushed the steering wheel to make the corner.

"Easy does it, Mill." Teddy flicked his cigarette out the window. "So what do you need with Vegas?"

I pressed the gas pedal too hard and we lurched forward, picking up speed.

"There you go. You're improving," he said. "'Cept you're headin' north. Vegas is south." He gave me a crooked look that made me bite my cheek. I held my tongue against the torn inside of my mouth. Against the memory of his lip and its scar, the taste of metal and honey, I hit the gas pedal instead of the brake and drove into the ditch.

When Teddy finished laughing, he took the driver's seat. "Give you a proper tour and all, if you're taking off. Which casino is it gonna be?" He pulled past the sugar factory and back over the tracks, towards downtown. "Well?"

I delayed as long as I could before answering him, watching the street ahead of us. I rolled up the window and closed my eyes for a moment. "The Flamingo," I said, opening my eyes to see him again.

He smiled at the windshield. "Pink fairy tale in the desert."

I wondered what he had heard, to say such a thing. "I think I have a job there, that's all." I wanted to keep the Flamingo for myself. *I have to leave*, I thought, fiercely, illogically, *you make me cruel.* Which didn't make me want him any less.

He drove out of the train yards through my silence, drove down the street that had once been Japantown, before the war. We drove past Oppenheimer Park—the hawkers, the peddlers, herb sellers, fishmongers, even the kids playing baseball, they had all disappeared. No shoppers jostled each other for the best orange or cucumber, no one sold bean curd cakes, that strange fermented smell no longer part of the street, all of it gone.

Teddy drove along Water Street, past Dermot's calm bar, only a few drinkers visible through the glass windows as we went by. Tomorrow would be the first of the month and Dermot would be finished with the place. The letters over the door had already been painted over—it would be another's concern, but I couldn't imagine a new owner standing in the same place, polishing glasses, measuring foam on the beer. Time to go, I thought, time to—I risked another glance at Teddy, who was tapping his fingers against the red steering wheel in time to a song on the radio.

He drove past the entrance to Deadman's Island. The Navy boys were busy beyond the gate, flags and insignias polished. Maybe I had some kind of premonition, I don't know. But really, Deadman's Island, what a name.

The island was set aside for the dead by the first people here. I thought about all the bedtime stories I had once told Teddy, when our mothers were out working, when I was still his real and best friend, stories I'd told him while holding out cards, this for you, this for me. Driving by that island, I wished he were still the same, that we both were the way we used to be. Though who that would be, I had no idea—aren't we all overlaid with everything that happens? The memory of a person or a moment, isn't that just one more picture, a slide shown on a wall, and then another one, overlaid on top, so everything blurs, like rain on a windshield.

The road took a curve away from the seawall and into the trees. Teddy said, "Remember all the stories you used to tell me? The bodies in the branches and all that?"

"I wasn't making it up."

He laughed. "'And they put his body in a carved cedar box high in the branches of the highest tree on Deadman's Island, where it could rest until his spirit was free.'"

He could mimic my tone too well, but I was flattered that he remembered the story. I hadn't quite told him the whole saga, that after the Indian burial ground, before the military post, Vancouver's upstanding citizens built a wooden house here. They called it the Pest House, a little wooden building filled with beds, where they sent prostitutes who were sick. A lot of the girls got smallpox, and to keep them away from the general genteel populace, the sick were tucked over here to die. The building still stood when I was young. Haunted, it was said, and when I had nightmares, sometimes that building came into my dreams, with those wasted lives in narrow beds like coffins and no fortunate card for any girl there.

. The road led us away from the little island and I wondered if the boys in uniform ever heard voices at night, and if they did, were the voices good or bad, kind or lonesome? My mother had told me about the Pest House because I'd made a rude remark about a girl we passed on the street, called her a name I'd only just learned in the schoolyard. My mother stopped and slapped me. She told me her mother, my grandmother, had made her bed in Paradise Alley. That's what it was called, there being no street to be a street-walker upon, so to speak. All through the tiny northern towns, it was a kind of living, and my mother's mother had kept two brats on it, until the younger one, a boy, had started coughing up blood and died. And I should remember there was nothing wrong with streetwalking, it was no more dishonest than any other way to make a living, and I wasn't to call any girls rude names, whatever their business was.

I thought now that my mother's views on streetwalking did not gel with her hatred for my chosen living. Was it not as honest a choice?

Teddy touched my hair. "Where've you gone, Mill?"

He pulled the car off the road and parked in the public lot near one of the park's viewpoints. Teddy got out of the car and didn't wait for me, head down, walking towards the seawall. There were no mountains to see, the rain clouds so low, West Vancouver barely visible on the far side of the water. I stepped in a puddle and paused to put up my umbrella, then I followed. There wasn't anything else for me to do.

He turned as I caught up with him, there at the point of the seawall, with the rain slanting in harder than ever. "You're leaving now, aren't you? Leaving tonight or first thing tomorrow. That's why you called me. Damn decent an' all."

I didn't trust the look he had. I said, "It's a fresh start."

"You coming back?"

There wasn't a good answer for that.

"I owe you money, you know. Haven't forgiven you for that."

"That's a fresh start too. Has nothing to do with Nevada."

"Has a lot to do with me."

I opened my mouth to argue, but he didn't notice. He was already walking back to the car. He opened the passenger door for me, waiting for me to close my umbrella and get in. Then he leaned down, one hand against the armrest of the door, the other hand against the edge of the roof, the new key ring looped around his index finger. "Take the car and drive to Vegas. Don't take the train. You should stay away from those old games, anyways. Makes me worry about you. The car's yours. I owe you one, don't I?"

"No, you don't."

"Just take the car. Make me happy. I want you to be...."

I put my hand on his mouth, felt his lips close underneath my uneasy fingers. He looked beautiful, damaged though he was by bad choices and bad luck. The rain suited him. He took my hand off his mouth, put the key ring against my palm and folded my fingers around it.

"You're such an idiot," he said, "what do I have to do?"

I opened my mouth but couldn't make any sound. And when I did speak, I sounded hoarse, I spoke too low and the words came out wrongly. "I do love you. I just...." And then I stopped, because I hadn't meant to say that at all.

Gambling is about losing. The same way living is about dying: you gamble and you lose, same way that you live and you die. Period. There's nothing unpredictable apart from the game itself. Risk, yes, luck, absolutely, and skill—of course, I have skill. But there was never any playing field, no skills I could acquire that would help me live with Teddy. Or maybe live with anyone.

That's what I should have told him, that I didn't trust anyone. He needn't have felt singled out. But he straightened and looked at me sitting there. Then he turned and walked away. Through the rain, of course it was still raining. I watched him go, as if I thought he might turn, even at the corner, turn and wink or wave or—I don't know, the rain made it hard to see. When I finally looked down, I uncurled my hand and there were the keys.

13

Gambling and dying—you may as well get yourself to Vegas in the meantime. The Flamingo was exactly the tropical bird Max had predicted, and I seized that fortune, divested as I was of everything else. My hands cold, I took the winding coast road to Bellingham, barely giving the mountains a glance. I stopped for a sandwich at a diner and it took me a bit of time to get going again—I'd parked, without thinking, on a slight incline, and it was tricky getting the car into reverse. But eventually I was driving again, along the highway that paralleled the train tracks, a route to Seattle that I knew all too well, past oyster joints and nightclubs perched on the cliff overlooking the Pacific. I glanced at the train when it overtook me, and I turned up the radio, I think I even smiled pointedly.

I detoured around downtown Seattle, following the highway signs obediently. There was no need to stop in a motel for the night—I kept going, through Portland and Eugene, the car engine pulling me further south. I drove with the windows rolled down, rain be damned, trailing radio waves, stations changing from polite talk radio to all manner of song stations and religious music. Destiny, destination, I played with the words, humming them nearly. I drove through forty-two little towns; I counted the signs, then I counted how many trucks passed—fourteen through the night, logging, mostly, and seventeen the following day. I bought fried egg sandwiches on brown bread and drove on, through Redding and down the Sacramento Valley, the weather beautiful, cool and sunny. The land reminded me of the Interior, small towns that fanned into nothingness.

I didn't look in the rearview mirror once, only partly because I had forgotten to adjust it for my height. Hours, alone behind the wheel, until I reached Bakersfield and there was a sign MOJAVE DESERT – TRAVEL WITH WATER. I stopped and bought a gallon for the car, along with a bottle of Howel's Root Beer for myself. I had no idea how to put water into the car, but at least I was prepared, should such an eventuality arise.

By the time I reached the Nevada state line, dawn was coming up across the desert's red-brown canyon land. Earth worn fine as dust drifted into my nose, my eyes, my hair, and my hands on the steering wheel stopped aching. I can look back at that moment, see the route into Vegas the way it used to be, nothing but a single road travelling through drought. Every now and then, I glimpsed an empty train track. Nothing but reddish dust and strange distant hills—a barren space where people had to invent themselves.

I thought of a story that begins after a war. The men all rush across a sea to kill each other, because someone has stolen one of their wives. There's something about a golden apple, and desire. The war continues for too long, and eventually, the men who haven't died in battle begin sailing home, and become lost. A storm comes up, because someone releases the wind, or perhaps the survivors are irresolute and they don't really want to get home too quickly. They've been away so long. And they drift through a series of adventures. They land on islands inhabited by monsters. They are enchanted by sorceresses, who weep tears of blood when the men leave. They are trapped by one-eyed giants who eat their friends alive. They are seduced and leave brokenhearted.

Las Vegas is one of those islands, trapped though it is in the desert. The casinos take the place of immortals. People arrive here as if they have strayed, they give themselves up to the capriciousness of Lady Luck, she who masquerades as Fate. No one can resist her siren song, coming as it does with all kinds of neon lights, free drinks, and a real bang-up floor show. Driving in, the pale dawn sky was vast with a mysterious haze over the hills—a heat haze which I now know never really goes away. I travelled towards that haze, through the desert, past the cacti and prickly plants and dust, towards the sun as it rose. I knew I was no sorceress, but I went willingly to work for Lady Luck out there in the desert. I went to lend my hands to the witch's work.

I drove past a crooked road sign, WELCOME TO CITY OF LAS VEGAS, INCORPORATED 1911. I knew Luck's looks could be deceiving, I tried not to be dismayed by my first glimpse of the so-called city. The town was only a handful of seemingly empty buildings and dusty false fronts. I stopped at the first service station I came to—I needed to pause, get my bearings. When I stepped from the car, the ground seemed to move beneath my feet.

I got myself a fresh bottle of soda and took it to the counter, where the guy running the shop was rolling a cigarette. He had the kind of walrus skin that comes from decades of harsh labour. I waited for him to light the cigarette, tiny against his broken face. Through his first exhaled cloud of smoke, he said, "This your first trip to Vegas, missy?"

I nodded.

"Can tell. Bet you been staring at them hills. Don't notice them after a while, they just get to be normal. But they are somethin', aren't they? Creepy." He paused to drag on his cigarette again. "Dead men's hills," he said, inhaling deeply. "But don't say I said so."

"I wouldn't dream of it."

"You'll dream of the place. If you stay. You goin' for a job?"

"I have that look about me, do I?"

"Yep." He sucked on his cigarette.

"You're entirely right."

"Lotsa hotel work. Can see you're not the cocktail type, that's just as well. There're plenty of decent jobs. Don't let anyone talk you into a job you're not happy with. Stick with the decent above board places, missy."

"Thank you for the advice."

"And stay away from gamblin' men. They're no good for a girl."

I kept my face serious. "You don't gamble yourself?"

"I do. I have. An' I regret it. Lost the best things in my life through gamblin'. Every time I swear I'll never return to it, I find myself back at the table emptyin' my pockets. Lost my wife that way. Lost my daughter too. Lost every friend I had. My brother don't speak to me. I still have my second wife, for now, but you'll notice I'm by myself. The wife is visitin' her sister in China Lake. Horrible town, is China Lake. Military men're just as bad as gamblin' ones."

"The two can overlap." I thought of Teddy. How could I not?

"That is the truth. Except in my own case." He held out his right hand flat, a little shaky. His ring finger and pinkie were mere stubs, missing their two upper joints. I'd not noticed earlier, when he was rolling his cigarette, proof I was kind of shaky myself. "With fingers like this, none too many'll give me a gun. But anyone at all's willin' to give me a pair of dice. Lost those fingerprints at the Grand Coulee, diggin' in a pump. Out in the dust."

I gave him a dime to pay for the soda.

He took the coin. "Don't bother me. I'd rather have dust than water. Water's just plain mean. I hate that dam. A body can't trust all that water, stuck in one place. Muck, mud, and lake weeds. I hate the damp. Give me the desert anytime. You know where you stand with a desert—it don't care about you and that's final. Whereas water has it in for a person, sneaky-like."

"I know what you mean," I said.

He nodded his head and waved the cigarette towards the scrub outside the window. "If someone knew a use for sage, he'd be a millionaire. Where're you goin' first?"

"The Flamingo."

"Flamingo's an upright joint. Good choice. But you might wanna wash up some before you go on over there. You're proper, I can see that, but you're lookin' a little off your feed. There's a diner just down the road some. Keep drivin' straight."

So these few dusty buildings weren't the entire town, there was more to the place—I was glad to hear it. Back in the car, I furled and unfurled my fingers against the steering wheel. The dusty main street was more interesting than the outskirts of town, but only slightly. Despite its oasis-inspired name, Las Vegas was no meadow. It was a baked sand-coloured little town, nothing like today's Vegas, no lights, no crowds. When I got there, the place was dusty and unimpressive, like me. Its talents had yet to be revealed. The only reason to be in Vegas was to gamble or to get a divorce, and I felt like I was doing both, here in this strangely most perfect place I could ever have invented for myself, where my hands were surely worth exactly their value. The air seemed to shimmer slightly above the sawdust gambling joints. The town was a daughter of the sun, a Circe disguised with low familiar buildings, as if it were no different from Lethbridge or Kamloops or any other stop on my old train routes. A few shops had fashionable window mannequins, brand new addresses with fresh paint, Lucky Strike cigarettes ads and "Camels Don't Get Your Wind" in big writing. The rest were dim and faded, false fronts like the shacks near the gas station where I'd stopped. It was all familiar, the signs, street, shops, but the colour of the light was wrong. A good kind of wrong, if you know what I mean.

The diner was very turquoise and bright enough to compete with the white light of outside. Behind the counter, a woman with too much cotton-candy-blond hair piled on her head was rearranging the coffee cups. "Be with you in a second sweetie," she said, and she was. "What'll it be? We've got a blueberry pancake special that'll perk you right up."

"Don't I look perky?"

"A little tired, sweetie. Just arrived?"

I nodded.

"I'll bring you the pancake special. Coffee?"

"Tea, if you don't mind."

I went to the washroom and let the tap pour cool water across my neck and wrists. I smoothed my hair such as I could, and pulled a pale yellow shirt from my bag. In the little toilet space, I changed into a skirt that was wrinkled but businesslike. When I returned to my seat, the waitress brought me a pile of pancakes on a plate the size of a football field.

"How do I get to the Flamingo?" I asked.

"Easy as pie, sweetie, head straight on out of here. Only the one road. You'll pass El Rancho, then the Flamingo. Take your pick. The Flamingo's the classiest. The other one's a dude ranch, if you know what I mean."

I didn't have any idea what a dude ranch might be. "The Flamingo's where I'm headed," I assured her. "The pancakes are fantastic."

"Everybody needs a good breakfast," she said. "Good luck."

I left seventy-five cents to cover my meal and a gratuity for her friendliness to a plain and hungry stranger, and I went back to my dust-streaked white car. I turned the key and wondered if the sedanette felt as tired as I did. First, as the waitress had warned me, I drove past El Rancho, which had an affair that looked like a lighthouse stuck on the top—later I found out it was supposed to be a windmill, clearly built by someone with only the slightest idea of what a windmill did. After the Rancho, there was a long stretch of emptiness, a lovely warm expanse of air that shimmered, sliding in the windows of the car as if it were velour. The whole view shivered with the day heating up; the resulting blur was completely different from the smear that rain gives Vancouver. At the far end of the road, as if through a flipped-around telescope, I caught sight of the Flamingo. I imagined the Flamingo, I admit this, as a bird. A tall pink bird in the landscape, maybe because that's what Max the doorman had predicted. But the Flamingo didn't look anything like a bird. It was definitely pink, though. A wavering solid stretch of pastel architecture came up along the highway.

Someone described the Flamingo as a movie set with no budget limits and in retrospect, that seems about right. I stopped the car at the edge of the long curving driveway, and getting out of the car was like walking into a Fred Astaire movie—the sweep of driveway, the elegant entrance, the absurdly pink low building with its crazy tall sign, the *F* a stylized swerve that looked more like a bird in flight, a flamingo, I suppose, than any letter of the alphabet. The low suave pink building was framed by all sorts of pines and twisting palms that couldn't be natural to the desert. I paused just before the lobby entrance, purse over my arm; I pinched a pine needle from the nearest shrub, crushed the green pine between two fingers and held it under my nostrils. My need for this job, my desire to work here, crowded my head, and the pine reassured me. I closed my eyes and inhaled the scent of the woods in Vancouver, the hobo jungles with their appalling liquor made of pine sap, Teddy convincing me to lie down in a bed of pine needles, a long, long time ago. The soft mattress of the coast I'd abandoned. Knocked off-course by memory, I might have hesitated there for too long if the tree in front of me hadn't rustled. I opened my eyes as the pine bush swayed wildly and a man in a black tuxedo backed out.

I coughed to warn him I was there—nothing worse than not knowing you have an audience. He pulled himself completely out of the underbrush and shook his head, holding something small and broken in his hands. "Poor thing," he said. "Got hisself run over. I saw the delivery truck did it, bounced right off the bumper. I was with a guest, didn't have a chance to get him out."

He was holding a black and white kitten, still breathing, but one of its back legs bent awkwardly, and its whole side scraped furless from the asphalt. I stepped closer, put a finger on the kitten's unhappy head, between the ears, and rubbed, then ran my hand over the back legs. It was a small female kitten. She didn't hiss or scratch, which wasn't encouraging. The cats I'd known in Vancouver, even when tiny, were fierce—isn't that the point of cats? But this kitten wasn't in any fit state to argue with me as I felt along its leg. As my fingers found the right place, its hip popped back into its tiny socket. The kitten shrieked as the leg fell back into a healthy position, but then the creature moved its head to peer back at its paw, relieved of the immediate worst of the pain. I moved my hand away, almost as surprised as the kitten itself.

"What'd you do there?" said the man, "Lookit that." The kitten, sensing new possibilities, hissed at me and began to make a tentative attempt at washing its side. "Poor thing, gonna go bandage him up," said the man in the tux, leaving me on the doorstep of the Flamingo with grit and cat fur all over my hands. I didn't want to wipe my fingers on my skirt, and if I stayed in the driveway, I'd get myself run over, too. I tried dusting my palms together, to no great effect.

In the reception area, the first person I saw was a big man with a face like a broken plate. "Excuse me, is there somewhere I could wash my hands?"

"What happened to you?" he said.

"A cat got itself run over in your driveway."

"Do I know you?"

"No sir," I said, my confidence wavering. I swallowed and started again. "My name's Millard Lacouvy. I came to have a word with Mr. Chappell if I could. I thought I'd wash my hands first."

"Lavatory's that way." He gestured towards the left. "Ah, hell, I'll walk you there. What happened to the cat?"

"Your porter's fixing him up." We walked through a green lounge. I didn't have time to look around properly, I was nearly skipping to keep up with his inconvenient big-legged walk.

"Ladies to the left. Where're you from?"

"Vancouver, got in this morning." I leaned against the swinging door of the lavatory. "I'll be right back." Soap, hot water, clean hand towels—I washed my hands, staring at my wan face in the mirror over the sink. I pinched my cheeks and bared my teeth at my reflection. Maybe fresh lipstick would help. I powdered my face and checked my hair and threw back my shoulders. This was it, my chance to get a job, an actual job, one I really wanted, at least until I built a bankroll; I smiled at my reflection and tried to stay convinced.

The big man was waiting for me, staring out the window at the elaborate garden. He turned. "So what d'you want to see Dick about?" He leaned against a round table in the green lounge and nodded to the seat opposite. "Please...."

The chair was a kind of triangle, sloped towards the back, so I perched on its edge—if I sat down properly, I would tip over with my feet stuck straight out stiff. I felt worse than before, positively silly, balancing there like the bird I wasn't, hoping to convince this bear of a man that I could deal cards. I tried to ignore the sweat on the back of my neck. "A friend of mine, Sam Lazar, suggested I speak to Mr. Chappell."

"We're about all in for chamber maids."

I was sure of who he was, then. "I'm not applying to be a chamber maid, sir. You're Mr. Chappell, aren't you sir?"

The big man smiled. "How'd you know Lazar?"

"We met on a train, crossing Canada."

"He should get himself down here. I haven't seen the guy in months."

"He's looking well."

"How'd you meet Sam exactly?"

I looked out at the manicured garden of the hotel, and I told him the truth. "I met Mr. Lazar in a card game." I turned and held his gaze. "Sam knows I play good poker. Please...." I could see he was about to cut me off, so I ran on, "I'm serious. I'm good. That's how I know Mr. Lazar, who says to tell you, excuse me for saying this but, he says he's sent you the best hands he knows, because he figures you need them right about now. He sends his best regards." I tried to remember if Lazar had given me any other message for Chappell, but all I could remember were the runny eggs Benedict we'd eaten for breakfast at the Dine in the Sky.

Chappell laughed, more of a snort. "Sam thinks you're a poker player. A girl poker player. No wonder you wanted to wash your hands. We should talk in my office."

His office turned out to be behind the hotel check-in, a perfectly square room with a one-way mirror looking into the casino. There wasn't much to see as yet—it was too late in the morning for the nightlife, too early for the afternoon players. On the wall behind Chappell's desk hung a carefully-drawn map of the hotel grounds; later I discovered that the location of every tree was marked on this map, each plant species identified, along with every room, every parking space, everything except the exact details of Siegel's own suite in the hotel, which he had good reason for keeping private. I sat down on one of the hard chairs opposite the desk and Dick Chappell took out a pack of cards, broke the seal, and handed the deck to me. I shuffled and arranged the cards in the arc that always precedes a casino game—I felt more awake, just touching the cards. I couldn't help glancing sidelong out through the mirror, admiring the bright, organized casino floor where I aspired to work.

Chappell nodded his head very slightly. "We only have men dealing blackjack."

"I'm better at poker."

"No, definitely only men deal poker. No one'll play cards with a girl dealing poker."

"I understand, but I'm a better class of dealer than the men Mr. Lazar implied were currently working for you."

Dick raised his eyebrows. "You're not shy, are you."

"Can't afford to be at this size."

"No poker. Can you see over a blackjack table?"

I let that pass. If I had to start with blackjack, then so be it—at least let me get that much. I was in Vegas, I could play poker on my own time. I wanted the protection of a casino and here I was. I gathered up the cards in front of me and dealt out a round of blackjack, which I'd tried out years ago at Dermot's. None of the men there liked blackjack, so I had abandoned the effort. Now I was glad for the experience.

Chappell picked up his phone, grey and clunky and without a dial, and barked, "Get Savage in here."

I picked up the deck and reshuffled a few times, no tricks, and fanned the cards in an arc. Using the joker, I flipped the line of cards over like dominoes, so all the faces showed. I gathered them up and dealt a round of cards, picked them up again, reshuffled, stripped the cards, and laid them out in a fresh round of blackjack. It was something to pass the time while we waited for Savage, whoever that might be. At the end of my first imaginary round, I glanced up through the one-way mirror and saw a dark-haired man, medium height, serious, crossing the casino floor. As he put his hand on the door to come in, he turned his face towards the glass, as if he could look through the mirror into Dick's office. Which is when I recognized him.

My fickle confidence fell out of my chest and pooled around my shoes before I could even gather up the cards. I picked up the pack and shuffled again, then I put my confidence back where my heart ought to be. The dark-haired man who called himself Savage was the one man in the country who wasn't likely to hire me—I'd called him a cheat years ago, when I'd left him on Water Street in Vancouver.

I was amazed I recognized him so quickly. But he looked just the same, easy to remember, whether he was calling himself Roberts or Savage. That's how fortune works – luck has an unfortunate sense of humour. When he came through the door, his smile was turned full force on me, as if he'd been expecting me all along. The lines at the corners of his mouth only improved him. He looked older and more reliable, not the shark I recalled. Nearly ten years ago, I was back in that laundry at the hotel, and his eyes were still hazel, cold clear starbursts. He showed no surprise as he walked in.

"Millard Lacouvy, I knew I'd see you again."

Chappell was astonished. "You know each other?"

I didn't like the idea of a card cheat strolling into Chappell's office at the Flamingo, it seemed wrong. But I needed the job, so when Roberts put out his hand, I put down the cards I had been shuffling and stood up to shake his hand. My fingers weren't going to tremble, I could control that—if you're going to play poker, you'd better have hands that don't quiver whenever there's hard change in the wind. But I was darned if I was going to demonstrate my skills like a one-trick pony. He took his other hand and covered mine, so I was held fast.

"This," Roberts said to Chappell ceremoniously, not letting go of my hand, "is the girl I once invited to be my card partner. She's the best player I've ever seen. Bar none, present company included. And she turned me down flat."

"Did she?"

"I was underage." I had to say something. I slid my fingers from his and sat down, because my legs suddenly weren't reliable. My legs wanted to take it upon themselves to run me straight out that casino and keep running until I was far from Vegas; my legs didn't mind if I got lost in the desert, as long as they got me far from this casino office. An illogical feeling, but there it was.

Both men stared at me. Then Chappell grinned. "Never heard of a girl mechanic."

"If she'll deign to work for me—as I say, she's refused before—if she'll work for me, I recommend you take her. Girl, on the short side, and all."

"We'll put her on a blackjack table and see how she does."

"Blackjack's a waste of her skills."

"Start her there," said Chappell. "Well? Alright with you?"

I swallowed the shiver that came just from looking at Roberts. The only paid job I'd ever had was at the Hotel Vancouver, and he'd been my inspiration to quit. Now here we were. I put down the pride that made me want to deal poker. "Blackjack will be wonderful," I said. "Thank you, gentlemen."

"Welcome aboard then," said Chappell, and shook my hand, engulfing it easily in his ham fist, though his touch was gentle.

"I'll give you a tour of the grounds," said Roberts.

Chappell picked up the telephone, paused and looked at me. "You have a place to stay?"

"I'll find something."

"Talk to my wife. She's a gold mine for that sort of thing."

"Allow me, I'll introduce you." Roberts held the door and ushered me out into the lounge. "The casino leads out to the pool," he said. "It's a damn fine view. I'll show you around."

We walked past the high tables of the blackjack, where the dealers stood and players sat on tall stools. I studied the dealer nearest me, a gangly redhead with no style in card handling. His lack of skill conflicted with the beautiful lighting, the calm atmosphere, the spanking new game table—I knew I was more than qualified to do his job. Roberts waited for me at the doors that led outside. When I caught up with him, he pushed the door open and went out into the gardens behind the casino, taking slow steps the way he had walked with me once in Vancouver.

"Your name is what exactly, now?" I said.

His smile hadn't tarnished with use, and I suspected he used it often. "Savage. Foolish name, but it's my own."

"My name hasn't changed any."

"I knew you'd end up working for me."

I didn't like the idea of working for a cheat, but I managed to stay quiet.

He said, "You've come at a good time. We need some dealers with talent." He escorted me through the gardens, showing me different trees as if they were each his idea, oleander and hibiscus, brightly-coloured things I'd never thought about before, with scents I would gradually get used to. The place smelled nothing like Vancouver—the air filled with the dusty green of the different plants around us and the chlorine of the swimming pool. I flexed my hands, I couldn't help it.

"Siegel is mad for plant life. You wouldn't think it, a guy of his reputation. But he loves all this. Takes the gardening more seriously than the rest of it." He nodded to the gardeners working in the grounds—very Lord of the Manor, he was, pointing out the buildings. "Stables there, golf course starts at the far end." We circled around until we were level with a row of small cottages at the back of the lot. "Chappell lives in the bungalow furthest to the left. Wife's name is Mavis."

"Thank you."

"And call me Stan. Please. I'll see you later." He smiled again, I couldn't tell if he was simply happy to see a familiar face, or if he thought I'd be useful to him. I wondered if he lived in one of the little bungalows, too, as I watched him walk back to the casino. What did it say about the Flamingo, that a cardsharp was in charge of the floor? Roberts be darned, I thought, and knocked on the door of Chappell's bungalow. When no one answered, I knocked again.

"Round here," called a voice from around the corner. I followed the sound. A dark-haired woman in a red bathing suit sat up from her lounge chair. "You caught me," she said, her Southern accent clearer now. "My pre-lunch treat. I love the sun."

"Mrs. Chappell?"

"Mavis," she said, stretching out her hand.

I introduced myself as a newly-hired dealer, and Mavis was too polite to say what her expression gave away. I gave her my most encouraging smile. "Your husband said you'd know where I might find a room."

"Dick believes I know everything."

"Don't you?"

She picked up her robe and led me back to the bungalow. Inside, the little company house was immaculate, sun streaming in through the Venetian blind. "I hope you're a good dealer," she said, disappearing into the bedroom. "We need players to lose more money in this joint."

I looked through the slats of the Venetian blind, out at the perfectly-land-scaped garden, until Mavis reappeared in an orange shirtwaist dress; she was one of those brunettes that looked like a house afire in bright colours.

"Don't tell Dick I was out sunbathing here. Mr. Ben wants me at the pool every morning, showing some leg, as he so kindly puts it. But some days, I just don't feel social."

"The pool's lovely."

Mavis smiled. She had a mouth that went just a tiny bit down at one edge, a mouth that gave itself away, and I trusted her just for that—Mavis was the real thing, even in the absurd dreamed-up pink Flamingo. And clearly she wasn't sure what to do with me.

"I'm looking forward to working here," I said, trying to reassure her. "Once I find a place to live. You probably know what I'll be able to afford on the salary."

"Yes," she said, picking up the phone and dialing. She listened to it ring somewhere, then there was a click. "George," she said, without giving the click a moment to speak, "dear, look, I've got someone here. She's new, one of our dealers. Yes, she. Do you have room? Good, yes, do. I'll send her right over, or no, I'll make lunch first. She'll be over in the afternoon. Of course I will. Yes."

She hung up the receiver. "George manages a building down off Fremont. Not noisy. Or nosy, come to think of it. He's a trooper, won't overcharge you. He mothers his boarders a bit. A good man, which I can't honestly say of everyone in this town."

I wasn't sure I wanted to be mothered by a man named George.

"Now lunch," she said, "I'd planned sandwiches, but with you here we should have something more substantial."

"There's no...."

"You seem hungry. I'll do up pork chops." She headed to the kitchen, paused at the fridge. "You like pork chops?"

I became friends with Mavis Chappell not by impressing her with any fancy dealing, but because I topped and tailed green beans for lunch, to go with the pork chops, and when the food was ready, I appreciated the meal, though I felt smudged, my three days of driving catching up with me.

We sat down to the meal, Mr. Dick Chappell across from me and Mavis at the end of the table. Chappell was a big chewer; he didn't spend much time worrying about me. He took moments between bites to gaze at his wife as if he was surprised to find her here, surprised in a good way. Mavis Chappell didn't fit with the clichés of women who looked like she did—she could have auditioned for the role of Calypso, seducing any sailor she pleased. She could have beaten any Californian movie star as a pinup. But she cooked pork chops in the middle of the Flamingo's well-landscaped grounds, to make a tired stranger feel at home. She was from the desert, not what I expected from a woman with a flowery Southern accent. Texas may not be known for its deserts. "But the desert's there, nonetheless," said Mavis. "Not all perfect pasture, is Texas. Dry as death, some of it." She shook her head. "I grew up in a dried-out little town called Muleshoe. Dust here's just like home. You get to like it."

She recognized the heat in Vegas, and the strange local plants, and the shimmering distant hills, she felt at ease, while everyone else sweated against the atmosphere, watering their lawns and filling up their swimming pools. Mavis didn't see the point of swimming pools, she said. "A girl can sunbathe just as well in the dust."

Chappell was managing a gambling boat off the coast of LA. He and Mavis were living in Santa Monica—she hadn't liked all that water, and the gambling boats made her nervous. "The whole thing feels likely to sink, don't you think?" So when the bosses said go to the desert, give Siegel some advice for God's sake, Chappell said of course. He packed a suitcase, set it on the passenger seat beside him and drove off into the Mojave Desert, promising Mavis he'd send for her as soon as he could.

Chappell worked exactly as he was supposed to, managing the Flamingo, calling in men he knew from running the horse racing wire, Mavis told me.

She listed names, and the only one I recognized was Stan Savage. Mavis wasn't crazy about the racing men—she wasn't crazy about a lot in the business—but she loved her husband. So after Chappell spent January sorting out Siegel's business knots, he sent for Mavis, to make the move permanent, and she did what any devoted wife would do: she packed their belongings and bought a train ticket for Vegas, no questions asked.

I can picture this in my head. She probably arrived looking like she'd spent a night in a five-star hotel with a makeup girl fussing over her, though she sat up for the short train trip in a hard coach seat to save the dollar. She told me she was a girl who had grown up with no shoes; only the horses were decently shod where she came from. She wasn't much older than me and she'd made it out of the dust bowl without even cards on her side—a girl who'd worn dresses made out of flour sacks and had turned out beautiful, built on dust as she was. When the train stopped in Las Vegas, I imagine she paused on the top stair of the train, surveying the knockdown town. She took a long look at the dust that hung in the air, and I imagine she smiled. Dick Chappell would have known everything would be okay, because of that smile.

After lunch, Chappell went back to the casino, saying he'd see me at six for the start of the evening shift. Mavis gave me directions to George's. "How long have you been dealing cards?"

"I'm older than I look."

"So you've been in this business since you could walk."

I had to laugh, she was so serious about it. "Your husband was right, you do know everything."

"George here is a good egg. He'll look after you."

It was my height, I guess, made her assume I needed looking after. Or maybe she knew there are times when everyone needs looking after.

🐭

I have to keep reminding myself how the town looked back then, as if I could overlay a series of slides in my head, there, and pull each one away—buildings disappear, sidewalks roll up, trees aren't planted yet, the strip malls don't exist, swimming pools haven't been dug—take each addition away until there is only the road I drove down, not even really a highway. Nowadays I miss the wide-open emptiness of the Vegas I first saw. It's gone now. You won't find it if you come here.

I veered to avoid a cat playing with something on the highway. Maybe killing a rat. Mavis said Benny Siegel had a thing for felines, and the cats returned his faith by clearing the place of rats. The desert is full of vermin, every kind of mouse, gerbil, rat, and every time Vegas added a street, the rodents got bigger. As the city changed from a dusty station siren to a trumped-up harlot, the rats turned from fierce honest desert rats to crafty dishonest casino rats. Those cats had their work cut out for them.

The landscape leaked over and around the car, showing more horizon than I was used to seeing in the middle of a town. I drove down Fremont, following the directions Mavis had given me. I passed the less-than-discrete sign for the Apache and took the next two blocks at speed. I pulled up in front of an old but well-kept wood frame house, the upper storey spreading out on either side onto an empty shop front, a barbershop, a corner store. The house didn't look tremendous, but it looked cheap and reasonably respectable, the only qualities I was fussy about. I got my suitcase out of the trunk and went up the stairs to the front door. I set the shabby suitcase at my feet and rang the bell. After a suitable delay, I raised my hand to knock in case the bell didn't work, when the door was forcefully swung open. A man in an emerald green dressing gown glared down at me from the doorway. I looked up at his face, and then gaped back down at his dressing-gown, which went to the floor in extravagant satin-shiny green folds. I probably opened my eyes a little wider than usual—someone who wasn't a poker player might have fainted.

"You Mavis's friend?"

"Yes." I held out my hand. "Millard Lacouvy, pleased to meet you."

"George." He put out his wide hand. While we shook, I realized he wasn't glowering at me, he was peering shortsightedly. "What's your name? Milly?"

"Millard."

"Millard. Okey-dokey. I'm George. Your room's on the top floor, two bucks a week. In advance. Breakfast's included, every morning in the kitchen. Which is in back, I'll show you. Come in," he said, sweeping his arm grandly into the dim wallpapered interior.

"I don't know what you've heard about me," he said, as I passed him. "The kitchen's back this way. These are my rooms downstairs, if you ever need me. Phone's here in the hall...."

Going up the uncarpeted wooden stairs behind him, I noticed he wore high-heeled velvet slippers with a little pouf of marabou feather stuck over the toes. As if he needed extra height. Catching me looking at his shoes, he pointed out the uneven step on the first landing. "Twisted my ankle on that, when I first fixed up the place."

"I hope you weren't badly hurt."

"I'm not as fragile as I look."

He looked about as fragile as a rhinoceros, but a sensitive one whose feelings had been trampled in the past.

The room for rent had a good-sized window with rose-patterned curtains, walls papered all over in small rose posies, and a rose bedspread to match. A lace runner covered the dark wooden dresser. It wasn't at all my taste, but I said, "It's perfect," because I wanted it to be, even if it was only halfway good.

"I did it up myself," he said, preening a bit. "I like things to be pretty."

I nodded, though I wondered how such a large man, with such hairy hands, had ever traipsed into Nevada wearing feathered mules, yearning for prettiness.

"Two of my brothers work at the Apache," he said, as if he too sometimes wondered what he was doing in Vegas. "You'll be better off at the Flamingo, much classier joint. Mavis'll look after you. We're going to be friends, you and me." He stepped back into the hallway. "You look right beat. Have yourself a nap. We'll talk later."

"It's...." I started, but George cut me off.

"If Mavis recommends a girl, I take her in. No questions asked."

"Thank you." I meant it more than I could say. I closed the door, took off my shoes and stockings and lay down on the bed. I stared at the rose-coloured posies. Finally, after days of driving, and the casino, and lunch with Mavis, I was so tired, falling and falling into sleep. And while I slept, Teddy was in rainy Vancouver, I hoped unbothered by my absence. I hoped he was smiling at the too-green mountains, making plans about that fool amethyst mine.

14

The amethyst sank into my dreams. I dreamed of purple water, a lake so huge and glowing there were no edges to it, a lake that went on as far as the eye could see, so no matter what direction I gazed in, all I saw was water, violet, not blue, stretched like a taut fabric across the landscape. I dreamed that a lake covered this whole Death Valley; only later did I learn that the lake had been real, a vast body of water that dried up twenty thousand years ago, vanishing with no excuse, the amethyst mirror of its surface suddenly sinking into the ground and leaving dust in its wake, the reverse of a tidal wave. No one knew why the lake disappeared, though in my dream the water shimmered, shivered as if alive, transforming and divining itself into an invisible lure, evaporating into the dusty sage-scented air.

When their lake disappeared, the Indians who lived on its shores were appalled, but they remained fond of the place, despite its dryness. They became experts in lack; they dealt with the new conditions by creating games of chance. They worked gambling into a belief system—bones like dice, thrown into patterns. Fortune and chance as religion. Really, if you've grown up beside a nice purple lake and suddenly one day it up and vanishes, after that, everything starts to look like a crap shoot.

I woke up flailing in George's rose-patterned room, as if the lake threatened to drown me. When I'd washed the dream from my face in the mauve bathroom down the hall, I dressed in clean clothes, I put on mascara, lipstick, blotted my face with powder, as if a well-made face might make a difference to my success as a blackjack dealer.

Benny Siegel decreed that everyone in the Flamingo would wear tuxedoes, from the dealers on up, from the housekeepers on down. Everyone wore black penguin gear except the management—Savage, Chappell and such wore whatever suits they chose. So when I returned to the Flamingo, finding a tuxedo to fit me became the first order of the day. With a certain amount of searching, the wardrobe mistress came up with a jacket that might have been ideal for a boy tap dancer. It didn't take into consideration the shape of a short woman, but I wasn't in the mood to fuss, and as I never did have that much of a chest, the jacket was fine as long as I left it unbuttoned. The skirt, well, the wardrobe mistress did her best, mouth full of pins, grumbling Polish-accented instructions. I took only one thing from my purse: I slipped the purple stone, that amethyst from Teddy, into the breast pocket of the tuxedo jacket. Not sentimentality, exactly. Just something that actually belonged to me, unlike the borrowed black tux.

Suitably done up, I went to find Roberts. Savage. I ended up saying "Stan," when I saw him, as he'd asked me to, because it was easier than remembering which last name was rightly his. He had changed into a darker suit for the evening shift, all steely grey silk with a pale blue shirt that set off his tan. Despite myself, I thought he looked fine. He knew the importance of costume—to be taken seriously at a cards table, you need to look the part.

I on the other hand looked foolish. "This tuxedo isn't...."

Stan ignored my complaint; he took my arm as though escorting me to dinner, except he held my arm a bit too hard, as if he thought I was going to shake him off. "You're at table nine for the first shift. Bear in mind you're working in a legal joint, not a backroom, okay Millard?" He lightened his grip. "Follow the rules as I give them to you."

"Not much of a challenge if you don't follow the rules," I murmured, annoyed that a man I knew was a cheat was reminding me to stay above board. But as we walked through the shining new casino, I was too impressed by the surroundings to begrudge him much. He had landed well, I thought. As we passed the roulette section, the men behind the tables—not dealers, I mean the watchers, the pit bosses—they all nodded to Savage respectfully. The roulette wheels spinning, the customers leaning in to watch their numbers, the pretty women in colourful dresses and diamond necklaces—yes, it was a good start to the night, walking through the Flamingo. If I played my cards right, I could get used to such a shiny safe place. I watched one of the roulette wheels for a moment as the croupier released the ball into the spinning wheel.

A discrete door was set in the wall behind the roulette wheels. Stan Savage led me into a little room with no windows, where a table was littered with racing papers and ashtrays, with a big clock above and a hulking grey television in the corner tuned to static fuzz. Fourteen men, all dealers, all more or less in tuxedoes, sat in the room, some with their jackets off and their shirts open, sleeves undone. All but one was my age—I mean, too young to be reliable as casino dealers. Cards recognize age and experience; unless you make a special arrangement with them, they'll take advantage of you. I couldn't help but wonder where these dealers had come from. Most didn't look as if they could find an ace in a stacked deck, and they regarded me just as dubiously, clearly thinking, "A girl? A midget girl dealing blackjack? God, the joint's in worse shape than we thought." They scrunched their eyes and calculated how soon they should start looking for new employment.

Despite the more or less audible comments, Stan Savage introduced me like a quick round of cards. The names waterfall from my memory: Walter, Joe, Jake, Howie, Daniel, Charlie....

"This is Millard Lacouvy," Stan said, "on table nine to start. Gentlemen, please note, she plays cards as well or better than any of you lot. I'm relying on you to make her feel welcome."

The men didn't answer. No one was wearing a nametag that matched the name Stan introduced them as—nametags were obligatory for dealers, and I was unsurprised no one chose their real names. Every guy had a tag that read as standard as possible: John or Mike, except for one bright spark whose nametag read Roscoe—the only old guy in the bunch, Walter looked sixty, easily three times the age of the other dealers. I learned later that his nickname had always been Roscoe, he'd had the nametag made specially. I didn't expect to like the man; he chewed a stubby cigar and the lapels of his tuxedo were spotted with ash.

"So you're the girl dealer." Roscoe screwed up his small eyes to give me the once-over as Stan finished the introductions.

"Nice to meet you," I said.

"Don't hold with girls at blackjack, myself." Roscoe took the cigar out of his mouth and squinted at it; there was no smoke, the tobacco's glow had gone out. Savage held out a lighter. Roscoe shook his head, his jowls moving slower than the rest of his face, as if they weren't connected to the main nerve centre. "Nah, I'll just chew for a while." He was pasty white, the colour you turn if you don't go outside very often. "So're we done here?" he said to Stan, "I have things to do."

I tried not to sigh. Stan gave me a nametag that read "Leslie"—at least I could pretend it was a woman's name, though no doubt the tag had been made for a man, one of the dealers fired after the disastrous Christmas opening. It didn't matter what the tag said, as long as it wasn't a name that could be traced in the phone book—as a dealer, the last thing you need is some player harassing you outside casino hours.

Jake and Roscoe were the two senior cardmen on my shift, and clearly they were unimpressed about having to work with a woman. I suppose if I'd been leggy and blond, they might have been more forgiving. I wanted them to like me, but that was probably unrealistic, and really, why did it matter? Their opinion was irrelevant to the cards.

Back on the floor, the contrast of colours was mind-boggling compared to the little windowless room. The casino was like an ice cream shop dreamed up by a demobbed man on junk. It was blue, purple, orange, fuchsia, and green. The chairs were shaped like triangles. The waitresses were all curves and up-do. The wood and brass fixtures on the gaming tables shone with polish; the red felt on the roulette tables was smooth as a prostitute's blush. The staff's black tuxedoes gave the impression players had stumbled onto a cruise ship, a kind of casino-ballroom where Ginger and Fred just might dance past, a trail of magenta feathers in their wake. But despite the riot of colours, table nine turned out to be the slowest table, tucked away towards the back corner. A low table limit, out of the main traffic—a sensible if disappointing place to start out. Seeing me look at the feeble players, Stan said, "You won't be back here for long, Millard, don't worry."

"I'm not worrying," I lied.

He frowned, the shifting colour of his eyes changing intensity. "It's harder than it looks. You should worry. I do." He shook his head, as if remembering something. "If there's a fire, stay with the chips 'til someone locks them down. Okay?"

"If there's a fire?"

"Mmhm, if there's a fire, you lie down on the table on top of the chips, to protect them."

I did my darnedest not to laugh. If there were a fire, I'd be running out the door along with everyone else. I certainly wouldn't be lying down on the table to protect the casino's symbols. But I nodded, silently holding my tongue against my teeth.

"This is Parry, your pit boss." Stan took his hand from my arm and shook hands with a thug wearing a navy blue suit. Parry was my first experience with a professional pit boss. He was a Mormon. Most of the pit bosses in Vegas were Mormons back then; with time I learned that Mormons are, from an employer's point of view, ideal for a casino—they're obsessed with money, they don't drink, and they don't touch cards or dice, as their religion forbids it. Parry was exemplary for the breed. He depended on his eyes, kept everyone honest by staring down our necks and glaring at the patrons. He made sure we dealers laid the money cleanly on the table, he eyeballed the chips we counted out; he was a live recording of everything we did. Each pit boss had four to six tables to oversee. We played with our backs to him while he glared over our shoulders at the game's surface. Parry didn't touch chips or money, he just watched, and it seemed his God had punished him for this obsessive watching, for the man had small warts outlining the upper edge of his eyelids, as if tiny flesh-lumpen insects weighed upon his eyes, trying to get at the rest of his face. The effect was unnerving, to put it mildly. I was glad to turn my back on him.

"Dust your hands," said Stan, to talk me through the opening ritual for dealing. He swatted his hands back and forth.

I imitated him, clapping and shaking out my cuffs, proving there were no chips or cards hidden in my sleeves or in my palms.

"When you've done that to Parry's satisfaction, break open the deck and do a wash."

I spread the cards out in an arc, in numerical order, and washed them as instructed, pushing them into a big pile, face-down and mixed up as if I were about to play Fish with a child. Not at all like washing sheets in a laundry, despite the name. When I felt the cards were nicely clean, I reassembled them into a deck. Stan watched as I shuffled and stripped the deck—like pulling bark off a branch, rough little groups of cards being pulled away from the main pack. It was a ritual whereby the new cards and I got to know one another, we sized each other up before any players tilted our relationship. I felt the cards become my allies, even if we were only going to play blackjack.

Before Stan left me to work, he grinned at me, a flashing instant of delight breaking through his reserve. His joy made me look down at my hands. I pinched a speck of imaginary fluff from the immaculate felt in front of me. I'd never had such conditions for work, such elegant lighting, impeccably-groomed operating surface, brand new chips lined up in front of me in a shiny brass holder. I wanted to revel a little, though it was only blackjack. Behind me Parry made a hissing noise with his teeth. I glanced sideways to discover him smiling at me, an expression in no way suiting his wart-loaded eyes. The smile emphasized how his face was shaped, as if fists had planed off his jaw during some previous enterprise. It did not make him a joy to look at.

"Makin' yourself happy over here? Know what you're up against, got everything set out for yourself, all's okay...."

"Yes, sir."

His smile vanished. "Keep your nose clean. Run into any trouble, I'm right behind you."

"You're right behind me anyway."

"Not used to having someone watchin' your back, are you? Savage better not be bluffing on you. I got no sympathy for hard luck cases, you better be some kind of rabbit's foot. What d'you call yourself, Millie...."

"Millard."

"Melissa, fine, watch yourself. My eye's on you. Live up to it."

Fortunately, he moved on to harass the dealer beside me at the next black-jack table, who happened to be the red-haired employee I'd glimpsed earlier, tired, nearing the end of his shift. Daniel was pale and gangly, able to move cards yet equally able to screw anything up on a moment's notice. Parry took a sadist's pleasure in messing with Daniel, but my immediate concern was limited to my table; the rest of the world could fall off the edges of that green baize. I set my hands out on the table like spiders, limbering up my fingers, well-trained black widows.

Two men wandered over; one put out some chips and nodded to me, so I would deal him a game, while his friend pushed two hundred and fifty dollars across the table towards me. I laid the money out in shelves, hundred-dollar piles, to confirm the amount, and handed over the appropriate chips. Blackjack is dead easy to deal, especially in a casino; the dealer's hands are simply an efficient machine, allowing the game to function. But I was excited to be holding cards at the Flamingo. My hands felt at home.

We played another round. Another, then another after that. Another. Mostly I, as dealer, won. Mostly, the customers lost. I tried my darnedest to keep them losing. But I couldn't fall into blackjack the way I fell into poker, my mind kept wandering off into its own corners, the way a girl might get distracted out on a bad date. Passion keeps the mind focused; passion and curiosity—and whatever else it may be, poker is passionate, whereas blackjack dealing is skill and routine. Blackjack is not passionate. It is not like a kiss.

I kept my eyes on the game in front of me, dealt the Ace of Spades onto the table, then six of Hearts, then Queen of Diamonds, which made me think of my mother. I should have gone to see her before I left town. Why this should matter to me, at such a late date—I sighed to myself, not so that anyone at the table would hear me. The Queen of Diamonds, sharp-edged queen of ice, she hadn't flung any shoes at me lately. Why did she remain enamoured of Teddy, and so unimpressed with me? At least I was a success, some of the time.

Both the men across from me tapped the table, kept me here, in the present. The tapping meant "hit me," so I gave them each another card. Ten of Spades—bad news for him; two of Clubs—disappointment for the next guy; five of Spades for myself—reversal but fortune will soon turn in my favour. Both men tapped the table, hit them again, not bothering to talk, one blowing smoke in my face. I gazed steadily at him while dealing the next card; his face was grey, pouchy, his eyes malevolent. The card was the eight of Diamonds—financial ups and downs. The man blew smoke in my face again, intentionally, but I won the round and kept myself from sneering at him as he went away.

The next round, I dealt a Jack of Spades for myself as dealer. The black Jack—I nearly, very nearly, kept Teddy out of my head. His card, I couldn't help it, always made me think ever so fleetingly of sex. Not a ladylike preoccupation, but cards aren't ladylike—they encompass all of life. I was better off alone, I had gotten myself this far to be alone, to sink or swim on my own abilities. The amethyst-coloured lake from my dream, that's what suddenly swirled into my head.

One of the players slapped the table, startling me.

"Daydreaming?" he said nastily.

"Another game, sir?"

The players were our audience, the cards and I, the talent, the acrobats. But for blackjack, there are so few contortions, so few leaps from the flying trapeze. All I had to do was deal and play, the faster the better—whenever I won a hand as dealer, the money went to the house, so it was in the Flamingo's favour if I dealt fast and won often. My goal was finding favour with the house, so I won as often, as quickly, as I could.

No players handed me money directly; they placed their cash on the table, whether it was money for betting or money they were giving me as a tip, either way I set the money out in hundred dollar shelves as Savage had told me to do, strips of cash, left to right. Then I took the customer's money and placed chips equaling the amount, arranged in piles this time, stretched out for an instant to prove how many chips were in each pile. It was easy to become a blackjack automaton. I concentrated to keep my movements ship-shape, with Parry's warty eyes boring into my back; I was working too hard to notice the time passing, though every now and then I'd glance enviously at the rest of the casino, my eyes seeking the poker tables.

"Break after this," Parry murmured finally. He'd kept me on much longer than the normal forty-five minute stint. I wrapped up with the Jack of Hearts and nine of Clubs. Dealer won. Parry was testing me, not wanting to take me off the table as long as I was winning for the house. I dusted my hands, and Howie took over my table, casting a practiced eye over the chips in their rows. On my way to the backroom, I looked longingly at the poker section. The dealers were seated at their tables, cards set out in interesting patterns. Poker looked to me as desirable as a ballroom, as unattainable as a gentleman's club, while I was Cinderella, stuck at blackjack until I could afford a fairy godmother.

Somehow I survived the remaining five hours of my shift. Afterwards, I was so tired from standing, I actually stumbled in the staff washroom, caught myself with one exhausted hand against the wooden stall door. I wanted to see more of the casino, watch the Flamingo slip seductively from night into dawn, but I was so dog tired, I could barely drive myself back to George's to collapse into my new bed.

❧

On my second night, I dealt pedestrian hands: seven of Clubs, four of Diamonds—an improvement in finances, a promise that cheered me up—then the ten of Spades alongside a pouting Queen of Spades, the Ace of Clubs, later another ten of Spades—that repeated card of misfortune and worry. I gave the ten a dirty look, but I kept leaning on black cards. The players relinquished their chips and sighed.

"Hit me," they said sometimes, or they tapped the table; only surrender had to be a verbal signal, they couldn't merely wave a vague hand over their cards. Players had to be clear about their intentions—I was conscious of Parry's warty eyes upon me.

The only real changes from my first shift to my second were that Roscoe said hello to me, and on my way back to the staff room for a break, Savage intercepted me to ask, "Everything going well?"

I nodded.

"Free after your shift?" But he walked away without waiting for my answer. I could have chased after him and demanded what he meant, but I didn't want to talk to Savage more than I had to, he was too distracting. So I went outside and stood by the pool, long enough to smoke a cigarette, looking at the water lit from below, supernatural-like. Cats' eyes shone from the bushes, and someone giggled just out of sight, music slipped from a bungalow doorway.

Too many hours, forty-five minutes on, fifteen off, until three in the morning. My cards behaved and I switched tables, always under Parry's eye. It bothered me to be watched so hard, but Parry had no reason to trust me—it's too easy to cheat with chips, they're so small and they're not counted up in packs the way cards are.

Back in the staff room on my final break of the night, I found Roscoe reading the sports pages. He pulled out a lighter when I fumbled with a cigarette—my fingers were tired and clumsy. I thanked him.

"You're doin' okay."

"The chips are slippery, I guess they're so new," I said.

He grunted. "Parry spotted a guy puttin' chips in his mouth, openin' night. Slippery alright."

A fast dealer could hand out a round of blackjack, play it, pay chips out to players and in an instant, slip a chip into his mouth, imperceptibly, in a tiny smooth movement, to retrieve later for himself. The idea didn't appeal to me. I said, "Then what?"

"Parry left him on shift for two hours, kid damn near choked on the chip. Didn't even need to fire the dimwit, he took off so goddamn fast."

I imagine it took about two seconds for the guy to get into his car and drive as far from the Flamingo as he possibly could, probably didn't stop until he was in Mexico. Parry would have that effect on a person.

"You were here in December?"

"Hell no. They fired everyone from the first opening. No-talents. I got here just before you. Where're you from?"

"Vancouver. Up in Canada."

"I'm from New York, like a lot of the guys."

I went back to my table, trying to figure out if he was being friendly, or if he was trying to find out about me. I dealt an eight of Diamonds—financial instability—and then a nine of Diamonds—surprise with money. Surprise can really go either way. I dealt a three of Spades, for unfaithfulness, and on and on, I tried to stay focused but it was difficult. I was tired, bored, when finally Parry said, "That's it, you're off. Sweet dreams." He was the last person you might want wishing you sweet dreams; he made it sound so permanent.

I signed myself out, a ritual I'd been introduced to the night before. This time, I went through it on my own, three types of paperwork, initials to write on the card boxes, to prove I had taken out new decks and checked them back in, initials on the chip sheet, initials for the tip box. I went into the staffroom to remove my nametag and change my shirt. I left the tuxedo jacket and bow tie on a hanger in the staff washroom, careful of my footing, knowing I was just as exhausted as I had been the night before. Then I went out to get my cut of the night's tips. "Chips or bills?" asked the count girl.

"Chips," I said, and signed "ML" in wide cursive script that didn't look much like my usual handwriting. I put the chips in my purse, feeling their texture and pattern as if they were a kind of Braille.

It was two in the morning. I drove home avoiding the shiny lights of Fremont, unwilling to be lured in just yet—I needed to save the chips in my purse, give them time to add up. I parked the white sedanette and thought of Teddy, choosing this car for me, buying me a car so I could leave. I fumbled with my keys as I went up George's front steps. A car passed the house and I ignored it until it slowed and stopped. A man got out and I was surprised to see that it was Stan.

"I wasn't planning to run halfway across town," he said.

"Have you run halfway across town?"

He might have been frowning, I couldn't rightly see, it was too dark. He walked around and opened the car's passenger door. The car had suicide doors and the inside looked completely black, as if any light had been snuffed out. "If you don't hurry up and get in the car we're going to be late."

"For what?"

"You want to deal more than just blackjack? Or maybe I'm mistaken and you're going upstairs to sleep, long day tomorrow." But he didn't close the door, he just leaned there, one foot on the curb, watching me. Confident, because he knew he had a sweet offer, sweetened by his own thin self.

I frowned at him. "What do you want dealt?"

"A guy asked for you in particular. We need a poker dealer."

"Strictly a dealer?"

"Mmhm. Deal for us. The tip'll make it worth your while." He made it sound like a bribe. "Be a pleasure to see you at a real game."

I wanted to play poker, not deal, he knew that, but even dealing would be so much more interesting than blackjack. My fingers shivered. "I can drive myself," I said, stalling.

"No, I drive. You're too tired. We're in a hurry."

I went. Because it was Savage, and it was poker, and I couldn't resist. Maybe I should have had more backbone, but I stepped into the big car, Savage slammed the door closed and walked back to the driver's side. We headed down the highway out of town and I sank further into the luxurious car seat.

"His name is Roland Jackson. He's from Mississippi but made himself over into a Texan, that's where he got rich. He plays a good game but sloppy. He was playing blackjack a while back at your table, you'll recognize him. He wants you to deal. Asked specifically."

That didn't surprise me. Gamblers are attracted to anything that might sway their luck; just as some people dislike the number thirteen, or never sit down with left-handed poker-players, other gamblers court such oddities. Some players seek out the red-haired dealer. Some don't play when it's a full moon. Sure it's superstition, but if you believe in it, you're going to be affected. Some players don't like the idea of a girl dealing cards, and some do. Some gamblers believe dwarves are lucky. So sure, a really short girl dealer might just double someone's luck. Worth a try, wasn't it? No doubt, this was the reason Jackson asked for me as a dealer. Maybe it would turn to my advantage, make Chappell think I was a bonus at a poker table. A girl can hope, surely?

Savage drove too fast, his profile lit by the faint gold glow of the car's expensive dashboard. It was a nice profile, it had character, but I turned my head sternly to look straight out through the windshield, the stretch of road ahead illuminated only by our headlights. Oh, Vegas was dark back then. The lights of downtown lasted only a few blocks. I was as pleased by the darkness as I was by Stan's profile, I savoured the prospect of dealing a real card game and not the pabulum of casino blackjack. The sky suddenly went gooey, pouring past us, not quite properly black as the Flamingo came into view.

Savage drove around the back of the building, behind the bungalows, parked, got out. He put his hat on as he walked around the car, opened the passenger door and gave me his hand. His fingers were cold, though I couldn't imagine he was nervous.

"Are you playing?" I asked, which brought me such a clear image of Dermot's backroom, that single night I'd seen him play cards.

Perhaps he had the same memory, for he said, "You'll keep us honest."

I wondered. Once out of the car, I took my hand from his and adjusted my collar. I followed Stan along the gravel path to a guest cottage. Roses twined up in front of the door, as if we were in an English garden. He turned as we reached the stoop. "I look forward to playing cards with you."

"Dealing is fine." Maybe I didn't want to play cards with him. I wouldn't be able to trust such a game—surely while I had gotten better at my playing over the past years, he'd become a better cheat, too.

But Savage didn't seem to follow my reasoning. "The house had better take you up. I'm working on it."

"Where the hell've you been?" said the Texan, as Savage stepped aside to usher me in. "Roland Jackson," he said, putting out his hand. "We're nearly givin' up on you. Let's get down to business."

"You in that much of a hurry?" murmured Savage.

A dining table had been pulled into the middle of the room and six chairs set up around it. Tactfully, they'd reserved a high upholstered chair for me. The Texan smiled with too many teeth as I was introduced to him as Miss Taylor, Stan making that up on the spot.

"Mind if I keep callin' you Leslie? I like the name."

"Of course, Mr. Jackson. Please do." That casino nametag would do better than my real name. You know the real name of something and you have power over it—Leslie Taylor, I thought, why not.

We played with fresh packs of cards from the casino; I broke them open and washed them just as I'd been doing for blackjack, then the players cut the deck for the order of play, and I began to deal. The cards demanded to be heard, though they favoured no one in particular. Savage got decent cards, steady, and I was surprised by how much I liked watching him—his hands with the cards, his expression. He played with tiny hints of emotion, parceling them out as false lures. Jackson was the fish, and Stan focused his tells on him, wrinkling his brow, adjusting his tie, rubbing his eyebrows, always when Jackson was sure to notice. It sounds so overt in my description, but these were miniscule gestures, almost imperceptible, as Savage played Jackson, led him to believe the cards weren't going his way. I was intrigued—I rarely used fake tells; my very presence as a girl at the table was so distracting, I hardly needed an extra tic. But Savage played his very well.

At the end of every round, I gathered up the pack, tore the cards, tossed them into a wastepaper basket, and washed a fresh pack. Gradually, I got used to the different styles of players. Savage was the most interesting to watch; I found it difficult to keep my eyes off him. It took four hours for him to bust the Texan out properly and as far as I could see, he did it honestly. Of the other players, an actor named Lapeyre from Hollywood nodded whenever his hands were bad and tipped me nicely on the rare occasions the cards went his way. Across from him, the Texan had almost no tells, though he seemed to fidget with his chips while deciding if his hand was worthwhile. I made a note of that, for future use.

Lapeyre folded halfway through, staying on to watch, polite and interested. When the game finished and Savage raked in his last chips, the Texan wrote me an IOU as a tip on the back of a cocktail napkin, folding it up before handing it to me. I took the flimsy bit of paper, hoping it really was worth something, and put it neatly away in my purse. The Texan showed me his teeth, like a horse, this time not even pretending to smile. He didn't bother saying goodbye but merely walked away to another room in the suite. A door slammed and we heard water running. I stood up and wished I too had a bedroom so close. I felt as if the room were wavering as I stood. Seven hours of blackjack, then these hours dealing poker, with none of the excitement of actually playing the game. My fingers were actually sore, the edges of my nails worn ragged. Just the same, Lapeyre kissed my hand, bowing nearly double to do so. "I look forward to playing at your table, my next trip here, Miss Taylor," he said, charming as only an actor can be. He saw me to the door.

Savage followed. "I'll drive you back. Least I can do."

Out on the gravel path, I concentrated, one foot after another. Savage held open the suicide door, and I crawled into the expensive seat and fell asleep. I didn't even feel the car start moving.

❦

I woke up confused, staring at the walls papered with rose-coloured posies. I blinked at the repetitive flowers. I remembered dealing poker, getting into the car, and nothing. I shivered, even though I was too warm, the rose quilt over me, all my clothes on except for my shoes—I rolled over to check the floor, and sure enough, my shoes were set neatly beside the bed. No one in the room but me. I held my wrist out, my watch reading twenty minutes to four, only a couple of hours before my next shift started. My purse, sitting upright on the bureau, caught my eye. I untangled myself from the quilt and emptied out the contents. My chips from blackjack tips were all there when I counted them, the cocktail napkin still neatly folded beside my powder compact. I took out the purple stone and rubbed it with my fingers; the colour didn't change. The amethyst had no insight. It was just a rock, a pretty rock.

On my way to the bathroom, I passed a girl tall as a giraffe, who peered at me sleepily. She had thick cold cream around her eyes and across her fore-head. "You new?" she said. "I'm Elena. There's no more hot water." She swayed down the hallway to her room and I tried not to stare after her. I washed, coldly, and went downstairs to see what was left for breakfast. George was in the kitchen, wearing a sky-coloured silk robe. Little gold and blue embroi-dered Chinese pagodas frolicked up and down the sides. I blinked at him.

"Sleeping beauty, you're going to need sustenance to keep up with that schedule of yours. Sit down."

"Did I wake you, coming in so late?"

George shrugged, an elaborate gesture with the big sleeves of his robe, but he rolled up the cuffs and set in to making me a late afternoon breakfast. "Eggs how?"

"However you like to make them."

"Don't be polite, girlie. This is no town for politeness. You think that big boss of yours got to where he is by using restraint? You meet him yet?"

"Sorry?"

"Mister Siegel, my dear, wears the loudest silk shirts you have ever seen. Last time I caught sight of him, he was in a houndstooth jacket, yellow shirt and tie, green trousers and real nice alligator shoes. You could see him from the far end of Freemont Street. He looked like a neon daffodil. You have to understand, shrinking violets don't thrive in Nevada sunlight, girlie. You make up your mind what you want in this town, and you go about getting it. So?" He picked up two eggs in his left hand and waved them at me.

"Over easy," I said. He cracked the eggs against the iron skillet and tossed the shells into an empty tin can beside the sink.

"For the garden. Gotta help the plants along with what comes to hand. The Flamingo uses sewage on the golf course, keeping it green. You don't play golf, do you?"

"Won't plan on learning, now."

George laughed. "Good walk ruined, someone said. And you can't wear nice shoes, so what's the point? Here my dear. Cup of coffee'll set you up."

"Would you mind if I had tea?"

"I don't mind if you have gin, as long as you're a pleasant drunk. Which I'm not. It's never good news when I have a drink in my hand. Rosemary," he said, as he crumbled some scruffy green twigs over the eggs. "*He was in love with a girl named Rosemary...*" he added, singing some tune I didn't know.

He made me eggs over easy, with toast, and a tomato arranged in segments at the edge of the plate, as if I were eating in a Canadian Pacific train's first class dining room. Except that I was somewhere safer, stranger.

"Eat up." The plate banged down in front of me, a fork and knife, a linen napkin. Really, as elegant as any train's dining room. I wanted to ask how I'd ended up in my bed, but I wasn't sure I wanted to hear him describe the details. He balanced on the back of the chair opposite me, a curious operation, a man his size perching like a sparrow. "I like cooking for little girls like you. It's a pleasure to see you eat."

"My mother worked as a cook. I like to eat."

"My mother was Italian. She fattened people up." He sighed and rubbed his eyes with a corner of his silk sleeve. "God rest." After a respectful pause, he shook his head. "On Mondays I make spaghetti for all the girls, you'll meet everyone. And we're going to get along fine, you and all of us, you can trust me on that." He stood up and squeezed his bulk delicately past the table. "Now clean your plate. It's the only thing I absolutely demand." He went off to his front room, humming.

When I finished my breakfast, good girl that I was, I started on the dishes. The hot water made my worn cuticles sting. George came puttering back in and stood watching. "You're sure that's good for your hardworking fingertips?"

I submerged my teacup. "Soap's a nice change. Cards aren't the cleanest thing in the world."

"Move along dearie, I'm mistress of this house. And you've done your time with bleach."

"Bleach?"

"Waste of your hands. No wonder you got out of the laundry."

I dried my hands on the dishtowel. "Who told you that?"

George didn't answer, just pushed me playfully aside and put his big hands in the suds.

I hung up the dishtowel and folded my arms across my chest. "Stan Savage told you that, didn't he?"

"I asked him."

"He has no business saying that."

"Girlie, you remember being brought home this morning? No, because you were out cold.... Don't interrupt, it was nine in the morning. I was getting breakfast for two of the girls. You were brought home by a guy I happen to know is not the kind of man who brings dames back at that hour. Normally, and believe me when I say this, he opens the door of the hotel room and that's that. He doesn't even hope for the best. I said, don't interrupt. I realize this was a different thing. But don't go taking some moral high road with me. I asked him what the hell was going on, my new lodger coming home like that. He said you were exhausted, not drunk, and that he knew you from way back, when you were just a kid, working in a hotel laundry up the coast."

"That's not true, I beat him in a card game. That's how we met."

"But you were working in a laundry."

I opened my mouth to say, *and he was cheating at that card game when we met.* But I didn't. I tried to remember coming home, out cold as I was, but all I could imagine was an embarrassing vision of Stan carrying me, which seemed like a bad movie. I'm not leading lady material—I'm more likely to be cast as the freak. Unless maybe it was a film about Napoleon, maybe I could play his sister. "I wasn't a kid, working at the laundry. I was eighteen." Almost."And then I quit."

"Nothing to be ashamed of, girlie. My family's in laundering. I don't let it bother me."

It was difficult to stay mad at George, for all his queeny airs and bossiness. He had dug through so much strangeness in his own life that once he decided to like you, he liked you, no matter what.

He gave me a serious look. "I want you to know, and I like Stan Savage, I'm saying this for your own good, he's got a wife over in California that he's still married to. A woman he abandoned. Now I'm not saying she was necessarily a good woman or any kind of wife, but there are things you should know. Come home so late."

"I was dealing cards, George, that's all." But I filed away that information about the man's wife, because details are useful, whatever game you're playing.

"All I care about is, you ate your breakfast. Girls clean their plates, in this house." He winked at me and turned back to the dishes, while I went upstairs to get ready for my shift.

When I arrived at the Flamingo, I cashed in my cocktail napkin at the cashier cage. Amazingly, the woman accepted it as a valid marker and gave me three chips, patterned pink and green, each worth one hundred dollars—a pretty fine tip for four hours' work, enough to bankroll a game after my shift. Well worth the extra dealing last night, even if I'd passed out afterwards. I put the chips in my purse in the staff room when I went on shift, and I tried not to think of them there, waiting for me, waiting for my shift to end so I could take them out to play.

I needed a low-ball game, not here at the Flamingo—employees can't play where they work, anyhow, so I would go to one of the smaller joints downtown. I was so excited I had to pause and take a deep breath before I reached my table. Parry glared at me by way of greeting, and I got down to the business of standing behind a blackjack table, moving cards.

At eleven, on my third short break of the night, I went outside and lit a cigarette and sat on one of the lounge chairs by the swimming pool. The air was hard and dry, the absolute opposite of Vancouver—no softening salt or damp mold in the air, just oleander and dust with a knife of wild sage through the pool's chlorine smell. A lone swimmer glided back and forth in the pool; I focused on the way he touched the far side, turned, returned, watery reflections rippling through the pool, glowing pale in the middle of the garden's darkness, the swimmer going back and forth and the dark shrubbery beyond. The rows of bubbles swirling through the water in his wake made me think of Teddy's trail of tiny scars, down his shoulder blade and across his back. Soon I'd be back at a poker table. I'd be able to justify what I was doing here—as if I needed the game as my excuse for having left Teddy and the touch of Vancouver's damp air.

Past the glow of the water, a trail of globe-topped lamps led to the guest cottages and bungalows. As I finished my cigarette, someone came up the path. I recognized the thin dark silhouette. "Stan," I said, as he reached the reflected light of the pool.

He smiled sharply at me. "I hope George was decent to you when you woke up."

"It wasn't very professional of me, I was...."

"Exhausted." He stood at the edge of the pool, the green watery light throwing shadows across his face. "You were exhausted."

"It's just dealing, standing up," I said. "I'll get used to it."

"Mmhm."

I leaned forward and knocked the ash from my cigarette into the ashtray beside my lounge chair. "The tip was a nice surprise."

"Jackson's an ass," said Savage. "It's a pleasure to bust a guy like that."

Beyond the pool, there was a rustling in the shrubbery—the cats prowling through the gardens, their eyes appeared as bright pinpricks in the darkness and blinked away again. Savage glanced over at them, then gave me a lingering appraisal before going into the casino. He left me wondering about his choice of words—busting Jackson. I wondered how it was that Savage played poker in a bungalow on the Flamingo grounds, how his game connected to the casino profits.

For the rest of the night, I watched the cards go through my hands and into the fates. By the end of my shift, I was almost too tired to contemplate a game of poker. Almost. I signed out, looping my initials, hardly like handwriting at all, my fingers so worn. But back in my own clothes, my purse on my arm, once I was outside and opening the door of the sedanette, I sparked back to life.

I tried to hold caution in my teeth, however much I wanted to play. I drove downtown and parked outside the Apache Hotel and stood on the sidewalk for a moment, letting the bright neon of the signs give me courage. My legs and arms were tired from blackjack; my brain was fine. My fingers would come onboard. I shivered, I couldn't help thinking of Gerald Avison, such an ugly boy, such an unattractive man, leaving me with fear like vinegar in my mouth. Vegas would not be like that. I held my purse close to my body and I went past the Hotel Apache and into the Boulder casino next door.

The wood panels around the bar were carved, framing red velvet wallpaper with little wooden pillars. Barmen in clean shirts and black Western ties tended the long dark bar, but the mirror behind the cash was shattered, long shards missing near the tobacco-stained ceiling. When the men at the bar turned to stare, I threw back my shoulders. Women played one-armed bandits the way teenagers played jukeboxes, and maybe they stood at the craps tables, not because they understood the rules, but they shook the dice for their man, blew on the numbers for luck. But I wasn't suited to that kind of endeavour.

Poker was serious in old Vegas, in that not-yet-a-city, that place which no longer exists. I looked past the bar and saw a space at one of the low-bet poker tables. I had the money to ante, so there was no reason for them to deny me a place. My nerves struck hard dissonant chords through my fingers. I had to concentrate on each fingertip, steadying myself. I'm just tired, I told myself, and I greeted the floorman and sat down at the five-dollar table.

I was determined to play only $150 of the tip money—the only way I could build a bankroll was by being restrained, practical. But when the cards happily began speaking to me, my fingers were too filled with noise to listen. Like a metronome, a clinking repeated flat note, I lost a hundred dollars, the small green chips disappearing from my fingers. I knew nothing of the players here, workers from the dam project, army guys, ranchers. Some were lousy players, some unpredictable, none recognizable types from my train games, and nothing like the high-rollers at the Flamingo. Listen harder, I thought, trying to adjust my play to suit the men the Boulder attracted, but however readily I calculated their odds, I failed to predict their moves.

It took me three hours to lure back the hundred dollars I'd lost. I was incapable of pulling off any bluff, I might have wept from the effort. Finally the cards gave me two tens, Clubs and Spades, with the ten of Hearts showing, the ten of luck and happiness—I made back my money, just. But that was all I did: I walked out even, with my faith stuttering.

For three days after that, I went no further than my blackjack shift at the Flamingo. Players came and went, while the cards went through their rituals, while I washed and shuffled and stripped the decks. I worked as hard as any sailor. I watched the cards, waiting. Was the freckled guy to my left, with the too-big palms, doing anything notorious with his blackjack cards, or was he just awkward with them, uneasy, as he probably was with women? Was the too-tanned man stabbing my cards in pseudo enthusiasm to make a nail-dent in the Ace, something he would recognize in the next shuffle? Washing the cards gave me a chance to catch such things, take a close look, make sure the backs of the deck weren't marked in any way. I hadn't expected this to be a big problem in Vegas, with all the pit bosses and security men on the floor, watching the players.

"You kiddin'?" said Roscoe, when I bummed a cigarette in the staff room. "Those decks sleep sound in the safe, stacked up like the money sleepin' beside 'em. You got Lissoni yet? Bastard. You watch him, guy's a toad. Too stupid to count. He'll call Parry on you when he loses. You got the card counters yet?"

"Not as yet," I said.

"You know what you're lookin' for? Parry'll have 'em thrown out."

It was easy to spot a card counter—blackjack normally has such predictable bets, that if a guy started making illogical decisions that came out right, he was probably counting cards. Not that it really mattered—the house still made money. But the Flamingo believed the game's mood was ruined by counters, even when the house edge more than compensated for anything a counter could do. I had no doubt Parry would have a counter removed and roughed up with delight. I must have looked a bit sick, for Roscoe said, "The house not agreein' with you?"

"I'm fine."

"Not used to workin' for a house?" he said. "You get used to it. Doesn't mean you've sold your soul."

His tone was reassuring, but I suddenly found myself wondering about my soul. I mean, my card-playing soul—I wanted to let my fingers ease back into their listening, their reading of the cards, but how long did I have to wait, to get my bearings? I wasn't feeling patient. Savage hadn't invited me to deal any more poker games—the weekend fish came and went and I was disappointed. I was sorry not to be dealing a bigger game, to be earning another wild tip that I could add to my bankroll. Maybe I was disappointed that Savage hadn't stopped to say hello, whenever I glimpsed him walking through the casino.

Ten of Spades, two of Diamonds, nine of Spades—blackjack, dealer wins. I played with other people's fortunes and counted the hours in my shifts until Monday, my first day off. I wondered how long I could deal this game before boredom made me too sloppy for Parry's warty glare.

The town of Vegas wasn't much to look at, but at least on Mondays it was peaceful. On Mondays, the casinos were quiet—everyone had run out of crazy money, and the weekend crowd had gone home. On Mondays, the G.I.s went back in their barracks, the dam workers returned to Hoover, the ranchers drove out to their cows on the range. The only busy place in town on Mondays was the courthouse, which doled out no-fault divorces. "So don't go there on Monday you'll be standin' in line," said Roscoe, when I signed out, Sunday night.

"I'm not married," I reminded him.

"Blackjack treatin' you okay?"

"Not bad," I said.

Roscoe laughed. "I've got that damn upstairs table. Poker'll go on all night."

"I didn't know you dealt poker." Most nights, I saw him at blackjack, the only decent dealer in the place, a sense of style despite his weight and the ghastly grey of his skin.

"Yeah, gotta hope I don't get Lissoni. He keeps threatenin' to play." Cigar wedged against his lips, he cracked his knuckles. "Dealin' that table, you do what you're told. You get my drift."

I nodded, remembering how Samuel Lazar had warned me away from the crooked upstairs table. "Enough action for me elsewhere," I said, and Roscoe smiled. Not a pretty sight, but well-intentioned, his smile.

"Enjoy your day off, kid."

I thought I might sleep all day long on Monday, but I woke up early and decided I may as well explore the town. In my five days of work, I hadn't seen anything beyond the Flamingo and my one unfortunate foray into the Boulder. I'd had no time.

The main drag was impressive enough; it was the side streets that were strange. They literally stopped, veering off from Fremont with great conviction, as if they were normal city streets, and then, after two or three blocks, their optimism dead-ended in dust. Sidewalks trailed off into dirt, which became sand, which was grown-over with sagebrush and cacti. Or not grown-over, no, I mean it had never been disturbed—the sage had been there since time immemorial, reaching all the way to the horizon, only stopped by blue hazy hills. I turned on my heel and went back to Fremont, tried a cross-street a few blocks down. This led into houses on wide lots, but then this street too tapered off, the addresses ran out of steam, lost their way, until one last house stood on the edge of the desert, and the street ended. A lone Joshua tree stood there, parsing the landscape. I got dust in my eye and stopped there for some time, weeping, trying to get the speck of dirt out with my tears.

I walked back to the main strip, and Vegas was suddenly a city again: drugstore counters and a chapel down the block, with the Boulder Club and Golden Nugget and the Eldorado, lined up, their three tall signs weighed down by the wide blue sky above. I thought of Vancouver, terminal city with nothing in its favour but location, its loggers and railway workers, remittance men and ex-sailors, a motley assortment of jobs and needs that metamorphosed into a city. Vegas might do the very same thing, take this odd collection of signs and sunshine, lure enough players out here, and the place could turn itself into a real city. Already it seemed real enough for me.

I stood on the street corner opposite the Apache, looking down at the card parlours, sawdust joints interspersed with more upright places. I tried to hear whether my hands were ready, yet, but I heard nothing. I sighed and went back to George's house to run myself a bath. The cards hadn't abandoned me, they were just taking a pause, a rest—I had to wait. The hot bath made me gasp, the skin along my fingernails stinging like needles in the bath water.

Dealing cards nonstop for a week had done my fingers as much damage as the hotel laundry.

Everyone who roomed at George's had their day off on Monday. Just the girls, as George put it, seven of us around the kitchen table for dinner, with George presiding. He stood at the stove, talking, passing out plate after plate of spaghetti. For the showgirls I think it was the one meal a week they could really go for—the rest of the time, they were haunted by the spectacle of standing around in nothing but tights and feathers through the dinner hour. It put a girl off her feed.

Elena, the best-looking, showed off her newest coat. Why anyone would wear fur, in the warm air of Vegas, was beyond me, and I said so. But girls like Elena used fur as insurance.

"She pawns them when times are less generous," explained George. "Don't you, girlie?"

"Pawn is such a nasty word. I pass them on to people," she said, shrugging out of the silvery fur and tucking into her meal.

I liked the showgirls. They were a new species to me, exotic crested herons at the table, all long limbs and unusual heads. The two cocktail waitresses were less interesting—their conversation revolved around tips and how uncomfortable their shoes were. And there was the other recent addition to the household, Sabina, who'd arrived only a week before me.

"Where do you waitress?"

"The Steakhouse. But I'm really a showgirl."

"You're a dancer?"

She shook her head. "Not yet. I'm going to be. I'm keeping my ears open."

Sabina had tiny ears attached to an absolutely symmetrical round head; she had brown eyes and brown hair, and her skin was what romantic writers would describe as porcelain. She didn't look anything like porcelain; she was much too curvy and the light in her eyes was anything but china doll when she stood up to get some more lemonade. "Anything's better than waitressing at the Steakhouse."

"Don't say that, girlie," said George, handing her a bowl of grated cheese.

"Aren't the tips good?" I asked innocently.

Sabina did a little pas-de-deux, or whatever those little ballet steps are called, across the kitchen floor, holding the lemonade and cheese as a partner. "I'd rather wear feathers." She put a fresh glass of lemonade down for me. "You're like my littlest sister," she said.

I put cheese on my spaghetti and though I was the ugliest girl in the room, for once I didn't mind. Sabina's smile had made me feel that I had as much right to be here as anyone else. A real family dinner, that's what it was, the kind of family I'd never had. "God bless this house," George said, "enjoy your dinner." And we did. It was proper and homey, even if it was a home created by showgirls and a matriarchal patriarch.

15

I waited for my hands to give me some kind of signal—that sounds crazy, but that was the truth. A whole month passed that way, it felt like a year, all that blackjack. The cards moved from blackjack shoe to tabletop as I turned them over on the green island of my table, and I cared less and less about their performance. Players clung to the rim of my table, blood leaving their fingers as their skin went white, but I was indifferent. I spent my shifts on blackjack hoping Savage would invite me to deal a poker game. Then I'd wash my hands and shuffle rounds of poker for as many hours as necessary. I watched Stan Savage play—I told myself it was because I didn't trust his skill, but honestly, I enjoyed it—and he wasn't cheating, so far as I could tell. I watched the other players just as carefully—when I became a player again, I would use what I remembered against them. And Savage watched me, every card I dealt, staying 'til the end of every game.

After a particularly long night in a particularly floral-patterned bungalow, Savage escorted the last player to the door and came back to the table where I was tearing the decks from the game. Routine, at the Flamingo—every day new packs were put into play. The old ones, we tore up, laboriously. By the end of the night, my hands only had enough strength to tear about twelve cards at a time.

Savage sat back and folded his arms on his chest.

"You're not fooling me, Millard Lacouvy. You could give a damn about dealing these poker games. You should be playing your own cards."

Instead of answering him, I picked up a deck that hadn't been torn yet and fanned it onto the table. "Pick a card."

Savage leaned forward, pulled out a card, glanced at it and slipped it back into the fan. I slid the pack together, shuffled, and dealt face-up, one by one. At the nine of Diamonds, I paused.

"This one," I said.

He caught my wrist. "I've known that trick since I was a kid."

"It's still a good trick," I said. It wasn't a trick, exactly; it was just memory and card manipulation. "Red nine, restless ambition."

"You need a card to figure that out about me?" He let my wrist go and laughed. "Leave the rest, I'll tear them. Sit and keep me company."

I didn't want to stay. The blackjack shift, the poker dealing—all those hours took a toll, and the pink and green pattern of the wallpaper was starting to wink at me. But Savage smiled as if I was the best hand in a long night of good cards.

"I hoped I was going to see you again," he said.

"How nice to be a wish come true."

He laughed. "You give no quarter, little girl. I like that."

"I'm not a...." Then I saw he was still laughing at me. I searched for a way to make him stop. "So how's your wife? She not in Vegas much?"

He tore a pile of cards and threw them into the rubbish. "No quarter, like I said." He evened up a fresh set of cards. "My wife has never been to Vegas. We haven't seen each other in, let me see...." He tore the cards. "A year and a half, more than that, two years? She and I were a bad... let's say we were a bad bet." He took a new pile of cards and tapped them into line.

"But you did marry her."

"She thought I was quite the catch."

I stood up, got my coat, my purse. "You weren't?"

He tore the cards and laughed, a hard sound like a cough, like he'd gotten a nine of Diamonds stuck in his chest and was trying to dislodge it.

Much as I could see he was no great catch, I'd watched his hands, his game, I'd watched his face, and I liked the way his lips stayed closed around his thoughts. I rubbed my forehead. The darn flowers in the wallpaper never existed in nature and their weird plant pattern made me nauseous. I put my hand over my eyes. "This room bothers me."

"You should get yourself playing again."

I looked at him through my fingers, then lowered my arm. "What makes you say that? Who says I'm not playing?"

"Well, are you?"

It was none of his business. I looked for my cigarette case and took out my lighter.

Savage tore and threw away the remaining cards. "I've played cards for as long as you've been alive. You don't think I've had some slumps?"

"I'm not having a slump."

"You should get yourself back to a table, keep your hand in."

"What would you know about it?" I gave him my best aggrieved expression, but it didn't have the desired effect, because he reached over and took the lighter, holding it for me so I could get the cigarette lit.

"I'll walk you to your...."

"I'm fine." I went out alone. I drove myself slowly home, being careful of every car I passed. The sunlight hurt my eyes.

A day later, George's household was woken by screeching tires and a shrieking Elena, followed by a man swearing at her. Confused, I got out of bed, slunk to the stairs and peered down to the front hall. A man filled our front doorway like a metal filing cabinet—all grey, suit, skin, hair, his arms crossed on his chest, everything sealed and with sharp corners which had crashed into Elena. She screamed at him some more, incoherent. I didn't like the look of the man, but when George's door opened, I skulked back to my bedroom.

By the time I crept down to the kitchen, Elena sat defiantly at the table, mopping her eyes with one of George's enormous handkerchiefs, her pink dress torn at the sleeve. Her mouth was swollen. I put the kettle on for tea, stepping around Sabina, who was putting the finishing touches on her latest evening gown. George held the green satin fabric and was fussing with the pattern. Sabina had succeeded in her ambition: she'd gotten a job as a chorus girl alongside Elena, dancing in one of the evening reviews.

When I sat down at the table, George said, "The low-down creep hit her. Look at that... don't worry honey, it'll heal up fine." He caught my gaze. "'Course, she did try to run him over. Too bad you didn't, girlie. Nicky Rutowsky deserves to be mowed down. You should have used a bigger car. Not just girls but full grown men would thank you for it. From coast to coast. He'd be no loss to anyone, not even his mother."

Elena sniffled with dignity and stood up unsteadily. "I am going to have a bath and go to bed." She lisped a bit because of her split lip.

"Get some sleep, honey. Makeup'll cover that fine, tonight. No one'll notice." We were silent as she stalked from the room.

"Everyone'll notice," said Sabina. "She should never have gone with him. Made men. Feh." She curled her perfect lips in disgust.

"That's not strictly true, girlie. Millard, help yourself to cinnamon buns. There's fruit salad in the fridge. No time to cook this morning, you understand. Sabina honey, Rutowsky is not part of... he's not family. He's mean misbegotten scum, pretends to be a big guy. Cheap and brutal. Always involved in the worst schemes. His partners always take the fall. Trail of dead men behind him." George shuddered. "If she'd run him over, would have been a favour to everyone. I told her to stay away from him."

Sabina shook her head. "You tell Elena to stay away from him, you tell us not to date dealers, you tell me to stay away from army boys... you don't want us dating anybody." She took the pins from the sleeve of her dress and rearranged it.

"That's different," said George. "Rutowsky's an ugly piece of work. Are you still seeing that Jim? Not that he's anything like Rutowsky."

"No reason to be so opposed to the military," said Sabina, talking very precisely around the pins she held in her mouth.

"Well, I don't trust them," said George. "Living out there in the desert in all that nothing. Running those fake bombing missions."

I looked at him quizzically.

"They do," he said. "You never notice the airplanes? Coming in low and fast and making a hell of a racket. They fly down through the state, pretending to bomb the bejesus out of us. I call that impolite."

Sabina took the last pin from her mouth and anchored the collar of her dress. "Well Jim's very nice to come to the show. Spends all that time working in the hot sun out there and drives in specially to see me. I think that's nice."

"No one should live out in the desert. A whole lot of nothing," said George categorically.

I looked at George, his arms full of green satin. I had driven through that desert, and it wasn't nothing. I thought hard about the dust and scrappy small trees out there, remembering the Lethbridge grit against Teddy's skin, before the war. I stretched my arm across to the plate of cinnamon buns. I couldn't get the dust out of my head.

My expression must have been very strange, for Sabina clicked her tongue. "You're grouchy these days."

"I'm tired. Waking up to a girl screaming is no way to start the day."

"Well, no," agreed George. "I hope you didn't hear his language. Curled my hair, it did."

Sabina put on the sleeves of her dress, adjusting the décolletage, putting in new pins. "Come to the show tonight, cheer you up. A few headliners, a few cocktails...."

"A few feathers." I stood to go upstairs.

"What's wrong with feathers? Do you good."

"I have to work."

"Switch one of your shifts. Get an hour off and come see me." She lifted her arms so George could measure the underarm zipper for the dress.

"Would do you good," said George.

"Why is everyone worried about my public good?" I said, too sharply I guess, because Sabina and George both turned to stare. "Alright, I'll go see the show."

"Come 'round backstage, it'll be more fun. Want to drive up with me? I'm leaving, soon as I get out of this dress."

Sabina's army boyfriend had loaned her a car, a red Roadmaster with so much rust on the undercarriage, it was barely a legitimate form of transport.

"No thanks."

Sabina refused to feel embarrassed by her car's pedigree. When she was ready, George and I stood on the stoop, watching her peel away from the curb, smoke billowing from the exhaust. She honked the horn cheerfully and waved, leaving a lingering burning smell in her wake. But later, when I went into work, I remembered her offer and I convinced Roscoe to take one of my shifts, squeezed in before his own. A one-hour window, freed from blackjack, to see Sabina's show.

In my dealer's tuxedo, I was the most dressed woman backstage; I was also the shortest, by well over a foot, and that was before they put on their shoes. They wore feathers and baby oil and not a whole lot else. I knew what to expect, but I was still startled. Sabina gave me an effusive kiss and introduced me to everyone. "This is Millard, she lives at the same house as me. She plays cards."

The nearly-naked chorus girls giggled and cheered and readjusted their lipstick. Sabina caught my eye, smiled hugely, and settled me on a stool in the wings, where I wouldn't be in the way. I noticed that Elena had taken the night off; I don't know how that affected the chorus line, maybe they just danced a little faster. I watched as the wardrobe boy adjusted the feathers on the girls' headdresses and bustles. Sabina put Vaseline on her teeth, so the lipstick wouldn't stain them during the two hours of smiling. The wardrobe boy handed her a styrofoam vase, for the Grecian tableau that opened the show, all silver and pale blue, and the girls rushed onstage.

"Mostly it's important to keep the body makeup off the vases," he murmured to me as the curtain went up. Applause bellowed out over the music. "The next number, the white hoop skirts, they're the worst."

When the curtain fell, Sabina came roaring back into the wings, tearing off her headdress, reaching for new feathers. While a comedian did his act out front, backstage was choreographed chaos. Behind the blue velvet curtains, the girls stripped off their pale Grecian stockings, grabbed towels, and rolled on their harlequin body stockings, keeping all their crucial bits in place without mussing their make-up. I cowered in my corner, avoiding flung feathers and styrofoam. The wardrobe boy ran back and forth in silent hysterics, adjusting the skeletal hoop skirts that were made of white feathers until, as the comic relief took a break, the girls rushed back onstage, their lipstick perfect. As the curtain went up, Sabina did a back-flip, the other girls high-kicked, and that ambition in Sabina's eyes when I first met her? It was being realized.

Showgirls in those days weren't whores, despite what the movies would have you believe. Working full-time, showgirls didn't really have a lot of spare energy for moonlighting as call girls, and from what little I heard of it, call girls were pretty tired out by the job such as it was, they didn't feel like high-kicking during their off-hours.

When my time was up, I whispered my thanks to the wardrobe boy and slipped away; Sabina was on stage in a fruit-based tableau involving feather bustles with pineapples—it looked better than it sounds. I went back across the floor, dodging Parry's filthy look.

"You gettin' sloppy?" he said.

"I had to see a friend." I made a mental note to buy Roscoe a box of cigars, since he'd endured Parry on my behalf. And then the cards took my attention, slipping from deck to table, each fortune in my hands hesitating for just the barest of instants before falling open on the table. I thought about Sabina, knowing exactly what she wanted, and getting into the show. I knew what I wanted, too. I'd just been waiting for some symbol, I guess, some moment when it would be all right to return to poker, when I was no longer afraid.

Which is why, when my shift was finally done, the sun just coming up, I got into that white car Teddy bought for me, and I drove downtown. I parked on Fremont Street. I had one hundred dollars in my purse, enough for a game in a sawdust joint. If I didn't have enough money to be picky, so be it. The Frontier was the shiniest casino on this part of the strip, its entrance wider than the Golden Nugget or the Boulder. I didn't have the bankroll for such a place, not yet.

Every casino proclaimed glamour and money in blinking lights and twirling lassoes and sparkling mirrors. But in between and in behind the shiny Fremont addresses were greasy little places that specialized in every kind of game a person could want. It was quite a litany, the variety of games that people could want, but all I sought was a reasonably above board game. The décor wasn't going to bother me—I've never been too fussy as long as the table is flat and the light is even. I didn't mind being one of the only women in the place; the Boulder had steeled my nerve. After a month of watching this town, I had a fair idea of whom I'd be playing.

The place I chose was hardly a casino at all, just a bar, really, shoehorned between the brick wall of the Boulder and Herman's Dime Store window. I walked past Herman's astonishing assortment of lead soldiers, balsam airplane kits and cheap stockings, and paused at the dark window next-door, which wasn't honoured with a name at all. A fan of cards was painted over the door, along with what once had been a lamp, shaped like a pair of dice— except someone had taken a rock to it and only one corner of a black-spotted white glass cube was left, dangling uneasily above the sidewalk. This was the place I chose to make my comeback. I knew there would be a coin table in a place as run-down as this, a table cheap enough for me to ante in with just a quarter, or maybe fifty cents. It would make the hundred last longer.

I pushed against the wooden door and as the door opened, fetid air puffed out into the morning, all smoke and disappointment. I coughed, but stepped inside. I knew it would be dark—it was dark—and I knew it would be dirty—it was dirty—but I hadn't been prepared for the smell. It's a visceral thing, smell. Sweat, cheap tobacco, rancid beer, and through it all, that under- lying strange sage smell Vegas used to have, it permeated everything, even the dingiest of card joints. A man stood up in the further reaches of the bar and came towards me through the gloom. "Yeah? You lookin' for someone?" he said, a cigarette attached to his lip, stuck there with saliva.

"A game," I said. "Twenty-five cent ante's about right for me."

"No ladies in the bar," he said.

"Far as I know, this isn't exactly a bar. It's a cards club. I want to join."

A voice called out from further inside. "Screw it Pete, bring it on, whatever it is. Some kid, deal her in. Dang, can't get nothin' done at this blasted table..."

The now-named Pete looked at me and picked the cigarette off his lip, letting spew an impressive stream of spit onto the floor. I didn't know how he could do that without chewing tobacco, but underfoot, the inch-deep sawdust seemed used to such abuse. I was glad to be wearing heels. I stepped past Pete and saw two tables, the one on the left occupied by three men. Chips in front of two of them, a pile of loose change in front of the third.

"I'm just getting outta this, myself," said the man with the coins in front of him. He didn't seem particularly surprised by the fact he was talking to a girl.

"There's a chair if you want it. I'm gettin' onto a good streak here," said the man to his left, unshaven, fatter, wearing the clothes of an army sergeant who hadn't been back to his barracks for a few days.

I made myself smile as hesitantly as I could, so they wouldn't know how pleased I was to see them. "Well it's mighty kind of you to let me play," I said. "I used to love playing with my daddy and his friends. I kind of got hooked on the game."

At that dingy table, the cards greeted me like a long-lost friend. They romanced me with their lovely songs, giving me high pairs, Ace-King, and suits with an Ace of Diamonds. I nodded an invisible greeting to the showgirl Ace, I was glad to see her. It was the showgirls who made me realize where I belonged—back here at the table, not dealing blackjack at the Flamingo, watching feathers float past. I didn't care that the table's baize was stained and pockmarked with cigarette burns. After my first hand, I didn't even notice the smell. The day went past, and when I finally glanced at my watch, I saw I'd have to wind things up or I'd never get to my shift at the Flamingo. The cards loved me even then, knowing I had to leave—they obliterated the sergeant in the very next round.

"That daddy o' yours musta been one helluva player," he murmured.

The guy remaining between us folded and shrugged and said, "Y'know, I'm thinkin' of goin' home, findin' my wife, must be wonderin'...."

"That's a good idea, sir," I said. "She's probably waiting."

Pete counted my cash, making no comment as he paid out the $562 I'd made playing for small change. It added up alright. It was the luck I'd been looking for. I walked out of that filthy card club feeling like Napoleon after a successful battle; I didn't care that I hadn't slept and was going to have to squint through my Flamingo shift.

Funny thing was, the blackjack seemed to fly by that night. My legs hurt, but I watched the cards and fed the players what luck I could—I finally had a little bit to spare. I wasn't as bright-eyed as I thought, however, for when I headed off for my third break of the night, I didn't notice Savage circle over to walk beside me.

"I'm moving you out from Parry's watch, up to one of the front tables," he said softly.

"Thank you." Blackjack would be marginally more interesting at a table with better action, and maybe I'd get a new pit boss. I wanted to escape Parry's warty suspicious looks.

Savage touched my shoulder, as if straightening my tuxedo jacket. "You look happier tonight."

I shrugged against his hand.

"You should have a drink with me sometime," he said.

I thought of how he'd invited me for dinner years ago—how he'd made my mouth water. I remembered what George had said about him. George, who didn't know anything about my hands, who worried about my affections, such as they were. "Maybe," I said.

"We can talk about getting you off blackjack."

We were almost at the door that led to the windowless room. Savage moved his hand from my shoulder, touched my sharp chin for an instant and walked away. I clamped my teeth together hard to jolt myself awake. The rest of the shift went by in a haze of near-sleep. Black spots seeped across the green baize until I bit the inside of my cheek to keep the card patterns clear.

For another month, I dealt blackjack, slightly mollified by the better table. My attention was distracted by card-counters—I gave them a hard warning glance before reporting them. Some got my message and avoided my table before I had to finger them—I didn't want to be responsible for having someone roughed up. Card counters seemed so harmless in the grand scheme.

When I dealt poker for Savage, he said nothing more about that drink. I thought of Teddy, alongside my fickle heart, but he surfaced less and less often, even as I drove the car he'd given me. Even sleeping, I barely dreamed of him. I dreamed only of cards—patterns, colours, symbols. And once a week, it wasn't just dreaming—once a week, on Sunday nights, I took myself down to Fremont Street. Sunday nights, there were still some weekend fish, and I didn't need to see the Flamingo until Tuesday evening. I had time to play at the Broken Dice with relaxed fingers, easy cards.

I sat down for a ten-hour game with two cowpokes; I use the word cowpoke specifically. I mean, they wore actual spurs, and they put their big black hats under their chairs for the game. This was Vegas in the beginning of its first prime, when I sat across from these two cowboys alongside an ugly-faced Miami man in a silk suit, who barely spoke but when he did, his most beautifully-cultured voice was as smooth as the cloth of his suit jacket, his vocabulary as foul as I'd expected from the cowpokes.

My hands felt like thoroughbreds kept in the stable for too long, free now, on the track, stretching their muscles, ready to race. The cards went so nicely, well into the next night, that I missed Monday night dinner at George's. I forgot everything—the Flamingo, dealing for Savage—nothing in my head except the cards. It was blissful. The last few hours of that particular game, an old guy in a beard came pretty close to cleaning everyone out until I got a serious lady, the Queen of Clubs, topping a whole steel wheel, which I used to close the table. The old guy looked like an old-timer from my Silver Rush childhood, wearing clothes that had seen so much darning it was hard to be sure what colour they'd originally been. I dragged the pot towards me feeling exhausted but so exhilarated, I felt able to walk through walls, appear and disappear at will. At least the old guy was polite about my win. When I left the table, he shook my hand. Mister Miami though, he swore at me good and loud in his fine cultured voice.

The old-style road guys understood the power of name-calling, that what you called something tended to define the thing, if you used the words right. Maybe I was a witch, or a bitch, or something worse. No surprise that gamblers used to have nicknames. There was Doby Doc Caudill, who liked to decorate his bib overalls with a diamond stickpin or two—a cowboy and junk collector and a road gambler, he was never a doctor. There was Blondie Forbes, and Amarillo Slim, and Titanic Thomson. Johnny Moss was one of the few who hadn't bothered to get himself a nickname; without planning to, I ended up like him, with no clever moniker. I'd have been honoured to have one, but the players already had my diminutive gender to contend with. Perhaps I didn't need any witty name to make me memorable.

I cashed out and the rush of the cards kept me from feeling tired until I got into the car. I stopped at a diner before going home to George's—I wanted the satisfaction of breaking one of those new hundred dollar bills I'd won, even if all I was buying was a grilled cheese sandwich. The nearest place was the Corner Diner, with its horseshoe-shaped lunch counter and unfortunate lighting. Breakfast was served anytime, day or night, a plus for someone of my profession, with my appetite. Nothing ever looked appetizing under fluorescence, but I ordered breakfast anyhow.

The guy behind the counter worked his way through the options. "Over-easy or scrambled? Brown or white toast? Sausage or bacon or both?"

I was impressed when a plate arrived with eggs over-easy exactly as I liked them, hashbrowns greasy as they should be, and a generous pile of bacon with two perfectly-cooked sausages. The brown toast was buttery and hot. No one would go to the Corner for a romantic meal, or for the view—the windows looked out onto a deserted stretch of downtown, despite all the action one block away. Around the corner from the Boulder, the Corner's sidewalk was patrolled by exhausted hookers and burnout cases, the dregs of Freemont Street. There was a sports betting parlour further down the block, a couple of empty shopfronts, a taxidermist right across the street from the diner. But the diner was clean and I came 'round to liking the place—the way the horseshoe counter curved, its row of green stools, the linoleum with its little gold chevrons, and the calm mood of the guy behind the counter. He was always cheerful. Quiet, but friendly. Never inquisitive.

It wasn't even on the corner of the street; it had a bay window that jutted out a little, creating a sort of angle. That morning, I sat with a view across the milkshake machines and over the grill, the mirror reflecting not me, but rows and rows of clean glasses. I turned my head just slightly to see out that angled window, down the street, plain though it was, and right at the end, three blocks away, where the street finished and the desert began, there were the hazy distant hills. Sunrise coming up, the Corner was almost pretty. I sat at the Corner in my new town, and I was happy.

I worked a long week at the Flamingo. Home, finally, I stood in the hallway, thinking that blackjack was making my back hurt. I was too tired to immediately climb the stairs to my room, and the light was on in the kitchen, so I wandered slowly down the hall. George sat at the kitchen table staring at three empty glasses, a blue bottle of sherry standing two-thirds empty in the centre.

"You missed company," he said.

"Anyone I know?"

He shook his big head. "Bad news." George wore a dark suit, a white shirt, and a grey tie, loosely knotted.

I sat down in one of the chairs opposite him. "Nothing wrong with you, is there?"

"No. Siegel. They've killed him off."

"I don't think... he wasn't at the Flamingo tonight but that doesn't...."

"He was in L.A. They did him in his very own house." George looked down the hallway and I swear he shivered in the warm night air.

"I didn't realize you knew him well."

"That's not it, girlie. There're going to be some changes in this town. Lansky's taking direct control of that Flamingo of yours." He paused. "You might have to change jobs."

I knew very little about Meyer Lansky, Siegel's boss. I'd heard he didn't get his hands dirty unless it was absolutely necessary. I suppose that meant bumping off Siegel was necessary, by someone's definition of the word. I got a clean glass from the cabinet and poured a thimbleful from the blue bottle. The sherry tasted like cough syrup—maybe George found it medicinal. I refilled his glass.

"Shooting the dreamers doesn't seem right." George pulled the sherry glass closer. "You'll need to watch your back. There'll be changes. Wonder if that boss of yours will stick it through."

"Chappell's solid."

"No, Savage, I mean. Chappell sticks 'til he's sent somewhere new. He's a fixer, they'll keep him."

"And you're not betting on...."

"I'm not a betting type, girlie." George put his head in his hands. "I have to get some sleep. Breakfast time's gonna be here before we know it."

Up in my room, I took out an old pack of cards from my bureau, shuffled them, burned the top one and laid the next three in front of me—Mary Ellen's simplest fortune. I glanced at the walls of my room at George's house, thinking of Mary Ellen, missing her, after all this time. Then I looked down at the three cards laid out on the bedspread. Three of Hearts—caution, eight of Spades—disappointment, and the King of Clubs—an affectionate dark-haired man. None of it helpful in any way. I shuffled the cards back into the deck. I wanted easier dreams, but a girl can't bank on that sort of luck.

16

Even if George hadn't warned me, even if the cards had been good, the atmosphere at the pink bird changed. The next evening, from the pit bosses on down, everyone was sharp with suspicious looks. Dealers edged around Chappell as if he was contagious, knowing their job was gone if they were called into his office. I continued dealing cards, blackjack only, with no after-hours invitations to deal poker. Savage avoided me; when I did catch his eye, across the casino floor, he frowned and looked away.

Everyone knew Siegel was crazy as a bedbug, but maybe he'd been right to keep his suite at the Flamingo secret as a fortified bomb shelter. Paranoia ran through the Flamingo casino hierarchy from top to bottom—it kept everyone as close to honest as they could be. But with Siegel dead, no one knew where suspicion might fall next. No one spoke to each other in the staff room. Dealers and floormen were replaced with older guys. Stan Savage remained, his edges more knife-like than ever, and Chappell didn't seem any different, he just looked tired.

I didn't like dealing blackjack, but I had grown accustomed to my routine. I had enough security to play cards, and the casino itself made me happy, really, honestly, happy. I liked the crazy colours, I liked some of the dealers, Roscoe and some of those guys, and I liked Chappell. I didn't want to be called into the office. I only knew one person who might be able to tilt the cards in my favour: I went to see Mavis. I got up early and I put on my lucky red dress and I dropped by her bungalow at teatime, before my shift started.

When she came to the door, she had dark circles under her pretty eyes. She was wearing a pair of yellow silk lounge pyjamas with navy trim, her hair tied up in a pink bandanna.

"I'm spring cleaning," she said, "But it's a perfect time for a break. Come in."

"Hard days for Dick, I guess," I said. The living room was in the throes of total reorganization, the furniture pulled away from the walls, the sofa pillows stacked to one side, a bucket of water and a cloth on an empty shelf on the far side of the bungalow.

"Excuse the mess," said Mavis. "I'll just put on some coffee."

"Would you mind if..." but then I stopped, looked at the mess of the living room. It wasn't worth asking for tea—Mavis was worried enough without my being a difficult guest.

"I have some pecan squares," she called from the kitchen. "Do you like pecans?"

I went into the kitchen, edging around an A-frame ladder. A broom was balanced on the top rungs.

"Cobwebs," said Mavis. "You'd be amazed, the spiders in a bungalow like this."

"I don't know that I've ever eaten pecans," I said, to distract her from the spiders. Surely her industrious cleaning had more to do with the casino's reshuffling than with cobwebs.

Mavis put her hands on her hips, staring out at the living room. She shook her head. "I think we should sit in the bedroom. It's the only room I've finished. You go on in, there's a settee by the window."

The bedroom window framed a view of the golf course. I thought of George's story about the sewage; the grass did look nice and green. In the distance, a few men stood, doing whatever it was one did at golf. I sat down on the tan chaise longue, beneath the window. On the far side of the neatly-made bed, a narrow mirrored teak dressing table held the usual collection of perfumes and lotions, the necessary apparatus for a good-looking woman.

Mavis brought in a tray with the coffee and pecan squares and two pink rippled glass coffee cups; she balanced the tray on the bedside table and curled up at the foot of the bed. She looked like a tired film star, lounging in pajamas between movie shoots. I took a pecan square and said, "So am I getting fired, along with everyone else?"

"Not everyone's getting fired," she protested. "There's the slot machine guys, they're happy. Aren't the new machines pretty? And Walter's promoted."

"Roscoe?"

She nodded. "He moved over to watch the count-room. Haven't you noticed, how he has the eyes of a prison superintendent?"

"But he was dealing."

"He can deal cards," she said. "One of the only ones. Apart from you, of course." She poured me a cup of coffee and I tried to like it. Mavis sipped her coffee. "Meyer had him dealing these past months to keep an eye on things. He and Meyer go back, they went to school together, such as it was."

"I didn't know," I said.

"Meyer's very educated," said Mavis, misunderstanding me. "He can quote entire sections from *The Merchant of Venice*. I've heard him."

I stared at her, surprised that she had met Lansky, I guess, and, well, *The Merchant of Venice*? That made me stare too. A nice choice for Lansky, to have memorized that play in particular, don't you think? The good guys in that piece are such pansy-wits. Then I realized Mavis probably figured I hadn't read any Shakespeare either.

Facing my silence, Mavis said, "Doesn't mean I approve of the man. It's just business."

"So Roscoe's watching the count-room now?"

Mavis sighed and explained how the skim, which she politely insisted on calling "the dividend," now depended on Roscoe. I didn't ask what had happened to Siegel's man. As a dealer, I already knew the money from the Flamingo slid out from the casino's backroom, swam away to Florida where it was divvied up and cut into appropriate percentages. Our hard-won dollars moved all across the country and seeped out its borders in neat satchels, by plane, train, automobile, boat, to each investor of the Flamingo. Mavis knew everything about it; she explained the twelve-way splits to me despite the circles under her eyes, outlined the transfers moving gradually into Cuban bank accounts, proportional according to who was out of favour and who was in control.

"So Roscoe keeps the dividend from slipping, from now on. Meyer's relying on him," she concluded.

I didn't ask Mavis how she knew all this; I imagine she weaseled the story from her husband without his noticing. I said, "Funny move, factory worker to factory overseer."

"Factory book-keeper," replied Mavis. "Well, there aren't any books. Just memory."

No books, I thought, no incriminating evidence if anyone ever did come down on the operation. I heard the kitchen clock chime five o'clock. "I'm going to be late for my shift," I said. "I stayed longer than I meant to. It was the pecan squares."

Mavis walked me to the door, stood looking grimly out at the casino grounds. "I hate spring cleaning." She gave me a quick kiss on the cheek. "I'm glad you came by."

As I passed the swimming pool, I realized she hadn't answered the question about my job. It didn't reassure me one bit. Inside the casino, I turned at the noisiest of the new changes—slot machines, installed in a long row. I didn't like one-armed bandits, all clashing gears and flashing lights and little automatic bells; Mavis liked them, but watching the pictures of fruit spin by, I wondered why. Casino lore held that women were bored by poker, that they liked sparkly lights and noise much better than mere cards. If that was true, I would never understand my gender. I walked quickly past the machines that lived off lost nickels.

A girl stood at the end of the row, just before the door leading to the windowless room. She seemed to have misplaced her shoes. Her face had been reapplied crookedly and the slot machine was doing its best to hold her up. Her ruined mouth and shoplifted ambitions were just part of the scenery. Showgirls like Sabina made a dime and fifty a week, but too many girls came to this city and couldn't get jobs as dancers. There was the Vegas I was proud to be part of, the city that was shiny with money, stacked with colourful chips, filled with explosive wonder, and then there was the other Vegas, the real one, that I was half-ashamed by, but only half, because I was also afraid of it. The fear was completely rational. It was the admiration that didn't quite make sense.

I wasn't going to end up like the shoeless girl at the one-armed bandit. I needed to move off blackjack. I wanted to play real games at the casino; I wanted to play here, even with the grim men in dark suits, even with Roscoe watching the skim and Savage in the corner, unwilling to meet my eyes. I tried not to think about why he was avoiding me. I got out on the floor in my tuxedo, dusted my hands, stripped the cards, and began dealing.

A player won a decent hand of blackjack and I paid out what the house owed him. Parry had been shuffled up to my table, so he stood behind me, coughing irritably. He was in his predictable bad mood, a bleak silhouette hovering at the edges of every play. For a religious man, Parry never seemed filled with any kind of holy spirit. I guess that's the Mormons for you. I suspected they'd be better off if they drank something stronger than orange juice, every now and then. Towards the end of my shift, I changed a customer's seven hundred dollars into chips, and as I glanced up, I noticed Stan, prowling past the tables.

He paused to murmur, "At the bar after?" and drifted away again, a well-dressed shadow. I dealt my last game, finished my shift, and signed out. I changed into my red dress and went dutifully to find Savage. He leaned against the gold and rose bar that nestled in the swoop of a half-wall, near the roulette tables. The bartender was mixing a pair of whiskey sours, which I recognized by their pale colour—the blackjack players at my table often ordered such things.

When the sours were ready, Savage picked up the two tall glasses and headed for a gold-topped round table in the furthest corner, not bothering to check that I followed. He put the sours down and pulled out a pink chair for me. It was considerate of him to give me the chair; the gold banquettes were not designed for short women.

"José makes a good whiskey sour. Thought you might like to try it."

I didn't usually drink, but the glass was a decent stage prop, giving me something to do with my hands while I waited for Savage to speak.

"Your health," he said, holding up his glass.

I raised mine, politely, and took a tiny sip, tasting mostly lemon juice and sugar. I fished the cherry out of the drink and set it aside; I wasn't quite convinced maraschino cherries were edible. They looked like plastic to me.

"I've got an idea," he said, "that Chappell finally likes."

I didn't say anything; I wondered if Mavis knew about the idea. With my straw, I nudged the maraschino cherry on the table. It didn't move.

"They like it too," said Savage.

"They?"

"The new management."

After a while, with me saying nothing and Stan rearranging his hands on the gold-coloured table between us as if he were trying to find a comfortable position, he sighed and put his hands flat on the table's surface. His signet ring clinked against the tabletop.

"Sometimes, Millard, it would be nice if you made small talk."

"I never learned drawing room arts in the wilds of Canada."

"Was it as wild as all that? Vancouver seemed civilized when I was there."

I couldn't decide if he was being sarcastic or not. Maybe he wasn't. But I was sensitive about it—I wasn't very civilized when he met me in Vancouver. But he hadn't said that, exactly. I set my drink to one side. "It's about my job, you wanted to talk to me about the job."

He made a funny sound, almost a laugh. "Nice having this drink with you," he said. "Very relaxing."

"Yes, thanks for the drink. It's very...." I looked at the drink in its tall glass. "It's very strong." I didn't know what else to say about it.

He did laugh, then, but instead of speaking his mind, he took out a black and silver case and offered me a cigarette. I shook my head. He took one for himself and lit it with a silver lighter from his breast pocket. The lighter had a wind-blown Vargas girl in a red raincoat embossed on it, expensive but tacky, not really the kind of accessory I expected him to use.

"It was a gift." He looked sheepish as he pocketed the lighter. I wondered if his wife had given it to him. "You have to move off blackjack."

I threw away my interest in his wife. "I make better odds than anyone else."

"They don't like the idea of a girl dealing blackjack."

"So let me deal poker."

"They don't like the girl dealer, period."

"I'm the best you've got," I said. "Especially with Roscoe moved to the count-room."

"I know that."

I drank some of the whiskey sour, as if having a really strong drink would help me think of an answer. A defense. The drink was cold; I put it back down on the table.

"If you're just going to fire me...."

"We're not firing you."

"I can't wait around, dealing poker games after hours," I said.

"That's why you're going to like this idea of mine."

"I will?"

"I'm taking you off blackjack, turning you loose as a mechanic."

"I'm not a mechanic."

Savage raised his eyebrows, as if to say, Yes you are. You know you're a mechanic. Cards listen to you like you wrote the mechanical book on their engine.

"You know darn well what I mean," I said.

A card mechanic is a cheat, pretty much by definition. It was one thing for Sam Lazar to call me a mechanic—I liked Lazar. It was entirely a different thing with Savage. Because I wanted Savage to admire me? No, something else, but before I could sort out what bothered me, Savage said, "I mean an honest mechanic. We need a new shill."

"Something unpleasant happen to the guy you had?"

I wondered who it had been. I didn't much care where he had gotten to; I didn't like the word or the job. A shill plays with house money that's handed back at the end of a game. There's no motivation to win, save that you're hired for your time and paid by the hour to win a game. I shook my head, my earrings knocking against the sharp angle of my jawbone. "I don't want to be bought. Thanks."

Stan sighed again. "I suppose you had some kind of upright contract in that dive in Vancouver? When you were twelve?"

"I was seventeen."

"By the time I met you. But you'd been playing for years. You were a pro. I never saw anything like it. You'd started, when, ten years before?"

"I was a regular Mozart of cards."

Savage ignored my sarcasm. "So you can be the Flamingo's prodigy. A freak of nature."

"Being a performing monkey isn't one of my ambitions." I stared at the whiskey sour until I had my voice back under control. "I'm no one's ace in the hole. There's no point if it's not my own bankroll. I'm not going to be a one-trick pony, trotted out when a game's going too well for a customer."

Savage started to laugh. "What do you think I was doing at those games you dealt?"

The games suddenly made sense. Savage hadn't needed to cheat—he wasn't playing with his own money. He was breaking the banks of players who had taken too much money away from the house, in private invitation-only games. The fact that I'd been his witness, privy to the players' legitimately-devised demise, didn't make me like the work he was doing any better.

"I'm not going to bust suckers out for your murderous bosses."

"So many ugly words in one sentence."

"Like a sideshow shell game. Distracting the crowd while carnival owners steal the mark's pocketbook. How can you stand it?"

Savage brought his hands together and leaned his chin on his interlaced fingers. "In this scenario, you mean I'm the one stealing pocketbooks?"

If I was the dealer at the poker games he was busting, if I was the honest gatekeeper, then yes, he was the thief. Playing beautifully above board, robbing in the pay of the casino, but a thief just the same. The idea must have hurt his pride, because there was a tiny shift in his usual expression.

"I'm not saying you weren't playing an honest game," I said. "I just don't want to do it."

"How noble of you." He picked up his cigarette from the ashtray, tapped off the ash, and took a long drag of smoke. He leaned back and the smoke came out his nose, an effect that made me smile. Even though I was being fired, I thought how funny he looked, a man pretending to be a thoughtful dragon. It makes me smile now, just remembering it, even with everything that came after.

Savage said, "Can't you think of me as a friend, Millard? I'm trying to get you the best deal from the house. It's not easy."

I must have looked dubious, for Savage pressed on.

"It's the best I can get for you. You're off blackjack, as of now. I'm sorry." When I didn't say anything, he added, "It's a promotion."

If I'd eaten the maraschino cherry, maybe the conversation would have turned out better. I stood and picked up my purse.

"Don't go. Think about the offer."

"You've fired me. What happens next is, I leave."

Savage stood too and took my hand. I slid my fingers out of his cool grasp.

"The house doesn't want you playing somewhere else. They want you here. I convinced them of that. Don't make me look bad for recommending you."

"Your reputation is really not my problem."

He took my elbow, as if he were accompanying me. There wasn't much I could do without causing a scene, so I allowed him to walk with me to the cage. I wanted to cash out the Flamingo chips I had in my purse. I had a great desire to get rid of anything to do with the house.

Savage murmured, "You know Truman played pot-limit stud before dropping that bomb on Japan?"

"What?" I was concentrating on the cashier cage. All I heard were his last three words. The thought of Teddy seized me, Teddy and a country he'd never spoken of. A bomb that ended his imprisonment, finished the war and set him free. I thought of the way his eyelashes shadowed his cheek when he closed his eyes.

But Savage misunderstood my silence. He was filled up with the story he wanted to tell. "Really," he said, "Truman was in Europe, meetings with Churchill, with Stalin. He was travelling home on the USS Augusta. He'd pretty well decided he was going to bomb the bejesus out of Japan. He didn't want to talk to anyone who might disagree, so he locked himself in a room with the card-playing newspapermen on the boat with him. They played poker. You can't disturb a man when he's playing a game, even if he is President."

I tried to imagine playing poker with the American president. "And you're telling me this because?"

"Cards. You're not the president, I'm sure you have no desire to bomb the bejesus out of anyplace—it's about cards."

"I see." I didn't see, not at all.

"A game," persisted Savage, "a good game, gets rid of all the noise. You know that's the truth. You can't be disturbed by anything, if you're at a good table."

"Playing as a shill doesn't count as a good table."

"Does for me. You don't know, you haven't tried it." Savage paused, looking across the floor. "I liked it."

"I am not going to work as a shill."

I thought the tone of my voice was as final as it needed to be, but he didn't leave. I became increasingly aware of his hand. It was warm in the casino, but his hand didn't feel sweaty. It was pleasant, or would have been, if he weren't trying to convince me to take a job I didn't want. I saw the pit boss at a craps table whip his head up and nod at Savage.

Savage slipped his fingers gently along my arm. "I have to go. Take the offer."

I stayed in line, but I watched him cross the floor, sharp and unhurried. He wanted me to be the same kind of player he was. He knew I'd be able to keep players at the table, that I could bust players who were too good for the house's taste. But I didn't think there should be extra gamblers pulling for the house—a casino makes enough money without that extra tilt. Working as a shill was underhanded, dirty—like politics, like a bomb.

I'd been naïve, to think Savage was playing his own money at those games I'd dealt. Maybe I was naïve saying any kind of poker was clean. But it can be. Straight-played and above board—you play at a casino to get a clean table. You pay your fee, every game, and in return, the casino gives you honest dealers, level tables, and new decks of cards. It's a perfectly equitable arrangement.

I reached the cashier and I pushed my chips beneath the zoo-like brass bars. The gambler behind me coughed, impatient to get his turn at the wicket. I gathered up my bills and coins and shuffled to the side, organizing my purse. I watched the cocktail waitresses in their tight black skirts and tuxedo jackets churning through the thinning crowd. Savage had disappeared. I slipped through the casino unnoticed, past the pit bosses and middlemen and guards, walked past them, below their gaze. All of them watched the room, observing the customers, the games, as the night turned slowly into morning. I felt angry at each and every one of those men—why should they work at the Flamingo in legitimate jobs, when I couldn't? Because I was a girl, I was allowed to work only as a shill—even the word left me with a bad taste in my mouth.

At the door, I noticed Roscoe leaning on one of the brass dividers. I was angry with him, too, why not? He had a place here and I didn't. He caught my eye, grumbled something.

"Sorry?"

"Lookin' under the weather." He waved his half-finished Caesar at me.

"It's the lights."

"Nah, you look crummy. Read any good detective stories lately? Really takes the edge off a lousy mood. But I'm outta Christie novels, can't loan ya one."

I'd seen him once or twice shoving a paperback into his tuxedo pocket. Maybe he was inspired by his boss, Meyer; maybe he, too, had memorized some Shakespeare. Even with my anger at Savage, my anger at the casino, I started imagining Roscoe's idea of a nice evening—go home, eat a solid Italian meal made by his housekeeper, and tuck himself into bed to read a detective mystery.

"I haven't read anything lately. I was just leaving."

"That's too bad, kid. I need to keep my head level, y'know. Can't get crummy. An' those newspapers are buggin' me. Believin' our Vegas isn't really American, even though it's the American Dream personified. That's what worries 'em." Roscoe downed his drink as if the Caesar were water and he was a plant. "We're the cornerstone of America." He slammed his drink down on the tray of a passing waitress. She scurried away on fast-moving long legs. I'd never seen Roscoe so irritated.

"I've had a bad night too," I said.

"Bah. We came out of the U.S. of A. smoothly, there was a bit of blood, sure, like any child comin' into the world. Mother Mary. The American Dream. There was no space for Eye-talians like me in that dream, no space if you're a fuckin' Jew, you know what I'm saying, you know I'm a dark little wop, hell yes. I know that too."

Roscoe was neither dark nor little, but I wasn't going to argue.

"I don't mean nothin' personal to you, doll," said Roscoe. "But where I come from there was nowhere to go, you know what I'm sayin'. Eye-talian? Jewboy? Paddy? What else could we do with our dreams? We ended up with the stuff the world didn't wanna touch, kinda stuff that leaves your hands dirty."

I thought of Teddy, boxing. "That's just how it works," I said. My hands were probably dirty enough to work as a shill, if you looked at it from that point of view.

"You want a Caesar? They do 'em fine here, good an' spicy. I'll get you one...."

Roscoe flagged over a different waitress before I could protest and suddenly I was holding a tall glass edged with salt and far too much celery. It tasted of Tabasco. I fished the greenery out of my drink and held the celery awkwardly to one side, the way a Catholic leaves church on Palm Sunday, holding a little cross. Maybe Roscoe thought the same thing. He cleared his throat.

"Don't get me wrong, Luciano's a good Catholic like me, but it's all the same big Rotten Apple. Chairman's a Shylock Polak from New York, no wonder those guys hate him so much."

I wondered who Luciano was, though maybe I didn't want to know. "Someone getting your goat, Roscoe?"

"Bah, forget it. Some guys get my goats, kid, that's life. You're Canadian, right? Wide open space."

I nodded.

"Spent a bit of time there, fell in with the Jewish Navy, Lake Erie. You know."

I didn't know, but before I could answer, he grabbed the celery I was holding. "You mind?"

While I stared, he ate the celery stick—I would say he ate it thoughtfully, but he didn't have a face that ever looked thoughtful, he only looked more or less thuggish.

When he'd finished the celery, down to the last leaf, he said, "You gotta eat the veg, my wife used to tell me. Me, I was always good at the numbers. Never worried about the veg so much. Might be we got that in common. You're a short kid with good numbers, am I right?"

"Sometimes."

"So this is the place for you."

"Savage just fired me, Roscoe."

"Well, from the blackjack, yeah, but…."

I shook my head, wishing I could get rid of the Caesar and get out of the casino.

Roscoe said, "Consider your options, kid. Where're the numbers gonna treat you good?" He gestured across the Flamingo's floor with his half-empty glass. "This is the place for you."

I looked around the room, and then out the glass doors towards the too-bright dawn.

"Ya know I'm right," said Roscoe. He patted my shoulder with his big hand. It was more of a thump than a pat, but he meant to be reassuring.

There was no discernible change in the casino floor but suddenly Roscoe was alert, looking across the tables. "Gotta go," he said, tossing his empty glass at a passing waitress. I handed her my barely-touched Caesar and went outside. I wasn't sure why Roscoe cared whether I worked as a shill or not. When I reached my white car, I had to leave the door open for a while, the air was searing inside. I waited while it cooled down, looking at the pink stretch that was the Flamingo, its perfect evergreens in a row. I wondered how that kitten was, if it had found itself a safe haven in the back shrubbery, near the swimming pool. I was going to miss working here. Any more of this, I thought, I'll make myself cry. I got into the car, hot as it was, and drove downtown, squinting in the sunlight. When I reached the boardinghouse it took me while to muster the energy to get out of the car. I knew I'd have to discuss the whole problem with George. I felt as if I'd been arguing for days.

My landlord was at the kitchen table wearing his orange dressing gown, doing his monthly books. At least my rent wasn't owing. There was a massive plate of cinnamon buns on the table, a trail of raisins between the plate and his papers.

"They fired me," I said without preamble.

He looked at me. "You're the best thing they've got." When I didn't answer, he said, "Have a cinnamon bun."

I sat and took a bun to please him. "It's not like I want to leave." I felt pathetic now, too tired to stay angry.

"We can get you rehired somewhere."

"No one's going to hire me if the Flamingo's cut me loose. They'll think I was cheating."

George leaned his shadowed chin on his big hands. "You sure they're firing you?"

The morning light from the kitchen window made him look like a home-making angel, even if he was unshaven.

"I don't like what they're offering me, comes down to the same thing. Management doesn't like girl dealers."

"Their loss." He looked at me strategically. "What did they offer you?"

I explained.

"Shill's not so bad," he said. "Would be okay."

"Nice cinnamon bun, George."

"What?"

I glared at him, but he seemed willing to wait me out. "I don't like working for an hourly wage. Not playing with my own money. Breaking guys' wallets when they've worked them up. Where's the challenge in playing for the house?"

"Well." He sat silently for a while, going through the rest of his paper-work while I finished the bun and ate another. My head started to weigh too much for my neck, but George suddenly snapped his big fingers. "How 'bout a proposition player, you like that better?"

"An invited prop? How's that more legitimate than a shill?"

George shook his head as if I were an idiot. "No house money riding on you," he said, "first off, so you're breaking the wallets, but it's your game, your wallet, on the line. And you'd still get a salary to turn up at the best games. Have your own bets. Play your own games. Get some inside invitations, go to their tables, play for a while, leave when they ask you to. Keep games going. Keep games moving."

"I don't play with a fix."

George nodded, impressed with his own idea, thought I still couldn't quite see it. "Flamingo wouldn't want you on a fix," he said. "That's the point. No one expects a little thing like you to play for the house. You're perfect." He was looking at me speculatively, as if he might put some money on me himself.

"Perfect?"

"Think, missy, the house has a game going, a big fish, a guy they want to stay at the table. They want the game to be good, to keep him involved, inter-ested, happy—and losing money. That's where you come in. You show up and keep the game going, in case other players fold or lose or walk away—the game keeps going, the big fish is happy, the house is pleased, everyone's happy."

Except that I didn't have a stake to sit down at real games, to stay the course. "I only have the cash for sawdust games, George, I haven't had a chance to build up a bankroll."

"So get out there and do it."

I sighed. "It's luck, might take three nights, might take three months. I can't play the Flamingo's games without the backing cash." I felt as if George were trying to sell me on the very same job as Stan, only from a slightly different angle. "Whose side are you on, anyway? My bankroll's not nearly serious enough for their games."

"That can be fixed."

"I don't play slant, George."

He adjusted his hair-do. "Of course you don't. I wasn't implying that, silly girl."

I finished the second cinnamon bun and tried to dust off my sticky hands. "I'm going to sleep," I said.

"Hold your horses. This town needs special girls like you and me. So I need to think this through, you hear me, girlie?"

I put my elbows on the table, which wasn't polite but I needed to hold up my head.

George swept his paperwork into a pile and closed his accounts book. "You're thinking about the prop, right? You'd do it, wouldn't you? If I could get them to stake you, it would be a sweet deal."

"The Flamingo won't go for that."

"Savage'll go for it. He'll convince them it's a good deal. They'll take a percentage, but it won't be bad."

When I didn't say anything, he nodded. "You're supposed to be here, girlie. This here's a perfect town in just one or two ways, and one of those perfect things is exactly what you're good at. Least, I hear you're good at it. So let me talk to some people." He spread his big arms wide, then folded them behind his head in a gesture stolen from Rita Hayworth, but all wrong. "Friends look out for each other."

I went upstairs to bed. I thought I'd have terrible dreams, but I didn't— maybe the cinnamon buns took care of that. When I woke, it was night, and I didn't have a blackjack shift, I didn't have to go to the Flamingo, I had nothing to do—which meant only one thing. I put on a pair of plain brown slacks and a short-sleeved white sweater and I walked out of the boardinghouse with my purse over my arm. I had two hundred dollars that I could play with, and if I was at a table, I wouldn't worry about Stan, or George, or anyone else. I could listen to the cards. I remembered what Savage had said, at the cashier's cage, about not hearing any noise, if the game was good. He was right. The fact didn't please me.

The hazy light in Pete's eyes brightened when I showed up, and I played through the night and into the following day, a good straightforward table at the sign of the Broken Dice. I don't think Pete slept much. Night or day seemed to make no difference to him, he just spat on the floor and dealt cards and paid out what guys won at the table. Every now and again, fools came to play craps, and Pete took their money—craps was his game, and I didn't entirely trust his dice. But the cards were dealt fair in that horrible place, and they were more than kind to me.

"You're a funny one," said Pete, when I left.

"I like the game," I said.

"Yeah, there's that," he said, and spat heartily onto the sawdust.

I managed not to wince. After all, he was counting out an extra six hundred dollars I'd just earned at his table.

"You're always welcome here," he said. "Word gets out you're here, guys might come out special."

"Don't count on it, now," I told him, putting the money in my purse. He came around and opened the door for me. We shielded our eyes from the sunlight.

"Sheeit," he said, "that sun." I edged out onto the sidewalk and he slammed the door tightly behind me.

I had barely fallen asleep when George knocked on my door, calling me to the phone. When I slumped down the stairs, he handed me the receiver with a big stage wink.

"Hello?"

"Millard, it's Stan."

"Oh."

"I can tell you're glad to hear my voice."

I had been dreaming of water, of canoeing.

"I have this new idea," said Stan.

"Do you?"

There was a slight cough on the other side of the line. "The other day, I hadn't thought things through."

I waited.

Stan said, "What about working at our invitation as a prop player?"

George really gave the man a script. My landlord hovered beside me, peering at me coyly, pleased as only a shortsighted six-foot man in an orange silk dressing gown can be.

"Being a prop instead of a shill?" I turned my back on George.

Savage sighed. "Millard, yes, make your own bets, no house money riding on you. With a salary."

When I still didn't say anything, Stan added, "It's a very straight-up offer."

Working as a prop was a way to stay in Vegas. The salary would pay for incidentals like room and board, gas for my car, and I could still play poker, on my own time. This reminded me of the obvious. "I need a stake to play real poker for you," I said.

There was barely any pause. "We'll stake you $20,000 for a month. Pay us $25,000 back, we're even."

"Steep markup." And it wasn't enough, if I was going to play properly at high roller games. "If I'm at the big table, I need twice that."

There was a longer pause at the other end. I wondered if Stan was smiling. "Thirty-seven thousand, does that suit you?"

"And the markup?"

"Pay us back fifty, give you three months to pay. Forgot to say, compensate for the salary, we get a percentage of your take."

"You forgot?" When he didn't answer, I said, "What percentage?"

"Well, forty-eight." To his credit, he managed to sound embarrassed.

"Forty-eight? Big chunk of money to lose to the house."

"It's not losing it. We're paying you."

It was my turn to be quiet.

"Look," he said, "it's the best deal anyone's going to offer you, Millard. The house wanted sixty-two. I argued for you."

"How kind."

George coughed. I turned and he waved his hands in an encouraging gesture.

"Get yourself back here for the end of the week, and the deal is signed and sealed. No shill, no fix. My word on it." Savage hung up, leaving me with the receiver against my ear. I wanted to believe him, but how much was a card cheat's word really worth? A prop was an employee—the way a mechanic works in a garage, on cars he's told to repair. I wouldn't be wearing a uniform, but I'd be employed just the same as any of the tuxedo-wearing dealers.

But the offer would allow me to get a bankroll going. If I could get myself a bankroll, I could gradually get out of the Flamingo deal and play poker. Not just small sawdust games. Real games, the kind of poker I'd been trying to play all my life—games where the money was serious, but so was the skill. Just a few months of being a shill, I thought, and maybe I could build up a real bankroll; once I'd paid back the pink bird's stake, I'd be a free agent. I could keep up my numbers and slowly move into real games, with no percentage disappearing to the house.

George beamed as I came into the kitchen. "Oh, I knew my girl had talent. I thought you were a card shark from that first game you came home so late. Full of talent. I knew they'd promote you, girlie. A fix is just your ticket."

"I'm not a fix," I protested. "Anyway, I haven't agreed yet."

"Yes you have," he said. "And I am going to make you the best breakfast."

17

I drove to the Flamingo to work out the details of the stake—such a discouraging word, the stake gave me visions of myself as a vampire, with a wooden spear through my heart, my hands pinned to the ground. I shook my head, got out of the car and went directly to Chappell's office. I wanted to deal with him rather than Savage, confirm everything Stan had claimed was true.

"Good to see you, Millard," said the big man when I appeared at his office door.

"I miss my uniform," I said, to make a joke of this re-hiring.

"Mavis wants to make you dinner, tomorrow night. Suit you?" When I nodded, Chappell stood up and leaned over the desk to engulf my fingers in his huge hand. "I'm glad you've taken up the offer. It's good to have an honest player on our side."

Through the window, I could see the gaming tables. Chappell opened a drawer in his desk and brought out a piece of paper, which he made out to me—a house IOU for thirty-seven thousand. He signed it with a wide blue-inked signature.

"Dinner at six?"

"Yes sir." I took that paper out across the floor, not quite meeting anyone's eyes. When the cashier counted out the money, not one of the bills looked real. But I took the money, putting most of it into one of the casino boxes, to use at their tables later. I took only the tiniest portion with me.

I drove downtown tapping impatient fingers against the steering wheel; I would have to play well on my own time, to make the stake back and pay off the Flamingo. And there were plenty of possibilities for my black arts downtown—the Golden Nugget, the Boulder Club, the Majestic, that familiar row down Fremont Boulevard. Each casino's neon sign hardly made up for the plain gambling hall interiors. I parked in front of the Golden Nugget's glittering display and along with the military types and their dates, alongside the out-of-towners and the obvious marks, right beside the cowboys and the dam workers, I found my place at a table and anted in. Taking my cards, I tried to imagine how I would feel, playing for the Flamingo. I didn't wonder for long— the immediate game is always more important than the future. I studied the men around me, considered their cards along with my own. Which reminded me of Savage, telling me about Harry Truman dropping the atom bomb. Maybe he was right: poker was a kind of bomb, clearing everything else out of its way. It made demands. Its destructive power was intrinsic to its nature. Every game, every round, demanded more losers than winners.

❧

When I went to the Flamingo, the colour was beginning to leach from the landscape as evening came on. Downtown's neon was coming into its own. The Mint had an eye-popping new sign, blinking in syncopation to the Fremont's burst of violet cascading lights. Then there was a quiet spell of emptiness along the Strip before El Rancho. Cars whipped past me, pastel candies on their way to the Flamingo.

I parked around the back of the hotel and walked through the garden to Chappell's bungalow. The lights glowed against the encroaching twilight. The air was sage and dust and possibility. Mavis had put candles outside on either side of the door—a beautiful picture, the little house and the lights glowing inside and the candles, flickering, unique, my memory of it.

I raised my hand to knock but Dick Chappell opened the door before my fist touched the wood. "Right on time," he said.

Despite the heat, Mavis had roasted a chicken, with steamed collard greens and grits instead of potatoes. A bowl of fresh green beans alongside. "In case you don't like collard," she said.

"I like everything." And I did, even the grits, which were something like porridge, only not sweet and not for breakfast.

We talked about all kinds of things. I remember having an opinion about the new Dodge that Chappell wanted to buy. Mavis asked only that it be yellow. "I like yellow for cars," she said, "it's sunny. Black is so funereal. And impractical, what with the heat."

"My practical Southern flower," said Dick, fond, not teasing. I suspected that if he bought the car, it would be yellow inside and out. I didn't blame him.

Mavis served us second helpings and refilled our glasses of iced tea. She said, "I get lonesome for home cooking."

"She means, her mom's kind of cooking."

"Everything's delicious," I said.

Dick mashed butter into the grits on his plate. "She's also wondering about you."

I put down my glass of iced tea. "About me?"

"She is the cat's mother," said Mavis, giving her husband a slanted look.

"True, true. Sorry my dear. What I mean is, Mavis doesn't think we're treating you in an upright way."

I took a bite of chicken.

"I don't think it's fair," said Mavis, leaning forward, the fabric of her dress pulling a little at the neck, emphasizing the tan line left by the strap of her bathing suit.

I swallowed. "I'm looking forward to playing." I wondered if that was the right thing to say. I looked at the remaining food, as if the grits might give me some indication of what Mavis meant.

Chappell sensed my confusion. "Mavis thinks I'm putting you in a delicate position, with this proposition of Stan's. Of ours."

"Oh?"

"I'm going to get you going tomorrow. Tonight you should just relax. Enjoy dinner. We'll get to work tomorrow evening."

"Richard," said Mavis. I'd never heard her use his full Christian name.

Dick blushed. Really, the big man turned a peculiarly rosy colour that had nothing to do with the heat. He wiped his mouth with his napkin. "Mavis feels that you're too honest a girl for this business," he said, staring down at his empty plate. "I've told her that's the whole idea."

"I've played a lot of poker. I know what it involves."

"Thank you, Millard. I couldn't have put it better myself. You see, my dear?" He glanced over at her, almost shyly.

Mavis shook her dark head. "You've never cheated at cards."

"I don't play a fixed game. That's established." I looked searchingly at Dick Chappell's big face. He was impassive. "Stan Savage made that clear, didn't he?"

"No one expects you to play any game you don't want to play."

"She's supposed to walk away from some of those men?" Mavis pushed herself away from the table. "More iced tea?"

"No dear, I'm fine. Sit down."

Mavis cleared the empty plates, clattering the cutlery just enough to express her disapproval. I stood to help her and carried the mostly-finished grits back into the kitchen along with the empty bowl from the collard greens. I stacked the dishes on the yellow Formica counter.

"I'll be fine," I said.

"You don't know some of those men, Stan and those other men." Mavis kept her back to me, rinsing our dinner plates and stacking them in the sink.

I considered this. I couldn't let her think I was all that innocent, much as I might have liked her to. She had invited me into her house as a friend—better she know exactly what I was. "You know why I came to work here, really?"

She glanced over her shoulder. "You needed a job. You're a dealer. Of course you'd come here."

"But the Flamingo in particular? I'm here because an acquaintance of mine, Sam Lazar, recommended I look up your husband, because it was a good idea for me to leave the games I had been working."

Mavis didn't nod in understanding, and I realized I'd have to be more specific. "I needed a job somewhere safer, Lazar knew that, wanted to help. Lazar has always been a perfect gentleman to me. But I know he's not a gentle man. He's leagues beyond someone like Stan—I mean in the way that you worry about."

"You don't know," said Mavis.

"I'd rather take my chances here than anywhere else on the continent. Play real games, the kind I'm good at."

"The people here aren't...." She paused.

"Aren't likely to have me assaulted if I win their money, Mavis, so long as I keep to the rules. The casino protects its own. That's what I'm here for. To play with protection." I didn't want to explain the mugging at Banff, the trains, even as I could feel the very solid floor of her bungalow shifting under my feet. As if it were a train corridor, a compartment.

Mavis glanced again over her shoulder, her expression thoughtful.

I met her eyes. "I grew up with these people, Mavis, people just like the men here." I suddenly thought of the way Stan Savage held his cigarette, very studied, posed. Stan wasn't from anywhere elegant or beautiful; he'd created whatever he was, on his own. He hadn't had any natural easy gift for charm, not like Teddy, say. No, Savage was more like me than I might normally admit. Older. Less honest. But still—I took a breath and said, "I'm more like them than I look, maybe."

Mavis didn't answer. She dried her hands and opened the cabinet to bring out three pale pink dessert plates. I took them and held them to my chest. "I'm not a cheat. I play an honest game, and the men you're talking about know that. They understand being upright, for all their other ways of doing business. Sam Lazar, and Roscoe and all the rest of them, I suppose, certainly your husband. I know what I've gotten myself into."

"What did Stan say to you, to make you agree to be a prop?"

"Why would it be Stan?"

"Who else would it be?"

"George convinced me to take the offer."

I took the dessert plates into the dining room and Chappell put out his hand as if stopping traffic. "Don't let Mavis confuse the issue. You're always free to quit. I'll stand by you, if you ever decide you don't like the set up." I could have shuffled and dealt an entire round of cards, waiting for him to speak again, but eventually he smiled, a crease that ran up to his eyes and fanned outwards. "You're free, Millard, whenever you pay back the initial stake. You can keep playing on our salary, with the percentage, or walk away. See how you feel. Anyone tell you different, talk to me."

I shook my head but he scrinched up his eyes.

Mavis called from the kitchen, "Is he treating you right?"

"Always, my dear, always," he replied. "Miss Millard here can look after herself."

Mavis smiled sadly from the doorway. She brought out an iced lemon cake, an elaborately-decorated thing that she put on the table in front of her husband. He reached out to touch her cheek and she turned her head, to rest her chin in his wide hand for an instant.

On Saturday night, my first call to work, Sabina walked into my room without knocking. I was zipping up my dress, a sleeveless green affair she insisted I buy for the occasion.

"Good," she said, surveying the dress. "Don't you have any jewelry? You need...." She opened my bureau drawer, rummaging through the cards, cigarette packages and casino chips I kept there. "What about this?" She turned, holding the silver bracelet from Teddy. She breathed on the blue iridescent stones and polished them with her finger, then held the bracelet out to admire its shine.

I shook my head.

"Don't be silly, it's pretty." She clamped the bracelet onto my left wrist and adjusted the safety chain. I didn't move my arm away. "Now you look sophisticated," she said.

"Sophisticated?"

She laughed while I looked at the silver band, its filigree pattern, its three stones. The way he knew the width of my wrist. The same way he'd chosen the small car, the way he knew me. A history, I thought, same as any game has, and I left the bracelet on my wrist. Maybe it would be some kind of luck.

When I got to the casino, the floor was jammed, the roulette and craps tables decorated with pretty girls, expensive jewels glinting down their cleavage. Men bet lucky numbers and laughed or groaned depending on the whims of fortune. The big fish had settled in for the weekend; no doubt Roscoe eyed the long night with relish.

I was glad to be wearing the sleeveless dress with its short-sleeved jacket. I liked the texture of the fabric, like reed wallpaper only softer. Good for the heat, for Las Vegas was getting warmer as the summer progressed. While there was something resembling air conditioning in the casino, it wasn't what you'd call cool. I wore the shoes Sabina had recommended—very high heels, not easy to walk in, but I was almost the height of a normal woman, wearing them. I imagine it was the height that made Stan Savage look curiously at me as I walked towards him.

"So?" I said, when I reached him.

"You look nice."

"I mean the table. Where am I playing?"

He smiled, and it was as pleasing a sight as ever. "Table three, McLaren. Our problem of the moment."

I glanced across the floor to the table in question; there were six men there, one with an absurdly massive red moustache.

"No," said Savage. "To the right of Yosemite Sam there. But take out anyone you want." And he grinned so widely that his teeth gleamed, really, like a wolf's.

A woman won a pot from the one-armed bandits and the clattering drowned out whatever Savage said next. He escorted me across the floor to the poker section, as if I were a new player, introducing me to the dealer, a guy named George.

I sat on the leather chair Stan pulled out for me, and I marveled at how beautiful the table was—not the men playing, I mean the light, perfectly angled from hanging ceiling lamps with gold fabric shades, shining upon the immaculate green surface of the baize, and the dealer's alacrity and skill. The blue stones in my bracelet gleamed as I set my hands on the table. I relished the smell of new cards and tobacco smoke, the beer set down beside my neighbour's cards, it all delighted me. To get into the fresh round, I anted, and the dealer doled out our three cards each, two hole cards and the third up for a door card; mine was two of Hearts, the lowest showing. My hidden cards weren't much better, a random five of Clubs and a ten of Diamonds; I folded. The first three rounds sat that way—it's a sad truth, the better the game, the more often I tended to fold.

"Where're you from, little lady?"

"Oh, way up in Canada," I said.

"Cold up there," said the man with the cartoon moustache. "I'm from Wisconsin myself, I know what I'm talking about."

"She won't be able to handle the heat," said the big guy opposite me. This was McLaren. He stood up and scratched his crotch—Vegas was about as classy as poker got, and it wasn't very classy. Wisconsin was pleasant enough, but when he stood, McLaren smelled of rotting eggplant, overpowering the scent of new cards and cigarettes. And soon he would smell even worse—losing makes a man like that sweat.

As the hours went by, I saw that Stan Savage was right about working as a mechanic. I liked it. Mechanics sounds like so much automobile maintenance, and maybe that isn't wrong. Many of the players required only the most basit of poker strategy to beat. I enjoyed the game, even knowing I was there on salary, with a borrowed stake. I looked at the Kings of Spades and Clubs, along with the nine of Hearts and nine of Diamonds already on the table. The cards I held included the one card the big guy needed to close me out—the Ace of Spades. But it was mine, and he ought to have known better than to bet the pot against me. When I won, McLaren threw his hand onto the table and spat, "Hell with you, bitch."

"Watch your language." I pushed my cards towards the impassive dealer.

"You can't handle the heat?"

"Not at all," I said. "But you might expand your vocabulary."

One of his fellow players coughed and the big man glared at him.

"Nice bet, lady," said the man from Wisconsin. "I'm staying in," he said. "Next," said the dealer. "Ante."

And so it went, I might say, rather well. Savage didn't pull me from that first game but let me play to the end. I cashed out with a sense of accomplishment, and stashed most of the money in the safe. When I turned from the cashier, Roscoe was standing behind me. "How'd it go, doll?" Roscoe had his usual cigar stapled to his mouth, lit for once, smoking.

"Not badly."

"If you run into any grief, don't hesitate. Tell me." He patted me on the shoulder and walked heavily back towards the count-room.

I was invited to every high-end Flamingo game that was going against the house. It was beautiful. I sat down to a table with George Raft, the movie star—he was a passable card player. People said that he came to Vegas to study the mobsters, but I think it was quite the opposite—the mobsters were studying him. I watched, while we played cards. So many men at the Flamingo had no idea how to be gentlemen, and Raft was a natural. Sure, he grew up in the same rough New York neighbourhood as the rest of them, but he was a handsome man, smart in his way. He invented himself as a Hollywood gent, and even with his career wrecked, he was still handsome. All the made men paid attention to his style. They watched the way he held his hands, the way he talked, smooth but slightly affected. Was control the affectation? Or threat? Just so, the way he smiled. George said that even Bugsy Siegel imitated Raft—while extorting money from him. At the table that night, I wasn't immune to the man's charm. The game was more attractive while he played opposite me. I barely noticed the other players, I watched Raft and did my job, kept him there, betting.

I played him for the fish he was. But after three hours, Savage sent a gopher with a message to leave the game—I wasn't needed any longer. I sighed and moved to the next table, as instructed, where two nondescript Baltimore businessmen were trying to recoup their losses at a game dominated by the ugliest man I had ever seen. The dealer seemed cowed, murmuring, "Yes, Mister Lissoni." or "No, Mister Lissoni," whenever the toad croaked at him.

I studied this toad as I took my seat. Lissoni smoked cigars the size of zucchinis that smelled the way atomic waste ought to smell. He trailed ash and attitude with a sense of blessed entitlement. I tried to work what magic I could with the cards, but after a single round, Lissoni threw his losing hand on the table and said, "No time for this crap. Who's this fucking girl? I want the upstairs table. Now. None of this bullshit."

The dealer tried to soothe him. "Upstairs is only on Sunday nights, Mister Lissoni. I'm sorry."

I shrugged at the two Baltimore men as we sat waiting for the ugly man to sort out his chips.

"What the hell do you want?" he growled, dusting us with ash.

I smiled and anted in for the next game.

Despite the occasional boor, I enjoyed the work. The pretty lights and the cards and the games—I liked the job, much as I regretted proving Stan Savage right. Even the prospect of paying back the stake they'd lent me didn't worry me too much; if I wasn't called in to play at the Flamingo, I spent my time at the sawdust joints downtown. I worked my way out of the Broken Dice over to a nice no-limit game at the Boulder. It was cleaner than Pete's place, and while I missed the easy acceptance from the guys gathered around Pete's much-abused baize table, I appreciated the higher pots I pulled down at the Boulder.

I played for two months like that; I know I was there, but the details blur because of what came after. How memory smears whole summers into a single night and stretches a few days into a scar. Memory and history, all those nights the Flamingo called me in to play. I sat at obvious casino games with the weekend fish, and Stan called me for poker games in the hotel bungalows as well. The same games I had dealt before—now I played them, very much as Savage had. The dealers didn't know me—they were new, hired after Siegel's death. I learned to sip a whiskey while I played, a tiny bit of whiskey with a great deal of ice. It was very hot in those bungalows, even late at night. Sometimes I wondered if Savage missed working these games. No longer the house shill, he managed the poker games, kept track of which fish were in town, playing which table, how their money was holding out. When needed, he'd call me.

Once he caught me just as I was leaving, the telephone ringing as I walked down George's hallway. When I answered it, I said, "But I'm heading to the Boulder."

"That's your nickel. We need you here."

I had to go upstairs and change; I couldn't go to the Flamingo in trousers.

"You on your way?" said Savage.

"'The game will have to hang in until I get there."

"Hurry up. We'll give the guys some drinks, meanwhile."

When I did walk into the Flamingo, Savage was pacing up and down the floor. But he smiled when he saw me. To have him look happy, seeing me, oh to be honest, I didn't give a darn about his wife. I didn't care that he used to cheat at cards. All I wanted was that smile, alongside the weekend crowd coming in the doors, the shine of their optimism, the coins in their pockets.

"I should be upstairs by now," he said. "I had to send some girls up as distraction."

"Upstairs?" Then I realized what he meant.

"I'm dealing it now," he said, "you bet it's upstairs. Steadier game than it was. Sunday nights."

I remembered Sam Lazar warning me about Ben Siegel's tilted private table. "I never want to play upstairs."

We reached the velvet rope that divided the high stake tables from the rest of the floor; Savage bent his head to murmur, "You'd be fine at the upstairs table. Be a treat." He kissed my cheek and walked away. I stood like a cat caught staring too fixedly at some object of desire, even as the floorman, waiting to take me to my seat, politely said, "Miss Lacouvy?"

"Yes," I stuttered, and I blinked, not at all like a cat. I was much more like the rats I'd seen all those years ago, running from their demolished home, ready to make a place for themselves in the next good thing that came along. If any animal was to be my familiar, it would be one of those rodents. Small and grey and practical and fast with cards. Well. Sex is so distracting, might be the only thing to compete with cards. But I said appropriate greetings to the men at the table, and I took my seat, and fortunately, my first hand dragged my thoughts from Stan Savage.

I bluffed solidly through the game, taking one of the men's twenty-three thousand, not that much, really, for the kind of stakes we were playing, but he was numb afterwards, his eyes wide, caught in the game's too-bright headlights. And when I got word to leave the table, somewhere towards Monday morning, I felt a little bit peculiar—it's one thing to take a man's money with my own hands; it's another thing to do it for the house. Walking past the bar, I saw the numb guy sitting at the bar, staring fixedly ahead. He hadn't ordered a drink. The chair beside him was free, but when I sat down beside him, he didn't react. The bartender called over, "Weak or strong, Miss?" knowing I usually ordered tea at this hour of the night.

I looked at the slumped man beside me. "Strong tea, thanks."

Bringing my tea, the bartender prodded the guy's elbow. "You want something?"

The man swiveled his head, lizard-like eyes looked at me, slowly recognizing. "You took my money." His voice cigarette-thick.

"We were playing poker. It's a risk of the game."

"Wasn't my money."

"Whose was it then?"

"The devil's. I'm going to hell."

"No guarantee of that." I signaled the bartender. "We need a glass of water and a ginger ale, something soothing for the guts." I wasn't willing to give the devil's money back, but I didn't want him to die of dehydration, either. Vegas sucked at players, changed us with its dollar bills, its numbers and symbols, the greenish glow of cards and dice and money, not to mention the heat, the dust, the lack of water. If this man didn't pay attention, he'd keel over, right at the bar, drown in all this dust and strangeness.

I rested my forearms against the wood. As I stirred my tea, I looked at the bracelet clamped on my wrist. For the first time, I saw how harsh the cards had made me, how limited my regrets were. How little I had really suffered, clearing out Teddy's money at Dermot's game. I frowned at the stupefied man beside me but he didn't notice. I might never have sat down and cleaned him out at the Flamingo table except that Savage set me upon him. Was that being honest with luck?

I finished my tea. I asked the bartender to get the guy beside me a whiskey, I owed him at least that much. Then I went to count out the Flamingo's cut of my winnings, that painful forty-eight percent. I gave the cash to Chappell in his office—it felt less suspicious than going to the backroom as a girl, not in uniform, going in there from the high stake tables. Players might have suspected the truth.

18

I played for the Flamingo and fell into bed at dawn, as usual. Except that I woke to a sharp knock on my door.

"Millard?" George's voice. "Sorry to wake you girlie...."

I groaned.

"Good, you're awake," said George from the other side of the door. "You should get up. Someone just called on the telephone, says I have to tell you he's on his way. Wanted directions on how to get here. Didn't catch his name. You awake in there?"

"Yes," I called out. I dragged my legs from bed and opened the rose-patterned curtains to the searingly bright morning. I pushed the window up as far as it would go and leaned against the frame. I hadn't seen Teddy for six months, but I was sure it was him. He wasn't in Vancouver, or in Pearl, or who knows where else. The way a hand floats across the table distributing chips, a failed hope, a wrong decision on the right card, an incorrect time to play—I knew Theodore Ahern was in my new town of Vegas, driving down Fremont Street. I could imagine him already, driving a Cadillac and singing "That Lucky Old Sun" along with the radio.

An hour later, Teddy's voice drifted up from the kitchen. And there he was, large as life, wearing a disheveled too-striped blue suit, a wrinkled pale blue shirt, an undone polka-dotted tie. George was pouring him a cup of coffee. I couldn't believe he'd found me.

"Mill...."

Teddy stood up and opened his arms. His left hand glinted with a gold wedding band.

"You're married?"

George looked at me while Teddy stared at his own hand, as if he'd forgotten the gold ring on his finger. He shrugged. "Well you weren't gonna marry me, were you? Kind of like the ring, suits me, don't you think? Aren't you glad to see me?"

My feet stuck to the kitchen threshold. "How'd you get...."

"I was thinking you'd say how glad you are to see me. I couldn't wait to see you." He came over and hugged me, hard enough that he lifted my feet from the ground.

"I'm glad to see you," I said dully. When he put me down, he left his arm around my shoulders for a moment and I shivered. Maybe it was the wedding ring on his finger. Maybe it was the way he smelled, a mixture of gin and aftershave, not unpleasant, but definitely unfamiliar.

"You never told me you had a cousin who played cards good as you," said George, sitting down to preside over our reunion.

"A cousin?" I squeaked, right at the same moment that Teddy nudged my wrist.

"Craps are more my style," Teddy interrupted. His eyes caught on my bracelet. He turned his face away, as if stifling a yawn.

"But you can deal cards, can't you?" George stirred sugar into his coffee. "Millard, maybe you can talk to that Stan of yours, see if there are any jobs."

"Stan?" Teddy's eyes slid to my face. His expression metamorphosed before my eyes to perfectly benevolent disinterest. "Yeah, do that. I've got a week's worth of business in Mexico, then I'm back. Figured my cousin would think of something to keep me out of trouble."

"There are amethysts in Mexico now?"

He smiled a little coldly. "Oh yeah, labradorite and sodalite. Princesses, too, so I hear."

I wondered if any of those tiny stones brought him pleasure.

"John hasn't even been to a casino yet, Millard. He came straight to see you. Isn't that sweet?" said George, smiling at Teddy with delight.

"John?"

Teddy grinned at me. "Yeah, how about we drive up to the pink bird, get some breakfast?"

The phone rang down the hall and George got up, silk dressing gown fluttering behind him. I leaned towards Teddy. "What exactly are you doing?"

"Dropped in to say hello, Mill, been too long."

"I mean, the name John? Why the...."

George came back into the kitchen. "So are you kids off for breakfast, or should I rustle up some grub?"

I stood up. "You're a marvel in the kitchen, George, but we'll go out."

"Yeah, catch up," said Teddy.

"You are going to love the Flamingo." George adjusted his hair coquettishly. "If I were dressed I'd go with you. But Millard is the girl to show you 'round. Best fix they've ever had." When I started to protest, George held out an authoritative hand. "Don't argue with me, girlie. I've heard it from a few sources. Everyone agrees."

"A fix?" interrupted Teddy, giving me an uneasy glance.

I shook my head. "Not that kind of fix."

Teddy stood up but he seemed off-balance. He cut his eyes away from me and smiled at George. "So did you meet Mr. Siegel before he was popped?"

"Oh, well." George shrugged his satin-covered shoulders in a gesture that was pure Betty Grable. "You'd have liked the man, I can tell from your taste in suits. Crooked though he was." He fanned himself a little with his fingers. "I only ever agreed with Ben on one thing—the heat. He said this town was a goddamn hellhole, pardon the language."

Teddy laughed and held out his hand. "Good meetin' you, George, I'll look forward to seein' you when I get back to this hellhole."

I went upstairs to get my purse. I glanced in the mirror and smiled as I applied pink lipstick. My mouth frowned back at me.

Downstairs, George followed Teddy to the front door. I rummaged through my purse to get my car keys, but Teddy waved a careless hand. "I'll drive, Mill. Take you for a spin."

"Don't trust her driving?" asked George.

Teddy laughed. "Nah, I was the one taught her to drive, bought her the car...." He paused. "Maybe I don't trust her driving. Everything else, though, I'd trust my life with Mill. Wouldn't I, sugar?" He brushed my hair behind my ear.

I was going to say how the sedanette was wonderful, how, oh, I don't know, I was going to say something nice. I meant to say that I appreciated the car, that I liked driving it. But the words tangled, unsaid. There was an enormous blue-finned Cadillac parked in front of the house, dwarfing my car.

"George says you got a helluva stake from that pink bird of yours. Surprised you didn't trade up the car." Teddy put his hand on the roof of the sedanette as if patting a horse.

I wished George had kept his mouth shut about the stake.

"No dents in the fenders. Your driving improved, huh? Or d'you not drive it?"

"I drive it everywhere."

He opened the Cadillac's passenger door for me before going around to the driver's side. The car sported a pale blue interior, the seat wide enough for three of me.

Teddy drove with his right hand, his left arm resting on the rolled-down window, his eyes on the road. He turned down Fremont without even glancing at the casino signs.

"What's the pink bird staking you for?"

I searched through my purse for my cigarette case, paused, and lit the cigarette. "I work as a prop at the Flamingo. Not a fix," I said, pulling the smoke into my lungs.

He frowned. "Dangerous choice, don't you think?"

"No."

Teddy looked sideways at me and raised an eyebrow. I turned to blow smoke out the open window. The air was dusty with sage and car fumes, that hot tarmac smell coming in as the day heated up. The long gap of desert stretched into the distance—it was always surprising when the Flamingo's long unlikely pink outline appeared. At the entrance, Teddy pulled to the curb and tossed his keys to the valet who opened my door. "Very classy joint, Mill."

But with him beside me, I couldn't admire anything. I glanced to the far side of the floor, towards the glass doors that led out to the garden—the pool was probably filled with pretty girls and wives, tanning and swimming. Just Teddy's cup of tea, I thought, which was hardly fair—what should I be bitter about? I spotted Stan Savage at the far end, near the slot machines. It seemed early for him to be on the floor, but maybe that was just the way I felt, that it was too early for me to be here.

"Should get myself a job," said Teddy. "I could see myself working in a place like this."

"I don't think they're hiring."

"There was a time, if I said I was gonna get a job, you'd have been pleased."

"The Flamingo's not… maybe it's not the best place for…." But I couldn't finish the sentence—I wanted him to leave, immediately, as much for his own good as for mine.

"You worried I'll mess up your fix?"

"No, that's not… it's just a complicated place, Teddy."

"John," he said.

A woman in a dress patterned with turquoise top hats hit the jackpot on a slot machine, and Stan turned wearily towards the clanging bells. At that moment, Teddy put his arm around my shoulders, pulled me close to kiss the top of my head, then let me go. "So show me the sights," he said.

I walked towards the far door, keeping as much of the casino as possible between me and Stan. "Why the name John, what kind of craziness is that?"

"Mill, let it alone."

I made a disgusted noise, and Teddy held his hand out in front of me.

"This ring," he said, "comes with a father-in-law who wants to skin me alive. And a few too many creditors. I figured it'd be good to take a break. John seems as good as any...."

"I'm not going to call you John."

"You call me whatever you like." He ran his hand through his hair. Two women turned to look at him; one actually licked her lips.

"Let's have breakfast downtown," I said, "we'll look at the gardens and then we'll...."

Teddy touched my shoulder, as if to reassure me. "Whatever you want, Mill."

Only one of the craps tables was occupied—a gang of sleepless Hollywood types clustered around it, one of the men still in tails, his shirtfront untucked, and a girl in very high class pyjamas and skyscraper heels. An older woman in a fur shrug—how could she stand it in this heat?—held the dice in her hand and blew on them playfully before rolling twelve.

"Boxcars," she said joyfully. She turned and saw Teddy. "Hi honey, knew you'd be back."

Teddy said, "Hi sugar," then glanced down at me. "Had to drop in here, didn't know how else to find you. That boss of yours, Chappell, good guy, very helpful."

Teddy took a long look across the casino, taking it all in—the bar, the gamblers on their way to the tables, the lights overhead, the dark men in suits. He smiled lazily and followed me out to the crowded pool.

"Beautiful, don't you think?" I said. Did he notice my enthusiasm was brittle? I showed him the grounds, the garden, told him about Siegel's plant obsession.

"So how 'bout Siegel's private suite, you gonna show me that? Where'd he live? What's it like?"

"I haven't seen his suite," I said. "I don't know what it's like."

"Good, give me somethin' to find out for you."

"I thought you were going to Mexico."

"I thought we were going for breakfast."

I had him drive us to the Corner Diner, where I ordered two of pretty well everything—sausages and eggs, pancakes and bacon, French toast and ordinary toast, juice and coffee. And tea, for me.

When the food arrived, Teddy looked at the spread and raised an eyebrow. "Haven't eaten lately?"

I didn't want to say that he made me hungry—he might think it an innuendo-laden compliment. Because he worried me, and fear made me hungry. His grin, when I didn't answer, reminded me for an instant of the boy I knew back on East Pender Street.

"Spent a couple of weeks in Spokane," he said, taking a piece of bacon with his fingers. "I had a helluva breakfast every mornin' in that hotel."

"Spokane?"

He nodded, eating the bacon. He wrapped his other hand around the coffee cup in front of him.

I stared at his gold ring. "That where you got married?"

"Mill, forget it. Maybe I'll get divorced. I'm here, right? Divorce capital of the world? That George—he's a character—he said he knows some girl at the courthouse, makes her living dressing people up for their divorces. Makin' the world a safer place for marriage. I like that."

"Spokane?" I repeated.

"Yeah, it's an okay town. The hotel's good, could have spent a few more weeks there. But I wanted to see you."

"What have I got to do with Spokane?" I said.

"Nothin'," he said, cutting into the pancakes. "At the hotel, I met this old woman, Russian. Old lady left during the Red uprising, that's how she called it. She came over here with three big jeweled Fabergés sewn into the hem of her dress." Teddy paused, waiting for recognition. When none came, he said, "Fabergés, Mill, they're, uh, jeweled eggs. They're worth about six thou each, depends. So... she's an enterprising old dame, I tell you. Tiny, too. Like you."

I pushed the hot toast into the runny eggs. At least the food was straightforward.

"She said I reminded her of her first husband. The Russian one. She got a kick outta that. That's how we got in touch, I met her son-in-law...." He paused and scratched the stubble on his face.

"What?" I poured myself more tea.

"Doesn't matter," said Teddy, dismissing the detail with his fingers. "You've got to picture Wasa, big make-up, hair dyed orange, most incredible rings on her gnarled-up fingers. She's ancient, kinda special. I listened to her stories, that's really what she wanted, an audience. She deserves an audience. So...."

Teddy became the old lady's friend, her young man of ideas. And eventually, this old lady leaned forward over her teacup, as she and Teddy sat in the hotel's tearoom, and she said, in her thick Russian accent, *Maybe you would like to see something?*

"Invited me up to see her dusty old family portraits. Showed me how I looked like her first husband. And she showed me the Fabergé egg. The one left, that she hadn't sold." Seeing my expression, he put down his fork. "Nah, Mill, I didn't steal the damn egg. Give me credit for some heart. I borrowed it from her, got it appraised. When she marveled at how much it was worth, I offered to sell it for her. Sold that last Fabergé. Made her a thoroughly comfortable retirement."

"I suppose you made something like a commission?"

His eyes sparkled briefly. "She's a generous old bat."

"Why are you telling me this?"

"You asked what I was doin' here."

"Spokane is nowhere near Vegas."

He laughed and dug back into his food. "You finally learn some geography?"

"I always knew my geography." I knew he was teasing me, but some mascara had gotten into my eye. I rummaged in my purse for a handkerchief.

"Honest, Mill, I have a bit of money for now, figured this would be a nice town to spend it in. After this week in Mexico, I've got nothin' going on. Could shack up here. What do you think?"

When I didn't answer, he said, "Or how about, Mill, you drive down to Mexico with me. We'll have a good time. Then we come back and hit your town with style."

"You have a poker game in Mexico? I'm not going to play it for you."

He put down his fork again. "Why do you always think the worst of me?"

"But it is a poker game."

He made a noise very like a growl and closed his eyes. When he opened them again, he still looked angry. "Yes, it's a game. Old army buddy... I'm goin' to Mexico to collect on a favour the guy owes me. Nothing to do with you. I thought you'd might wanna come 'cause it would be fun. But it's a bad idea, you're right."

"That's not what I said."

He looked hard at me and then glared out the window. After a while, he said, "So you're liking this place?"

I nodded.

"No one leans on you? The casino guys?"

"No, it's a job, Teddy. I just do my job."

"So you ever been to Mexico?"

"No, Teddy." I was surprised at how vehemently I spoke his name.

"John," he corrected.

"Still no."

Teddy was quiet then. He ate, his eyes half-closed. He finished the pancakes and watched me eat. Finally, he shrugged and leaned back in the booth, expansive, very much the man about town. "Well that's fine, Mill. So much the better. I'll get going. Not gonna cramp your style. I'll be back this way in a bit, we'll catch up then." He stood, hesitated, then blew me a kiss. "Be good, now."

🐭

But that night, for the first time, I barely broke even at the Flamingo tables.

"You catch a bug or something, Millard?" said Chappell, when I went to his office at the end of the game.

"No guarantee how the cards are going to be," I said. "I'll get some sleep, things will be better tomorrow."

Chappell sat down heavily behind his desk and waved his beefy hand at me. "Rest up."

I drove home wondering if Mexico looked like Nevada, if it was dusty and sunny there too. I parked and let myself in, and the aroma of cooking dragged me into the kitchen.

George was serving Sabina pancakes. He turned to stare at me, spatula in hand. "That handsome cousin of yours didn't convince you to go to Mexico?"

"I have a job, George."

"I would've gone in a pinch. Just one pinch." He grinned.

Sabina groaned. "Way George's taste goes, means John *must* be a snake."

"He's the girl's cousin," said George, "don't speak mean of family. It's not right."

"He's not exactly family," I said.

"It's true you don't look much alike."

Sabina said, "You're changing for the barbecue, right?"

I turned to look at her more carefully. As far as I could tell, she was wearing her nightgown. "I'm going to bed," I said.

"No, no, no," she said. "You're going upstairs to shower and then you're coming with me to Betty's barbecue."

"Betty?"

"Betty who used to dance at the Flamingo. You met her. Everyone'll be there." Sabina pushed me upstairs. "Get you out in the sunshine for a change," she said. "Betty's got it all planned out. They're going to set off fireworks at sunset."

"Fine." But I was thinking of Teddy, flinching at the fireworks of New Year's Eve. I couldn't help it. Teddy, who was in Mexico by now, for some darn reason or another.

Sabina insisted on taking her terrible car to her friend's new house. I lit one of her menthol cigarettes to counteract the car's smell of burning rubber and hauled myself from the passenger seat. Guests stood on lawns as green as game tables, neighbours' children splashed in the kidney-shaped pool, and more than a few of the women wore bathing suits, ruffled at the sides to great effect. Beyond the splashing water and the perfectly-groomed garden trees, the low gold of the desert was framed by the far ceramic-coloured hills— giant sandbox piles massed up by some deity in his off-hours. It was a typical desert day, the air clear, tasting ever so slightly of dust.

Stan Savage, overdressed but somehow perfect in a blue silk suit, stood beside the host. While I watched, he picked a fresh gardenia from a shrub and put it in the buttonhole of his jacket. The gesture pleased me; it was meticulous, though a gardenia is an absurd flower to have in the desert. The plant is from Hawaii or some hot humid place like that. But I like the scent of gardenia, and I was thinking this as he turned and saw me. Which made me blush. Maybe I was still recovering from the oxygen deprivation of Sabina's car.

"You had a nice run until last night." He handed me a drink which looked a lot like lemonade and I took a long, unladylike swallow.

"You shouldn't be watching my cards." The drink was not lemonade.

"One of these days I'll find myself playing against you. It'll be my advantage to have watched those cards."

I frowned at the scraggy sage, the way it began just at the edge of the lawns, as if it were specially planted there. No fence to keep the desert at bay, just a line of jagged dusty plants.

"Thought I saw you on the floor yesterday morning. Showing the place off for someone?"

I glanced at him. He smiled so effectively that I forgot to worry about Teddy for a moment.

"Ever go see the horses?" he said.

"The horses?"

"The Downs is a good-looking track. I'll take you out there some afternoon."

I shook my head. Horses frighten me—all that obvious insanity in a race-horse's eye. Sheer terror, that's what fills those eyes. And I thought, unreasonably, about how black Teddy's eyes could be, how wild. I sat in a lawn chair. "I don't follow the horses."

"Not even to see them race?"

I shook my head.

"You might have a point. No matter how many wires I worked, I didn't get good at calling the horses."

"Isn't fair, betting on a game the horse runs for you. No game in that." The bookie wire for horse betting was a strange vicious business. From the jockeys on up to the bettors, there was a lot of money wrapped up in horseflesh.

He smiled. "Because you thoroughbred types prefer racing on your own legs."

I wasn't sure if that was complimentary. "You don't?"

He shrugged. "Then I'd be a thoroughbred too." He squinted in the sun, waiting for me to answer. It seemed like the day wasn't quite in focus, or Savage himself was uncertain at the edges, unusual for him. "Do you want another drink?"

I leaned my cheek against the cold empty glass in my hand. "No. Won't help my mood."

He sat in the chair beside me. "Why the bad mood? You're sitting in the sun. The afternoon's beautiful. I'm willing to get you a drink, or whatever you want. And you have the night off. Cheer up."

He glanced away from me and I noticed Sabina coming towards us, steady despite her absurd high-heeled Roman sandals.

"Do you know Sabina?"

Savage shook his head and stood to introduce himself. He offered to get her a drink. Sabina eyed him speculatively as he made his way through the crowd.

"He's married," I said.

"Well," said Sabina, "so many men are." She adjusted the single strap of her sundress, a toga affair that didn't leave much to the imagination.

A man I didn't know came up to us and looked deeply into Sabina's eyes. Or into her cleavage—it was difficult to tell, from where I was sitting. He said, "How about I get you a nice hot dog?"

He said it with such a leer that Sabina didn't even bother laughing. She pulled me to my feet and we tottered off towards the barbecue. The short husband stood nearby in chef's hat and apron, handing plates around, being the perfect foil to his leggy Minnesotan bride. Betty's main claim to fame was that she posed for *Life* magazine, lounging in a bathing suit by the Flamingo's swimming pool. Everyone admired her picture. But Miss Swimsuit was no idiot; she had invited her mother-in-law to stay for a month, and the mother-in-law coordinated the party. Alongside the all-American burgers, there were potato pancakes, there were several kinds of fish, all pickled, and there were meat-filled cabbage rolls in a sauce strongly related to Heinz catsup. Alongside the food table, one of the Flamingo's bartenders mixed cocktails— Betty's mother-in-law was no prude.

Sabina accepted a drink from a man I didn't know, and looked around admiringly. "A showgirl with all this, she's done good. Betty's no dummy. She's got her mother-in-law right onboard."

After I'd eaten, I sat at the edge of the party and watched Miss Swimsuit, circulating among the guests. Sabina was right—Betty didn't need to impress her husband, nor her husband's friends, who were happy just seeing her legs. No, she knew that she needed to convince her mother-in-law that a honky from dustbowl farmland could be an upright wife. Betty had managed to win over the older woman with a mixture of deference and good humour, a combination I would never master. At the barbeque, it was clear the tall natural blond and the round mother-in-law were allies. What clinched the deal was the obvious—the showgirl had happily given up her job, to get down to the serious business of producing sons.

The mother-in-law made the announcement, made everyone pause, even the kids in the pool. Holding a glass in the air, she yelled, "Howie! You have a toast to make! The sun's going down! Where are the fireworks?"

The showgirl beamed. The husband raised his arm towards the reddening sun. We all clinked glasses to celebrate. She was due twenty-one weeks from that moment. I wondered if this was the kind of dream Sabina pictured, when she moved to Vegas, or if this was the dream Stan Savage hoped for, when he married—the barbecue and the blond and the sons-to-be. That popular family dream that didn't include me. Even Teddy was married, apparently. I wasn't sure why this fact bothered me so much—I didn't want to marry him, so why did I care? I leaned back in a lawn chair and closed my eyes.

Someone nudged the toe of my shoe. I opened my eyes to see Savage standing between me and the setting sun.

"Another drink?"

"No. I'm just leaving."

"Then leave with me," he said.

I shook my head. "Might give you the idea that I enjoy your company."

"I'll manage with my illusions. I have to go to work. Why not have a drink with me at the Flamingo?"

He put out his hand, as if I needed help getting up from the lounge chair. As I placed my fingers in his, he smiled in straightforward invitation.

In the car, I leaned back against the seat so I could look at Stan's profile, but the car was too comfortable. I closed my eyes and listened to the engine's droning hum. Then I blinked and realized the car had stopped—I had fallen asleep. Savage had driven past the Flamingo's foolish pink sign while I slept. He'd parked on the far side of the garden, near the last wing of bungalows.

When I rubbed my eyes, he said, "I can't decide if it's me or the car, that keeps putting you to sleep." He took out his cigarette case, offered me one, and when I refused, lit one for himself. "I can take you home. I should have seen you were tired."

I watched his hands. Long thin fingers. He took a drag of his cigarette and I caught myself staring at his lips.

"We could be quite a pair in this town," he said.

Maybe it was because we were in the car and through the dusty windshield, the golden tint of setting sun fell on his face, maybe that's what was so appealing. I put my hand against his arm, and when he leaned towards me, thinking I was going to speak, I suppose, I reached my other hand to his neck. I meant to kiss him for only an instant, but it was a more involved gesture than I expected; he pulled me from the seat. I had forgotten how desire feels like an engine, how oil snakes through the blood and plows every other thought out of its way.

"Just one minute," he said, and got out of the car. I might have had second thoughts, but I didn't. I opened the passenger door and met him on the gravel pathway.

"Here," he said against my ear. We walked a few steps towards one of the bungalows. "This room's empty." He threw away his cigarette.

He opened the unlocked door with his free hand and didn't turn on the light. He closed the door by pushing my back against the wood. I felt the door latch into place. It was like being alone in a room with a wolf; he was all teeth, not bothering to undo my jacket but trying to pull it over my head.

"It doesn't do that," I protested, undoing the buttons.

That made him laugh, I don't know why. As he turned, he tripped against the coffee table in the dark. There was a sound of wood cracking.

"Damn that," he said, pulling himself out of the debris, falling into an armchair, bringing me on top of him.

Still half dressed, I struggled with limbs and clothes and a hilarity that made me gasp for breath. The armchair complicated things. My knee turned to an awkward angle while we tried to untangle and recombine ourselves. I would say I was seducing the man but there wasn't much calculation in how quickly we shed our clothes. It was more like diving, a smooth desired plunge into a swimming pool, how the water is cold and surprising, a new element, expected and not expected. Not expected at all. I kicked him unintentionally, turning, which made him laugh again. He brought his mouth, still laughing, against my shoulder blade, my spine, his hands across my bare hips. I pulled his right hand up against my mouth so I could taste his skin, bite the flesh below his thumb.

"Ouch. Sharp teeth."

He pushed his hand against my chin and tilted my head back against him. I hadn't realized how I missed being touched—the push and grab of the body, I mean, with no unspoken regrets. I stayed there, his hand against my throat, breath against my skin. The way blood moves around the body, pulsing. I folded up suddenly against him, closed my eyes and listened to his breathing, ragged, then gradually calmer. When we were both still, quiet, his palm against my collarbone, I pushed myself away from his chest and stood.

I saw my purse, where it had fallen not far from the door. I grabbed it and what clothes I could see and retreated to the bathroom. The bathroom tiles were swirly pink, which made me look even more flushed than I was. I spent an inordinate amount of time trying to dampen my hair down to its usual lines. When I put on my dress, I noticed a tear, underneath the arm, where the seam had given way. I smoothed the fabric—at least that would be easy to mend.

When I came out of the bathroom, Savage had turned on the lamp by the bed. He examined the wreckage of the coffee table.

"Cheap glue. Siegel probably paid a fortune for it. Want to break something else?"

"No."

He picked up my jacket and laid it on the still-made bed. He stood, buttoning his shirt. "I haven't laughed so much in months."

I blushed again, I could feel it, a red rush through to my ears.

"You annoy me," I said, moving my head to save the lipstick I'd just reapplied, so that he missed my mouth and kissed my ear.

"I noticed." He sat down on the bed. "You could stay, the hotel maids aren't going to throw you out. Unless you prefer to sleep in my car."

"It's a comfortable car."

"I'll drive you back."

I shook my head and put on my jacket to cover the tear in my dress. "I'll get myself home. You were going to work."

I let myself out of that hotel bungalow and remembered what George had said about Stan Savage. I suppose I was proving him right, except Stan was something I wanted, at least for a moment. Because Teddy was still in Mexico, and had a wedding ring on his finger. Because I wanted my heart to be beyond breaking. Because my hands wanted distraction.

Through the taxi's open window, I breathed in the cooling heat of the evening. Sage and asphalt, tobacco and the old leather interior of the cab. I felt scrubbed all over, my skin's edges rough and alive. I looked in my purse for a dollar to pay the taxi and saw that silver bracelet still on my wrist. As if the only cards I ever held were ambition and hunger. No hearts at all.

19

When Teddy returned from Mexico, he had acquired a monkey, a monkey he called Melville, though it never paid much attention to its name. Its white furry ears were too big for its black fur-capped head, and its agate eyes blinked out from an owl-like white mask. Its chest bore a white ruff against reddish squirrel-like fur. It was a clever creature with leathery hands and feet, and a long red-brown tail with a white tuft at the end.

I wasn't expecting the monkey when it arrived. I wasn't exactly expecting Teddy either—I secretly hoped he wouldn't come back. But when the car horn sounded outside George's house, the noise pulled me down the stairs. I knew it was him. I stood on George's front stoop as a disgruntled welcoming committee.

Teddy stood beside the Cadillac, stretching. Then he reached back into the car, I assumed to get a briefcase. But a fast small shape whipped out of the car and up Teddy's arm, stopped at his shoulder and sat there. When Teddy turned towards me, I saw the shape was a monkey, there on his shoulder. A red monkey, at that.

"Hello, sugar." His voice sounded heavy.

"Look what the cat dragged in."

He stopped two steps below me, so we were at eye level. I wrapped my hands under my armpits to keep from touching him. I wondered if I looked as unpredictable as he did. At least I didn't have a monkey on my shoulder.

"You're lookin' tired." He kissed me on the cheek. "Long hours at the pink bird?"

He smelled worn. There was a coating of dust over the mingled gin and aftershave, along with a faint musky smell, no doubt from the monkey.

"You're not bringing that animal in here."

"Melville? Come on darlin', Melville here is the best-bred monkey in the world. Aren't you, champ?"

The monkey stared at me with credulous eyes and reached out its paw. Despite my better judgment, I held out my hand. It had tiny black fingernails and shook my hand most professionally. Which is when I thought of the obvious.

"Have you taught it to play cards?"

"Can a guy get a coffee around here or are you going to leave Melville and me out on the steps?"

I led them through the house and out the kitchen's back door, he and the monkey settling on the patio in the shade while I went back inside and put some water on for tea. I knew Teddy didn't care, coffee or tea, so I set out the teapot along with two willow-patterned cups George was collecting. I grabbed a handful of ginger snaps cooling on the counter. George was doing his mysterious Thursday afternoon rounds, so no one witnessed me setting a banana and a couple of figs on a plate for the monkey. When the tea was ready, I brought out the tray.

"So where'd you get it?" I said.

"Really, they workin' you too hard or what? You shoulda come to Mexico with me. Was a good time."

"The monkey," I said.

"Melville?"

"The monkey."

"This monkey, I'll have you know, is a squirrel monkey from the Andes Mountains. He is not just any monkey. I won him off a Mexican. He was workin' in the circus. He's damn smart."

"The monkey or the circus guy, for giving you a monkey instead of paying a debt?"

Teddy offered the banana to the monkey, who shrank from it. Teddy shrugged, the little animal moving up and down with his shoulder. "I guess he's shy."

"Maybe it doesn't like bananas."

"Monkeys like everything, that's what the Mexican told me."

"How long have you had it?"

"Three days. He's been eatin' donuts." He moved the animal gently off his shoulder, its small claws catching a bit in the loose weave of his shirt. He set the monkey down on the table. This seemed to please the little beast. It reached one long red fur arm across the plate, picked up a ginger snap, sniffed it with interest, snapped the cookie in half, discarded it, then took a fig. This it held to its chest, using its other three paws to climb back up Teddy's arm, quickly, quickly, and sat back down on his shoulder, where it happily ate the fig, very neatly, I must admit.

"Why are you here?"

Teddy gave me his very best smile, pleasure tempered with more steel than there used to be. "I'm in town to get a job, sugar. Maybe teach the monkey some tricks."

"You got a monkey off a Mexican in a circus act and it doesn't know any tricks?"

"He doesn't do much. Curls up in the glove compartment. Seems happy being warm. I thought you'd like him."

The monkey looked at me with its small eyes. It licked the fig from its fingers, then it groomed the white fur mask on its face, as if to make itself as presentable as possible. And I swear it smiled. Like a candidate at a job inter-view—choose me, please. I wondered what kind of job Teddy was thinking of getting, while he was here. I suddenly wondered if he'd driven back to the Flamingo, before coming here. I closed my eyes for a moment, trying not to imagine him talking to Chappell, or worse, talking to Savage. He had no reason to care about that, I thought, but the blood ran from my face. I opened my eyes. I poured the tea, adding sugar to Teddy's before setting the cup in front of him.

"Where are you planning to stay?" I asked.

"I was thinking the Thunderbird. Looks cheap."

"You better tell them about the monkey. It could probably be a little destructive, if you leave it alone."

"Actually, Mill, that's where you come in."

"Really?" I dunked a ginger cookie in my tea.

"Well...." He scrunched his eyes up as if he were trying to convince me of his earnestness. I laughed, I couldn't help it.

"What?" he said.

"You... forget it."

"I was thinking you might want to look after him for while."

I suddenly understood the fool expression he'd made. "You're pawning the monkey off on me?"

"You always said you wanted a pet."

"I said no such thing."

"He's a smart little bastard. You'll enjoy him."

"I can just imagine."

Teddy was immune to sarcasm, always had been, but the monkey understood my tone. It groomed the fur around its face and blinked at me, and I nearly forgave Teddy for turning up with such a joke on his shoulder—not that I forgave him for being here, but the monkey, well, it wasn't the animal's fault. I watched the creature's small fingers.

"So you'll teach it to pick pockets?"

"Oh, maybe a necklace here or there, y'know." His grin had a new wrinkle, the same line on his left cheek that Mary Ellen's smile once had. I bit my lip to see it. The monkey ruffled the fur on its chest and folded its fingers neatly, clearly waiting to see what happened next.

"How about cards? I said.

"The monkey? Don't be an idiot."

"You wait."

I left him there and went inside, upstairs, and took a well-battered pack of cards from my bureau drawer—I wasn't going to break in a new deck on the monkey. Coming back downstairs, alone, I said aloud, "Damn you, Theodore Ahern, I bet I can teach this monkey to play cards better than you ever learned."

Outside, I cleared the tea things out of the way, lit a cigarette, and spread out the cards. Face cards, in order, on down the numeric line, finishing with Aces, those old dancing girls. Teddy and the monkey watched me silently.

"This is blackjack, monkey, so pay attention."

"You can't teach him like that. He's not a kid; he's more like a dog."

"Want to bet?"

Teddy grinned again and held out his hand. "The monkey's yours if you can do it."

"I don't want the monkey."

"What then?"

I looked at him, sitting there in the shade of George's backyard, waiting for me to set terms we both knew he'd ignore. He wasn't going to help my game. I thought of Mary Ellen and her advice about the suit of Hearts. Her son was volatile, here in the desert, and I felt like a dangerous spark—the sooner he left my vicinity, the safer we'd both be. One of the neighbours was burning weeds and the shifting wind brought the smoke towards us for an instant, the air filling with a bitter smell, like a perfume gone wrong.

I shuffled the cards and set the deck down on the table. "If I teach the monkey to play, if he really learns, you'll take the rodent and get out of here. You don't need to work here, Teddy. I do."

He looked surprised, pained, and he shook his head. "Melville's not a rodent, Mill. He's a squirrel monkey. Not a squirrel."

"Rat, monkey, no difference to me."

He looked up at the house. The monkey watched him; it had been travelling with Teddy, maybe it could read him better than I could. When Teddy met my gaze, his eyes reflected nothing but light, black and shining. Then he looked down at the cards, his eyelashes shadowing his cheek. As if only a minute had passed since I'd woken up next to him in Vancouver, when he'd slept so peacefully beside me and I'd felt obliged to shatter his momentary peace.

He rested his palms on the table, on either side of the deck. "Tell me a fortune," he said.

"Why?"

He picked up the deck and shuffled the cards. "Because it's been a while."

"I haven't read your fortune since we were kids."

"So? 'Bout time, don't you think?" He handed me the pack. The monkey watched us curiously. I burned the top card and turned up the next three cards. Three of Hearts. Eight of Clubs. Seven of Spades. We stared at the cards together. The three was the least troubling—an exercise in caution, it told the bearer to say nothing that might be turned against you. But the eight of Clubs—I stared at it sadly, a card that brought trouble between people. And the seven was worse—loss of friendship or loss of a friend. Sorrow sat in every card. Teddy nudged the seven. "That's not good."

I didn't know how well he remembered Mary Ellen's fortune telling. "Could go either way," I bluffed.

"Christ, don't lie to me about cards."

I shuffled the bad luck out of sight. "I'll teach the monkey," I said.

"In return for?"

"Get out of here, Teddy. It's not a good town for you."

"I figured this was the perfect place for rats."

"I never thought you were a rat."

"Not anymore?" He stood and leaned across the table to kiss my cheek. "Nice to hear. But it's a okay town for you?"

"Teddy... I have a good job. Let me alone."

"The monkey," he said. "Sure. Let's call it a done deal. How 'bout, you teach the monkey to play blackjack in twenty-one days. If you do, I'll get me and the monkey outta town."

My fingers felt like shards of metal. "You promise?"

"Worry about teaching the monkey." He shook my hand, formally sealing his word. "'Course I promise."

The animal chittered and held out its paw, so I shook hands with the monkey too, for good measure. Its tiny paw hesitated in my hand. Teddy reached into the breast pocket of his jacket and brought out a fine silver chain. He threaded the fragile choke chain around the monkey's neck and tied it to the chair. The monkey looked worried but did nothing. Teddy smiled and brushed his finger against my lips, warm touch of memory. Then he walked back into the house.

The monkey and I listened to the slam of the front door, both of us unclear on Teddy's next move. I sized up the monkey. I wondered what it thought of Teddy, if sitting there it sensed the history stretched between us. You might laugh, me thinking this of a monkey, but animals aren't stupid. They don't bluff. They don't speak. But they understand emotion—hunger, want, desire. All the essential instincts. The monkey clicked its small teeth, very softly—as good a comment on the situation as any I could come up with.

To be a good poker player, you need to thoroughly understand the game. You need to calculate probabilities—which cards have been dealt and what's still out there. You need psychological understanding, a feeling for how the other players bet, and an ability to read tells. None of these qualities is necessary to be a good blackjack player.

"Okay monkey," I said. "It's you and me. We're going to play blackjack. Want a drink?"

The longer I played for the Flamingo, the more I appreciated the taste of scotch. A single glass lasted me an entire evening. It was less destructive than kicking back mixed drinks—I was always pleased when the cocktail waitress brought yet another round of jewel-coloured cocktails to my opponents. Teaching a monkey to play cards was an occasion that seemed to demand a dose from George's front room whiskey stash. So I went inside and got myself a scotch, a small serving in a big water tumbler. I added two handfuls of ice. Part of the appeal of whiskey was the way ice melted slowly as the cards played out; by the end of most games, I was drinking barely-flavoured water.

I didn't think the monkey needed a whiskey—though who knows, coming from a Mexican circus, maybe it liked tequila. I poured milk into a small bowl and filled a second dish with water. I carried all this outside. The monkey splashed around in the milk and drank the water. I wiped down the table, had a sip of my drink, dried my hand from the condensation on the glass, and got down to business.

"Okay monkey, the goal is to get twenty-one. Or as close as you can. Are you paying attention?"

The little animal blinked.

"Good. The game developed out of Faro, used to be played in New Orleans. You're going to like blackjack, it's all about counting. This is how you count." I counted from one to twenty-one aloud, very slowly.

It wasn't an immediate success. Melville didn't have experience with cards, or with numbers, or with anything much, really. I don't know what tricks he performed at that Mexican circus, but he certainly wasn't doing anything useful. I spread the cards out in front of him and tried to show him what a card was. If you've ever tried explaining the concept of a card to a child, you might have an idea. Only more so—children recognize the importance of symbols. Monkeys, I'm not so sure. But I tried, I held up those Hearts, Clubs, Diamonds. I struggled to demonstrate the concept of the number seven, using cookies. Every number, every suit, to a monkey. It took some time. It took some conviction. I guess, really, I had nothing better to do. At least the monkey kept me from worrying about Teddy, or wondering what I might say to Stan. Could I simply turn up for work, with no mention of the weekend? I was better off playing cards, even with a monkey.

I persisted with the basic counting skills. Sure, you can argue that monkeys don't know how to count. I beg to differ. With enough practice, Melville counted just fine. Maybe he couldn't do higher math, I don't know, and who cares? For blackjack, he needed to understand numbers one through ten. After that, it was just repetition. And I admit, that first afternoon was uphill—he kept picking up the cards and putting them in his mouth. Then, discovering the card wasn't edible, he'd tear it up.

"There are players who do that," I told the monkey. "They get thrown out of the casino. Bad monkey. No."

He looked at me. I scowled at him. My scowl had long ago stopped working on Teddy, but surely it could frighten a monkey. I swear the animal shrugged. By evening, we'd gone through an entire pack of cards, along with I don't know how many figs, three apples (he ate the core, seeds and all, but carefully spat out any brown spots) and five of George's slightly stale peanut butter cookies—I know, not healthy food for a monkey, but by then I had run out of fruit. Finally, he was content to look at the cards, pick them up gently, and hold them in his fingers. Though he couldn't shuffle yet, he was fine dealing individual cards.

"Hit me," I told him, tapping the table in front of me. Obediently, he gave me a fresh card. "Good monkey."

We became friends, that afternoon—if one can be friends with a monkey. Animals have deep and I think quite rational mistrust for humans. I can understand that feeling; I don't trust people either. I believe in luck—people are more complicated. The monkey had a similar value system—it believed in food. Everything else, well, it reserved judgment until it had ascertained whether or not you were edible.

You could say I empathized with the monkey—I played poker as the house pet, didn't I? Maybe that's what Teddy meant by bringing me the monkey.

I gave the animal the last peanut butter cookie just as George came home. I swept the cards into a pile as he came into the backyard.

"Girlie, what have we here?"

"It's a monkey. Its name is Melville."

"I can see it's a monkey."

George was wearing one of his "outside suits," as he referred to his conservative masculine attire. Today, because of the heat, he'd chosen a white and tan seersucker suit, closely fitted to his substantial form.

The monkey held out its small paw. George stared at it.

"He wants to shake your hand," I said.

George put out his great hairy mitt of a hand, which the monkey shook, formally.

"Does it have any diseases?"

"No. It's a very clean monkey. My cousin John brought him."

Suddenly a beaming smile lit up George's face. "John! How is he? It's his monkey, of course it is!"

"He asked if I could look after it for a little while. Do you mind, George? I owe Te.... He bought me that car, when I left Vancouver. I said I'd keep an eye on the animal for a bit."

I didn't feel like explaining that I was teaching Melville cards. I was beginning to think of the bet as being a rescue operation—I couldn't see Teddy looking after anyone. Maybe I hadn't forgiven him for leaving me alone, at Christmas, in the Ivanhoe, when I'd so needed his company. He might similarly abandon the monkey—a creature unable to look after itself.

George put his hands on his hips. "So you're taking on a monkey as a roommate?"

I hadn't really thought about it that way, but George didn't give me time to reply.

"It could sleep in a bureau drawer," he said. "My mama always put babies in drawers. Like cradles, you know."

The monkey looked at me quizzically as I picked him up by his scruff, tucked him under my arm, and followed George into the kitchen.

"He'll be good company."

"The monkey?"

"When you're out playing at the Flamingo, this here monkey and I will get to know one another. You can hardly play cards with Mister Peep on your shoulder."

"You're a gem, George."

"I think of myself as one of those Greek types, you know, lots of weapons, an elephant, maybe a monkey. Presiding over the Vestal Virgins."

"Didn't they get sacrificed?"

"Okay, forget the virgins. I prefer living with you girls anyhow."

Before I left, George helped me set up a home for the monkey in the half-opened top drawer of the bureau in my room. Melville seemed calmest curled into the back of the drawer, in the shadows. I tucked the half-chewed pack of cards beside him and gave him an old pillowcase as a blanket. And maybe he was plain old tuckered out by the travelling or the cards, because he didn't cause any trouble at all when I closed the door and went to the Flamingo.

❧

I parked at the far end of the lot, and walked through the gardens, stopping to say hello to Mavis. She came to the door in a pale yellow dress, a towel over her shoulders, her hair in curlers.

"I wasn't expecting company," she said, as she led me to the kitchen. She put her pink rubber gloves on to finish the dishes.

"I kind of hope I don't count as company."

"Is your stake going along alright?'

I picked up a dishcloth and dried the plates as she stacked them in the rack. "Well?"

"Does Dick tell you everything?"

She laughed. "Only what I'm interested in. So, when you pay it back, will you still work here?"

"I like Vegas."

She let the water out of the sink. "I'll fix my hair and walk over with you. I haven't been on the floor for at least a week. Maybe I'll go see that new act in the lounge. Dick tells me the comedian's very funny."

While Mavis combed her hair, I curled up on the living room sofa and read the newspaper—the headline announced the air force had captured a flying saucer in New Mexico.

"You think they've found aliens?" asked Mavis. Her hair looked movie-star perfect, the sort of coif George would kill for.

"New Mexico can have the aliens, Las Vegas is strange enough already."

We went into the casino arm in arm. I scanned the floor, wondering if Teddy was here, dreading the possibility.

"Here's your job…" said Mavis, slipping her arm from mine.

Stan Savage threaded his way between the crowded tables towards us. He dodged a cocktail waitress as Mavis headed off to the lounge. "Right on time," he said.

"I try."

"You'll be amused. It's a private game out back." He held the door and I stepped outside again.

"Amused?"

People were dancing by the pool. A woman sang *It's a sin darling how I love you*, off-key, as a man dove neatly into the deep end. Water splashed us as we walked around them. Stan wore a new suit, twilight-coloured. His blue shirt collar very sharp against the skin of his neck. I paused to get myself a cigarette.

"Full moon," said Stan, lighting my cigarette. The moon was just rising, tinted gold by the dust in the desert air. "Long crazy night ahead."

"Because of the moon?"

"Always."

He led the way down past the pool, and I glanced again at the moon. I wouldn't have pegged him for a superstitious type, no more than any gambler. As the path turned off towards the same bungalow door we had so recently been in, he shrugged in a way that was very close to an invitation. His expression was so odd, I laughed.

"It wasn't exactly my choice of location," he said. "But I thought you might find it funny...."

"They replace the coffee table?"

"Mmhm."

He held the door of the bungalow open, and just before he introduced me to the other players, he murmured, "After the game, see if I'm around, will you?"

I didn't have a chance to be distracted by that prospect, for the young dealer in the room shuffled the cards messily, and all too quickly, nothing was easy. Four of Clubs, nine of Spades, seven of Hearts—lies, death, broken promises in every hand. I wanted the cards to stop deriding me with poor fortunes, but every possible disaster appeared on the table. I played for a difficult eternity, fighting to get decent pots, regretting the cut I had to pay the house. At least Savage let me play the game through to the end, the cards foretelling terrible fates every step of the way.

The explanation for the dark cards was obvious as soon as I left the game. I walked through the gardens, wondering where Savage might be, and suddenly stopped as if I'd hit a wall. Teddy sat by himself at the edge of the Flamingo swimming pool.

"Hi, sugar," he said. "Good game?"

"Fine."

"Was hopin' I'd run into you. Got myself a job today. If you're going to be taking three weeks on that monkey, I need somethin' to do with myself."

"You never have trouble finding things to do with yourself," I muttered, edging closer to the pool.

"That Chappell thinks the world of you."

My fingers tensed against my purse. "You got hired here?"

"Yeah." He stubbed out his cigarette. "The pay's not bad. I start tomorrow afternoon."

"As what?"

"Dealin' blackjack."

I was speechless.

"I thought you'd be happy," he said. "Chappell said you used to deal blackjack. Looks dead easy. Waste of your skills, I can see why you quit it."

"I didn't...." I stumbled against one of the flagstones and Teddy stood up to steady me.

"Careful," he said.

I shook his hand off my elbow and sat down on the edge of the diving board.

"I thought you'd be pleased, gainful employment an' all."

I wondered if he'd met Stan, too, what he might have said about me, or about himself. "To heck with it, Teddy, do what you like."

"John," he corrected.

"Whatever godforsaken name you want."

"It'll work out okay, Mill." He sounded uncertain. "You're gonna like having me in town. I won't get in your way."

I buried my face in my hands. When I looked up again, Teddy was gone. I stared at the empty pool, a glowing green square of light and water.

🐁

I don't know if monkeys see in colour, but patterns definitely appealed to Melville. The animal no longer tried to eat the deck. He recognized face cards, caressing them and licked his fingers most thoughtfully afterwards. We sat in the backyard, the monkey and I, practicing how to deal, doling out the cards in the correct layout for blackjack.

The monkey picked up the teaspoon I used to stir my tea and offered me the spoon, handle first. I accepted the spoon and gave the animal the pack of cards. He studied the cards for a moment, then arranged them in his left paw and neatly dealt out a card for me, face up. I praised him lavishly. I didn't take my anger at Teddy out on the monkey; I liked the little beast, and what's more, he was my ticket to Teddy's departure—the sooner I managed to teach him cards, the sooner my so-called cousin might leave town. There were two obvious flaws in this plan—first, Teddy was unlikely to keep his end of the bargain, and more importantly, I wasn't convinced the monkey could learn the game. He might fake his way through enough blackjack to win my bet. Some players I'd seen at the Flamingo couldn't even count. I leaned back in my patio chair while the monkey contemplated the cards. We spent so many hours out there I began to tan.

George brought me out a piece of coffeecake and stared. "Cards, Millard? With a monkey? I thought you were playing solitaire."

"It's a bet I'm going to win."

"I don't doubt you'll win," said George.

I wished I had the same certainty; I took a forkful of the coffeecake.

"Stan Savage called a few minutes ago. You're free, slow night, he says. And he wants to know where you got to, the other night. Whatever that's supposed to mean?" He pursed his lips.

"Lovely cake," I said, "we'd all starve without you, George."

Unable to resist a compliment, my landlord beamed at me. He leaned towards the monkey and offered it the square satin sleeve of his orange dressing gown. "Want to come up?" he said.

The monkey eyed him warily.

"Doesn't want to tear the silk with his claws. Smart monkey."

George laughed and rumpled the little animal's head affectionately. Within a second, the monkey was busily chewing the lead out of the pencil I'd placed on the table.

"No, bad monkey," I said.

With his tiny hands and bright eyes, the monkey kept a constant eye out for odd bits and pieces to sample. It had already discovered that ballpoint pen caps were not edible, and that sugar cubes were. I disentangled the pencil from its grasp.

"And John called," George said.

"Why?"

"Wanted to know if you were free for dinner. So now you are."

"I don't want dinner. I'm eating cake."

But when the horn of Teddy's car sounded outside, the monkey swiveled his head, chittered, and ran up my arm. George opened the front door as Teddy reached the bottom step. He was eye-popping in a green and white striped suit, the blue polka-dotted tie loose around the collar of his white shirt.

"Made us a reservation at the Beachcomber," he announced, coming up the stairs. The monkey made a neat jump from my shoulder to Teddy's arm, climbing it like a branch.

George surveyed Teddy's ensemble. "The tie's a fine choice. But let me know how the waiters react to the monkey on your shoulder."

I shook my head. "We aren't going to...."

"The waiters," said Teddy, "are going to love us."

I gave Teddy my very best disgusted look, though he seemed impervious. "Why would I go to dinner with you? I'm waiting for you to get out of town."

"Still mad at me, huh?" He cut his eyes to George. "I get a job, she's peeved." He shrugged as if to say, what's a guy to do?

I frowned. But George, bless him, said, "What's the job?"

"Blackjack. Figured she'd have told you all about it."

George made a "humph" sort of noise. "You got a job she was told she couldn't do. No wonder she's annoyed."

Teddy raised an eyebrow.

"The pink bird doesn't have any girl dealers. Didn't you notice?" said George.

"But a fix is okay? That's half-assed." The monkey put its fingers in Teddy's ear and he winced. "So's that why you're mad at me, sugar?" He pried the monkey's paw out of his ear and I noticed he had a new pair of square polished gold cufflinks. "How's teaching the monkey goin'? You can tell me about it over dinner."

"That monkey's learning all kinds of things," said George, just as I said firmly, "I'm not hungry."

Teddy laughed. "That's a first. Well, forget dinner, I have a surprise for you, you'll like it."

"I don't like surprises."

"Come on, Mill, you used to like surprises just fine."

I rolled my eyes but picked up my purse and reluctantly went out to his car. He handed me the monkey and opened the car door with a flourish; the monkey crouched on the dash as we drove up Fremont. Teddy kept his left hand on the steering wheel and, with his right hand, fished a glittery silver key out of his breast pocket. I took it before the monkey could grab it. The key was attached to a Flamingo key ring.

"So, aren't you curious?"

"I'm not happy you're working there, Teddy."

"I got the key to Ben's suite. Whatcha say, you haven't seen it, have you?"

"Where'd you get that?"

Teddy shrugged, keeping his eyes on the road. "Oh, I was talking to a chambermaid... she wanted to show me something I hadn't seen."

"Wonderful."

"Management doesn't know what to do with the big man's suite. Keep it clean and wait...."

"It's not like he's coming back."

"You never know. Maybe it's haunted. Wanna see the suite?"

"Why would I want to see that?"

Teddy smiled at the road, as if we were co-conspirators. "'Course you do, Mill. The guy had a creepin' feeling, you know, when he built the place. There're false hallways and secret staircases and stuff. 'Course you want to see it. And I've got this extra key to the place, just for you."

The dealers at the Flamingo whispered that the doors of Siegel's suite were set up with gun portals, that there was a secret movable bookcase that led to a bomb shelter, specifically to confuse the hit men. I'd even heard there was a gun rack hidden in the canopy of the bed. Lot of good it did Siegel.

"Why?"

"Come on. Benjamin Siegel, an' his red-haired girl? You work for the house, might as well see where the legends come from."

"I mean, why are you making keys for the suite, what's the...."

"We'll just take a little peek."

The monkey leaped from the dash onto Teddy's shoulder as we stopped in the casino's side lot. Walking towards the building, we must have been quite the sight—Teddy filled up with his latest secret, the monkey on his shoulder, and me playing the dwarf. A complete circus act in one easy outing. I shrugged his arm off my shoulders. The heat was a sage-scented wall of warmth, even with the sun easing down towards the mountains, turning the casino grounds into a candy-coloured painting, sweet. It left a bitter taste on my tongue.

Teddy pushed open the door leading into the casino. I looked around anxiously and saw Roscoe on the far side of the floor; I acknowledged him, barely, with a tiny smile. I didn't think he noticed Teddy, walking ahead of me. I paused before going upstairs to the dark red hallway.

In front of the suite's unnumbered door, Teddy tossed the monkey in the air and caught him, the animal chittering with fear or pleasure, I couldn't tell.

"Go on, open the door."

I unlocked the door and stepped inside. The room didn't have that unused, immobile scent that places have when they're empty. No, the air was ordinary, slightly perfumed by the objects there or by the cleaning staff—in fact, the air smelled ever so slightly of a familiar aftershave. I didn't imagine

Siegel's cologne would have lingered for so long. Teddy closed the door gently behind us and turned on the light switch. The room was wallpapered in a dark leaf pattern with twining stems. The huge pool table was the most noticeable piece of furniture—carved wooden legs like totem poles, lots of fringe surrounding green baize, spotless as the gaming tables downstairs. Suspended over the pool table was a green glass lampshade lit from within, polished brass arms leading up to the fabric-covered ceiling.

Teddy tapped the rack of cues. "Want to play?"

"Not really a girl's game." Pool never appealed to me—all that leaning and reaching, with a pool cue practically taller than I was.

"And poker is?" Teddy allowed the monkey to jump onto the pool table. "Never thought of you as a traditional kinda girl, Mill."

I ran my hand over the smooth grain of the wood, while Melville snuck down into one of the pockets, exploring the tunnels. I went over to the bookshelves. Expensive editions. I looked more closely, reading with my head at a tilt.

"Good books?"

"Yes."

Teddy came over to stand beside me as I took down a copy of *Brideshead Revisited*, wedged between *The Ghost and Mrs. Muir* and *The Age of Reason*, which didn't sound like much of a novel to me. The age of reason had to be older than I was then, certainly.

"Take whatever book you want. No one's gonna notice." I must have seemed disapproving, because he said, "What? You think his ghost's gonna mind? No one's reading them here, trust me. The guy I'm meetin', he's not a big reader like you."

"Who are you meeting?"

"No one you know."

I opened *Brideshead Revisited*. The binding was loose, with a dog-eared page towards the end. I tried to imagine Siegel sitting up in bed, reading this English novel—unlikely scenario. Did he worry he might leave the book unfinished, spine bent back on the silk bedcovers? I put the book back on the shelf as Teddy went into the next room. I followed him to the doorway. The bedroom had a massive canopied bed, all carved, as though it had landed from a fortified castle in the Alps. It was swathed with apricot silk in all directions, sheets, pillows, drapes, anchored with more silk on the walls.

"You ever see the girlfriend, when Siegel was around?"

"From a distance. She never played at my table. Too busy being a bag-girl. She delivered cash to Swiss bank accounts." I wondered what she was doing now.

"She must've gotten this junk over in Europe." He waved his hand at the swirly dressing table with gold drawer pulls, the mirror encrusted with cut crystal, the chandelier dangling so low with extra glass grapes and beading, Teddy had to duck his head to cross the room. A pair of solid marble tables squatted imperially on either side of the bed—nothing like the wooden coffee table Savage had broken. On the wall opposite, there was an ornate cuckoo clock. Teddy leaned down to push back the heavy fringed rug; a trapdoor was cut into the floor, with a simple finger hole to pull it up. I glanced back at the clock, realized it was stopped. Maybe Siegel hadn't liked the bird popping out at him.

"Bet you've never seen such a thing," said Teddy.

"A cuckoo clock?"

"The trapdoor, idiot." He crouched down beside it.

"There was one beside the sink in our kitchen, to the crawl space under your house. Don't you remember?"

"Sometimes I dunno what I remember." He pulled up the trapdoor.

I looked down at the plain board staircase leading into the dark. "How did you know this was here?"

"Oh," he said. "I told you. A chambermaid. She was showing off what all she knew."

"You already said that. I mean...." But I couldn't remember what I meant, exactly, because Teddy stepped onto the first step and hit a switch and a series of light bulbs came on, snaking down the stairs to a narrow corridor. When he held out his hand, I leaned my fingers against him for balance on the open stairs.

When we reached the foot of the long steps, I couldn't tell if the corridor was in the basement, or merely a back hallway hidden on the ground floor. I wondered where we were on that map in Dick Chappell's office—and then I felt a familiar choking smell of bleach. We were near the hotel laundry. I coughed, a memory I could do without, those singe marks still faint on my forearms, steam closing my throat. I stepped ahead of Teddy, wondering what he wanted with this tunnel. The corridor twisted sharply to the left and I stopped. There were wide beams ahead, crisscrossing the ceiling like the underside of a railway bridge.

"It's not going to cave in on you."

"Why are we here?" The lights of the tunnel snaked forwards and the rough concrete walls seemed to narrow as we went on around a turn. I could no longer see the stairs. It was cool, which in other circumstances might have been enjoyable. He wanted to impress me, I thought, that was all, an entirely innocent secret, Teddy showing off, how he'd gotten to know the place in only a week, while all I ever did was play cards. But when I turned, his expression was serious.

"Could hide anything down here," he said. "Every wonder if he did?"

"Sure, a thousand necklaces."

"It's a great meeting place, huh?"

The corridor smelled of dirt and bleach and I swallowed with difficulty. "Maybe if you're meeting ghosts or rats or something."

He laughed. "Nah, this guy, Rutowsky...." He stopped, as if rethinking his approach. "We could make some serious money, you an' me."

I recognized the name. Rutowsky was the man who hit Elena.

Teddy put his hands gently on my shoulders. "You could bring a whole new angle to the team."

"We've never been a team, Teddy."

"We were, once," he said.

"I have a job. I like this job. And you're leaving. You promised."

"I thought it would be good to talk here," he said, continuing down the tunnel. "So you can think about it."

I should have turned and gone back up the stairs, but I followed him, I thought it would become clearer, I thought—oh, it's been too long now, I don't know what I thought. Teddy went around another sharp corner. The tunnel twisted as if the route had been built to imitate the Grand Canyon or some other great mystery. The cold seemed to increase, until I was shivering, following him there, underground. The smell of earth and bleach in my nostrils, in my mouth. Teddy seemed so intent, so filled with his new scheme, and I recognized that look. It never bore good fruit.

"I met this guy," said Teddy. "You don't have to do much, really..."

"I'm not doing anything, especially when you start with I met this guy."

Teddy shrugged. "I want to give you the option. You need to pay back that stake, get yourself free of this place."

"This place," I caught up with him and poked his arm, "is where I want to be. I'm fine."

"Yeah, you've said that before, Mill."

"I don't...."

"You don't need my help, I know. But I want yours."

"What are we doing in this godforsaken tunnel?"

I must have sounded truly angry, for Teddy took my hand, held it tightly in his own, our fingers interlaced as he looked down at me. "Nothin'. We're doing nothin'. You're seeing Siegel's escape route. You're a tourist, seein' the sights. Forget I said anything. I wasn't tryin' to upset you."

"I want out of here."

And then, as if by magic, when we walked around the next turn in the tunnel, there was a metal door. The concrete walls, the hard floor, the beams overhead—the tunnel led to this inexplicable metal door.

"Not locked from this side," Teddy said. "I'm goin' back to pick up Melville, before he scares the dickens outta the maids. This'll take you into the garden. Siegel kept a car there. Meet me 'round the front, we can get a bite to eat... you hungry yet?"

"How can you?" I pulled my hand free and rubbed my eyes, as if they were stinging with bleach. "I'm not hungry. I'll get home on my own." I pushed at the door, and Teddy reached past me to turn the doorknob. I sagged against the cool metal. "Can you drop off the monkey, maybe give him to George, when you can...."

He half-laughed. "Yeah, after all, you have that bet to win." He left me in the doorway. I didn't even know then why I'd come to hate the place.

Siegel's former garage held only a row of empty planters and some gardening tools. I kicked one of the planters in disgust, realizing I still clutched the key to the suite. I put the key in the outer pocket of my purse, to give back to Teddy when I next saw him—give it to him or fling it in his face, either one. I hated the feeling that Teddy was sneaking around the Flamingo. Ben Siegel's suite gave me the creeps.

I played cards downtown for a while, but they weren't tremendous, and eventually I went back to the casino and met Sabina for a drink after her show. I carefully avoided the blackjack tables, in case Teddy was working the late shift. I didn't think I could bear to see him, just then. Instead, I paused in the lounge and chatted with a new croupier, very blond and square-jawed. His colouring reminded me of Adam, especially when Sabina emerged from the dressing room—she mussed his hair and the man blushed a most amazing shade of pink. Sabina smiled as he walked away.

"That one's a godsend."

"Why?"

"You know those big-spending fish, the kind they're always telling us to be nice to? Feh." She made a face. One of her army boys had recently broken a mobster's nose for looking sideways at her. Chappell had managed to smooth everyone's feathers—Mavis told me Dick secretly agreed with the army boy, and the mobster's nose hadn't been anything much to look at, before being busted. Sabina licked her well-glossed red lips. "Turns out, one of the made men has no interest in girls. He comes out here to escape his wife. I was the one who told Dick, for goodness sake, find the man someone to his taste. Find him someone who isn't a girl. Mavis understood what I was saying, put it more plainly. Anyway, they've hired, well… Bill, who you were speaking to. Isn't he lovely?"

She nodded towards the croupier, who was back at his roulette table. She put her hand on my shoulder. "Imagine thinking that everyone likes show-girls. Not everyone does."

I glanced up at her and had to smile, she was such a gorgeous example of the type. "Most men like showgirls."

"Well," she said. "If they like girls. But in this case, Bill's the solution. He's cute, don't you think? And the man's happy as a clam now, losing money under Bill's handsome gaze. The boy's not a bad croupier, either. Everyone wins, and I don't have to sit on the poor man's lap anymore. Let's go down to the Riviera for a drink, I'm tired of this place."

20

The Flamingo was packed with all the usual unlikely hopes of Friday night, those dreams that get rusty on Saturday and can't even be traded for a cup of coffee, Sunday morning. Roscoe was taking a break, propped up at the bar. He sucked in his jowls, as if thinking really hard, and the bartender went to get fresh celery for another Caesar.

Roscoe cleared his throat, all phlegm and old man rumbling. "I'm not the hard guy I used to be, doll."

"Long day?"

He groaned. "Old age takes its portion, you know what I'm sayin'. I sent two kids to expensive schools, my wife lived a good life 'til the cancer got her. But I tire out easier than I used to. I'm glad my kids are outta this business."

The bartender brought over the fresh Caesar and Roscoe tossed it back, barely pausing in his complaint.

"Not sayin' I was ever an honest guy, but you hear what I'm sayin'. Family or no, a guy's always in this business for himself. No one else. You hear me?"

"Don't worry, I'm in it for myself." I was concentrating on my bankroll, wasn't I? I was aware of every chip I needed to win, in order to pay the casino back its fifty thousand. I had always been in the world for myself, I thought—no one else was around.

The second Caesar seemed to be just right, for Roscoe smiled, something like contentment settling on his old gorilla face. "You're at table five. Fatso needs to stay at the trough."

I reached up to touch Roscoe's shoulder in thanks and went over to the poker tables. At table five, a disturbingly skinny man skulked behind a wall of chips. Fatso, I thought, understanding Roscoe's humour. I took my seat at the table and studied the cards, as I was teaching the monkey to do. The pattern on the two of Clubs is just as interesting as the elaborate design of an Ace. There is no hierarchy, really, only positions of usefulness—a hand with four twos will beat Queens full of Aces.

The players included two Chinese guys who finessed an impeccable game and the table would have been a pleasure except for skinny Fatso, who insisted on constant patter, calling Kings "cowboys," Queens "tits," threes "treacherous." Every time anyone drew a seven, he drawled "easy seven." It wore on a person, over time. When the Ace of Spades appeared as a river, Fatso yelled, "Chicago!"

The Chinese guys each allowed themselves a brief sigh of dismay. The Flamingo dealer cleared his throat, and the cards, well, they didn't like being called silly nicknames. I did nicely, despite the vexatious banter. But just as I was getting comfortable, a gopher came over with a note—irritating symbol of my employment—which read, "As soon as you can." Code for me to leave the game, since the players were now well hooked. I hated being pulled by the Flamingo—how could I play seriously if I had to stop whenever my cards gleamed too brightly? What was a minor annoyance when I started propping had grown large and awkward, especially as I edged closer to earning my stake.

When I stepped down to the main part of the casino floor, I swung past the blackjack tables. Strictly to torture myself, I stood and watched Teddy work. I couldn't help staring at the ladies leaning into Teddy's table; the other games on the floor were crowded with men, but at Teddy's table, the players were almost all women. They were entranced by his current incarnation as dealer, they watched him nearly as closely as I did. They played cards against him and the house, but they were thinking about sex—not that there's much harm in that, really, except Teddy wanted to give them something to watch.

The cocktail waitress found me and brought me a cup of tea with a smile. "Good night?" she asked.

"So-so."

"Good tips tonight," she said, "I ain't complainin'."

Maybe it was the wedding ring on his finger, maybe the desert air illuminated his smile more perfectly than ever, or maybe Nicky Rutowsky's scheme gave him an extra shine. Teddy couldn't help it—ladies came to his table, thick as any cliché, ready to singe their pretty wings. I was nearly immune, but I could still feel the overall effect of his glow; I knew what drew women to his table. It bothered me that the only man at Teddy's table, tonight, was the hard-cornered Rutowsky, sitting at the edge of the game, egging on the girls, no doubt making callous jokes and putting his hands in all the wrong places.

I wanted to win my bet. I wanted Teddy to leave town before the place harmed him. I thought of George Raft, the movie star—Teddy was similarly able to invent and reinvent himself to reflect desire. The surface you saw when you looked at him became whatever you wanted. At the Flamingo, Teddy shimmered, a kind of mirage destined to disappear once he got what he wanted. Whatever it was. I turned away—I didn't want him to see me, watching him. He might think I was admiring him, or worse, considering his scheme.

"So how are you two related, exactly?" said Stan. He stood behind me, had been watching me stare across the floor at Teddy. His hazel eyes looked greenish in the casino's sparkling light.

"We grew up together."

Stan moved closer to let a huddle of men lurch to the far end of the bar, their faces shiny with excitement. I wondered what game they had played, what they had won.

"In that tumble-down town of yours?" Stan's smile was more believable than anything else I'd seen that night.

Unfortunately, it reminded me of my stake, and how many days remained—how many chips, dollars, cards. "Wish you hadn't taken me off that last game," I said. "I was just starting to...."

Savage shrugged gently, as if there were some things he could do nothing about. "I can redeem myself in other ways."

I looked past him, towards the blackjack tables, and when he put his arm around my waist, I shifted aside. "I have a stake to pay back," I said.

Savage leaned towards me and brushed my mouth with his. I stepped back sharply, hitting my back hard against the brass rail that curved out from the bar.

He narrowed his eyes as he did when studying a hand of cards. Then he said, low so only I could hear him, "So you can fuck me behind closed doors but God forbid you kiss me in public."

I flinched and pushed past him, past the other bar patrons, until I reached the exit to the pool. Outside, two women sat on the diving board, singing and drinking cocktails, flamboyant as parrots. I headed away from the pool lights, hearing the door bang behind me. Hard footsteps hit the flagstones and then the gravel. I turned and crossed my arms as Savage caught up with me.

"First of all," I said, "you're married, so if I did have any qualms I would be entirely justified. And there's the fact you work here."

"How the hell does working here matter? I take you off games all the time."

"But it might occur to you, the being married." I interrupted.

"All kinds of things occur to me."

"Such as?"

He stared past me as if someone was nearby, though we were alone. After a moment, he cracked his knuckles and reached into his pocket for his cigarette case. He turned the black and silver case over in his hands.

"I shouldn't have said that, in the bar," he said.

He offered me a cigarette, and helped me light it, before taking one for himself. Behind him, there was a loud splash from the pool, accompanied by shrieks and laughter. He smoked for a while, clearly trying to find the right phrase. I saw no reason to help him. I tapped some ash off my cigarette and watched it flicker, pale grey, catching the light from the pool, scattering into minute pale flecks that drifted into the dark grass. A cat stalked a lizard or rat rustling through the underbrush.

"There's something not right about the floor tonight," Savage said. "I can't figure out what it is. But I'm going to assume it's not related to you. Alright?"

"What's that supposed to mean?"

He shook his head and walked back towards the casino. Just before the glass doors, he paused and straightened his shoulders. I'm sure he smoothed his expression, too, wiped any emotion, most professionally, from his face. Then he opened the door and stalked into the madness of the weekend floor.

At least the monkey was straightforward. I taught the animal a basic shuffle, then a waterfall, and we reviewed the rules of play, again and again. Really Melville just wanted to spend his afternoons doing the waterfall shuffle. I couldn't blame him. We sat in the backyard, a dusty wind coming down from the hills, the reddish earth in the distance folded into pyramids and cascades, the colour wrinkled like the monkey's paws as he shuffled the cards. He did a beautiful waterfall, despite his small hands.

With pieces of toast as a bribe, I tried to convince him to memorize the numbers. I set three peanuts out on top of the three of Clubs, four peanuts on the four of Spades and so on, but he got so distracted by the peanuts, we couldn't get anywhere with the numbers. I went back to toast. In the end, he seemed to recognize the patterns; he didn't grasp the addition involved, but it didn't matter if he understood the game—he only had to play it. I hadn't promised Teddy that the monkey would play *well*, only that the animal would play. I've seen humans play blackjack with far less comprehension than the monkey, and they still have the nerve to blow smoke in a dealer's face. The monkey dealt another hand, nine of Clubs, Queen of Spades. How much do any of us really understand our cards?

Melville was very well-behaved in George's house. When we weren't practicing, he sat on the half-empty shelf above the sink, where George kept the dish soap. Occasionally, I suppose when he thought no one was looking, Melville would reach a small fast paw over to the top of the soap bottle, run a finger along the top edge, where the dish liquid had stuck to the rim, whip his paw back to his mouth, and suck his finger. I guess he liked the lemon scent. Everyone thought he was cute. Only George knew I wanted to teach the beast blackjack to win a bet—and I hadn't told him exactly what winning entailed.

I spent too many hours there on the back patio, when I should have been adding up chips for my stake. I liked the monkey, I liked spending time outside for a change, far from my worries at the poker table. But as I grew convinced that the animal would learn enough blackjack for me to win, I felt regretful. I was going to miss the little beast. Not that the monkey was such a hot-shot player, or really any kind of a player, but he gave me the illusion that he understood the game. And who knows, maybe in some way, he did. He was having better luck than I was—whenever I sat at the Boulder, trying to make money, the cards squinted up at me with no energy. They didn't seem to appreciate that my stake was due in less than two weeks.

Returning home, I couldn't sleep. I had thirty-five thousand dollars, fifteen thousand short of my Flamingo stake, and ten days to go. I sat out with the monkey, practicing, and when the sun grew hotter overhead, I moved the table into the shade of the tree. When Sabina walked out of the kitchen onto the patio, the monkey was studying his cards thoughtfully, and I had finally stopped maniacally going over my numbers.

Sabina put her hands on her hips. "What in the world are you doing?" Her short green nightie, the one with real fur trim and matching high-heeled silk mules, looked especially outlandish in the midday sun.

The monkey looked at her briefly and went back to the game. He tapped the table—one of his favourite gestures—and I gave him another card. It was an eight. He hissed; he had to fold.

"Dealer wins," I said. I gathered up the cards.

Sabina flicked the ash off her just-waking-up cigarette. "Millard, you're playing cards with that monkey."

"He's not bad. Look…." I handed the pack to the monkey and gestured for him to deal.

He took the pack carefully, arranged it into his small hand, and shuffled the cards, first neatly and plainly, and then in an elegant waterfall. Sabina laughed. I pointed and the monkey scrupulously dealt cards for Sabina, then for me, and then for himself as dealer, methodically following where I placed my hand to guide him.

"Come on, play," I said, "he's dealt you a game."

Sabina pulled over a chair. So, there we were in our pyjamas, playing blackjack with a monkey, under the warm Vegas sun. We played four rounds; Sabina won three and the monkey as dealer took the last. I wasn't concentrating on my play—my hands were trying to encourage the monkey's sense of the game, and I preferred to save my luck for real games that might improve my bankroll. The fifteen thousand gap remained lodged in every one of my thoughts.

"Have to get ready for work." Sabina patted the monkey on the head. "Make sure John doesn't teach it to cheat. Would be a shame, looks like an honest monkey."

She went inside, and I wondered what it was about Teddy, that with only a glimpse of his dealing at the Flamingo, Sabina thought him likely to cheat. Teddy, who was due to drop by here in an hour or so—I wondered if I could win my bet now. The monkey was as ready as he'd ever be.

"You heard Sabina," I told the monkey. "Don't cheat. It's not correct. Especially not for an animal. You stay upright."

I wasn't really worried—the monkey was motivated by peanuts and praise. It's hard to cheat in those terms. The little beast couldn't help chewing the cards from time to time, he often forgot the rules—what he understood of them— and face cards still delighted him beyond all reason. But he didn't cheat.

I got a bowl of water for the monkey and tied his leash to the lowest branch of the magnolia tree, while I went upstairs and did my hair. When I returned, the little beast was nit-picking its tail—not that it had fleas, I think it's just a grooming habit that monkeys have. I heard Teddy come out the back door.

"Given up, sugar?"

"Not exactly."

"So, he learn much?" Teddy unhooked the chain and the monkey scampered up his arm, chittered in his ear, and settled comfortably on the shoulder of his pinstriped grey suit.

"You look sharp. Have a date?"

Teddy blushed. I swear he did it on purpose, for specific effect. "The date's with you, Mill. I'm here, aren't I?"

"Have time for a quick round of blackjack?"

How could he say no? He sat down and let the monkey run back along his arm to the table. I gave the cards to the monkey and he shuffled. I gestured for the monkey to deal a hand for me, a hand for Teddy, and one for himself as dealer. Seven of hearts, two of Clubs, seven of Spades. I wondered how the bet would play out.

The monkey dealt us each another card. A lock of hair fell into Teddy's eyes and he smoothed it back without taking his gaze from the game, a gesture it hurt to watch, too familiar. The same cowlick he'd always had, which I'd smoothed from his eyes in the roundhouse, what felt like a lifetime ago. While the monkey considered its cards, I watched Teddy's face change from bored to intrigued. He cut his dark eyes to me, then looked back at the table. He ran his tongue along the groove in his lower lip and shook his head as we sat through the late hot afternoon. Our cards were low and the monkey dealt us each a third card. Teddy went out, with twenty-seven; I was at nineteen, which seemed pretty good, but the monkey turned his third card—two of Diamonds. Twenty-one, dealer wins.

Teddy squinted at me as if the sun were in his eyes, though I knew it wasn't. "Blackjack," he said.

Melville put the two of Diamonds into its mouth.

"No, bad monkey," I said.

"Nah, he's a good monkey, Mill. Give him credit. He won the bet for you." Teddy offered Melville his arm, and the little beast scampered up, still holding the two triumphantly. "I'll be damned." He leaned back, balancing his weight on the two back legs of the garden chair. He tilted his head as if listening to some unheard tune in the distance. "Want to go for dinner?"

I looked at his wrist, to check the time on the watch visible below his white cuff. He caught my glance and slammed the chair legs back onto the patio. The monkey dropped its card in dismay and leapt back onto the table.

"You've got a game to go to. Of course."

"I have a job to go to, Teddy. As do you."

The monkey picked up the remaining pack of cards and fidgeted them into a half-shuffle.

Teddy raked his hands through his hair. "I can't believe this."

"What?"

He gestured at the table. "You still expectin' me to leave town?"

"I won the bet."

"Yeah, but I just got the job. I can't leave now."

"You didn't think of that earlier?"

"There was no way you were gonna win. How'd I know the monkey was so smart?"

I folded my arms across my chest and glared across the table as Teddy picked up the discarded half-chewed two of Diamonds—the card means a love affair or a business partnership. I wondered if he remembered that. He raised one eyebrow, card in his fingers.

"Well? What if I stay, for a little while?"

"You're better leaving now. I'm worried about you."

He put the card in his breast pocket. "I'd be flattered, Mill, by this sudden concern of yours, but you could care less about me."

"What do you mean?"

"It's about your stake, you don't want me messin' up your...."

"The Flamingo isn't a place to mess around with."

"I just need to wrap things up a little. How 'bout a week? Isn't that when your stake's due? We can have us a big celebration, and then I'll split. Promise."

"My stake's up in ten days. But that doesn't...."

Teddy pushed his chair back and stood up, offering his arm to the monkey. Melville clambered up to sit on his shoulder without a backwards glance at me.

"Where are you going?"

"Melville must get bored, spendin' all his time here. Don't you, champ? I gotta get busy, if we're outta here in a week. Ten days, Mill, that's perfect. All I need. Then this desert town is all yours. It's too dusty for me, anyways." He leaned down to kiss my cheek as the monkey chittered. "Have a good game. Work hard."

I was left in the backyard by myself, the deck in a pile on the table. I stared at the cards. I couldn't stand myself. I wasn't even sure what the stake was, not then. I tore up the remaining cards.

☙

I got to the pink bird late. Stan was staring at the casino floor. He touched my hand without looking at me and nodded towards the poker section. "Table three. Keep them all there, if you can."

I moved my hand as if flicking water off my fingertips. At the green baize tables, I wanted to forget everyone. I played through the night without stopping, and I was happy to do it, I wanted to be under the beautiful lights, I wanted to do exactly what I was told, sit at a specific table and get up when the house sent me a note to leave the game. I didn't want to think, I wanted to play the cards I was given and add to my stake, every card, every chip.

When I'd finished the last game for the night, it was well into the pre-dawn hours of Monday morning. I looked around the floor and realized Savage was upstairs, dealing cards at the crooked table. I wondered if his job was to stack the deck, or if the players were the cheats. Which was worse, I wasn't sure. I stopped at Chappell's office and paid out the house cut. I noticed an unusual clump of people at the edge of the bar. Roscoe stood at the furthest edge of the crowd.

"Blackjack," murmured Roscoe when I went over to say good morning to him. "Seen that monkey play?"

"What?"

"The monkey, Johnny-o's monkey. Helluva blackjack player, that thing. Somethin' not right there, 'gainst nature, is what it is."

"Here?"

"Yep." Roscoe pushed me ahead of him, so I could see through the crowd at the lounge. There was no show going on, too late for that. But sitting at the edge of the bar, surrounded by dealers who had finished their shifts but who hadn't managed to get home yet, there was Teddy, dressed in his grey suit, the monkey beside him on the bar, presiding over a game of cards. I made my way closer with a sense of dread.

The bartender nodded to me. "You got some money on that thing?"

"Not yet."

"Tea? Whiskey?"

"Nothing, thanks."

Teddy glanced up slyly as I came over and gave me a million-dollar welcome. "My cousin, who convinced me to come to Vegas in the first place...."

I ignored Teddy's outstretched arm. I shook the monkey's small paw, its fingers lingering in mine. I taught Teddy to play cards, but the monkey was a far better student—it played a pure version of the game, based on pattern and a desire to please. So I'd created a perfect foil for Teddy, without meaning to—he was all-too-willing to be the man with a secret, a mystery, the good-looking guy with a monkey on his shoulder, *hey, have time for a game of blackjack?* How could anyone resist an offer like that? My very own mistake, in action.

"The monkey must be tired," I said.

Teddy looked from me to Melville and made a sympathetic grimace. "Yeah, show's over. Come on champ, time to call it quits."

The dealers laughed and drifted away, and one of them winked at me as he went past. "Ya got it to stop before ya lost anything to it, huh?"

I felt like crying as Teddy gathered up his IOU's. Whatever he'd promised, Teddy might never leave Vegas, not if things went well for him. He smiled as he went by and I shrank from him.

"You taught him good, Mill."

Driving home, I called myself every bad name in the book.

On Tuesday night, I played downtown at the Boulder, and instead of improving my stake, I got Aces and eights not once, not twice, no, I got that cursed hand three times. I tossed it out, looking over my shoulder every time. Dermot had told me the original Ace-eight story so long ago—how Wild Bill Hickok was shot dead, holding two Aces, two eights, and one other card. No one was quite sure what that last card was, but those two Aces and eights were enough to make anyone skittish. I knew bad news was coming; I just didn't know precisely what form it would take.

Shaken by those cards, worried by the hole in my stake, I met Mavis for tea. The Flamingo's rose and gold lounge was quiet—during the day, the little café tables offered a calm, foolishly pretty place to meet. We sat at the far edge, looking towards the roulette tables, and the bartender brought us a platter of fried things, shrimp and such. Mavis had on a cream-coloured dress that made her look like a calla lily.

"That monkey could be an entire chorus line of Rockettes for the attention it's getting," she said.

"It's played here again?"

Mavis checked her lipstick, holding a knife sideways to see her reflection. "Three nights in a row, haven't you heard? John works his shift, leaves the monkey in his car, and after his shift, he sets up here." She put down the knife. "Dick can't decide if it's a draw or an embarrassment. The monkey's beaten two of Meyer's bagmen, but he makes that prince laugh. You know, the prince who's visiting from Luxembourg—where is Luxembourg?"

"Near France." I remembered newspaper maps of its invaded borders, during the War.

Mavis ate a batter-covered shrimp. "Dick's a little worried about Brazelton. His wife, your cousin, that monkey—it's going to be messy. Dick hates complications."

I didn't know Brazelton, but I imagined the wife had caught Teddy's eye. Or he had caught hers—some predictable story. I took a sip of my Mai Tai. "Sabina says he's the pet of every showgirl here."

Mavis laughed musically. "The monkey, or your cousin? Stan hates him."

I jerked my head up. "What?"

"He hates your cousin. Wants Dick to fire him."

I moved my drink so it was perfectly in line with the food platter. "Maybe Stan's right, maybe the monkey shouldn't be playing."

She gave me a funny look and I wondered what kind of gossip had reached her ears.

I took one of the crab balls, held it up on the end of its pink flamingo-topped toothpick. "Looks like an eyeball," I said.

"Tastes better," said Mavis. "Seriously. Nothing to do with the monkey. Stan wants that cousin of yours fired. He says there's some kind of history. Is there?"

"Dick tell you to ask me that?"

She stuck her tongue out at the remaining crab balls. "I told him it was none of my business."

"You're right."

She frowned tartly and selected a triangular fried thing on its toothpick. "What do you suppose this is?"

I took it from her. "Pineapple?" I wiggled it and set it back on the plate.

"Tropical fruit are so funny, growing in the ground like that."

"I don't think they...."

"They're like carrots," she said, "they grow with their tops sticking out the ground. I've seen them."

"Don't they grow on trees?" There weren't a whole lot of pineapples growing in Vancouver, at least not on East Pender Street. As we considered the pineapple, Chappell came over and kissed his wife hello.

"We were talking about pineapples, dear."

"Pineapple trees," I said.

"Tell her, Dick. They grow like beets, you know, pineapples do, under...."

Chappell kissed his wife a second time and sat down heavily in a chair opposite us. I felt even smaller, sunk in the booth as I was.

"Forget the pineapple," he said, picking up the mysterious fried triangle and putting it in his mouth. Chewing, he said, "Savage says you know something about this monkey."

"It's John's monkey," I said.

"Yeah, well, what's the idea?" said Dick. "We're gonna get guys coming in with trained tigers? Pet poodles? What next?"

"It's just a monkey," said Mavis. When her husband didn't answer, she got up. "I'm going to powder my nose." Tossing me a worried look as she left.

Chappell cleared his throat noisily. Mavis walked past the roulette tables and paused at the shiny one-armed bandits. She fussed with her purse. When I turned back to look at Chappell, Stan Savage was standing beside the table, all flawlessly pressed blade-sharp edges.

"The monkey," said Chappell, as if we'd strayed from the conversation.

Savage adjusted his red tie and sat in the booth beside me. "Why are you bothering Millard with that?"

"You said...."

"I said she'd taught it to play, I didn't say...."

I interrupted him. "Who said that?"

"Well, you did, didn't you?"

I stalled, getting a cigarette from my purse.

"I've watched it," Stan said, holding out his Vargas lighter. "Holds cards the way you do."

When my cigarette was lit, I said, "You're telling me I play cards like a monkey?"

Chappell snorted.

"No." Savage frowned. "But it shuffles cards exactly like you do. Plays well."

"Damn well, for a monkey," said Chappell.

I shook my head. "It's blackjack, there's nothing personal about blackjack. It just learned some patterns, that's all." I wondered what Teddy's scam was—knowing would make it easier to protect myself. "It's John's monkey," I repeated.

"I think we should ban it," said Chappell. "No point in having a damn monkey in the joint."

"Don't the players like it?" I said.

"We have girls for that."

"I'll leave you two to duke this out." Maybe I could join Mavis at the noisy one-armed bandit, spending loose change.

"No, this concerns you. It's your cousin," said Savage.

"Let the monkey be, it's just a monkey." I let the cigarette smoke surround me, soothe my nerves.

Chappell shrugged. "It's conflict of interest, what it is, John dealing cards for us and bringing that damn monkey through here like a carnival side show on his off-hours."

I suddenly saw where this conversation could go. I wasn't even being vindictive, exactly. I took another breath of cigarette smoke, remembering

Teddy, showing me the dimly lit escape route from Siegel's suite. How pleased he'd been. Did the tunnel snake right under our feet, underground beneath the lounge? I glanced at Savage, poised as a knife beside me. If I could get Teddy out of Vegas, if I could pay back my stake, my desires would be simple. "You could sack him, Dick," I said, "that would solve things."

Stan's shifting eyes narrowed.

Chappell said, "You suggesting I hire the monkey instead?" He roared at his own joke and clapped me on the shoulder, pretty much knocking my lungs into my nose. While I coughed, he added, "Yeah, I'm gonna have to fire him. Don't worry about it, your name won't come up. I'll talk to John after his shift tonight. The ladies'll miss him."

Before I could say anything, he stood, laughing to himself, and headed for the roulette tables. With the shape of the booth, I couldn't leave until Savage moved.

"We should've hired the monkey, not John. Be less trouble," he said.

There wasn't any part of the truth I could tell him, about Teddy or the monkey.

Savage tapped his fingers against my unfinished drink. "Not crazy about Mai Tais?" He folded down the drink's pink paper cocktail umbrella and laid it on the table. "How's the stake?"

"You must know my numbers as well as I do."

"I'm not psychic. I don't know how you're doing, downtown. Where are you playing?"

"Around and about."

He grinned. "And the stake? You're on target?"

"You counting the days?"

He put his hands on the table and pushed himself to his feet. "Could be. You never know."

I watched him glide through the gathering customers in the lounge, and out onto the floor. I liked watching him, foolish though it was.

❧

After work, I went to the Boulder—five days remained for me to pay back the Flamingo, and I was determined to make my deadline for the stake. Not that I was exactly afraid of Chappell or Roscoe, but I wanted to be out of the racket of the Flamingo's inner workings—I wanted to play cleanly, just for myself. In my last go-round at the Boulder, my pocket cards were Spades, a sorrowful seven and misfortunate ten.

I went home counting numbers. I needed $8,000 more and I would be able to pay off the Flamingo. Sabina caught my arm as she came down the stairs and dragged me to the kitchen. "That cousin of yours lost the monkey in a card game."

"That can't be right."

"That's what I heard," she said.

George turned from the counter, where he was forming meatballs and lining them up on brown paper. "John was offered fifty grand for the monkey. That's the story I heard. He sold Melville to Brazelton. You know, what lives over in that huge new house? The wife, Iris, wanted the monkey as a pet."

Fifty grand, and a woman named Iris—that sounded like Teddy. I wondered if he'd offered Chappell a deal, promised to get rid of the monkey in return for keeping his job at the Flamingo. "Poor Melville," I murmured.

Sabina stretched. "Monkey's well out of it, if you ask me. Iris gets a new diamond every week. Maybe the beastie'll get a diamond leash. Can't be worse than the life that cousin of yours was giving it."

A diamond leash, I thought, maybe that was Teddy's plan.

When I drove to the Flamingo that night, dust from a new construction site filled the car with the smell of dirt and sage. I got out of the car and brushed myself off and looked up at the sky. Back then, the lights of Vegas, even the Flamingo's swooping sign, couldn't swallow all the stars of the vast desert. I gazed at the Milky Way, that white streak, and I wondered why the gods had laundry to bleach. Seemed the only possible explanation for that white line of stars—Fortune washing her dirty hands in the sky, above us rats down here. I don't mind being a rat, I thought. But I wanted to be a simple Las Vegas rat—I wanted to play cards, make money, make love. I didn't want to worry about the monkey and who-knows-what crazy scheme of Teddy's. I squinted up and wished on all the stars at once, wished Teddy away.

Inside the casino, Savage gave me a brief distracted smile and sent me to table two, which forced me to walk past the blackjack tables. Right past Teddy, working his blackjack shift. I tried not to stare at him. Before I could walk on, Teddy caught my eye and winked, and I shivered despite the summer heat. A dealer's eyes belong on the cards and on the people at the table, and Teddy shouldn't have been looking at me. I noticed the ugly shape of Rutowsky, leaning at the edge of Teddy's table, teasing the ladies playing blackjack.

I took my seat at the poker table and managed to soothe my mind enough to play. I folded my first three hands but I felt the game was coming around to me, when I heard an odd sound, something wrong behind me, to the left. I heard a hint of Teddy's voice, I was sure of it, a suggestion of familiarity in the commotion behind me.

"Lord, you see that?" said one of the men at my table.

He turned towards the noise and I couldn't help glancing that way too. Teddy's head appeared above the melee in the aisle. His eyes grazed across mine, moved on. I shivered again, brought my gaze back to the poker table. The dealer caught up the dead cards and reshuffled, pausing before he dealt out a fresh game.

"Guy was stealing chips, you wouldn't believe, hundreds in there. My God," said the player across from me. "Just an ordinary Joe too, how'd he get his hands on so many chips? Stuff 'em into his pants or what?"

From across the room, security in dark suits came over, and soon some goons dragged a little guy away, brown suit, mess of greyish curling hair, his arms going up and down like a marionette. The floor of the aisle surrounded, one of the higher up security types said, "Everything's under control, folks. No problems here. Show's over...."

The pit boss got everyone back into position. A new hand was dealt and suddenly I had cards I couldn't fold, two Jacks, Clubs and Spades. I waited for Third Street, but when I took the pot, I didn't feel right. As a salvation, there was a dealer change-over at my table. One of the waitresses noticed we were paused and drifted over to me. "You see that?" she said.

"No."

"Little weedy guy must've been at it for hours. Three hundred chips, mostly thou's. Sheer weight busted his seams. Chips rainin' down."

I glanced back to where it had happened. "Whose table?"

"That's the thing, had to be just 'bout everybody's, was so many. That cousin of yours was just going off-shift when it happened. He'd never seen anything like it, those chips pourin' down. He's a pro, gotta say." She looked out at the floor, maybe hoping to catch another glimpse of Teddy. "He took action, just slammed the guy into the table, guy was tryin' to leave. Then security goons were all over. Now the pit bosses are comparing notes. Old bulldogs. I'm headin' off shift, glad I didn't miss it. All the excitement I can handle. They're talkin' to the guy. I hear Johnny-o's quittin', doesn't want to live with this madness. Lucky man, he's got a choice, huh? I'll miss him."

I turned into a wooden Tiki statue while the waitress spoke. When she moved away, I rubbed the hinges of my jaw until I could turn back to the cards. But for the rest of the game, I could barely distinguish Hearts from Spades. I folded every hand and finished the game barely two thousand to the good—lower than I'd started out. With the cut owed to the house, the stake was stuck further than ever in my heart, and a darker heartsickness seized me as I walked across the floor.

I can't explain how I knew Teddy was responsible, how I knew he was a thief. What was going to happen to the little man in the brown suit who'd been dragged away? Teddy had been "right there" to slam that innocent guy into the table. Only then did I wonder if the casino would link Teddy with me. In Chappell's empty office, I left the casino's cut in the usual drawer. Savage was nowhere in sight, nor was Roscoe. I looked at the map on Chappell's wall and tried not to wonder where the little weedy man might be, what backroom might be reserved for such things.

I drove home with the windows of my car rolled up tight, running the windshield wipers against the dust gathered on the glass. I tried not to notice I was shivering. I let myself into George's quiet house and as I got to the top of the stairs, the phone rang. I stood on the landing and looked down at it, as if it were a cartoon telephone that shook as it rang. On the fourth ring, because I didn't want George to come out of his room, I walked down and picked up the receiver, saying nothing.

"Come out for breakfast with me." Teddy's voice, steady as ever.

I found my voice behind my teeth, which I hadn't noticed I was grinding. "You should be on the road by now."

"Come on, I'm at the Corner."

I paused on the front stoop before going down to the white sedanette. I stood looking around, as if I expected Teddy to be watching me. How he'd known to telephone. He knew I would answer.

The Corner was never exactly crowded. A person went there to be alone, or else after a shift, tired and hungry, either very high or very low on luck. Teddy sat in the crook of the green curving horseshoe counter, hunched over a cup of coffee. When he looked my way, his eyes were smudged. He didn't show any other ill effects of his night—he'd changed into a light serge suit, clean white shirt, his chevron-patterned tie perfectly knotted.

"Mornin' Mill."

I felt sick seeing him there, but I sat down on the stool beside him just the same. The grill man was polishing parfait glasses, lining them up neatly. He paused in his work. "Usual special?"

I nodded. He headed into the backroom, taking in a bucket of potatoes, dirt still on them, then came back with a different bucket filled with clean sliced potatoes, which he got started on the grill.

Teddy wasn't eating, nor talking. We sat beside one another, that was about all. When my food arrived, he ordered another cup of coffee, then reached into his breast pocket for a flask and poured the dregs into the coffee. The grill man smiled wryly at me and glanced at my so-called cousin as if to say, *what's his story, what's an upright-lookin' guy like him doin' in here?*

I shook pepper all over my breakfast.

The grill man said, "Call if you need anything," and headed into the backroom.

I nudged Teddy's elbow. "Maybe plain straight-up coffee'd do you more good."

"I doubt it, sugar."

I sighed and broke the yoke of the eggs so the yellow ran into the hash browns. I took a forkful and in my mouth, the food was flavourful as yesterday's newspaper. I swallowed. "Your partner get out okay?"

"What are you saying?"

"Don't. Don't even try."

Teddy was silent. I took another bite of eggs. More newspaper.

"Nicky's a pain," he said.

I picked up my glass of orange juice and noticed my hand was shaking. I drank the juice anyway. "So, you called me. Why, exactly?"

"I'm clear, right?"

"You need an atmospheric gauge?"

"You know what I mean."

I ate a forkful of hash browns too fast and burned my mouth, welcoming the tiny moment of searing pain. "How am I supposed to know? If I were you, I'd be in Luxembourg by now."

His expression flickered, a will-o'-the-wisp passing through his eyes, as if he'd been about to tell me something, a different story entirely. "Luxembourg, huh?" As if he might concoct a new version of the truth, just for me. "Wanted to make sure I was clear. 'Cause you'd tell me if I needed to get outta town."

"You need to get out of town."

"You've been sayin' that since I got here."

"What happened with Melville?"

Teddy made an odd clicking noise with his teeth and stared past me. "You know, Mill, I won him off a Mexican, and a mobster won him off me. That's just the way it goes. Monkey gets to be a pet, now." He focused his unsteady eyes on the coffee cup. "You taught him well, sugar, just loves those cards. But I think he'll have a better life with Iris, calmer, know what I mean?"

He took a slug of his coffee and gave me what he thought was a smile, but it came across wrong. His eyes didn't match the shape of his lips. He looked scuffed at the edges, his hair a little greasy.

"The Flamingo isn't a small-time game, Teddy, it's...."

"I'm fine."

"What am I going to...."

"Oh," he said. "I shoulda known, it's about you. Makin' sure your fix comes through okay. Of course."

"That's not... forget it." I pushed the plate away from me and put my elbows on the counter. I was going to put my head in my hands, but Teddy leaned towards me and kissed my cheek. He smelled of whiskey and diner coffee and some indefinable underlying harshness, like acetone. I coughed.

"Don't worry, sugar. I don't have any kind of death wish."

"So leave now. Just start driving. I'll lend you... I'll think up some kind of story, I could buy you some time, say you've gone to visit my mother...."

He smiled, that wrinkle of Mary Ellen's more pronounced than ever. "I'm fine, Mill. I'm outta here tomorrow, stop worryin'." He finished his coffee and stood up. "Won't see you for a bit. Look after yourself."

He punched my shoulder gently and I turned to put my arms around him, but he'd already walked away. He left the diner and crossed the street, and he paused to glance back at me before getting into the immense blue car.

The grill man didn't blink at the hundred dollar bill I used to pay for breakfast. He made change impassively—such things didn't matter in Vegas. On the sidewalk, I passed a guy asking for change, and I gave him one of the twenties I held. He took the bill in what was left of his hands.

21

I had no idea what Teddy planned to do. I stood beside the white sedanette and realized there was no point going back to George's. My landlord would be starting breakfast for the girls by now, and I didn't know what I could say, about anything. So I left the car where it was and walked to Fremont. The sun was still low, making long morning shadows of the street signs against the white sidewalk—no matter how much desert dust blew across this town, the sidewalks stayed pale enough to burn my eyes. I walked in the shade of the White Cross Drugstore. Nothing in its windows would help what ailed me. Next door, Herman's dime store wasn't open yet. And then I was in front of the dangling, broken dice-shaped lamp. I hadn't darkened Pete's filthy estab-lishment for weeks, but when I pushed opened the door and walked through the gloom to the table, he greeted me cheerfully.

"Well, well. Deal in the lady," he said. "Goin' good with you?"

I tried to nod.

"Bit of pressure good for the game." He waved his hand at the two army guys at the table. "This one's hell on cards when she gets goin.'"

"Thanks, Pete." I set my wrists against the less-than-immaculate baize, hoping to keep my hands steady.

Men joined the game and fell away as the hours passed; chips came into the pot and I raked them in. I thought of nothing but card patterns. I watched the numbers, their shifting dance, the expressions of my fellow players, until I was so tired, I thought I might actually sleep.

When Pete cashed me out, he leaned conspiratorially across the counter. "It true they got a monkey playin' cards at the pink bird now? Hell, what're they thinkin' over there?"

"Dancing tigers, coming next," I said evenly. "Underwater ballet. Anything a person can want."

"I dunno," said Pete. "Don't like lookin' too close at what people want. Never much of a surprise."

The sun was still in the sky, but the shadows had moved to the other side of the street. On my way back to my car, I bought the evening paper from the newsboy—mostly because he said "Afternoon, Miss," and I've always appreciated a gentleman, even if he's only ten years old. I didn't read the front page until I'd given the kid a nickel. I took one step off the curb, to cross over to the car, and stopped. The headline was in huge black letters: CIRCUS TRICK. "Authorities are now searching for the perpetrators of a startling break-in in the normally serene neighbourhood of...."

I read the article. Brazelton's house had been robbed. Jewish New Year, everyone was at synagogue. I stood in the gutter, flipping the page to finish the article. Break-in, that was just a figure of speech: the thieves didn't have to break in. No one locked their front doors in those days, not in Vegas. Why lock your door, when every crook in the country had a stake in the town's success? When the cops walked into Brazelton's mansion, they found the bedroom safe's door swung wide, nothing broken, but the combination lock had been neatly opened and all of their lovely jewelry was gone. All those diamonds. Except for Melville's leash, which he was still wearing. I squinted at the paper for a long time, trying to focus on the words.

The monkey had surely opened the safe. I could think of no other reason for Teddy's odd look when I'd asked him about Melville. But I wondered why he hadn't taken the monkey with him, after the robbery. Surely Melville was the most precious tool in the kit, worth more than the diamonds in the long run. He was unique. But maybe he was interrupted, or Melville ran from him. Or maybe it wasn't Teddy, after all, in that mansion. Maybe he'd taken my advice, maybe he'd left town, leaving the plan with Rutowsky.

I shivered. The paper told me that Brazelton left the New Year's celebrations early to get back to his house, beautiful wife on his arm. They walked in the front door and noticed something amiss. They went upstairs. Did Brazelton know whom to suspect? Maybe Melville bit Brazelton—I hoped the monkey drew blood, made the bastard worry about getting rabies. There was no further mention of the little beast. I wondered again where Teddy had gotten to—why wasn't the monkey with him?

I folded the tabloid up carefully, as if it were a precious manuscript, and I managed to cross the street, as if the newspaper were nothing but a tiny injury, a paper cut. But when I looked up, I saw someone was standing beside my car. Wearing a twilight-coloured suit. Stan put his hat further back on his head and tossed away his cigarette.

I hesitated on the far side of the car. "What are you doing here?"

"Hoping to see you," he said. "Obviously."

I tucked the newspaper under my arm. I wondered if Stan knew about Brazelton, if he'd put it all together, the monkey, and Teddy, and me. What kind of pattern did it create in his mind?

"Maybe we can get a coffee," he said, nodding at the Corner diner behind him.

"No thanks." My voice sounded tiny. "I was reading the...." I stopped, tried again. "Where's the monkey?"

"The monkey?"

I moved my head slightly, up and down.

Stan came around the car towards me. "Brazelton killed it."

"Dead?"

"Usually goes with the...."

"How?" My voice was smaller every time I spoke.

"Millard, what does it...." He stopped on the curb. "Brazelton swung its diamond-studded leash into a wall. Its neck broke. Apparently Iris tried to stop him."

Someone always has to take the fall, I thought. Better Melville than Iris. "How do you know?"

Stan put his arm out as if to hold onto my shoulder. I shied away. I thought about Iris, a woman named for a tall thin flower, how she might suddenly have held Teddy in her mind, John as she would have called him, while the monkey, chittering when Brazelton grabbed its leash, was suddenly airborne. Crashing into the wall, its skull cracking into its neck. You can't sacrifice your familiar, I thought, it's not right.

"Millard? Maybe you want to sit down."

"Why?" I closed my eyes against the sun. I felt Stan put his arm around my waist and take my arm, as if he thought I might faint. I opened my eyes, but I didn't move away from him.

"We'll have a coffee, okay?"

He steered me back into the diner and set me down in the nearest booth. There was only one other customer, an elderly type sitting at the counter, reading the newspaper. He didn't bother to look around, merely watched our reflections in the mirror behind the milkshake glasses.

"Two coffees," Stan said to the grill man.

When the man came over, he carried one mug of coffee and one pot of tea, an empty cup looped on his finger. He set the tea in front of me, glanced at Stan, and went away.

Stan put sugar in his coffee. Then he poured the tea and pushed the teacup against my folded hands. "I need to talk to you."

I looked at the steam coming up from the tea. Simple.

"You haven't seen that cousin of yours, have you?"

"Cousin?" I said. "No." I ran my fingers along the rim of the teacup. Its damp warmth didn't comfort me.

"So he's not your cousin." He cracked his knuckles. "So who the hell is he? Were you married to him?"

"What?"

"Your so-called...."

"No."

He rubbed his eyes as if he were exhausted, propped his elbows on the table between us. "I'm not going about this right. I'm worried about you, can you see that?"

"What?" I wondered if Stan had really sought me out because he was worried, or because the casino had sent him.

He looked across the table, his eyes ragged. "There's a guy, Rutowsky," he said. "Tell me you don't know him. John was… you know about his hollow leg scam? It's hardly original."

I meant to shake my head, but I couldn't move.

Savage sighed, moved his coffee cup out of the way, and laid his hands on the table. "Imagine you're dealing blackjack," he said. "You have a partner at the table, making fussy gestures with his cards, talking too much, joking, distracting the other players. Even Parry gets distracted by this customer, which gives you, the dealer, a moment here and there." A quarter appeared between Stan's fingers. He palmed the coin and it disappeared again as he turned his hands over. "You can sew a sleeve into your tux, like a trouser pocket. Make the chips disappear. At break, you dust your hands, shake your cuffs…"

Which he did, adjusting his wrists, the movement of his elegant hands like the gesture he'd made long ago, at Dermot's. I had never understood the mechanics of how Savage had gotten that extra card into his hand. But now, he laid his hands, empty, on the table. "You meet your partner, somewhere, and you split the contents of the pocket." He shifted his hand and the quarter was back in his palm, shining at me.

"Why do you keep saying 'you'?" I took the quarter from his open hand.

"How can you not know any of this? Your cousin, or whatever the hell he is, was the sleeve."

"You sound so sure."

Stan put his hand to his face, as if to rub away the grim expression that had taken root there. "Rutowsky was John's partner." His hazel eyes darkly staring at me. "You know Rutowsky? Tell me you don't."

"No," I said dully, "I don't know him." Remembering Elena's split lip, the man's grinding anger in George's house that one morning.

"Millard, please, I'm trying to help you. Rutowsky wants to know where John is."

"Why?"

Stan folded his fingers against the edge of the table. "Rutowsky is the problem here. Listen to me," he said, lowering his head to keep his eyes level with my shifting gaze. "Chappell can work this out. He can't stand Rutowsky, he's looking for an excuse to get rid of him. Chappell can talk it through. The sleeve's irrelevant. Chappell doesn't give a damn, get the money back, it's done. Rutowsky, he's the problem. You have to find John."

"He left town," I said, hoping it was true.

"Come on, Millard, level with me. You think Chappell wants to make the papers again? No. Rutowsky's our problem. Believe me here. John should get his ass over to Chappell's before Rutowsky finds him. Rutowsky's partners, they always end up dead, Millard. Are you listening to me?"

I stared at the air behind Stan's head. Interesting patterns twisted in the empty air. All kinds of impossible fortunes.

"Millard." He put his hands on either side of my face, forcing me to meet his eyes. His palms hot. "Figure out where John is. Where he might be. Tell me."

A key on its silver keychain. Teddy tossing the monkey in the air. Everything is useful, I thought, Teddy showing me Siegel's escape route, how pleased he was, knowing about that tunnel. The key still in the side pocket of my purse.

"I have to go." I pulled away from his hands and dropped the quarter onto the table to pay for my untouched tea. I slipped out of the booth before Savage could stop me. I got into my car and screeched the tires of the seda-nette, getting away from the curb. I took the corner of Fremont too fast, nearly hitting the poor newsboy.

It was a good thing there was no one on the road as I drove to the Flamingo. For once, I stopped right at the entrance of the casino and threw my keys at the valet, pushing ahead of the customers.

"I won't be long," I said.

I wondered if Stan Savage was right behind me. I didn't care. Inside, I ran straight to the stairs, I brushed past a couple arguing—her hair askew, his crushed shoulders, too much money lost—and down the too-red hallway. I took the key from my purse, glanced over my shoulder and didn't see Savage, not yet. I swung the door to the suite closed behind me and locked it. The looming shape of the pool table was immense in the gloom. I flicked on the lights as I went through to the bedroom. The orange silk bedspread was mussed, as if someone had lain there. I remembered how easy it was to fall into Teddy, the shine of him.

The heavy hanging bed drapes, the weird crystal furniture, the silenced cuckoo clock—the room was a haunted house. I dragged the Persian rug back but the trapdoor was too heavy for me. I jammed the room key into the sliver of space between the boards, and levered the wood of the trap up enough to get my fingers underneath it. I wedged in the tip of my shoe and pulled the door up. The smell of dirt and bleach slithered up from the tunnel. I hit the electric switch with my elbow and followed the lights down the stairs.

Did I imagine Teddy would be there? I should have called his name, called ahead of me down that corridor. I wiped my eyes angrily with the back of my hand. Damn you Teddy, I thought, I can't believe I'm here. Did I expect him to have the diamonds belonging to Brazelton's wife? What did I expect? I inched along the hallway to the bend in the tunnel, where the beams criss-crossed like the underside of a bridge, the smell of bleach stronger than ever. Then at the turn in the tunnel, I ran forward as if I might be in time, might get there before anything was too late.

Teddy lay on the ground, the white sleeve of his shirt stained dark with blood. Nothing else in the tunnel but his body. What I saw first were his legs, the trousers he was wearing in the diner. Then his white shirt. He'd been shot twice, once in the head, which accounted for the blood, most of it, and then in the chest, where there was almost no blood, only the moment where it had torn his shirt. He had fallen against his arm, the blood soaking into his sleeve and into the ground. Part of his head was smudged through and across the dark plain earth. Blood on the grey concrete of the wall, too, but I turned my eyes from the wall, I refused to look at it.

I pressed my hand against his chest, but the colour of my skin was wrong against the shirt. My fingers risked touching the fabric, where it was torn. I dragged my fingertips across the pocket to the collar, the way the shirt was still mostly white, his shoulder still solidly his own beneath the fabric. A dead man is still himself, even with half his head gone and the blood from his face cold. Still himself, that much was utterly obvious, but surprising to me. I wanted it broadcast, announced, made specific and known so no one would ever again have to discover it this way. I'm sure the blood on his face was cold, because I put my hand across his eyelids and closed his eyes. I did not look in his eyes, I knew not to. I smoothed his hair, carefully. And when I brought my hand back to his shoulder, my fingertips were streaked almost black in that dim light.

It did no good to kneel on the ground beside a dead man, except that I couldn't think of any good reason to stop kneeling there. The tunnel was noisy with rough breath—my own, nothing else. I held my breath, and then all I could hear was my heart, solid as a left fist hitting a punching bag, again and again, training for some great impossible fight.

When I finally stood up, my ankle buckled under me and knocked my weight against the wall, to the far side of Teddy's body. My shoes, my feet, were wrong, uneven. The heel of the right shoe had snapped off. I took off first one shoe, then the other, held them both in my hand and noticed blood on my stocking. I tried to wipe my leg clean with my wrist, which made it worse. I ran, unevenly, with my ankle strange underneath me and my shoes still in my hands. I ran as if I were the one about to be shot, as if it was still going to happen, in the future, ahead of me. I ran down the tunnel until I reached the flat metal door and I wrenched the door handle open to run through the empty shed, daylight shocking my eyes.

The texture of the gravel under my stockinged feet was strange and sharp. I stopped and looked around the gardens. The oleander, the hibiscus, the bougainvillea were all in bloom, their shapes trimmed into hedges, their colours seemed awful to me. There were people at the pool. I turned away from them, surprised to see women, men, standing, talking. I imagined everyone had somehow disappeared, had left me entirely alone. But then the path I took was familiar, the soles of my feet sore on the gravel, unstoppable, set into motion, I went to the bungalow that belonged to Mavis and Chappell. I must have knocked at the door, because I know I stood inside the living room and Mavis tried to take my shoes from me.

Her dress was red and yellow, yellow and red, and there was a glass of water. I imagine she wanted me to drink the water, but I refused it. Everything was brightly coloured, too much so, shockingly light, as if the room was radioactive with sunshine, as if I'd left my sight in the tunnel and could see nothing without pain. The colours burned my retina. I shut my eyes and tried to think of some words to give Mavis.

"What happened?" she said again. "I'm going to have to call Dick, unless you tell me what's happened."

She sat with me on the sofa, rubbing my arm, waiting, I imagine, until I chose to explain.

"Did you cut yourself?"

She endured my silence. After a while, she stood up and dragged the water glass out of my dirty hand. I don't know if there was blood on the glass when she took it from me. I looked at my fingers, disconnected from me, streaked, blood the colour of earth. Mavis came back with a fresh glass; this time it did not smell like water.

"Drink it," she said.

I shook my head. I was still trying to find a word to offer her.

Someone knocked on the door and Mavis glanced at me before going to answer it. I unfolded myself from the sofa and followed her, not with any conscious goal, except that when she opened the door, I threw the glass I was holding at the man standing there. I don't know, now, who I expected to see standing at the door. But I threw the glass and whatever liquor that was in it, flung it with all my strength into Stan's face. I was going to leave, then. I wasn't sure why I was still in Mavis' house at all. Savage stood still for a moment, to get the whiskey out of his eyes, I guess. But when I went past him, he put his arms around me, catching my hands as if I had fallen.

☙

I woke up in my bedroom, evening light against the rose posies on the walls. George sat on the bed near my feet, weighing down the bedclothes. I was tucked in so thoroughly I couldn't move my arms; I rocked underneath the sheets and freed my shoulders, loosened the covers until I could slide my hands out. My hands looked white and strange. I let them lie flat on the pink coverlet.

"Nice to see you awake," said George. His green dressing gown seemed to shimmer at the edges. "I brought you some toast."

My foot ached. I moved my ankle and uneven pain warbled up my leg. I turned my head and saw a plate of toast on the bureau, alongside my bottle of perfume. Maybe it was the smell of melting butter that woke me. I looked at the toast and the perfume. Then I focused on the lace runner on the bureau. If I kept my eyes carefully on these details, I would have nothing else in my sight. Nothing in my head at all.

George put a hand on my legs; I could feel the weight against the covers. "Girlie," he said.

I couldn't remember Teddy's feet, their position. That bothered me— shouldn't I be able to picture every detail?

"I couldn't be more sorry for John," said George. "I'm doing up his funeral. I'm right thinking he's not a Catholic?"

"What?" It was the word funeral that confused me. I turned my head and stared carefully at George.

"Catholic. He wasn't Catholic. Your family's Episcopalian or something, right? The Episcopalian minister's very understanding, the funeral's going forward tomorrow, no sense waiting on it."

"No."

"I'm thinking you need a break, maybe even a holiday. Maybe go see your momma up in Vancouver? Stay away from the cards and have a rest. You've had a bad shock."

I would have to tell my mother that Teddy was dead. I closed my eyes while George talked. I couldn't really hear what he was saying. I pressed two fingers against the corners of my eyes until I saw sharp slivers of silver, of amethyst, explosions of light against my eyelids. I tried to make sense of the different shining pieces, but I kept finishing with Teddy dead and the Brazelton robbery inexplicable. I tried assembling the story as a deck of cards, but there were too many I couldn't seem to find.

"I just don't know." I opened my eyes.

George looked at me. I wondered what he'd been saying that I had interrupted, but he nodded as if in agreement. I closed my eyes again, and after a moment, I felt George stand and leave. I slitted my eyes open; the shapes in my room seemed very far away. George would organize a funeral. Nothing could be less important. Nothing would celebrate his life. I was angrier at Teddy now than I had even been before, but that only made me sick. I fought my way out from the covers and went to the bathroom to throw up, limping against the pain in my ankle. I stayed in there for much too long, I think, because when I hobbled back, Stan Savage stood at the foot of the bed, leaning on the window frame.

I rubbed my hands over my eyes. The window poured too much light behind him. He looked like some kind of mirage illuminated by a sinking sun.

"I'm sorry," he said.

I put my arm against the bureau, trying to stop the pain in my ankle, and I stared at him, hoping he'd disappear. The room did flutter a little bit at its edges, but Savage merely turned to look out at the hills, I suppose he saw landscape out there. I slid towards the bed and as he kept his back to me, I laboriously sat on the bed, pillow at my back, my hands on top of the sheet I'd pulled into my lap. My legs were weighed down by sinker lines, but I swung them painfully onto the bed, covering myself with the sheet.

"They want me to ask you to play a game," he said.

"A game?" I echoed. I thought about the word, trying to see if there was a meaning to it. They, I thought. "You mean, you want me to play a game."

He stared fixedly out the window. "Lissoni. He's coming in this evening, for the upstairs game. I said asking you was a bad idea."

"Lissoni?" I tried to get that word into my head and suddenly it appeared perfectly, like a movie projector getting itself into focus—Lissoni, the ugly man I'd played once before. Cigars, attitude, a face that had been smashed since birth. I wondered how it was that I could remember him, when really my mind was so far from here, partly underground, partly standing in Mavis' living room, partly—

"I offered to do it," said Savage, "but they want me to deal."

"You don't need a prop at that game," I said, as if we were having an ordinary conversation. I shook my head, too many images sliding into one another.

"It's not a tilted table anymore, Millard. Not since I started dealing it."

A test, I thought. "Make sure I had nothing to do with... That's what it is."

He glanced at me, winced, I swear he did, and he closed his eyes. When he opened them again, wide, the setting sun illuminated the sunflowers in his eyes. He took his hands out of his pockets and opened his cigarette case. He lit a cigarette and stared at it as if surprised.

I slid down in the bed until I could see over Stan's head. The white ceiling fascinated me, it shifted like a lake underneath a summer breeze. Waves shimmered across its surface, then lay still. "Lissoni," I said, slowly, as if the word were spraying up from the waves.

"He's an asshole. But that's... Millard, I said I'd speak to you. So I have. I'm going to tell Chappell you're unwell, and who would blame you. I'll say you're unconscious, you're... Mavis will stick up for you. She gave you two Seconals, Christ, you should be unconscious." He rubbed his neck and crossed the room, put his hand on the edge of the door, to close it after him.

I stared at his fingers, I think I expected them to stay there on the door after he was gone.

Stan's footsteps were too loud on the stairs. In the hallway, he said something, probably to George, too low for me to hear. The front door closed. The light was fading. Blue shadows streaked the walls. I looked up at the ceiling. Damn it Teddy, I thought, am I always to be your accomplice, is that what you want, to take me down with you? I rolled my hand against my mouth and bit my palm until my whole arm throbbed. I stared at the marks I had made in my skin, then I threw off the sheet and forced my feet onto the floor. I stood, my strained ankle sending a searing pain up my leg. Good, let it hurt. I am not going with you, Theodore Ahern, I said aloud. No matter how much I want you here. I am staying here alone.

I dressed, white trousers, a green blouse. I crouched, awkward, to reach my shoes, my gesture paused, reaching—the white leather was curiously luminous at the bottom of the closet. Should I wear black shoes, as if shoes might be a sign of mourning? I picked up the white T-straps and sat on the bed to buckle them. My ankle was so swollen, the strap barely fastened stretched to its furthest clasp, and when I stood, I enjoyed how much it hurt. How the body was important. I'd always wondered why Teddy didn't mind being hit, boxing, his innumerable black eyes, his nose broken, once, twice— maybe this was the answer, that actual pain made the noise easier to bear. The noise in my head. The noise of being alive.

Hesitating every time I put weight on my twisted ankle, I left George's house very quietly, my purse tucked under my arm. If George heard my sedanette start up, heard me drive away, I didn't know. I didn't care what he thought of me, because I was quickly around the corner and driving. My windshield couldn't reflect all the lights, the Mint and the Horseshoe and the Golden Nugget, every one of them too bright in the growing darkness. I passed the Fremont Hotel in all its shell-coloured splendor. The air was cooler than it had been in weeks. I concentrated just on that detail, breathing in the air, its temperature, breathing out, while my white car reflected the lights of Fremont, and then through the lull, beyond downtown, past the construction site. Its dust. When the Flamingo appeared, I turned off the highway and stopped the car in the parking lot.

I closed my eyes and leaned my head against the steering wheel. I tried to open my eyes; on the third try, I found I was staring at the odometer. How many miles travelled. I reached for my purse. I kept my eyes straight ahead, watching the hood of the car. I remembered my stake, the remaining money I needed. How it seemed so far from me, unimportant. But while I got out of the car and walked towards the casino, I tried to remember my numbers. I limped, I could do nothing else. The money in my purse combined with the money in the Flamingo deposit box and the numbers faltered in my mind. I shuddered and put my hand against the pillar of the entranceway.

I went through the main doors and walked straight across the floor. I might have eaten a pack of cards as I went by the blackjack tables, picked them up from the semi-circles of green baize and stuffed them into my mouth. Diamonds, Spades, Clubs, Hearts—I would stupefy myself with cards. I found myself standing at the bar, as if the floor had shifted to get in my way, to force me to halt.

The bartender saying, "Strong or weak?" And the blankness of my face made him say, "How 'bout I make you something different? You wait, I'll make you something, Miss Lacouvy."

Give me something to hold on to, is what I meant to say to him. Instead he made me a disturbingly red drink. I tried to put it down but it stayed in my hand.

"Millard?" said Chappell behind me. "You're here. Savage said you...."

I turned and looked at him, but I may as well have looked through him, I could see the casino floor through his big frame.

"I need part of my bankroll to play."

He held out his arm, for me to walk with him. "I'm sorry," he said, but I had trouble trusting his tone, even as I took his arm and leaned against him to ease my ankle. There was no change in its pain, every step. We walked to the wicket that held the deposit boxes and under Chappell's steady eyes, I set the drink down on the counter and took my money from the box. Thirty thousand dollars disappeared so easily into my purse, such a small pile of bills. I put the strap over my wrist and picked up the red drink. My ankle was on fire. I wanted it to keep feeling that way, as if the floor burned, step by step, as we crossed the casino and went up the stairs to the same hallway that led to Siegel's suite.

Chappell paused at the first door and murmured. "Millard, I am very sorry about this."

He raised his huge hand and knocked before opening the door. The layout of the suite was different from Siegel's—the same dark wallpaper, but in burgundy, not green. An air conditioner whirred in the curtained window. That noise blended harshly with the electrical current already running through my head. I couldn't hear the next words Chappell spoke. At the centre of the room, Stan slid his eyes to mine for only an instant. Two men I'd never seen sat on the far side of the table, bland-faced and older; they stood to shake my hand. Lissoni couldn't be bothered to acknowledge me. He watched Stan break open a second pack of cards. A fourth player turned, putting away a handkerchief. "Damn heat," he said. I knew him from previous downstairs games—he would give me no trouble.

But then Lissoni raised his head towards Chappell and waved his empty glass at me. "'Bout time the waitress got here. These fucking drinks are melting too fast."

I stared at Lissoni, I couldn't focus on his face, I simply knew it was him, ugly, mean. While Chappell said, "No, this is Miss Lacouvy. You've met. She's been looking forward to playing with you. And I'll send up a waitress. My apologies for the heat."

Apart from the burning pain of my ankle, I felt no warmth in the room, only ice. My fingers felt numb with cold. I glanced at the droning air conditioner and my gaze was caught by the redness of the chairs, the carpet, too, red as the drink that was still, yes, still in my left hand. I set down the drink as Chappell pulled my chair out. I didn't feel any different sitting down, the pain in my ankle continued. I pushed my hands against the edge of the table, as if I could push myself away from the chill I felt. My fingers clung to the wood. I suppose Chappell left the room, but I didn't pay attention.

I tried to focus on the table, the cards Savage shuffled. The deck blurred. Lissoni spoke, blowing cigar smoke towards the dealer. I paid no attention to his words, I don't know what they were. But my eyes cleared and the ugly man came perfectly into focus. His face hadn't changed, still that train wreck in motion. I set my teeth together when Lissoni spoke again to me. I didn't care to be polite. He could think I was a mute.

Savage shuffled the cards. How much do the cards choose their own patterns? How much is touched by the dealer? A great deal, I thought. A fair deal, a square deal, a rotten deal. This casino like a rotten fruit, tunnel out, underground. I forced my fingernails in the palm of my left hand. I had to stay aware of the room, could not risk thinking of anything but here, now, this place, these cards. I stared across the table at Stan. I wondered if he had told me the truth, that he didn't cheat, dealing this table. Or else I was a prop at a tilted table.

My hands set themselves to pick up the cards and my torn ankle counterbalanced the noise in my head. Our door cards weren't inspired; I had a four of Diamonds, the man next to me had a two of Hearts. The other players didn't care who I was, or whether I spoke to them. Surely we each held reasons to play, to remember, to play, to forget, to remember again. Did they know the table was tilted? Did they expect it to be? I held a dark pair of Aces—Clubs and Spades. I looked at their surface, the elaborate death ace, while Stan watched me. My hands did their work, I barely paid them any attention, their acrobatics. The cards tried to assure me that what was left would be all right.

I won the first pot, ten thousand, while Lissoni blew smoke across the table. I looked mostly at the green underneath my hands. When the cards brought me the Queen of Diamonds, I folded, wondering how I would tell my mother that Teddy was dead. Suddenly I was convinced that it wasn't true. There was no point to such a fact, a man like Teddy being dead. If he was not alive, there was no purpose to him. Whatever words I found, my mother would blame me. The table wavered beneath my fingers, and I spread my hands flat against the green felt, considered its surface, held steady. I took up my hands and found my cigarettes. I allowed the man beside me to hold out a light and I thanked him.

Lissoni swore at his cards and threw them down instead of folding neatly. He stood up, stormed over to the air conditioner and gave it a hard kick, as one of the other men at the table made soothing noises. I didn't even try to understand the words.

Stan dealt another hand. Did the cards console me? No. They had no interest in such things. The longer I played, the worse the cards. If my ankle hadn't burned so constantly, if the colours of the room weren't so painfully bright, if Savage had even once met my eyes, I might have put my head down on the table and given up. I picked up my cards. A seven of Hearts—card of broken promises. I glanced at the ceiling, the lamp, I followed the light down Stan's shoulders, his arms, to his hands. He wasn't dealing me any favours, and I didn't want him to. Jack of Diamonds, next, with which I could do nothing, and bad fortune to boot. Come on, cards, I whispered. Lissoni upped five hundred dollars, not so impressive except he flung his chips rudely into the middle of the table, splashing the pot. The faintest trace of disgust scudded across Stan's face. I force my gaze back to the table, away from his eyes. He dealt the last card of the porch and I folded.

My foot throbbed like a grandfather clock, slowly ticking, timing the hours as they slipped into cards. I felt the increasing weight of my head and hands. I glanced at the red drink still beside me but I couldn't seem to make my fingers connect with the glass. Despite my strong beginning, I was down half my bankroll. Lissoni re-raised me and I kept folding, until the ugly man won a twenty-one thousand dollar pot with the most unlikely hand: a pair of twos, Hearts and Clubs, along with a Seven of Diamonds, and a Queen of Clubs. Those cards didn't add up to anything—I should have caught his bluff.

I tried to pay closer attention to his tells. His tiny eyes rippled with dislike—not only towards me, no, he disliked everyone at the table, including and most especially Stan. I wondered if Lissoni expected the table to be tilted in his favour by the dealer, if that explained his style of play. Maybe he had no idea that the house had placed me here to break him. I calmed my eyes by looking down again at the green baize.

The next round was better for me: Lissoni folded, throwing his cards away at Third Street. Truly, throwing them—he tossed them on the ground in disgust, a move that wouldn't be tolerated downstairs. But here, apparently, anything might happen, for we finished the round and Stan merely gathered the fallen cards, tore the deck we'd been using, and opened a new one. He washed and stripped the cards impassively and put them into play. The man beside me, the one who'd made soothing sounds at Lissoni, went all in with his failing four hundred in chips. I cleared him out, not particularly interested in his demise. One of the other players stepped away from the game, made his excuses to Lissoni, who swore at him. I paid no attention. I waited, through the next rounds, herding my luck towards my stake, towards removing Lissoni and winning the rest of my stake.

And finally, I was granted a beautiful hand—no need to even bluff. Stan dealt me a full house, Queens full of Jacks. The Queen of Hearts and the rest, black cards. I didn't flinch at the Jack of Spades, I held it steadily, I thought of Teddy's eyes, how black. I made my bet. My only religion was here in front of me. Surely that's what Teddy believed, that I loved nothing else but these cards. I gazed at the Jack. Nothing changed. I raised, which teased Lissoni into making too large a bet. The pot totalled thirty-two thousand dollars. I picked up that red drink beside me, its ice long ago melted, and I drank it down, all of it, before turning over my hand.

I didn't look at Lissoni. I did not care when he rose and threw the butt of his still-lit cigar into the centre of the pot. He strode out of the room, slamming the door behind him. The remaining player shrugged, I heard him say something, but I paid no attention until he reached over, picked the smouldering cigar from the pile of bills and chips, and tossed it into the melting ice of Lissoni's finished drink. There was a slight sizzle as the burning cinders petered out and died.

"Well done, lady," the man said slowly. His face was as wide and grey as Roscoe's. "I'd gladly throw in another twenty thou, for seeing Lissy leave like that. Does my old heart good." He stood and leaned across the table to shake my limp hand. He slapped Savage on the back and tossed him a five hundred dollar chip as a tip. "For doin' it with style," he said, as he left the room.

I pushed the chair awkwardly away from the table, my legs graceless, my shoulders starkly frozen. I stood stiffly but my sprained ankle came very close to failing beneath me. My fingers clutched the chair. Stan came around the table to help me.

"Don't," I said. His kindness was unbearable. "Count out the chips."

Stan wrapped an arm across my shoulders, forcing me to lean against him. I shifted and propped my weight against the table, to keep from tipping my ankle. With his free hand, Stan raked the chips for me, laid them in shelves. I rubbed my eyes—somehow the pain in my ankle had spread through every part of my body. My shoulders, my neck, my head, even my eyelids burned.

"It more than pays off your stake," he said.

I wished I cared. I did care. Or, I knew I'd come round to the idea of caring. Just not yet. I pressed my hands against the rim of the table on either side of my waist; I could feel no solidity in the wood, only the furred texture of the felt. Savage took his arm from my shoulders and slid red chips into their metal box, stacked bills alongside and clicked the box shut. There was more than enough money to buy myself out of being a prop. My winnings would pay back my stake, even after the house cut. I could walk away. Roscoe was in the count-room right now, downstairs. I could pay him.

I couldn't imagine it. I was only an empty collection of sticks, a series of painful angles held together implausibly by a few torn muscles. Perhaps I was wavering visibly, back and forth, there at the table, for Savage pressed his hands against my arms as if trying to keep me in one place.

"I'll drive you home."

I shook my head. "Cash in the stake for me. Please."

He didn't move his hands. "I'll come and tell you how it goes," he said. "I'll come to George's. That's where you'll be?"

I looked at him for a long time, trying to decide if I would be there or not. I had no idea. Perhaps. I trusted him, though, and this surprised me. The sharp pain in my ankle made me open my mouth, but I had nothing to say. I moved away from Savage's hands carefully, favouring my sore ankle, pressing my palm against the wall. I leaned on the doorframe and forced myself into the hall, the ridged wallpaper absurd beneath my fingertips. My hand found the warm wooden banister of the stairs as a relief. I walked downstairs slowly.

I must have limped as I crossed the floor, but I don't remember; I might have floated, my legs, my arms released by the game. The physical solidity of the casino itself, its shining lights, seemed dim compared to the dawning morning on the far side of the glass doors. I went alone through the doors into the outside silence, into the city's smell of sage and dust. I walked towards my white car and when I reached it, I turned, pressing both my hands against the hood to take my weight off my torn ankle. I leaned there and stared back at the casino, the pink swoop of its entrance, the magic marker of flight in its sign. The sun was just starting to come up and the Flamingo seemed pinker than ever. I thought of the gardens, the blue swimming pool, the game tables, the rose and gold lounge, the reddish dust of the desert, the dirt and bleach smell of the tunnel. I let it go, all those chips, cards, bets, I kept only belief, only trust, and I got into the white sedanette and drove.